Please return/renew this item by the last date shown on this label, or on your self-service receipt.

To renew this item, visit **www.librarieswest.org.uk** or contact your library

Your borrower number and PIN are required.

LibrariesWest

Ann McIntosh was born in the tropics, lived in the frozen north for a number of years, and now resides in sunny central Florida with her husband. She's a proud mama to three grown children, loves tea, crafting, animals—except reptiles!—bacon and the ocean. She believes in the power of romance to heal, inspire, and provide hope in our complex world.

Deanne Anders was reading romance while her friends were still reading Nancy Drew, and she knew she'd hit the jackpot when she found a shelf of Harlequin Presents in her local library. Years later she discovered the fun of writing her own. Deanne lives in Florida, with her husband and their spoiled Pomeranian. During the day she works as a nursing supervisor. With her love of everything medical and romance, writing for Mills & Boon Medical Romance is a dream come true.

CHRISTMAS MIRACLE IN JAMAICA

ANN McINTOSH

DECEMBER REUNION IN CENTRAL PARK

DEANNE ANDERS

MILLS & BOON

Published in Great Britain 2021
by Mills & Boon, an imprint of HarperCollins*Publishers* Ltd,
1 London Bridge Street, London, SE1 9GF

www.harpercollins.co.uk

HarperCollins*Publishers*
1st Floor, Watermarque Building,
Ringsend Road, Dublin 4, Ireland

Christmas Miracle in Jamaica © 2021 by Harlequin Books S.A.

Special thanks and acknowledgement are given to Ann McIntosh
for her contribution to The Christmas Project miniseries.

December Reunion in Central Park © 2021 by Harlequin Books S.A.

Special thanks and acknowledgement are given to Deanne Anders
for her contribution to The Christmas Project miniseries.

ISBN: 978-0-263-29778-2

10/21

MIX
Paper from
responsible sources
FSC® C007454

This book is produced from independently certified FSC™ paper
to ensure responsible forest management.
For more information visit www.harpercollins.co.uk/green.

Printed and bound in Spain using 100% Renewable Electricity
at CPI Blackprint (Barcelona)

CHRISTMAS MIRACLE IN JAMAICA

ANN McINTOSH

MILLS & BOON

For my sister, Kathy.

Fruit is soaking,
and this year we're making Christmas pudding together!

PROLOGUE

IT'S A NEW BEGINNING.

Seated at the end of the hotel bar, her shoulder against the wall, Chloe Bailey took a sip of tonic water and considered the thought carefully. Beyond the plate-glass window rain fell steadily, the gloomy San Francisco evening mirroring her mood.

Shouldn't she feel happy about the dawn of this next part of her life, especially after the horrid couple of years preceding it?

Perhaps she should, but instead of sparking joy, the rumination echoed morosely in her head, reminding her that success hadn't created this change. Failure had.

She wasn't used to failing. Actually, she'd lived her entire life conscientiously trying to avoid doing so.

Coloring within the lines.

Always doing what was expected.

Working hard to be the best.

Only taking considered risks so as not to make big mistakes.

Living what others erroneously thought was the perfect life.

It hadn't always been easy. Often she'd wished she didn't have the reputation for being reliable, steady, dependable. Especially when her parents used her as an example her siblings would do well to emulate, which had led to resentment when they were all younger and created an unrealistic vision of who she really was. And now...

She groaned quietly, and reached for her glass. Waves of hurt and embarrassment made her skin burn even as a shiver ran along her spine.

No one in her family had ever gotten divorced, until now.

Waking up five thousand miles away from her London home to her solicitor's text saying the entire ordeal of getting free from Finn was over had made her equal parts sad and relieved. Finn had fought the divorce every step of the way, making what should have been a straightforward matter into a circus. Creating discord, spouting ridiculous demands and accusations, trying to force Chloe to go back to him rather than go through with severing the marriage.

The mess he'd caused even had her parents questioning her decision. And just like that, Chloe was no longer the "perfect" daughter, sister or friend but someone others looked at with pity. Or speculation, since there were few people she entrusted with the true reason for the breakup, and Finn was almost universally liked.

It was all highly unfair, and as she drained the last of her sparkling water, Chloe couldn't help feeling resentful.

She hadn't cheated or lied. Finn had. Yet here she was, left holding the bag.

As she twisted the empty glass back and forth between her fingers, she heard her grandmother's voice, clear as day, as though the older lady was beside her and whispered into her ear.

"Anyone who thinks life is always going to be easy is

*a jackass. When things get tough, lift up your head and
look for the advantage. There's always one, but usually
you have to seek it out."*

That was Gran's reaction anytime one of the family
was dispirited or gloomy, but the familiar refrain rang
hollow now.

"What possible advantage could there be to this
mess?" she muttered.

But her brain was already whirring, putting aside the
depressing, self-pitying thoughts and searching for the
elusive silver lining.

Professionally, the breakup hadn't changed anything.
Her position at the Royal Kensington Hospital was both
secure and rewarding, and the cutting-edge research she
was involved in gave her a great deal of satisfaction.

It was personally that she'd suffered, and perhaps that
was where she could benefit?

All her life she'd been so careful, terrified of dimin-
ishing her good name, constantly aware that her parents expected her to set the best possible example for
her younger siblings. Well, much of that had gone out
the window over the last couple of years, leaving her...

Free.

To do things she'd wanted to but shied away from because they were risky or could potentially make others
think less of her.

She'd always been so careful, so conservative and con-
ventional. Wasn't it time she let loose a little?

"Can I get you another tonic water?"

Startled, Chloe looked up at the bartender, and instinctively nodded. "Yes, thank you."

She wasn't ready to retire to her lonely hotel bed,
knowing she'd only lie sleepless while she wrestled

with all the ramifications of the life-changes she was going through.

But as the other woman began to turn away, Chloe was struck by a totally different type of impulse.

"Wait," she said, causing the bartender to pause. "Do you serve mojitos?"

"Sure," the woman replied with a smile. "Wouldn't be a real bar if we didn't."

"I've always wanted to try one," Chloe said, ignoring the whisper in her head telling her she rarely drank and she should be more careful, here in a strange city with no one to watch out for her.

"One mojito, coming up," the bartender said, her smile widening.

"Brilliant," Chloe replied, grinning in return.

When her drink came, she silently toasted her grandmother and her own quiet revolution, determined to make up for all the lost years of being so timid she'd forgotten how to actually *live*.

And when she found her gaze snagged by that of a very handsome man sitting across the bar, she refused to give in to the impulse to look away. Instead, she kept her eyes locked on his and raised her glass once more to her lips to sip the delicious liquid.

Then, as the gentleman in question rose and began to make his way toward her, she let herself smile, just a little, feeling excitement quicken her blood.

Here's to new beginnings.

CHAPTER ONE

WHEN THE PILOT announced they were beginning their descent, Chloe leaned closer to the airplane window and was once again disappointed. Thick clouds obscured the view below, just as they had for most of her flights from Heathrow to New York, and from there, toward her final destination: Jamaica.

Jamaica!

Just thinking the name made her smile again. Really, she'd hardly stopped smiling since hearing where she was going as part of the Kensington Project, which sent specialists to other hospitals outside the UK to share their expertise. While she'd expressed interest in the prestigious program months ago, she hadn't been informed of where she was being sent until just recently. And now here she was, on November first, winging her way to her destination.

She'd heard so much about the island but hadn't had a chance to visit, and now her heart raced as she waited to catch her first glimpse of its legendary beauty.

As though sensing her excitement and taking pity, the clouds suddenly thinned, then disappeared, revealing peaks and valleys of an almost startling green.

"Oh!"

Her soft exclamation attracted the attention of the lady next to her, and the older woman looked out the window too.

"It's beautiful, isn't it?" she asked, the pride in her voice evident, her accent definitively Jamaican.

"Lovely," Chloe agreed, giving her a grin before turning back to the window.

"No matter how many times I come back home, every time I see those hills, my heart is happy."

Glad to have someone to share her enthusiasm, Chloe asked, "I'm sure it is, with a view like that to come back to. Were you away for long?"

The lady laughed. "I've lived in New York for the last forty years, but no matter what, I always think of Jamaica as home."

Chloe chuckled. "My gran is the same. She's lived in England for probably sixty years and still talks about Jamaica as though she just left. She was so excited when she heard I was going."

"Is this your first visit?" the lady asked, her brow creasing as though she couldn't believe it. "Even though your grandmother is Jamaican?"

"It is," Chloe replied, wondering why the other woman thought that was so strange. "Both of my grandparents are Jamaican, but they met in England. Once they started a family, they couldn't afford to go back very often, and although I've wanted to visit, I've not had an opportunity until now."

Besides, Finn hadn't been at all interested in her Jamaican heritage and always vetoed the island as a vacation destination.

"How long will you be visiting?" The lady seemed intent on ferreting out every secret Chloe may possess.

"Do you have any family left here, or will you be going to one of the resorts?"

"Actually, I'll be here for two months," Chloe told her, feeling another little tingle of happiness at just saying the words. "And no relatives left, that I know of anyway. It's a working holiday, so I'll be in Jamaica for Christmas. Going by what my gran says, that should be fun."

"Oh, we Jamaicans love Christmas," the lady replied with a decisive nod. "Why do you think I come back almost every year, now that I'm retired? Will you be in town or in the country?"

Not being sure what the lady meant by *town*, Chloe simply answered, "I'll be working at Kingston General Hospital."

"You're a doctor?"

There was no skepticism in her voice. Instead, she was beaming as though that was great news, and her reaction caused a little glow of warmth to bloom in Chloe's chest.

"I am. A neurologist, to be exact."

"How wonderful. Your family must be so proud and pleased."

Then, thankfully, her new acquaintance leaned over and started to point out landmarks below and Chloe didn't have to reply.

The reality was her family members—with the exception of her grandmother—were anything but pleased with her at this point, and that still stung.

When she'd called, excited to share being chosen as a part of the Kensington Project, her mum had been less than enthusiastic.

"We've hardly seen you in months," she'd complained. "First, too busy with work, then off to San Francisco for a conference, and now, hardly back a month and you're off again."

To hear her you'd think Chris Taylor, Chloe's boss, had decided to include Chloe in the project just to spite her mother.

"It's a great opportunity, Mum. I'll get to share some of the research and advancements we've made at the hospital and to see Jamaica at the same time."

"But to be away for Christmas?" Her mum sounded outraged, as though she'd discovered a plot against her and the family. "Why on earth would they send you off into the wilds now?"

"Jamaica is hardly 'the wilds,' Mum—"

"Well, I think it's very poor form, sending folks away over the holidays."

Hearing that particular tone in Mum's voice, Chloe's first impulse was to try to placate her and calm her down. That's what she'd always done, and it was probably expected, but after a lot of thought, she'd decided the habit was one that needed breaking.

Over the years, people—especially her family and Finn—had used her peacemaking tendencies to their own advantages, pushing her into corners with their anger. Hammering at her until, suddenly, she was doing what *they* wanted rather than what was best for her.

So while a litany of complaints flowed from Mum's lips, Chloe hadn't bothered to argue. Instead, she'd let Mum have her head, then reiterated firmly that she'd be going to Jamaica. While that had gone over like a lead balloon, the frosty silence and cool goodbye thereafter had almost been worth it.

Apparently, the expectation was that if you protested hard enough, Chloe would change her plans to accommodate. Well, they'd soon learn she wasn't inclined to give in anymore.

And truthfully, she was glad not to have to deal with that particular battle at Christmas. In the past it had been her favorite time of year. The lights and decorations. Bustling about to find perfect gifts for family and friends.

But since her split with Finn, and the reaction to it from her family, the season had definitely lost its luster. If she spent it with her family again this year, she'd once more be expected to take all comments with grace, as though having her family side with Finn wasn't painful. And if she decided to respond to anyone the way she'd want to, there would be hell to pay.

All things considered, she was glad to avoid fielding the inevitable questions about the divorce, not to mention remarks like those she'd been subjected to at the last family get-together. Aunt Gloria saying it was obvious being single didn't agree with Chloe, since she looked so 'sickly,' while Aunt Janice warned she shouldn't let herself go, since it would be harder to find a new husband.

As though after what Finn had put her through, she had any intention of looking for another relationship, much less getting married!

No.

She was just finding herself again after years of being a part of a couple. Rediscovering facets of her personality she'd forgotten or pushed aside in service of being Finn's wife. Embracing this new life with gusto and the kind of pleasure her family couldn't and wouldn't try to understand.

Like the excitement of a one-night stand with a handsome, sexy man.

Remembering the night in San Francisco gave Chloe a secret, delicious thrill.

It had been, in its own way, revelatory.

She'd only ever been with Finn and would be the first to admit their sex life had grown stale and flat, although she hadn't been able to put her finger on why. Then, when she found out he'd been cheating on her with a work colleague, she'd thought that explained their lackluster lovemaking.

Finn had a different idea about what the problem was.

"You're just not very sexual, Chloe. It's hard to get really excited when the woman you're with doesn't exactly seem to enjoy being made love to."

At least he'd stopped short of calling her "cold," but hearing him say that made her truly angry.

"You never complained before. Why is it, all of a sudden, that *your* cheating is *my* fault?"

As though realizing he was close to saying the unforgivable, he'd tried charm instead.

"Chloe, you know I love you. I always have. But we were so young when we started going out, I got curious about what it would be like with someone else. I made a horrible mistake, but it was a one-off. I'm sure if we work at it, we'll get back to where we were."

That conversation had put the final nail in the coffin of their marriage. Perhaps in time she might have forgiven him for cheating, as she had before. He didn't realize she knew about his previous indiscretions, since she'd kept the knowledge to herself, determined to make their marriage work. After all, she'd put so much into the relationship and had loved Finn for so long, she'd been scared of what it meant for them to no longer be a couple.

But she couldn't forgive him for lying nor for trying to make her the problem when it was clearly him.

Yet his assertion that their issues in bed stemmed from her lack of sexual interest had haunted her and left her with lingering doubts.

But what she'd discovered in San Francisco allayed them, forever.

Just thinking about that wildly passionate night still made her hot and bothered.

First, there was the fact that she'd actually agreed to sleep with a man without knowing anything about him except his first name—if the name he'd given her was even real.

Second, there had been absolutely nothing wrong with her libido when she was in his arms. In fact, she'd been a little shocked at the ferocity of her desires and how demanding she'd become in search of satisfaction.

The day after, as she settled in for the long plane ride back to England, she'd been both relieved to have Finn proven wrong and astounded at her newfound boldness. Yet while she regretted nothing about that night— especially since it had cemented her determination to take more risks—she had no intention of making a habit of picking up strange men. It had been a successful, exhilarating experiment but not one she was sure she felt comfortable repeating.

No, she told herself, as she shook off the memory of that night and tried to bring her wayward breathing back under control. It had been astounding, earth-shattering and brought her to life in a way nothing else could have, but it wasn't a high she'd be chasing often.

Irrespective of the nights spent tossing and turning as

her body remembered finding the ultimate satisfaction with a man clearly versed in how to pleasure a woman.

Going forward she had a plan to rebuild her life, which didn't include getting involved, even casually, with any men.

Dragging her thoughts back to the present, she was in time to have her seatmate point out the town of Portmore, which she described as a bedroom community for the capital city, Kingston.

"My daughter lives there," she explained, before pointing out the peninsula where both the airport and Port Royal were located. "You've heard of Port Royal, right? It used to be called the Wickedest City in Christendom before it was mostly destroyed by an earthquake, somewhere back in the seventeenth century. It shrank to a village, but now it's a heritage site with a cruise-ship terminal. They serve some of the best steamed fish there. Make sure you get someone to take you."

And as the pilot announced they were about to land, the lady added, "I hope you have a wonderful time in J.A."

Stuffing the research paper she'd been reading back into her bag, Chloe gave the older woman another wide smile. "Oh, I'm sure I will."

It was just the adventure she needed, and she intended to enjoy every moment.

Dr. Lemuel "Sam" Powell checked his watch, shifting restlessly from foot to foot. Around him swirled the cacophony of the arrivals area at the Norman Manley International Airport. Shouts of welcome, impatient honking of horns and the whistles of the police officers hurrying people along battered his ears, adding to his annoyance.

He was supposed to be at the golf club, playing dominoes and relaxing as he usually did on a Sunday afternoon, not at the airport waiting for a visiting neurologist.

But when the CEO of the hospital had called that Friday and asked for a favor, Sam knew it wasn't in his best interests to say no outright, even if they were also friends. That didn't mean he didn't try his best to get out of the chore.

"Shouldn't Gilbert Owens be meeting him, since he's head of neurology? Or even Dr. James?"

Kendrick Mattison sighed. "Listen, Sam, Owens isn't at all pleased to be hosting a visiting specialist. I think he's taking it as some kind of affront. You know how he can be."

Sam did know. They were extremely lucky to have Dr. Owens on staff and heading up the neurology department. The older man was well respected, both for the research he'd done and his spotless record, but also notoriously hard to please and inclined to take offense if he felt he wasn't being given his due. Perhaps he was wondering why, exactly, the Royal Kensington Hospital felt it would be advantageous to Kingston General to have this Dr. Bailey for two months.

"That's all well and good, but what about Simon James? As your second, he would be a good representative of the hospital."

"He's out of town, and before you even ask, Rashida's mother is throwing her a baby shower, and you know how peed off she'd be if I missed it."

Sam had snorted, trying not to laugh outright. Rashida Mattison was a four-foot-ten dynamo who both terrorized her husband and had him wrapped around her little finger.

"Yeah, laugh all you want, but your day will come," Kendrick said. "And when you're wrapped up in matrimony like I am, I'll be on the sidelines giving laughs for peas soup."

"Well, save your hilarity," Sam replied, letting obvious smugness color his voice. "Because it's not happening."

"Well, happening or happening not, we'll have to see, but I need you at the airport at four to pick up Dr. Bailey. Stop by the office before you leave. One of my admins will have a sign printed for you to hold so she knows who you are."

"She?"

But even as the question left his lips, he realized Kendrick had already hung up.

So with that in mind, Sam had been diligently watching the door, holding up a sign on which was printed Dr. Bailey, trying to spot the English neurologist. But besides one or two curious glances, no one had approached.

Sam shifted again, fighting the restlessness that had plagued him for the last month. This was never his favorite time of year to begin with, since it brought forward memories kept at bay most of the rest of the time by a constant whirl of activity. Company and the camaraderie to be found at the golf club or his favorite bar, where he sometimes went to play darts or pool, helped keep the ghosts asleep.

Being alone in his house made him hyperaware of the echoing spaces in his head, which, if given the chance, filled with old sorrows and questions he could neither answer nor seem to avoid. This year he'd had a brief respite in the form of an erotic night with a sensual stranger. But while he'd been able to forget Victoria and all that had happened for a few blissful hours, the aftermath had left him even edgier than before.

Lost in thought, Sam jumped as a loud altercation broke out behind him, where cars were stopping to pick up passengers. Spinning around, he saw two drivers arguing, threats and curse words flying left and right. Then a couple of police officers joined the fray while disembarking passengers and other gawkers crowded around to watch the spectacle.

Taking advantage of his height to keep an eye on the melee, Sam held the sign at an angle where it could be seen by people coming out of the doors.

Just as the officers were succeeding in breaking up the quarrel, he heard a strangely familiar voice say, "Sam?"

He froze, as shocked as she sounded, all the air rushing out of his lungs, disbelief holding him in place for a long, fraught moment.

Then he turned and found himself face-to-face with a woman who'd haunted his nights and bedeviled his days. One he thought he'd never see again after that one ecstatic night.

"Chloe?"

Her mouth had been open just a bit, obviously in disbelief, but at his question, it firmed. Grew almost grim.

"Yes. Dr. Chloe Bailey. I believe you're here to pick me up?"

CHAPTER TWO

CHLOE HAD STOPPED so abruptly, the porter had to swerve to avoid running into her heels with his trolley. Trying desperately to maintain some kind of composure, she locked her trembling knees and wiped as much expression from her face as she was able to, though her skin felt clammy and cold.

Even as she'd said his name, she'd been sure she was wrong—had expected him to turn and tell her she was mistaken. Surely when she saw him full face, she'd see her error and he'd look nothing at all like the man she'd slept with in San Francisco.

But instead, she was gobsmacked to realize it definitely was him, in the flesh, staring back at her with a look of intense shock. If she weren't so flabbergasted herself, she'd be inclined to laugh at his expression, but amusement was the last thing on her mind.

Even as her brain whirled with questions she was too stunned to ask, she was taking in every remembered feature of Sam's face.

The soft dark skin, his chin shaded with a hint of stubble, as it had been the night they'd spent together.

Wide-set eyes, with their almost black irises and ridiculously thick lashes.

The intelligent sweep of his forehead, eyebrows tipped high up in surprise.

Strong nose and jawline.

And that perfect, full-lipped mouth...

Focusing on those lips caused heat to explode in her belly and fan out over every inch of her body. All too well did she remember the deliciously wicked things his mouth—incongruously both soft and firm at the same time—was capable of. Fighting for control, Chloe tore her gaze away, reluctantly meeting his once more.

Yet Sam seemed as tongue-tied as she herself was, and who knew how long they might have stood there staring at each other if the porter hadn't intervened.

"Boss, we have-fi move. We blocking the way."

Sam blinked a couple times as though waking up, then looked at the porter.

"Yes," he said, his voice strained, like his throat was tight. "Take the lady to a spot on the curb, please, while I go for my car."

Then without another word, he turned on his heel and walked away, leaving Chloe to stare as he disappeared into the crowd.

"This way, miss," the porter said, swinging his trolley around her with an expert twist of his body.

Still reeling from the unexpected encounter, Chloe blindly followed the porter to a clear area on the pavement, where he started unloading her bags.

Despite the heat of the afternoon, she was shivering, her brain scrambling to come to terms with what she'd seen.

San Francisco Sam? Here?

No doubt working at the same hospital she was assigned to for the next two months?

How?

Why?

"You all right, miss?" The porter's question shook her out of her muddled thoughts, and she turned to see him watching her, concern clearly etched in his face. "You need to sit down?"

His solicitude brought her back to herself, and she took a deep, steadying breath.

"No, I'll be okay. Thank you." Finally remembering she had to pay him, she unzipped her handbag and rooted about for her purse. She retrieved a banknote and held it out.

"I'll stay here with you until your man comes back," he said, as he took the money from her hand.

Knowing the elderly porter was only being nice, Chloe bit her tongue so as not to snap that Sam was *not* her man.

Instead, she managed to dredge up a smile from somewhere and replied, "That's very kind of you but not necessary. I'll be fine."

But the porter only leaned on his trolley and tipped back his red cap.

"No problem, miss." The corners of his eyes crinkled as he smiled back. "Yuh remind mi of mi granddaughter. Mi nuh mind staying for a little, till you feel better."

And his gentle waffling about the weather and then his family had the benefit of calming her down. Her laughter at one of his stories about his son loosened her muscles, releasing the tension locking them.

Yet as soon as the vehicle pulled up in front of her and Sam got out of the driver's side, all the stress came flooding back.

She stood silently as the two men casually chatted while stowing her suitcases in the back of his 4X4. Sam even chuckled, as though nothing untoward had taken place, seemingly completely unconcerned about seeing her again.

Then he glanced her way and caught her staring. A flash, like lightning, jolted down her spine. Miffed at herself and his insouciance, she called out her thanks to the porter and opened the door to enter the vehicle. Once in the passenger seat, she pulled out her dark glasses and put them on, blocking both the tropical glare and Sam's gaze. Hopefully they'd hide whatever he might be able to read in her eyes.

What to do now? Bring up their prior meeting or wait for Sam to do so? There were so many questions she wanted to ask, but her emotions were all over the place and she was too flustered to figure out how best to approach the issue.

Never in a million years had she expected to see this man again, and ridiculously, her brain ping-ponged between pleasure and an emotion too close to fear to be comfortable.

When Sam got into the driver's seat, Chloe kept her gaze trained ahead, looking out the windscreen at the swirling crowd of people and vehicles. Yet it was impossible not to see his movements in her peripheral vision, and although she briefly thought about turning to look out the passenger-side window instead, she didn't.

In fact, as he buckled his seatbelt, she realized she was looking at him from the corner of her eye. When he put the vehicle in gear, the breath hitched in her throat at the sight of his strong, long-fingered hand, her body remembering with startling clarity the sensations it had created.

And the memory was delicious.

Dragging her eyes away, she stared straight ahead

again as Sam maneuvered the car through the throng and away from the departure area.

The silence lay thick between them, and Chloe was reluctant to break it. What would be worse, driving into Kingston in silence or engaging in discussion about this unbelievable encounter?

He'd left the airport behind and they'd traversed a roundabout before he said even a word.

"Well, this is a surprise."

From his tone it obviously wasn't a pleasant one, and a wave of heat—part embarrassment, part annoyance—flooded up into Chloe's face.

"For me, too," she said, keeping her voice level as best she could, hoping he didn't hear it wobble at the end.

"Really?"

Now he sounded downright skeptical, and as Chloe turned to look at him, she had to rein in rising anger, although some leaked through when she asked, "What are you implying?" Despite her best efforts, her voice rose. "That I followed you here?"

He was silent for a long moment, but his mouth tightened, lines forming at the corners as he frowned.

Finally, he said, "Well, what are the odds of us meeting a month ago in San Francisco and then you suddenly turning up in Jamaica?"

Astounded at his arrogance, all Chloe could do was stare. Then anger turned to ice-cold rage, all embarrassment disappearing.

"Get your ego under control," she snapped. "You're making yourself look like a git."

"I'm…" he sputtered, his head whipping about with satisfying alacrity to give her a shocked glance. "What—?"

"First off," she butted in, unrepentant at interrupting

whatever he wanted to say, glad he'd looked back at the road ahead, releasing her from his dark gaze. "I didn't get to choose where Royal Kensington was sending me and didn't know I was coming here until a few days ago. Secondly, I didn't even know you were Jamaican when we met last month. You sounded American—"

"I don't sound American at all."

"You certainly did when we werc talking at the bar," she retorted, wondering if he'd put on the accent then, although she still heard a trace of it now. "And, since we didn't get around to exchanging life stories, I assumed you were American."

"All that is well and good, but—"

On a roll, she spoke right over him, so incensed the words tumbled over one another.

"Finally, and most importantly—if I *were* interested in anything more than what we shared that night, wouldn't I have at least given you my contact information before leaving?"

Sam's mouth opened and closed a couple of times, but all that came out was an inarticulate sound. Satisfied she'd made her point, Chloe crossed her arms and firmly turned her head away, glad her words had at least seemed to shut him up.

Sam gripped the steering wheel so hard his knuckles hurt. He definitely wasn't used to being raked over the coals—except by his mother on occasion—and his first impulse was a swift, harsh rebuttal.

Why was she so surprised that he'd think she'd followed him to Jamaica? Wasn't it the kind of coincidence no one would believe? He was well within his rights to question her motivations.

Except, deep down he knew he actually deserved the tongue lashing he'd just received.

He'd been shocked when he turned around and saw her, and he knew without a doubt he wasn't the only one rocked by the encounter. Her eyes had been wide with surprise and her lips parted as though she were trying to speak but couldn't. But more than just being stunned by the sight of her here in Jamaica, Sam was even more dumbfounded by his instinctive reaction.

He'd wanted to grab, hug and kiss her. Take that luscious mouth beneath his, claiming it the way he had back in San Francisco.

One-night stands weren't something he usually indulged in, simply because they were inherently risky. Although, having long ago decided he wouldn't get seriously involved with anyone again, he made sure to steer clear of anything that seemed as if it might become a relationship. Instead, there'd been short-term flings or brief affairs.

What was strange about the San Francisco encounter was how hard it had been to get Chloe out of his mind. For a month he'd been trying to forget about her, but her memory had refused to be banished. That night had been an amazing, erotic experience, and the sheer sensuality of it invaded his thoughts with arousing and annoying regularity.

Now having been taken to task, he had to admit his response to her arrival back into his life had been brought on by an emotion he had no name for but somehow resented nonetheless.

His ruminations were interrupted by the need to hit the brakes as a fast-moving vehicle overtook his, squeezing into the lane ahead to avoid hitting an oncoming minibus. Realizing he wasn't giving the road the concentration it needed, he put on his indicator and pulled over to the curb, just past Gunboat Beach.

As he put the vehicle into park, Sam suppressed a sigh, dreading the upcoming confrontation.

Oh, he knew she was probably telling the truth. Everything she'd said had sounded convincing, and indignation had rung in her outraged tone. However, whether she was being completely honest, he had no way to know. He was in the habit of viewing coincidences and other people's words with a jaundiced eye.

Especially when the person involved was a woman.

That was a lesson he'd learned a long time ago and didn't need reminding of.

Chloe was still looking out the passenger window, her gaze seemingly fixed on Kingston Harbor or perhaps on the city beyond. With her arms tightly crossed over her chest, and the rather haughty tilt of her nose, her annoyance couldn't be clearer.

Well, he was annoyed too. Sam tried to convince himself it was because Chloe might suddenly expect there to be something more between them rather than anything else.

What on earth else could be causing this swirling emotion, which made it so hard to be conciliatory?

The sudden memory of her saying if she'd wanted anything more than that one night she'd have made her wishes clear had to be pushed aside. Sam took a steadying breath in preparation for wading into what felt like turbulent waters, but before he could even marshal his thoughts, Chloe rounded on him again. The expression of horror on her face made his heart rate pick up.

"Hello! Tell me you're not in neurology."

"I'm not," he replied, hearing the stiffness in his own tone. "I'm a surgeon."

"Oh, thank goodness."

She turned away again, leaving him once more speechless and even more embarrassed. Even though he didn't want her to think they could pick back up where they had left off, he also didn't want any awkwardness between them to seep through into the hospital. But where to start? Then he remembered one of her points and decided that was as good a place as any.

"Listen, I might have sounded American because I went to school there, from when I was seventeen until I finished my residency. It's not inconceivable that I fall back into the old speech patterns when I go back."

She threw him a narrow-eyed look, her lips pursed, but didn't reply, just turned to stare out the window again.

Then, before he could figure how best to continue, Chloe asked, "I take it that's Kingston over there?"

Apparently, she had no interest in continuing their prior conversation, and Sam couldn't decide whether to be annoyed or relieved.

"Yes, it is," he replied, leaning forward to point past her toward Victoria Pier, on the other side of the harbor. Dusk was falling and lights were beginning to come on, showing the sweep of the city climbing the hills in the distance. "That's downtown Kingston there and the corporate area spreading out behind. If you look past Long Mountain, over there, you can just make out the start of the Blue Mountains."

She seemed intent on examining the view, and Sam once again considered if he should say anything more. He should be pleased she seemed disinclined to discuss the strange circumstance they found themselves in, but something niggled at him. Whether it was conscience or a totally different impulse, he didn't know. All he knew was the entire situation had thrown him for a loop, and until he'd had a chance to sort through the events of the afternoon, he'd rather not say the wrong thing.

Again.

Yet he knew his attitude hadn't set the best stage for any future meetings and he should swallow his pride and apologize.

"Listen, let's just start over." In San Francisco she'd said she liked his smile, so when she finally turned to face him, he gave her one of his best.

She frowned in return.

Not particularly encouraging, but he forged ahead nonetheless.

"I'm not trying to make excuses, but seeing you like this has really thrown me."

He wished he could see her eyes, because perhaps then he'd have a better idea what she was thinking. Instead, all he saw was his own face reflected back at him in her shades, and the image of what looked like a leer on his face had his grin fading to nothing.

"Right," she said, and there was no mistaking the sharp tone. "It'll suit me to pretend we'd never met before."

Then she turned away again, leaving him with the impression the conversation was satisfactorily over.

Taking in a deep breath through his nose, Sam checked his mirrors and merged back into the fast-moving traffic.

"Oh." He suddenly remembered he'd been tasked with another job. Seeing her had driven it from his mind. "I was given a package for you. It's on the back seat, so please don't let me forget it when I drop you off."

She twisted to look into the rear of the vehicle.

"I see it," she said, before leaning between the front seats. "I think I can reach it."

She brushed his shoulder, leaving a hot, tingling spot behind. The scent of her hair rushed into his nostrils, bringing memories of burying his face in it as he shuddered with pleasure, trying not to lose control.

As she settled back into her seat, Sam realized it wasn't just the heavy Kingston traffic that was going to make the drive to Chloe's apartment a long one.

His heightened awareness, and the attendant desire raging through his blood, was going to make it everlasting.

CHAPTER THREE

CHLOE MANAGED TO hold it all together until Sam finally dropped her off at the flat the hospital had arranged for her. Then she collapsed onto the nearest chair and rubbed her nape.

The entire encounter had left her shaken, annoyed and—she was forced to admit—aroused.

When she thought there was no chance of ever seeing Sam again, she'd allowed herself to cast him in the role of perfect fantasy man. The kind of memory and image she'd be able to call on during those times when she was moved to pleasure herself in lieu of risking another anonymous encounter.

Now, having come face-to-face with him, she knew if they met again, it would take monumental willpower to continue the casually distant act she'd assumed for the rest of the drive.

Thankfully, she'd had the package from Kingston General to concentrate on, and it had, in turn, led to several topics of conversation she could effortlessly broach.

In the big manila envelope she'd found keys, a cell phone and a very nice letter from Kendrick Mattison, the hospital CEO, apologizing for not meeting her at the airport himself. At first, she'd been annoyed that he hadn't made the effort, thereby sparing her this uncomfortable journey. Then it came home to her how much more embarrassing it might have been had she and Sam seen each other for the first time at the hospital. Likely they'd have been surrounded by people who would surely have noticed their stunned reactions.

No, she decided. As shocking as this first meeting had been, far better for it to have been in private, than the alternative of having an audience.

The cell phone had been procured and activated by the hospital for her use while on the island and had been programmed with some numbers they thought she should have.

There would be a dinner to welcome her the following evening, and she would officially start at the hospital on Tuesday, giving her time to recover from her journey. Also, there were additional plans for her stay, covered separately in the attached itinerary.

Turning to the itinerary, she scanned the list. Along with the promised dinner, there was an orientation tour of the hospital on Tuesday morning. Reading further, she got a bit of a shock.

"Oh, they've arranged for me to do an interview with a newspaper. I wasn't expecting that."

Sam shrugged. "I'm not surprised. Having you here is a coup for Kingston General."

"Really?" She hadn't considered that an aspect of her trip. To her, it was simply a way to disseminate knowledge. "Why?"

He'd sent her a sideways glance, as though trying to figure out whether she was being disingenuous. Obviously whatever he saw in her expression had him taking her question seriously.

"Kingston General is a fairly new hospital, founded five years ago on the site of an older hospital that closed. Although it's classified as a private hospital, the aim has always been to offer specialized services to those who otherwise couldn't afford them, through a referral system. As a result, attracting specialists who can diagnose and treat less-prevalent diseases has always been a priority. Having a neurologist visiting from the UK, who's here to share new techniques and treatment options, is definitely something to advertise."

"I suppose so," she'd replied slowly, tamping down a nervous chill. "But I'm not used to being interviewed. Hopefully I do Royal Kensington and Kingston General—and myself—credit."

Sam sent her a smile. "I'm sure you'll be fine," he'd replied.

Blindly looking back down at the papers in her hand, she'd cursed herself as desire cascaded through her system, banishing her nerves and pretty much shorting out her brain.

He really had the most amazing smile.

It took her a moment to gather her thoughts.

"So health care isn't free here?"

"It is, in the public hospitals, but wait times can be long, and there's always been a demand for alternatives. Private hospitals fill that need."

"So there's a disparity in care?"

"There can be," he said slowly. "Wealthy patients can choose where they go and use a private doctor or surgeon, while everyone else has to wait. Which is why Kingston General is set up the way it is. Today I operated on a young boy with a bowel obstruction, from an inner-city community. He'd been referred from the public hospital because they didn't have a surgeon on hand and the case was urgent.

"It's always been the mandate that we don't turn patients away because of an inability to pay, but we usually only take referrals."

"What about medication costs?"

Shop talk seemed a safe enough subject, particularly since he was driving and had to keep a sharp eye on the roads. Originally, Chloe had considered renting a car, but if the Kingston traffic was anything to go by, she wasn't sure she'd feel confident about driving here. Drivers seemed inclined to do whatever they wanted, whenever it occurred to them, without use of indicators or, it seemed, their brake pedals. Luckily, the letter from Dr. Mattison included the information that the hospital had arranged for her to have a driver taking her back and forth to work during the week.

"Many medications are dispensed free of cost through the public hospitals and clinics, and there are a number of health-insurance schemes patients pay into to mitigate costs at pharmacies."

She'd continued to pepper him with work questions for the rest of the journey, not wanting silence to fall between them or, worse, to have him revert to their previous conversation. They'd actually passed the hospital, which he'd pointed out to her, and when he turned into the driveway of the small apartment complex, she realized it was only about ten minutes away from Kingston General.

"I could walk to work," she said, as she unbuckled her seatbelt. "It's close enough."

Sam paused with one foot out of the vehicle and gave her a stern look. "I wouldn't advise it."

"Why not?" Normally she'd be willing to take advice, but for some reason, she was reluctant to give Sam any leeway. Silly as it may seem, his very existence made her want to be contrary.

"It might not be safe."

"Why not?" she asked again, a little more forcefully. "It's probably, what, about three miles? And it seemed I'd be walking through a mostly residential area and then on a main road. I don't see the problem."

He was frowning, and although it should have been unattractive, Chloe's heart started pounding at the way his face fell into severe lines. He was suddenly even more gorgeous, and she couldn't help resenting him for it.

"Like most other cities in the world, Kingston can be dangerous to those who don't know it well. This isn't a tourist area, or out in the country where people look out for others. I'm sure the hospital made arrangements regarding your transportation, and it would be best if you took advantage of that."

She hadn't answered, just ignored the heat running along her spine and frowned back at him before getting out of the car.

He'd pulled her bags from the back of the vehicle, and they made their way into the building, using the keys Dr. Mattison had sent for her. The flat she was in was on the third floor, and her awareness of Sam was almost intolerable in the close proximity of the small elevator.

Trying to pull her thoughts away from reaching out, touching him to see if his skin was as soft as she remembered, was a battle that left her silent, tongue-tied with an intense surge of arousal.

Wrapped in his scent, seeing his reflection in the

stainless-steel walls, made it far too easy for the memories to flood in.

Tell me what you want.

His voice had been hoarse. His hand, which moments before had been sliding across her breast, had stilled, making her back arch with the desire to have the sinfully tormenting caresses continue.

Touch me, she'd demanded, before telling him exactly where, and how hard, and for how long.

Alone now, no longer needing to keep up her facade of unconcern, Chloe dropped her head into her hands, not sure whether to laugh or cry. The woman who'd had sex with Sam in San Francisco had been hardly recognizable. There had been no way to reconcile her with the old Chloe, who'd been passive and content to take whatever Finn gave rather than insisting on satisfaction.

While she'd been determined to hold on to the boost of confidence and personal power the night had brought out in her, she'd given no thought to what might happen should they meet again.

What she wanted was to call her best friend, Cora, and spill the entire story—including the encounter in San Francisco. Chloe had hugged the memory of that night close, wanting to savor it for a while before talking about it with anyone. Before she'd got to the stage where she was willing to share, both she and Cora had been chosen for the Kensington Project. Right now, Cora was in Stockholm, Sweden, where it would already be—Chloe checked her watch—after midnight. There was no way she would wake Cora up for this.

Besides, she told herself sternly as she got up to start moving her bags to the bedroom, she wasn't a child. She could handle it and whatever else came her way without anyone's support.

And, as she'd calmly told Sam before he left, since they wouldn't be directly working together, they probably wouldn't meet again.

At least, she heartily hoped so, for her own peace of mind.

Sam started the vehicle and sat for a moment, trying to sort out his thoughts—which Dr. Chloe Bailey had sent into a tailspin. He was positively flummoxed from seeing her again, his body taut, his heart still pounding although he was no longer in close proximity to the temptation she presented.

The last time he'd felt this confused and discombobulated, he'd been battling with grief and disbelief...

He tried pushing the thought away, shocked that it had even come to mind, although he shouldn't be.

Although the two instances had nothing in common, beyond this strange fight-or-flight impulse, he'd just been thinking about Victoria at the airport.

The car crash had been eight years ago, but every year around the time of that dreadful anniversary, the memories grew stronger—the agony harder to bear.

Yet ironically, without the lingering pain of Victoria's death—and that of the child he hadn't even known she was carrying—he probably wouldn't have slept with Chloe that night in California.

The sorrow still haunted him. Worse yet was not knowing why she'd withheld from him the fact she was pregnant. Every year he asked himself the interminable and unanswerable questions. Where had Victoria been going? Why—at four months pregnant—hadn't she told him about the baby? What else hadn't he been aware of in their relationship?

Was it something about him that had made her keep something so important and life changing to herself?

Had he inadvertently caused the disaster?

There was no way to know. Vicky had taken her secrets with her when she died. None of her friends had seemed to know what was going on and had declared themselves as shocked as he was. He'd met her brother a couple of times, but the siblings hadn't been particularly close, and when they saw each other at her funeral, the other man said he hadn't talked to his sister in months.

All of those memories had been bombarding him in San Francisco, and he'd been once more battling with them the night he'd seen Chloe across the bar. It was what had drawn him to her and led to that night of exquisite pleasure.

Pleasure that had driven the demons back into hiding and rendered Sam, in a strange and unfathomable way, renewed.

The old pain had been dulled, replaced by a memory of a woman so responsive, so intensely passionate he'd begun to wonder if he'd ever be able to forget her.

And now here she was. Slated to work in the same hospital he was in for two long months.

But Chloe had been right when she said they probably wouldn't see much of each other during her stay. They worked in different specialties and even would be in different wings of the hospital, so there was no need to come into contact, and they really could pretend they'd never met before.

Instead of making him feel better, the thought annoyed him more than anything else.

Dammit, the best thing he could do—for his sanity and his temper—was to forget he'd ever met Dr. Chloe Bailey and get on with his life.

Pulling out his phone, he sent Kendrick Mattison a text to let him know the visiting neurologist was safely at her apartment. Normally he'd call, but he had no interest in talking to his good friend right now. Not with all these crazy thoughts and feelings crashing about inside. Kendrick would hear in his voice that there was something off and demand to know what it was.

With a grim chuckle, he put the car in gear. Pulling out onto the road, he headed north out of the area adjacent to New Kingston toward his home above Manor Park. He'd just turned up the volume on his radio when the phone rang. Not wanting to answer but knowing it didn't make sense to avoid it, he hit the hands-free button to connect the call.

"Hey Kendrick. What's up?"

"I wanted to make sure everything went okay this afternoon."

He sounded rushed, and there was talk and laughter in the background, making it difficult to hear him.

"Yep. She arrived as scheduled, and I just dropped her off at the apartment as ordered."

Making sure he kept his voice even and casual took effort. He'd just decided to forget all about the darned woman, and here was an immediate—and completely unwanted—reminder of her existence.

"What's she like?"

Beautiful. Sexy. Infuriating.

"I didn't spend *that* much time with her," he temporized.

Kendrick made an impatient sound. "Just your general impression."

Sam bit back a sigh. "Seems nice enough."

"What?" Kendrick was practically roaring over the noise behind him, and Sam heard him kiss his teeth. "Listen, I'll talk to you later, or tomorrow. I can hardly hear you. I don't know why we have to go through this again."

Sam chuckled at his friend's disgruntled tone, knowing that for all his grousing, Kendrick didn't mind. He was a devoted husband and father. They may be expecting their third child, but Sam knew Kendrick was just as excited as he had been about the first.

That thought brought a pang of melancholy, which had to be ruthlessly suppressed as they said their goodbyes.

Sam drummed his fingers on the wheel, trying to decide whether to go straight home or not. The dominoes crew would still be at the clubhouse, and while the tournament would be well underway, they'd be company.

But at the same time, Sam wasn't sure he actually wanted company, or for someone to notice how out of sorts he was. Being alone at home would definitely be better than having to answer any nosy questions regarding his mood.

It was a clear choice between his own company and thoughts and whatever distraction his friends could provide. But since, despite being Sunday, traffic was crawling along Waterloo Road, it wasn't a decision that needed to be made right away.

His phone rang again, but this time he didn't mind the distraction.

"Mel, how're you?"

His sister let out an exaggerated sigh. "Frazzled. Allison had a meltdown of titanic proportions this evening when we wouldn't let her go to the movies with friends. Peter wanted to give in, but I put my foot down. She can't just throw a fit whenever she doesn't get her way, hoping her father will be afraid it'll bring on a seizure and let her do whatever she wants."

Sam could clearly hear the worry beneath his sister's exasperation, and his own stress level rose. His niece's epilepsy was a constant source of concern for the entire family, and Sam was often asked to explain things, both to the adults and to his niece, as well.

"Do you want me to speak to Ali about her behavior, from a medical perspective?" he asked.

Melanie hesitated for a moment and then said, "No. Let me talk to her first. If that doesn't work, maybe I'll ask you to try."

Sam was honest enough to recognize the wash of relief for what it was. Not that he didn't want to speak to Ali about her behavior, but he'd rather see if it became a health threat before he did. She was eleven, on the verge of puberty, and his speaking to her may exacerbate the issue, making teenage rebellion kick in, causing her to ignore his counsel.

One never knew how situations like that might play out.

"What I really called you about is Mummy's charity ball. Did you arrange for the bartenders and drinks?"

"Yes," he replied, glad of the change of subject. "And before you ask, David says he'll send the orchids up from the farm the evening before the party. Send me the florist's address so his delivery driver knows where to go."

"Great, thanks. I'll text it to you." In the background, he heard his brother-in-law's voice, and then Mel said, "I've got to go. See you on the weekend?"

"Sure. I promised to do Sunday dinner with Mummy and Daddy. Will you all be there?"

"Of course," she replied. "Okay, love you. Bye."

By the time he ended the call, he was driving up Constant Spring Road. Here the traffic was a lighter, and now he needed to decide about his destination.

In his mind's eye he pictured his living room, empty and silent. Then, before he knew what was happening, that image was replaced by one of Chloe Bailey. Not as he'd last seen her as the apartment door closed but as he'd seen her in San Francisco.

Naked.

Aroused.

Beckoning him closer. Making him wild with need.

Cursing under his breath, he put on his indicator and turned into the golf-club driveway.

Decision made.

CHAPTER FOUR

UNFORTUNATELY, CHLOE'S PLAN to not see Sam Powell again while in Jamaica was shattered the very next evening when he pulled up outside the building to take her to her welcome dinner.

"What the dickens?" she muttered to herself before walking out of the building, trying to ignore the way her body heated as he got out of his vehicle. Kendrick Mattison hadn't mentioned who was collecting her this evening, but Sam would have been her last thought.

He'd nodded emphatically the evening before when she'd said they probably wouldn't meet again, and she'd taken heart from his agreement.

Yet here he was, turning up again like a bad penny.

Silly to be glad that because she wasn't sure of the dress code she'd erred on the side of semiformal and thought she looked particularly nice, if she might say so herself.

"Before you say anything," Sam said, as he came around to open her door. "This wasn't my idea. Kendrick asked me to pick you up."

"It doesn't matter," she lied, keeping her voice cool and even.

"Well, I know you have no interest in being in my company," he replied. "But Kendrick wanted to be at the hotel early and asked me to swing by for you. If I'd refused, he'd definitely have asked me why, and I didn't think you'd want me to go into it with him."

It was on the tip of her tongue to agree, but once more the urge to be contrary came over her.

As she got into the passenger seat, she said, "I don't see why we couldn't say we met at the conference in San Francisco. We don't have to go into details, but it might be easier to let people know we're not complete strangers."

He paused, giving her a searching glance, but she turned away to buckle her seatbelt, unwilling to hold his dark gaze a moment longer than necessary. Bad enough to have been up half the night, the memories of the time they'd spent together making sleep elusive until jetlag and exhaustion had overwhelmed her senses. She still felt unsteady, on high alert, and looking into his eyes, shaded by those luxurious lashes, only heightened her disquiet.

But as he closed her door and started around the car, she took a deep breath and willed her heart rate to slow.

To survive being around Sam without making an ass of herself, she needed to be cool and collected. She'd rather eat bugs than let him know how off-kilter she was in his proximity.

As he got into the driver's seat, Chloe opened her clutch and checked to make sure she'd remembered to put her small pill case, stocked with anti-inflammatory pain medication, into the bag. When Sam pulled his door shut, she had to resist the childish impulse to hold her breath so the delicious scent of his cologne wouldn't penetrate her senses, but it was already too late.

Her body reacted as though touched, heating and tightening.

Get a hold of yourself, girl!

"You may be right," he said, as he put the vehicle into gear, pulling her out of her thoughts and back to the conversation. "Although Kendrick Mattison will ask why I didn't mention it before. I've spoken to him since I picked you up at the airport."

Chloe waved a hand in his general direction without looking his way. "Just tell him you met so many doctors at the conference, you didn't immediately remember me."

He snorted, the sound a mixture of amusement and what appeared to be derision. "Yeah, I'm sure he'll believe that."

Risking a glance at him, she sent him a frown but was secretly relieved when he was concentrating on the road.

"What do you mean?"

"I mean, you're a gorgeous woman. No man is going to believe I met you and then forgot. That's not how it works."

Chloe shook her head, ridiculously pleased to be so characterized but also ready to argue. Then, wondering what it was about him that made her so cranky, she thought better of it. "Well, tell him whatever you want. I don't care. But if it comes up, I *will* mention that we met before. I don't see the benefit in pretending otherwise."

"Okay. Okay." There was no mistaking the sharpness of his tone. "If it comes up, I'll say the same, but I won't volunteer the information."

"Fine." She was rather pleased with how unconcerned

she sounded. Not at all as though her heart was galloping along.

And she was equally happy when, not long after that, he turned into a driveway just five minutes away from where they'd started.

"What is this place?" she asked, admiring the verdant gardens, artfully groomed and accented by low lights shining up into the trees and casting the various shrubs into fantastical, shadowy shapes.

"It's a hotel," Sam said, steering the car under a portico. "With a fine dining restaurant and a small nightclub. They also have a few private rooms available for functions. It used to be someone's home, I think, back in the days of gracious old mansions in the colonial style."

When the car stopped, a valet stepped forward to open her door, giving her a wide smile and saying, "Good evening, miss."

"Good evening. And thank you."

"I'm going to park, then I'll be back to walk you in," Sam said, as she got out. "Won't be a minute."

Walking into the lobby, Chloe took a moment to catch her breath. Stepping over to a large colorful painting, she pretended to study it while willing herself to calm.

This was a work function, and she'd have to be on her toes. It would be naïve to think everyone would be pleased at the thought of her being here. The CEO of Royal Kensington had even said as much.

"There may be some staff members who view your arrival as an intrusion," he'd warned. "Or that you've been sent because we think their facilities and methods are somehow backward. It'll be up to you to prove that you haven't been sent to 'save' the neurology department or that you consider the way they operate to be outdated.

You're simply there to share information that may be helpful to them, based on the research we've been doing."

This first meeting with the doctors would be key in setting the tone, and she couldn't allow anything to put her off her game.

Especially not the incredible distraction Sam Powell presented.

Hearing the doors behind her open, she glanced toward them and silently cursed as her heart stuttered.

Why did Sam—dressed in a perfectly fitted suit, his loose, sexy stride somehow emphasizing his masculinity—have to be so damned attractive?

Worse when she considered what was beneath that suit...

"Do you like that painting?"

He was standing right behind her, and she had to stop herself from shivering at his low-voiced question.

"It's brilliant," she said sincerely. "I'd love to see more of the artist's work."

He didn't immediately reply, and the brief silence seemed to hum with electricity.

"There are other paintings by him in the National Gallery downtown. If you get a chance to go there, I think you'd enjoy it."

Why did his voice have to be so smooth—rich and dark like the finest chocolate? It made her want to drink it in, let it seduce her into all kinds of wickedly naughty adventures.

Chloe tightened her grip on her bag and fiercely reminded herself this was not a date...

Erotic images immediately arose in her head, causing her breath to hitch.

She knew only too well where a date with Sam could lead, but that would never happen again.

Tilting her chin up, she turned, intent on telling him they should get going, but the dark fire gleaming in his eyes caused the words to dry up in her mouth.

Then, in a blink, what seemed to be carnal interest on his part disappeared, leaving her to wonder if it had actually even existed, and Sam stepped back before offering her his arm.

"We should go in."

His voice was as unruffled as a slow-moving stream, and Chloe forced aside her hesitation to take the proffered elbow.

"Of course. Let's."

As they stepped through the door into the banquet room, Sam realized he was proud to have Chloe on his arm and tried—without much success—to curb the feeling.

They weren't together because they wanted to be but because of happenstance, and he knew he'd best be remembering that.

However, knowing that didn't negate the fact she was fabulous and, with that slightly pugnacious tilt of her chin, carried herself like a queen.

In her high heels she was almost as tall as he was, and the silky dress she was wearing hugged every luscious inch of her curvy figure while baring the smooth skin of her shoulders. Not just elegant, her outfit was meant to draw attention. From the brightly patterned material to the glittery gems on her sandals, her ensemble screamed confidence.

And confidence was extremely sexy in Sam's book.

As soon as they walked into the room, Kendrick came toward them, Rashida following on his heels.

"Ah, Dr. Bailey. I'm Kendrick Mattison. So nice to finally meet you."

As she shook Kendrick's hand, Rashida came up and introductions were made.

"I adore how tall you are," Rashida exclaimed, in her usual no-holds-barred way. "So stately and gorgeous. I've always wanted to be tall."

Chloe laughed, shaking her head. "You probably wouldn't feel that way if you had to go through the geeky, tripping-over-your-own-feet stage I did as a teenager."

"Well, you grew into your height perfectly. And I love that you don't hesitate to wear heels too."

Chloe stuck out one foot, showing her trim ankle and prettily painted toenails. Sam found himself staring and couldn't help wondering if he'd suddenly developed a foot fetish, since he found the sight so enticing.

"Oh, my ex-husband was only an inch or two taller than me and he complained if I wore shoes that made me taller than him. One of the first things I did after we split up was buy myself a whole new shoe wardrobe, all with high heels."

"You're my kind of woman," Rashida said, wrapping her arm through Chloe's and leading her away. "Let me introduce you around."

Sam was treated to the lovely sight of Chloe from the rear, hips swinging, her laughter floating back to him. The entire package was as intoxicating as twelve-year-old rum.

Kendrick's snort of annoyance brought Sam out of the spell he'd fallen under, and Sam tore his gaze away to look at his friend.

"Trust Rashida to just waltz off with Dr. Bailey, taking over my job." He sent Sam a piercing look. "And you didn't tell me she was a looker. I'd have thought that would be your first comment."

Seeing what could be made into an opening to come clean, Sam said, "We'd actually met before, and it didn't occur to me you'd want to hear what she looked like."

Now Kendrick's gaze sharpened until it could cut. "When did you meet her?"

It was clear he was looking for an in-depth explanation, but Sam didn't bite.

"She was at the conference in San Francisco. We met briefly."

"How briefly?"

Looking for a way out of the conversation, Sam said, "Shouldn't you introduce Chloe to Gilbert? You know how he can take offense if he feels slighted in any way."

Kendrick's gaze swung from Sam's carefully questioning face to where Chloe and Rashida were standing, talking to a small group of people, and then back again.

"We'll get back to our conversation later," he threatened, before striding away to scoop Chloe up and lead her toward where Gilbert Owens and his wife were standing.

Sam followed. He'd wondered if he should warn Chloe about the older neurologist's attitude toward having her at the hospital, but then he'd decided to let her handle it her own way. That didn't mean he wasn't interested in seeing how she managed.

He got to the group in time to hear Chloe say, "Dr. Owens, it's such an honor to be able to work with you. When I heard I was coming to Jamaica and realized you were in charge of the neurology department at Kingston General, I was so pleased."

Gilbert Owens looked unmoved as he replied, "That's kind of you."

"Not at all," Chloe said, her smile wide and her eyes sparkling. She was clearly ignoring the frost in his tone. "I read your paper on early-onset dementia a few years after you published it, and that was then I decided to become not just a doctor but a neurologist."

Gilbert's skepticism was palpable. "That paper was published in the 1990s. You couldn't have been out of your teens yet."

"I wasn't," Chloe admitted. "But my grandfather had just been diagnosed with it, and I realized my grandmother was having a very hard time understanding what was happening. I started reading up on the disease, and on a trip to a university medical library, I found your paper." She gave a smile—soft and almost shy—and continued, "I didn't understand much of it at the time, but with a *lot* of effort, I eventually was able to help Gran and Granddad by suggesting ways to keep him engaged, using your research as a template."

It was like watching someone fall in love, Sam thought, as all the starch went out of Gilbert's face, and his lips twitched.

"Well, I've had a chance to do some investigation, too, and I'm glad to know neurological research plays such a big part in the work you're doing at Royal Kensington. I'm particularly interested in what you've discovered about limbic-predominant, age-related TDP-43 encephalopathy, but we'll have time to discuss that in detail while you're here. In the meantime, the other members of the team are looking forward to meeting you."

And just like that, Gilbert and his wife whisked Chloe away, the older man squiring his young colleague about as though she were his long-lost daughter.

After a stunned, silent moment as Sam and Kendrick watched this miracle unfold, Kendrick said, "She's a magician. Or a witch. Owens looks like pleased puss, while here I was, preparing to shield her from his frosty reception."

Sam just shook his head, not wanting to express his opinion, which was that not one man alive would be immune to Chloe. That would be far too revealing.

As though reading his thoughts, Kendrick rounded on Sam.

"Now, just how *briefly* did you two meet?"

"Oh, for goodness' sake." He gave his friend a narrow-eyed glare even while acknowledging he was just putting off the inevitable. They'd known each other almost their whole lives, and Kendrick wouldn't rest until he'd heard the entire story. "I'm going to get a drink."

There was no way he'd be getting into any of it with Kendrick tonight.

Not when he still had the entire evening to get through and the attraction he felt toward the British neurologist refused to wane the way he wanted it to.

CHAPTER FIVE

THE FIRST THREE weeks of Chloe's Jamaican adventure practically flew by, a blur of work and the type of social whirl she'd never been a part of before. Jamaicans, she realized, thrived on community and casually got together almost every evening after work for dinner or a couple of drinks before heading home. She'd been invited to the Owenses' home for dinner one night and to Kendrick and Rashida Mattison's a few more, where she'd met their two adorable children.

Rashida had also taken Chloe under her wing in a big way. As the owner of a marketing and special-events management company, she seemed to know everyone everywhere they went and had dragged Chloe along to meet up with friends a number of evenings.

Those evenings, along with a full schedule at the hospital, were probably why Chloe hadn't awakened just before her five-thirty alarm, as she usually did. And was also why she was still lying in her bed at five forty.

"Get up, lazybones," she told herself, before finding the impetus to push back the sheets and stick her feet over the edge.

But it still took far more energy than it should to actually sit up, and then a concerted effort to stand. Once in an upright position, she yawned and stretched her way into the bathroom, checking her watch to see how much time she had before her usual Wednesday-morning call with her gran.

At six on the dot, she was sitting on the little patio outside her living room with her cup of tea, connecting to her gran on her tablet via a video chat. The hills behind Kingston were just being touched by the golden glow of the rising sun, while the sky lightened from gray to silken blue.

"Hello darling." Her gran was smiling, and for some reason, seeing her like that made tears gather at the back of Chloe's eyes. "How was your week? Are you having a good time?"

"I've been run off my feet, but in the best possible way," she said, before explaining all she'd been up to. "Everyone has been so welcoming, and Christmas is already in the air, although there's still one week left in November. Some places already have their lights up, and I've been invited to a few parties."

"I don't doubt it," her gran said with a little chuckle. "Christmas in Jamaica is always a big round of parties and jollification."

"Jollification? Not too sure I like the sound of that," Chloe teased. "But you know how much I love Christmas pudding, so that's something I'm really looking forward to."

Her gran chuckled. "I keep trying to tell you to learn how to make them yourself, but you won't listen."

"As long as I have you, you know I'm not going to bother to learn. Besides, I'm a disaster in the kitchen, as you well know."

They chatted for a little longer, and then Chloe had to hang up so as to get ready for work.

"Okay darling. Stay safe, and call me if you need anything at all," Gran said, as though Chloe were no more than twelve and away at summer camp. "I love you."

"I love you, too, Gran."

Silly to get teary-eyed again, and totally out of character really, but Chloe had to search out a tissue and wipe her cheeks.

"What on earth is wrong with me?" she groused, heading to the bathroom for her shower.

Then it struck her, like a blow to her solar plexus.

Frozen in place, she searched her memory.

She'd had her period just before going to San Francisco, hadn't she? Had she had one since then?

Galvanized, she stumbled over to the desk to retrieve her day planner and started thumbing back through the pages. Her hands were shaking, and she had to pause constantly to make sure she'd checked each date.

By the time she found the notation about her period, she was forced to sit down on the nearest chair as her legs threatened to give out.

Mid-September.

That was the last time, although there was a cryptic notation about spotting in early October.

And it wasn't as though her periods were regular. That spotting could have been one, couldn't it? And yet, because of her endometriosis and the pain that was part and parcel of her menstrual cycle, it was normally easy to figure out.

Realizing she was on the verge of hyperventilating, she forced herself to take a couple deep breaths and think it through logically.

It was more likely that stress was the culprit rather than anything else. After the breakup with Finn, there'd been a couple of months where her cycle had been completely disrupted. Her gynecologist had assured her it was nothing to worry about, and after a while, things had returned to normal.

That was probably all there was to it.

The trip to San Francisco, divorce, then finding out about being chosen for the Kensington Project were enough to throw even the staunchest character off-kilter.

At least she knew it wasn't that she was pregnant.

Even as her heart stuttered, she was shaking her head. The fertility specialist had been clear. With the scarring caused by the endometriosis being so severe, the chances of her becoming pregnant were slim to none. On top of that, the only time she'd been sexually active since September was with Sam, and they'd used condoms.

No. It just wasn't possible, and she'd come to terms with her infertility a long time ago. Even thinking about pregnancy as an option would just open her up to more heartache, and she wouldn't go through the pain again. She'd always wanted children but had been forced to shelve that dream years before.

"No."

She said it aloud, the one strident word enough to shake her out of the state she'd been working herself into.

"Don't be stupid. Get up, get dressed and go to work."

And even though she got her legs working and went through her daily preparations, the nagging possibility wouldn't leave her mind.

So, on the way to work, she asked her driver, Delroy,

to stop at a nearby pharmacy, and by lunchtime she had her answer.

Pregnant.

Impossible.

Yet, apparently not.

Her hands were shaking, the tester vibrating before her eyes so the plus sign wavered back and forth.

In fact, her entire body was vibrating, and a bubble of laughter tried to force its way up through her throat but couldn't get through. Realizing she was close to hysteria, she took a deep breath and the laughter, still trapped in her chest, caused her to hiccup. Putting a hand on her belly, she hunched over, fingers gently palpating the flesh as though trying to feel a difference.

Pregnant.

How?

Oh, she knew how, but not *how.* Had a condom broken? Had she and Sam slipped up in some way?

A wave of cold washed over her skin, freezing the laughter into trepidation.

Would Sam believe her when she told him she was pregnant, and that the baby was his?

Then she straightened and lifted her chin.

She didn't give a damn whether he did or didn't. *She* wanted this baby, desperately—wholeheartedly. And whatever decision he made about fatherhood was of no concern to her.

This was her chance to be a mother, and she wasn't just pleased, she was ecstatic, and no one—not Sam, or her family or friends—was going to make her feel otherwise.

Thus bolstered, she got a grip on her ragged and

wildly swinging emotions and went to wash her face before assisting Dr. Owens in the clinic.

Sam finally started closing his patient's incision after a marathon surgery that had started midmorning and gone all the way through to past three in the afternoon.

After being called up for the consult, and as the surgical team looked at the CT scan, Sam knew they were in for the long haul. Mr. Bogues had peritonitis, several large abscesses and what the radiologist agreed could be a fistula from complicated diverticulitis.

They'd gotten patient consent for the colon resection, and Sam had found someone to fill in for him at the afternoon clinic, then it was time to scrub in.

As the extent of the damage to the bowel, and the corresponding infection, was revealed, he marveled once more at his fellow human beings' capacity to withstand pain. Mr. Bogues must have been in constant agony for days, perhaps even a week, and if his wife hadn't insisted he go to the doctor that morning, he probably still would be.

By the time Mr. Bogues was in recovery and Sam had spoken to the patient's wife, it was gone four. As he walked back to his office, Sam's stomach grumbled, reminding him that breakfast—the only meal he'd had for the day—was far in the rearview mirror.

Closing his office door behind him, he checked his watch. He had time to write his report on the operation and then head up to the golf club for dominoes. Although there wouldn't be time to stop for anything to eat, it wasn't the first time he'd depended on the clubhouse kitchen for a meal.

Notes completed, he'd shut down his laptop and was putting it in the case when the phone on his desk rang.

"Dr. Powell here," he said mechanically, knowing it would be his secretary.

"There's a Dr. Bailey here to see you. She's asking if you can spare her a few minutes."

He froze, his body going from calm to red-hot in an instant, his heart rate going into overdrive just at the sound of her name.

He'd avoided her, assiduously, for the last three weeks—turning down all invitations when he knew or suspected she'd be there too. But that hadn't stopped his memories from eroding his determination to keep her at arm's length.

It had taken strength of will he hadn't known he had just to stay away. Especially when there was a little voice inside saying it wouldn't hurt to check up on her, and make sure her stay was going well. Just passing by her office or her apartment, casually, would be no big deal, right?

But he didn't dare. He'd seen her in the distance— once walking with Dr. Owens, another time leaving for the day—and realized the pull she exerted over him was too strong. If he allowed it to become irresistible…

"Dr. Powell?"

He was so deep in his own head, his secretary's voice startled him.

He wanted to say he didn't have time to see Chloe, but his brain was too frazzled to come up with a good excuse as to why, so he said, "Send her in."

Busying himself with securing his computer in its bag, needing something to do with his hands, he barely allowed himself a quick upward glance when she entered the room. May as well have stared, though, as his desk, bag—everything—disappeared, replaced by Chloe's image, now seemingly seared into his retinas.

She had on beige pants and a light pink linen shirt, both of which fit her to perfection, highlighting the delicious curves of her figure. Her face was serious—there were two little creases between her eyebrows—which he'd come to learn were usually a precursor to one of her frowns.

"Thanks for seeing me," she said, her voice brisk. "I hope I'm not interrupting."

He risked another glance, unable to stop himself, and his already rushing pulse picked up additional speed as their gazes met.

She looked away first, glancing around the room, and he could breathe again.

"I'm actually just on my way out," he replied, before clearing his throat, hoping he'd sound normal as he continued, "Will this take long? Or can it wait until tomorrow? We could go to lunch, if you're free?"

That would give him time to prepare, to shore up his tenuous defenses. She'd looked back at him as he spoke, and the expression that fleetingly crossed her face, smoothing out the lines between her brows, confused him.

Was it relief?

"Er, of course," she said, turning right back around and heading for the door. "If that's more convenient."

Then she paused with her hand on the handle and briefly dropped her chin to her chest. Spinning on her heel, she faced him again.

"No, I'm sorry. I won't take much of your time, but

I need to tell you something, and I'd rather just get it over with."

Walking to his consulting chair, she sat, placing her bag on her lap and hanging on to it as though it were a lifeline, her knuckles pale with the strain. Out of habit, once she was seated Sam pulled his chair out and sat, too, his gaze fixed on her face.

Chloe took a deep, audible breath and then said, "I'm pregnant."

The words made no sense to him. And yet they must have, because his heart stumbled and an icy pit opened up in his stomach. He tried to ask her to repeat what she'd said, but his larynx had seized, and when he opened his mouth, nothing came out.

"And before you ask, yes, the baby is yours. If it isn't, then we'll need to contact the Vatican about a miracle, because you're the only man I've been with since I left my husband two years ago."

Her words came at him as though from a distance. The frigid sensation had spread from his belly to form a band around his chest, causing the fleeting thought that perhaps he was having a myocardial infarction.

Then Chloe's face softened into an expression so beatific, all other thoughts flew from his head at the sight.

"It's actually a true miracle to me," she said, her voice low and so full of joy it melted the ice in his torso. "I was told I wasn't able to conceive because of endometriosis. So—" She paused, her chin tilting up to that pugnacious angle he'd come to know so well. "So what I wanted you to know is that I'm keeping this baby, and if you don't want to be involved in his or her life, I can assure you my child will lack for nothing."

He knew he should say something, but try as he might,

nothing came out. And it felt as though he'd been turned to stone. No, to some kind of gelatinous substance that precluded movement, so all he could do was watch as Chloe gave him a small smile and stood up.

"I'll let you get on with your afternoon," she said, and then she was gone.

Pregnant? With my child?

Sam's brain couldn't seem to grasp the concept, and he finally staggered to his feet, not knowing where exactly he planned to go.

Endometriosis...

His heart stopped, and a wave of nausea had him swallowing against the thickness rising in his throat.

Chloe's pregnancy was high-risk.

His legs gave way again, and he plopped back into his chair, momentarily overcome by fear so strong it dulled the edges of his sight to darkness.

What would be worse, he wondered dully: losing a child you never knew existed until it was gone or a second one you suddenly realized you wanted almost too much?

Because, just then, Sam realized the baby growing in Chloe Bailey's womb meant more to him than he'd have ever expected.

That baby—*his child*—was as much a miracle for him as it was for its mother.

CHAPTER SIX

CHLOE WASN'T SURE how she'd made it through the day, and even after speaking to Sam, a fog of disbelief still clouded her brain.

After getting back to the apartment, she closed the door behind her with a sigh and wandered straight through the living room and out onto the balcony. The entire day she'd felt unable to catch her breath, and now, as she lowered herself into a chair, she exhaled hard, searching for equilibrium.

Pregnant.

Tears of joy filled her eyes, causing the scene below to blur into a fantastical kaleidoscope as the reality slammed home again.

She'd been told conception wasn't possible—nor even probable. This was, indeed, a miracle, and she was determined to do everything she could to carry her baby to term.

But first she had to pull herself together so as to think it all through.

What she'd told Sam was true. If he didn't want to be a part of their child's life, that was fine. Hurtful, yes, but still fine. It wasn't as though they'd had a grand love affair or made promises to each other. When you got right down to it, they hardly knew each other at all, except in the most basic, physical way. She'd think him a heel if he abandoned his own flesh and blood, but not everyone was cut out for parenthood. Some people even actively avoided it, for whatever reason.

If he were one of those, then it was probably better he not be involved. Sometimes a reluctant parent was worse than one who never even tried.

Besides, they lived in different countries, a couple thousand-or-more miles apart. Logistically, it wouldn't be easy maintaining a relationship when he was in Jamaica and the child was in England.

England.

That brought her to another point she hadn't considered yet: Would she be endangering her child by staying in Jamaica for the full two months? Should she go home right away and seek a medical consultation with her ob-gyn?

While she'd never walked away from any assignment in her life, she'd do it in a heartbeat if it would be best for her baby.

Best to ask her doctor. Dr. Abdul would advise her as to the best course of action.

Chloe got up, glad there was something constructive she could do, and was crossing the living room for her phone when she remembered it would be going on eleven at night in London.

Pausing, she shook her head at her own nonsense. Hopefully this muddle-headedness wouldn't be a constant during her pregnancy. She'd call first thing in the morning.

She was about to go and change into something more comfortable when her phone rang and the doorbell sounded, simultaneously. Her phone was on the dining table, and she grabbed it as she made her way to look out through the peephole.

"Hi, Rashida. How are you?"

When a glance into the passageway showed a stern-faced Sam standing out there, whatever Rashida said got lost in the buzzing sound filling her ears. Chloe stepped back, as though Sam could see her, and tightened her grip on her phone.

Taking a deep breath, she willed herself to calm. Reaching for the handle to unlock the door, she strove for a breezy, unconcerned tone.

"I'm sorry, Rashida, but you faded out there for a moment. Could you repeat that, please?"

Chloe pulled the door open as Rashida replied, "I said I'm heading to Mayfair Hotel to meet up with some friends and I'll be passing your place in a little while, if you wanted to come."

Waving Sam in with a casual hand, Chloe turned away, leaving him to close the door.

"Sorry, I can't tonight. I have some paperwork to catch up on, but thanks for the invite."

"Aw, okay. Maybe tomorrow evening? If not, you're definitely coming out to Maiden Cay with us on Sunday. There's a session out there—a sort of pre-Christmas bash—and Kendrick's brother is taking us out there on his boat."

Sam hadn't moved from his spot just inside the door. Chloe could see him in the glass front of the dining room buffet. It gave her a little more time to gather her defenses.

"I'll let you know," she told Rashida, torn between

reluctance to get off the phone and a kind of terrifying anticipation of what Sam had to say.

"All right. Talk to you tomorrow."

"Bye," Chloe said, hearing the trepidation in her own voice but tilting her chin up as she ended the call.

Turning toward Sam, she raised her brows but didn't speak, waiting to hear what he had to say. His eyes were hidden behind dark glasses, but she saw him swallow, hard, before he spoke.

"You didn't give me a chance to say anything before you left my office."

It was obvious he was striving for an even tone, but all she heard was accusation, and her hackles rose.

"I thought you'd like a bit of time to think about what I said without me sitting there, staring at you."

Sam sighed, rubbing his chin. The rasp of his hand over stubble had a shiver running down Chloe's spine.

She knew, with breath-stealing clarity, exactly what it felt like to have that stubble against her skin.

Suddenly her perfectly adequate flat was too small—too close with Sam in it—and she spun away, saying, "Let's talk out on the balcony."

They settled at the table outside, and it felt too small, as well. Sam took off his dark glasses, and the distance between them seemed to shrink even farther. This close she could see his shifting expressions, the firmness of his lips and the tightness at the corner of his eyes. Those indications of stress heightened her own tension, and she twisted her fingers together beneath the table, where he wouldn't see.

She was still waiting for him to break the silence, refusing to say anything first. As far as she was concerned, she'd said what she needed to. It was his turn.

Instead of speaking immediately, he reached into the pocket of his white bush jacket and pulled out a slip of paper, which he slid across the table toward her.

"I made an appointment for you to see Dr. Millicent Hall. She's the best obstetrician I know, and when I explained your situation, she agreed to fit you in tomorrow evening. She suggested you ask your gynecologist to forward your records so she can see how bad your endometriosis is."

Chloe sat back, staring at him. Anger rippled through her, and although she tried to tamp it down, her voice came out higher than usual.

"You what?"

Sam's eyes narrowed. "Why do you sound upset? You need to see a doctor."

"You do realize I am a doctor, don't you?"

"A neurologist. Not an obstetrician."

"Listen." She leaned forward and jabbed a finger toward him. "If things had gone as we planned, you wouldn't even be aware of this baby, and that would have been fine. I'm perfectly capable of taking care of myself *and* my child."

Sam's eyes sparked, and his fingers, which had been flat on the table, curled to form fists. His mouth opened... and then closed again as he let out a long, loud exhale through his nose. His expression flashed from anger to pain and then smoothed into a calm, severe mask.

"You say you're pregnant with my child yet seem to expect that I'll just stand back and not try to do the right thing. That's not how this is going to work. So get used to it."

She drew in a breath, ready to fire back, but Sam held up his hand.

"If you want to, you can tell people what's going on and ask for advice as to which obstetrician to go to, but I'm telling you, everyone who's in the know will tell you to go to Millie. She's the best there is. There is the added bonus of her not working at Kingston General, so if you're hoping to keep your condition secret, she'd be a better bet than, say, Dr. Maynard."

Chloe was going to say she didn't care who knew she was pregnant, but bit back the words.

It was probably Sam who cared whether people knew about it or not, and if she was in a reasonable frame of mind, she'd understand why.

No one knew they'd slept together, and he was probably worried about how it would look should any of his friends find out.

"I'm not concerned about secrecy," she told him, making her opinion of his high-handedness clear by the sharpness of her tone. "But my plan is to contact my doctor in the morning and ask for her professional opinion as to whether I should return home immediately or if I can continue with the project. I'm not saying I *won't* see a doctor here, if my doctor says I can stay, but those are arrangements I'm quite capable of making myself."

Sam leaned back in his chair, his gaze boring into hers for what seemed like an eternity, lingering until she felt that familiar—and unwanted—tightening in her belly, and heat rose up into her face.

Suddenly he shook his head and asked, "Have you eaten yet?"

Surprised by the change of subject, Chloe replied, "No. I just got home and haven't given supper any thought."

"I haven't eaten since breakfast," he confessed. "I was in surgery since before noon."

Funny how just then she could see his weariness, when before all she had seen was sternness and strength. She felt herself softening, even as she tried to hold on to her annoyance at his autocratic behavior.

"And I can't be reasonable on an empty stomach," he continued, the corners of his mouth lifting slightly. "Come and have dinner with me, and then we can talk some more."

It was on the tip of her tongue to refuse. Everything about Sam Powell shrieked "danger." But she had to admit, if only just to herself, that his acceptance of what she'd told him about being pregnant with his baby was more than she'd had any right to expect. And his wanting to take responsibility, even if the way he was going about it got her back up, forced her to view him in a rather better light.

But was it wise to spend more time with him than was strictly necessary? How close did they really have to be to effectively coparent, especially long distance?

She sighed to herself. Those were questions that needed to be worked out, and pushing him away at this stage just meant putting off the inevitable.

She stood up.

"Okay. Give me a few minutes, and then we can go."

The look of relief on his face was unmistakable, and he smiled, causing Chloe's heart to stumble over itself.

"Great."

Quickly hustling inside to freshen up, Chloe tried to remind herself they had business to discuss: important issues regarding their child.

Looking at her reflection in the mirror, she gave herself a stern talking-to. All there was between them was one night of passion, and the new life they'd created. Nothing more.

When Chloe went inside, Sam let out a harsh breath and scrubbed at his cheek.

Why was she being so difficult when he was trying to do the right thing by their child—and her? What did Chloe see that made her so hostile to the idea of him being involved with her pregnancy?

What had Vicky seen that had made her hide the fact she was carrying his child all those years ago?

The memory of Chloe saying that if things had gone the way they'd originally planned, he wouldn't even know about her pregnancy speared right through him. That certainly hadn't been his plan eight years ago with Vicky. They'd been together for almost three years and had spoken, albeit in vague terms, about spending their lives together. He'd have thought she'd tell him she was pregnant as soon as she knew. Instead, she'd used the fact they were based in different cities—her busy with her doctorate in Philadelphia, him doing his residency in Baltimore—to hide her condition.

Once more the irony of Vicky's ghost inadvertently bringing Sam and Chloe together made him shake his head.

It had been the anniversary of Vicky's death when he'd first seen Chloe, and after noticing how gorgeous she was, he'd seen her pensive expression. The down-turned lips and lines between her brows. The pain in her eyes and restless confusion in the way she twisted her glass back and forth.

Although he couldn't say how, in her, he'd recognized a kindred spirit—another soul who'd been hurt by forces outside their control.

He'd been longing for some type of forgetfulness despite knowing it was something he'd never truly achieve. Away from home, he didn't have to pretend the day held no significance. In San Francisco he could spend the evening without anyone asking him what was wrong.

No one would care.

And it was strangely soothing to know he wasn't alone in the darkness of his mood, for there, in the same room, was someone else seemingly wrestling with a similar agony.

Even as he'd thought it, he'd seen Chloe's expression go through a slow but glorious transformation. From sad, she'd grown thoughtful, and then she'd smiled as though suddenly finding a way to cast aside whatever had caused her sorrow and to emerge into the light of a new day.

He'd wanted that.

Wanted her.

For succor and to hopefully somehow find a path back to happiness through her, if just for that one night.

And she'd given him all he'd dreamed of, and more.

For the first time in a long time—if ever—he'd lost himself in a woman's arms. It had not just been an erotic feast but an almost spiritual experience. In Chloe he'd found the forgetting he'd craved, along with an ecstasy he hadn't expected and, as he fell asleep, hadn't been sure he knew how to process.

When he'd awoken in the morning and found her gone, he'd been surprised at his own disappointment and anger.

Over the next days and weeks, he'd been intent on telling himself none of it mattered.

That it had been wonderful but was over, and that was for the best.

Now here he was, back in her presence and tied to her through the life she carried in her belly. A life he could hardly bear to think about and yet couldn't stop thinking about.

This was a second chance. Not with Chloe—he had no interest in giving his heart to any woman—but to be the father he hadn't been able to be before.

And no one—not Chloe, not even he, himself—was going to stop him from doing what needed to be done to protect this precious new life.

"I'm ready."

Lost in his torturous thoughts, he hadn't heard her approach and looked up, still dazed, to see she'd changed out of her work clothes. Instead of the tailored outfit she'd had on, she was wearing white capris and a floral blouse that beautifully showcased her curvy figure.

How would she look, round and bountiful with his child?

Desire, white-hot and unmistakable, cracked like lightning through his flesh, leaving him shaken.

There was no time for that—no place for it between them anymore.

So he forced it aside and rose, aware of her careful perusal. The caution in her gaze. He didn't smile, just nodded and waved toward the front door.

"Let's go."

When she turned away, he let out a silent breath before sweeping the piece of paper with the information about her appointment into his hand.

Whether Chloe knew it or not, or liked it or not, she'd be going.

Sam would make sure of it.

CHAPTER SEVEN

WHEN CHLOE EXPRESSED no preference as to where she wanted to eat, Sam took her to a small Chinese restaurant where, although the place itself was not much to look at, the food was amazing.

"Why is it that the Chinese food in Jamaica is so darn good?" she asked Sam, only half joking. It really was delicious.

He gave her a small smile. "My understanding is that most of the Chinese immigrants to Jamaica came from the Hakka region of China, and the food they popularized here differs from the more widespread Cantonese and Sichuan. Of course, the dash of Jamaican spice doesn't hurt."

"Whatever the reason, it's fabulous."

They'd kept the conversation light, as though skirting around the minefield of her pregnancy, and Sam seemed determined not to talk about any of it until he'd eaten.

"Have you tried Jamaican food since you got here?"

Chloe couldn't help chuckling. "I grew up eating Jamaican food. My dad's parents are Jamaican."

His brows lowered slightly. "I didn't know that."

She shrugged. "Not surprising, really."

Sam's eyes narrowed, and Chloe braced for whatever

was coming next, but all he asked was, "So, what's your favorite meal?"

"Gosh, I don't know," she said, looking down at her plate. Whenever their eyes met, a shiver of desire traveled along her skin, and keeping that kind of response to a minimum was imperative. "Maybe oxtail and rice and peas. Or stew peas."

"Did you get mackerel rundown?"

Chloe smiled and nodded, swallowing what she had in her mouth before replying, "That was Granddad's favorite, so we usually had it on his birthday. But you know what I'm really looking forward to?" Sam's eyebrows rose in response to her question, so she told him, "Christmas pudding. I love it, and this year, I get to taste more than just my Gran's."

His lips curved into a teasing smile, and the corners of his eyes crinkled. This time she couldn't seem to tear her gaze away.

"So, you have a sweet tooth."

"I do." No use denying it, and she found herself smiling back at Sam. "I try to keep it under control, though."

His gaze slid briefly down, then snapped back up to meet hers. "Looks to me like you're doing a good job."

There it was again: that tingling rush of interest firing along her spine and settling, warm and arousing, in her stomach. Her heart was racing, and gooseflesh shivered across her back and down her arms.

Mouth suddenly dry, she dragged her tongue across her lower lip and saw his eyelids droop as his eyes tracked the motion.

Then he blinked and focused on the dish of pork and *muknee* on the table, breaking the spell.

And when he next spoke, it was to ask how she was

getting on at the hospital, throwing a veneer of casualness over the tension that continued to shimmer in the air between them.

"It's going really well, I think. I've been seeing patients as well as doing informal training sessions with both the neurologists and the nurses in the department. Dr. Owens is very interested in a study we've been doing about the efficacy of already available drugs on certain symptoms of Alzheimer's disease and other forms of dementia. If they're able to prescribe drugs that already have generic variants, it can cut costs and make treatment more readily available for some of the patients. He's even asked me to take the evening clinic next week." She smiled down at her plate. "I think I've passed his test, and he's feeling a bit better about having me here."

"I think it's safe to say you were in from your welcome dinner. Kendrick and I saw you melt the ice right from the word *go*."

The little glow of satisfaction his words brought was ridiculous but unmistakable, and Chloe had to remind herself not to get caught back up in Sam's charm. She'd been down that road before and look where it had got her!

Not that she was complaining about being pregnant. Far from it. She was eternally grateful for the blessing. Yet it was coming home to her that she was now tied to this man forever, and she wasn't at all sure how she felt about that part of the equation.

"Do you have a particular area of neurology you specialize in?"

His curiosity seemed benign enough, so she didn't hesitate to answer.

"Most of the research I've been involved in leans toward unraveling the mysteries of dementia, but when it comes to patients, I treat all kinds of neurological disorders and diseases. Which is why Dr. Owens seems comfortable with me taking over the clinic for the evening. Apparently, his wife's receiving an award and he doesn't want to take the chance that the clinic runs late and he misses the ceremony."

"I don't blame him," Sam said, shaking his head and using his chopsticks to spear the last steamed dumpling. "That's the life of a doctor, isn't it? We have to be completely reliable when it comes to work but are often the worst when it comes to being available in our private lives."

Was that a warning, that although he was claiming to want to be involved in their child's life, she shouldn't count on him to be committed to raising him or her?

The question rose to the tip of her tongue and was bitten back.

She'd file that away for future consideration.

When they left the restaurant, the sun had set, and Chloe lifted her face to catch a little of the cooling breeze and smiled to herself.

"What's so funny?" Sam asked, having opened her car door so she could get in.

"Oh, just thinking about my family and friends back in London who are probably digging out their jumpers and carrying their macs and umbrellas wherever they go. And here I am wearing capris and a sleeveless top."

"Just wait until the Christmas breeze starts blowing." Sam chuckled, leaning on the door, his face alight with mischief. "Then you'll see Jamaicans bundled up like they're in the Arctic."

She couldn't help joining his laughter. It wasn't so much what he'd said but his expression. The twinkling eyes. A little bit of a wrinkling of his nose. That glorious smile, which did crazy things to her insides and caused the overwhelming urge to tug his face down so she could kiss him.

Thankfully, before she had a chance to turn thought into deed, he closed her door and, still smiling, walked around to get into the driver's seat.

"Are you in a rush to get home?" he asked, as he settled into his seat.

"Not really," she replied, before thinking it through. Then, in case he got the wrong idea, she added, "But I'm sure you have somewhere else to be."

"No, I don't," he assured her with far more intensity than she was expecting as he put the car in gear.

Where they ended up was Devon House, a heritage site that had been pointed out to her but Chloe hadn't visited yet.

"Oh, how stunning," she said, as they drove onto the grounds and she got a close-up view of the stately home. The trees and mansion were decorated with lights, and pots of poinsettias in full bloom had been dotted everywhere. "So festive."

"You like Christmas?"

"Usually," she replied, not wanting to get into why she wasn't as enthusiastic as she used to be. "I like decorating and gift giving, but of course this year will be very different."

"Without your family?"

"Mmm-hmm. And just being here rather than home in London. I'm just not sure what it'll look like."

He nodded as he put the vehicle in park. "It was a while back, but I remember my first Christmas away from Jamaica, when I was at school in the States. Definitely a bit disorienting."

"You didn't come home on break?"

They opened their doors and got out, then he replied.

"My parents couldn't afford to have me flying back and forth for the shorter breaks, so I stayed there most years and just came back for summers if I didn't have any courses planned. A couple of years, Kendrick and I spent Christmas together, but usually I was alone or with other classmates whose celebrations were very different from what I was used to."

"Where did you go to school?" she asked, as she followed him into the redbrick courtyard where various shops were housed.

"Maryland," he replied, naming a well-known university in that state.

"Winter there must have been a rude awakening after Jamaica."

"Oh, it was, believe me. For a while, I was considering staying in the US after my residency, but evenings like this make me glad I didn't."

She could see why. Pausing beneath the branches of a tree, she turned in a small circle, taking in the well-maintained buildings, the shops all aglow and decorated with bows, ornaments and the ubiquitous poinsettias in the windows. The air was warm but not sultry—perfect for sitting outside and enjoying the evening.

"Now comes the hard choice," he said, his voice so serious she spun around to face him, her heart giving a little leap of fear. But even before he spoke again, she saw the twinkle in his eyes, and her sudden spurt of trepidation waned. "Ice cream or baked goods?"

"Oh," she said, on a little gasp of relief. "Definitely ice cream."

"Girl after my own heart," he said, resting his hand lightly on the small of her back to guide her toward the store and leaving a tingling hotspot when he let go. "Take a look at the menu, so you know what you want when you get to the front of the line."

She chose a cup with two scoops—one fruit basket, the other sorrel, which she'd never realized could be used for ice cream, although she'd had the drink at Christmas. Sam got Devon Stout in a cone, and once they'd received their treats, they wandered out into the garden and sat on a bench.

"Do you know the history of this house?"

Chloe had to admit she didn't.

"It was built in the late 1800s by George Steibel, reputed to be Jamaica's first Black millionaire. He was a shipping magnate, and it's said that he could see all the way down to the harbor from the window at the very top of the house and would watch his ships come in. They've renovated the house and give tours, but it's too late to do one now. You'd have to come during the day."

"I think I will," she said, before taking a taste of her ice cream and giving a happy hum as the tropical flavors exploded on her tongue. "This is so good."

Sam shifted beside her, and a glance in his direction found him staring at her in a way that had heat trickling down her spine.

They both looked away at the same time.

It came to her then, just how dangerous this entire situation had become.

On first meeting Sam, it had been all about the physical attraction and the thrill of a tryst with a stranger, far from the prying eyes of anyone who knew her. Afterward for Chloe, the memory of Sam had taken on an almost mythical eroticism. She'd never see him again, and so it was safe to think about him. Fantasize about that night. Even imagine what other days—and nights—would be like with him.

Now, with her pregnancy, they were being forced to get to know each other on a totally different level. There could be no effective coparenting if they chose to remain strangers.

Not that the initial erotic interest had waned, at least on her part, but it had to take a back seat. There was no room for the kind of complications having even a short-term affair would bring, and no matter what, she wouldn't let herself even think of getting back into Sam's bed.

Sexual gratification was nowhere as important as her child's future relationship with its father, and it was up to Chloe to make sure nothing arose to jeopardize it.

And although she was enjoying this companionable interlude, there was one issue she needed to address, to make sure it didn't loom sometime in the future and cause problems.

Bracing herself, Chloe said, "You seem very calm about this entire situation. I'm actually surprised at how readily you've accepted the pregnancy."

Sam paused with his cone almost to his lips and then lowered it with a sigh. She wasn't surprised when his other hand came up and he rubbed his palm along his jawline to his chin. That seemed to be his reaction whenever he was tense or was taking a moment to think.

Finally, he replied, "Honestly, my first thought was to question it all. Whether you really were pregnant and, if you were, whether the baby was mine. I won't lie and tell you that none of the usual responses popped into my head. 'We used condoms.' 'How do I know she's telling the truth?'"

Sam paused, and Chloe realized she'd been holding her breath. Letting it out silently, she found the courage to ask, "So, what do you think now? I mean, I can understand if you want a paternity test after the baby is born—"

He stopped the flow of her words with an uplifted hand.

"Actually, I believe you."

There was no reason for his admission to make her smile. It wasn't approbation to be told someone thought you were telling the truth when you were, but somehow hearing it felt that way.

"Thank you."

He shook his head. "I saw the genuine happiness in your face when you called it a miracle, and realized you really were prepared to have and raise the child by yourself. In my mind, that means you have no reason to lie to me. In fact, you could have just kept the pregnancy to yourself and not bothered to even tell me about it. I'd be none the wiser, once you left Jamaica and went back home."

The thought shocked her, and she blurted, "I wouldn't do that. It wouldn't be right."

The look he gave her was unfathomable.

"Wouldn't it?"

"No. If we'd not met again, and I discovered the pregnancy without knowing your last name or where to find you, that would be one thing. But to know where you were and not tell you? That would be unfair to you and to our child too."

Sam nodded slowly but didn't reply, and Chloe wondered what the expression was that flashed through his eyes.

She could have sworn it was pain, but why would what she'd said be hurtful?

Finally, Sam said, "Listen, I know we don't know each other very well, but I think we should at least try to be friends."

"I agree," she replied, trying to sound firm and confident when she was anything but. "That will make it easier going forward."

"That's my way of thinking too. But I need you to realize that when I make suggestions, I'm doing so in your best interests—and the baby's too."

She knew where this was heading, and tried to sidestep. "I'm sure that's so, but I have a right to make my own decisions. It's not as though I'm without medical experience, so we're even on that front."

Sam let out a long breath through his nose and nodded, although there was that hand again, scraping back and forth across his chin.

"True, and I'll never try to say otherwise. Neither of us is an obstetrician, after all, but I'd personally feel better if you're under medical care while you're here."

Oh, she so wanted to argue, to say it was *her* body and *her* baby and she knew best.

Yet although the former was true, the latter really wasn't.

Sam had stepped up and accepted his responsibility far more readily than she'd had a right to expect, and if she shut him out now, it might make things more difficult in the future. And although neither of them had said it aloud, her pregnancy was high-risk. It really was in the baby's best interest that she see a qualified physician sooner rather than later.

"All right," she reluctantly agreed. "I'll go to the appointment tomorrow."

"Excellent." At least he had the good sense not to sound as though he was gloating as he took the piece of paper out of his pocket and handed it to her. "I'll pick you up at six thirty."

"I don't need—"

The look he sent her way had the rest of the sentence drying up in her throat.

"Six thirty."

CHAPTER EIGHT

DR. HALL TURNED out to be a matronly woman with kind eyes and the type of brisk, no-nonsense approach that Chloe appreciated. Besides a quick upward twitch of her brows when Chloe indicated Sam could come into the office, Millicent Hall had no questions about his involvement. Although she obviously knew Sam well, she treated them both with complete professionalism.

Earlier in the day her nurse had called Chloe to say the doctor had sent an order for blood tests to a lab independent of Kingston General, and Chloe had stopped there before work. After Dr. Hall examined Chloe and they were all sitting at her desk, she pulled a folder closer to her and placed her hands atop it.

"I've had a chance to look at the records Dr. Abdul sent, as well as your bloodwork, and to this point everything appears to be fine. Since there's nothing an ultrasound can tell me about the reduction or changes to your lesions, I think we'll wait to do one at your next visit."

Sam shifted, leaning forward to place his elbows on his knees, obviously intent on what Dr. Hall was saying although her comments were addressed to Chloe. It was silly to feel a little disappointed not to have the chance to see the baby via ultrasound, and Chloe simply nodded in agreement.

"But as you no doubt know, your endometriosis puts your pregnancy into the high-risk category. Dr. Abdul has classified your endometriosis as between levels two and three, and is worried there could be complications caused by your lesions. This means you'll need careful prenatal monitoring and to be on the watch for any signs of problems, not just in your first trimester."

It was what Chloe had expected to hear, but even so, her heart sank.

Sam reached over and took her hand, giving her fingers a squeeze.

The coldness of his fingers took her by surprise, and a quick glance his way showed tightness at the corners of his mouth and eyes.

She squeezed back, and he rubbed his thumb across her knuckles. Somehow, that soft brush of skin on skin calmed her, easing her tension and giving her a warm spurt of pleasure.

"We also have to be on the watch for placenta previa and preeclampsia. Some studies seem to indicate the risk of placenta previa is heightened in women who, like you, had surgical treatment for their endometriosis. And while it's not sure there is a correlation between endometriosis and gestational diabetes, you have other risk factors, as well."

Sam's hand seemed even colder than before, and another glance had Chloe thinking he looked positively gray.

"What can we do to minimize the risks?" he asked, his voice little better than a low rumble.

"Unfortunately, not a lot," Dr. Hall replied, her tone

conveying her sympathy. "However, Chloe will need to get ample rest, limit overexertion—both professionally and while exercising—and making sure she eats a fiber-rich diet."

The sound Sam made conveyed something akin to disbelief, which was backed up by his asking, "That's it? There's nothing else that can be done?"

"Just all the usual things pregnant women who want a healthy gestation and birth do," Dr. Hall briskly repeated, then blithely went on to outline those, ending up with, "And there's no reason to forego sexual activity, as long as there is no pain on penetration."

Sam dropped her hand as though suddenly stung. Chloe couldn't help noticing that before he let her fingers go, his had warmed considerably.

After Dr. Hall gave Chloe some pamphlets and additional instructions, including an appointment in two weeks' time, they took their leave and walked back out to Sam's vehicle.

"Have you eaten yet?" he asked, as he opened her door for her.

"I had something when I got home," she replied, doing her best not to touch him as she got into the vehicle. Something about that tender moment when he'd reached for her hand threatened to melt her resolve not to get any further entangled with him.

He closed her door without replying, but when he got into the driver's seat, he said, "Okay, good. I did, too, but there are some things you and I need to discuss. Do you mind going somewhere where we can talk?"

It was on the tip of her tongue to plead weariness, but instead she sighed silently and said, "Okay."

It wasn't that she didn't want to spend more time in

his company. On the contrary, she was eager to spend as much time with him as she could and knew she must be a little crazy to even feel that way. Better to get away posthaste, so she could give herself the stern lecture she so obviously needed, but it was too late for that now.

Instead of heading back toward New Kingston, Sam drove north.

"What are you up to this weekend?" he asked, his tone casual.

"I'm not sure yet." She leaned her head back against the seat and looked out the passenger window. Not really in the mood for small talk, she reminded herself to be glad he hadn't plunged right into whatever it was he wanted to discuss so urgently. "I usually take care of chores on Saturday, and Rashida invited me to go out on Kendrick's brother's boat to some island or the other."

"Maiden Cay. They have parties out there periodically, and I guess everyone is ramping up for Christmas, hence them having one so late in the year." He seemed to hesitate for a moment and then said, "They invited me too."

Now it was her turn to pause, trying to figure out exactly what he was trying to say.

"Do you want me to refuse the invitation?"

After all, Kendrick, Rashida and Sam had all been friends long before she came along.

"No, why should you?" He sounded genuinely confused. "Marlon's boat is big enough to handle it if the sea gets rough, so you won't get bounced around too much. You don't get seasick, do you? That would be my only worry, since it could lead to dehydration."

"No, I don't." Silly to feel once more gratified by his concern. "Do you think you'll be going?"

"Yeah, man. Sure. It's always a good time."

It was on the tip of her tongue to say she'd found it strange he'd never been around any of the times she'd hung out with Kendrick and Rashida, but she bit back the words. There was no need to maybe get him thinking she'd been disappointed—which she had been.

They were traveling along a road she recognized, and Sam confirmed it by pointing and saying, "That leads to where Kendrick and Rashida live."

As he said it, a car raced toward them on their side of the road, narrowly missing Sam's vehicle as it tucked in behind another vehicle to avoid a head-on collision. Chloe clutched the armrest on the door and pressed an imaginary brake pedal, suppressing a squeak of surprise. When she looked back over her shoulder, it was to see the car swerve back into the wrong lane and speed off again.

Sam threw her an amused glance.

"It's okay. I promise not to get into an accident."

"I don't know how you avoid one, with the way people drive. I thought about renting a car when I first got here, but honestly, I don't know how you do it."

He actually chuckled. "You get used to it, especially when you've grown up here, but yeah, it can be a hair-raising experience."

They were passing a shopping center, and the hills, which always seemed like a backdrop to the city, were suddenly right there. Sam turned off the main road, and they were immediately climbing, driving past houses built right onto the hillside on one side and below the level of the road on the other.

Sam touched a button on the rearview mirror, and Chloe saw a pair of wrought-iron gates start to open just ahead.

When he turned into the driveway, she asked, "Where are we?"

"My home," he said calmly, hitting the button again to close the gates behind them. "We can talk here without anyone interrupting us."

Why did she always feel as though she wanted to object whenever he said or did anything unexpected? It really wasn't like her—at least not the her she was familiar with—but something about his bossiness really was aggravating.

So when he drove into the garage, Chloe made no effort to get out of the car. When he came around and opened her door, she sat looking up at him for a long beat.

Sam looked back, seemingly unconcerned.

"Aren't you getting out? Or would you prefer to sit here while I go inside?"

Chloe huffed but swung her legs out of the vehicle and stepped down. "It would have been nice if you'd told me where we were going and *asked* if I was comfortable with it."

She would have moved past him, but Sam was blocking her way, his solid form suddenly too close, the warmth and scent of maleness suddenly too potent.

"I'm sorry," he said, and there was no hint of sarcasm in the quiet words. "I really am. I'm...so used to just doing whatever I want to, it didn't even occur to me you might object. If you don't feel safe—"

"Don't be silly." Why did he always make her feel wrong-footed? "If I didn't feel safe with you, I'd have never..."

And just like that, it was there between them.

The night in San Francisco. The passion.

Ecstasy.

Sam felt it too. It was obvious from the way his eyelids drooped and his mouth softened. They were close. Way too close. Yet Chloe couldn't find the strength to step back.

Instead, what she wanted to do was step forward into his arms. Lose herself once more in his kisses. His lovemaking.

But there was no room in her life for that kind of forgetting. Not anymore. With a baby to consider, she had to be smart and keep Sam at a distance so their relationship wouldn't mess up life going forward.

As though the same thought occurred to him, Sam stepped back, and Chloe could breathe freely again.

"Come on in," he said, as though that fraught moment had never happened, leaving Chloe wondering if she'd imagined it. But her nerves were all a-jangle, and the slam of the car door made her jump.

His home was multilevel, built into the side of the hill like its neighbors. After turning off the alarm system via a panel by the garage door, Sam bypassed the rooms on the ground floor and led Chloe up a short flight of stairs to the living room. As she hovered near the top of the steps, Sam crossed the room to pull back the curtains, revealing a stunning view of the city spread out below. After he opened the sliding glass door, letting in a cooling breeze, Chloe walked over and they both stepped outside.

Leaning against the balcony railing, she said, "How lovely. Seeing the city from this angle is amazing. Can you see the sea from here?"

"Way in the distance, with the Palisadoes Peninsula just a smudge on the horizon." He turned so he was facing her, but Chloe kept her gaze glued to the view. She hadn't fully recovered from the moment in the garage and didn't trust herself not to get drawn in by his magnetism again. "And it's not quite as nice a view on hazy days. Can I get you something to drink? Limeade or soda or water?"

"No. I'm fine, thank you."

She'd been dreading hearing whatever it was he wanted to talk about, but now wished he'd just get on with it. Being so close, knowing they were alone was doing insane things to her equilibrium.

"I've been thinking…"

Chloe didn't like the way his voice trailed off like that, and her heart rate went into double time at the slowly drawled words. Yet she didn't respond, just waited for him to go on.

"You should move in here with me, for the rest of your trip."

Sam kept his gaze trained on Chloe's profile, waiting for her to react to his words. It took her so long to do so, he was beginning to think she was planning on ignoring what he'd said, then she shook her head.

"No."

"You'll be more comfortable here. I have a lady who comes in to cook and clean three days a week, so you'll never have to worry about any of that. And, because we both work at Kingston General, I can drive you back and forth each day, without any issues."

She turned and looked at him then, her dark eyes searching his face.

Of course, the main reason was so he could keep an eye on her and make sure everything was going well. Be there for her if…

His mind shied away from that thought, just as Chloe shook her head again.

"No, thank you."

He couldn't take no for an answer. The emotions that had overtaken him as he'd listened to Millie Hall describe the risks inherent in Chloe's pregnancy demanded he do something—anything—to mitigate the chance of miscarriage. Having her here would allow him to keep a firm eye on her—make sure she ate properly, didn't work longer hours than necessary or take on more than she should.

Yet he knew saying those things wouldn't go over well with her, and as he struggled to find the right arguments to win her over, she lifted a hand.

"I can see you getting ready to ride roughshod over me," she said in a surprisingly gentle tone. "But it won't work. I have no intention of letting anyone—not even my family—know about this baby until I'm reasonably sure..."

He saw it then, as it flashed through her eyes. The same fear he battled with. Without thinking it through, he reached for her and gathered her close.

She resisted, her body tense and stiff for a long moment, and then she relaxed, almost melting against him as her arms went around his waist.

Burying his face in her hair, he said, "We'll get through this, Chloe. Everything will work out."

"Unfortunately, the outcome really isn't in our hands," she replied softly.

"No, but we can be in it together and support each other for as long as you're here." He was trying so hard to ignore the way she felt in his arms—the sweet weight of her resting against him. The way they fit so perfectly.

The moment was tender, and beautiful. Too special to let his outrageous desire destroy. "I know it's unconventional. Maybe some people will think it scandalous. But we're adults, and that shouldn't matter."

She leaned back slightly so as to meet his gaze, and in the dim light from the living room, her expression seemed to shift with varied emotions, one following the other. And then she inhaled so deeply he felt her breasts lift against his chest in what could only be an accidental caress but one that struck additional fire into his belly.

"I don't want to think right now, Sam. Don't want to search for answers. It feels too overwhelming and confusing. I just need simplicity—and something I'm absolutely sure of."

And with that, she raised her arms to loop around his neck, and pulled his lips down to meet hers.

CHAPTER NINE

CHLOE HAD SPOKEN the unvarnished truth.

She didn't want to think anymore. Not with all the turmoil rushing through her head, and the sensations bombarding her from being in Sam's arms.

Somehow, feeling—actual physical closeness—was suddenly more important.

In Sam's lovemaking could be found sweet forgetfulness and perhaps even a kind of clarity.

Yet those thoughts dissolved into nothingness under the onslaught of Sam's kisses, which left her weak-kneed and breathless with desire.

Oh, she knew the risks—to herself and her equilibrium—but his tenderness and acceptance had been her undoing.

Now she wanted his touch. Wanted to once more feel like the woman only he had ever moved her to be. Strong. Demanding. In control, until with a burst of pleasure, control was lost, leaving satiation behind.

Sam's breathing was as rushed as hers, and his hands roamed—restless and arousing—over her back and arms and bottom, pulling her impossibly closer with each hard caress.

And, oh, how he could kiss.

His mouth moved on hers, urging her to open for him,

to let their tongues dance against each other in sexy, provocative play. There was restrained ferocity in the way he kissed, and it drove Chloe wild.

Worming her arms between their bodies, she unbuttoned his shirt, baring his muscular chest to her roving palms. He was already in the process of returning the favor, and Chloe shivered as the cool night air touched her overheated skin when he pushed her top down her arms. It didn't take any coaxing at all for her to allow him to pull it off, and it sagged around her waist.

And still they kissed.

There were things she wanted to tell him—like how her nipples ached for his fingers or his mouth. Or how wet he would find her when he finally got her pants off.

These were things she'd never said to a man before. Not until that night in San Francisco, when inhibitions had fallen away as though they'd never existed.

Sam brought out the sexual being that had been trapped inside her all her life, and the freedom of letting go was more potent than tequila.

His mouth left hers only to latch on to her neck, and the sound she made was harsh with carnal pleasure.

"Yes," she said, arching her head back so as to give him access. "There. Oh…" They both groaned at the same time, and Chloe heard herself say, "You make me want to come, just from that."

A growl broke from Sam's throat and he picked her up. As she wrapped her legs around his waist, he turned to carry her back inside. The hard length of his erection resting right between her legs made her squirm, and she rubbed against it, feeling the tension in her belly tightening. Tightening.

"Dammit, Chloe." He lowered her to the couch, and

she spread her thighs, pulling him down on top of her. "You make me wild. I feel like a teenager again when you do things like that."

She would have laughed if she'd had the breath for it, but the need she felt had put her on a mission that demanded satisfaction.

"I don't want to wait, Sam. You make me feel better than I've ever felt before. Give me what I need."

He levered up to kneel between her legs, and the expression on his face had a hard shudder firing down her spine. It was the look of a man on the edge—feral, dangerous, aroused. Yet although he moved quickly, he was also surprisingly gentle as he removed the rest of her clothes until she lay bare and wanton before him.

Then, despite her egging him on, telling him to hurry, he shook his head.

"No," he said, taking her foot in his hand and kissing her ankle. "I *won't* hurry. We have all night."

"Take off your pants," she demanded, but he only laughed and shook his head.

"Not yet." He shifted slightly away when she tried to reach his fly herself. "You're so impatient."

By way of reply, since she couldn't do as she wanted and he was taking his own sweet time, she cupped her own breasts and pinched the nipples.

"God, yes," he growled. "Pinch them again. I love how responsive they are."

"I want you to do it." She pouted. "You should be touching them with your hands or mouth."

"I'm getting there," he replied, before kissing her calf.

"But so slowly," she said, before her voice was lost in a low gasp as he lifted her leg higher and his tongue swiped behind her knee.

And she'd been so intent on what his mouth was doing, she didn't realize his other hand had slid up and rested on her inner thigh until his thumb parted her folds, sending a shockwave through her system.

She cried out, arching her hips to deepen the contact, and Sam didn't disappoint. His knowing touch circled and pressed, enticing her arousal to a feverish peak until she came almost silently, no breath left for sound.

"There," he said, his voice deep and dark, almost dreamy. It made her shudder, not just from the timbre but also from the way his breath rushed across her thigh. "Was that enough?"

Opening her eyes, she realized he'd slipped off the couch and was kneeling beside it. Somehow, in the midst of her orgasm, he'd maneuvered her body over, so one leg was still on the cushion while the other was draped over his shoulder.

"No, it wasn't enough," she rasped, her throat tight, her body already craving another endorphin jolt from his loving.

"Tell me what you want," he said, his eyes gleaming behind slumberous lids, his lips soft, slightly upturned and seductive. "I love how you know what you want and how to ask for it."

So she did, her voice getting higher and more strained as his mouth and tongue, hot and slick against her flesh, took her over the edge once more.

Sam didn't give Chloe much time to come down off her orgasmic high before he surged to his feet and held out his hand.

"Come," he said, hardly able to get the word out

through the tightness of his throat. "Upstairs. I want you in my bed."

She rose, her legs wobbly, and he steadied her when she swayed before turning her toward the corner of the room and the staircase leading up to the bedrooms.

He was behind her as she climbed, and he couldn't keep his hands off her, so much so that when she reached the landing, he stepped up behind her, and pulled her back against his chest.

Her breasts were glorious weights in his hands, and when he found her nipples—tightly puckered—with his fingers, he reveled in her soft moan of delight.

Chloe made him crazy with need, but at the same time, he wanted this to last as long as he could. If she touched him right now, if he entered her body, he'd be done.

Done, done, done.

So he leaned against the wall, putting off the moment when they'd be on his bed together.

"Sam." Her voice was little more than a breath. "Oh, Sam. What are you doing to me?"

Loving you.

The thought ricocheted in his brain, but he didn't say it, just kept caressing her, teasing her, until she shivered in his arms, her hips rotating against his groin.

"Now, Sam," she said, her voice tight. "I can't wait."

Although he was touching her, his fingers slipping through folds so wet and hot he could hardly stand it, coaxing her toward another orgasm, he knew what she was asking.

And he couldn't resist.

Reluctantly moving his hands until they rested on

her hips, he nudged her up the last four steps to the corridor above.

"Last door on the right."

He hardly recognized his own voice. It came out like the rasp of a file over wood, rough and raw.

When he walked into his room behind her and turned on the light, there was a moment where his heart, which had been pounding, slowed and then missed a beat. He faltered, unsure what the sensation making him lightheaded could be. Then Chloe climbed into his bed and everything fell into place.

He followed, stopping to kick off his footwear and then remove his pants. The entire time he was watching her—seeing the restless way her fingers moved, the slow, sexy smile that tilted her luscious lips.

She held out her arms to him, and he didn't hesitate. Climbing in beside her, he pulled her close and kissed her over and over again, needing the closeness almost more than the physical satisfaction he knew awaited.

Habit had him reaching for a condom, respect for her had him putting it on, although there was nothing he wanted more than to be bareback inside her tight, wet heat.

Pulling her against his side, he said, "You drive, Chloe," and the look of sheer, sensual delight she gave him made him harder, if that was humanly possible.

She straddled his thighs and then, as though savoring every second, slowly slid home.

Sam screwed his eyes shut, fighting the need to move, thrust, to give in to the orgasm already building.

But this was Chloe's show, and he tried his best to let her have her way.

She chose a slow, rocking motion that had his breath

coming fast and heavy and took his control to the breaking point.

Yet she cried out first, as her hips suddenly picked up speed, her inner muscles contracting. Her orgasm took him over the edge so quickly, and with such intensity, an involuntary shout broke from his throat.

She collapsed down across his chest, and then after a few minutes where they both struggled with their breathing, she rolled to his side.

Sam floated, satiated and pleasure-drunk, sleep dragging at his eyelids. He tried to fight it, but when he looked down at Chloe, he realized she'd already dozed off and he allowed himself to follow suit.

"Sam. Sam."

Her voice called to him and he instinctively tightened his grip, keeping her flush against his chest. Even half-asleep he knew if he let her go, she would disappear again.

"Sam. Wake up."

A sharp jab to his ribs from a well-placed elbow brought him fully awake.

"Huh? What?"

"I need to go to the lav. And you need to take me home."

Loosening his arms from around her was a lot harder than it should have been, but Sam forced himself to do it, then watched as she made her way to the en suite bathroom. With a huge yawn, Sam rolled over and dragged his pillow into a more comfortable position.

When Chloe came out, she poked him.

"Come on, Sam. It's late, and I need to get back to my flat."

"Why don't you just stay here, and I'll take you home early in the morning."

"Nope. I'm sorry, but that won't work."

"All right," he grumbled, before rolling over and grabbing her to pull her back down on top of him. "All right."

She melted into him, just for a moment, and then she wriggled free.

"None of that, my lad. Up you get."

So, under duress, he complied when what he really wanted was for her to climb back into bed and go back to sleep in his arms.

Driving her home, the car was quiet except for the radio, both of them seemingly lost in thought. At her apartment, he walked her to her door and gently kissed her good-night.

"I meant what I said earlier," he told her. "I want you to move in with me."

The sweet, satisfied expression fell from her face, and those little lines between her brows came back.

"That's not a good idea, Sam, irrespective of what happened this evening. I'm not ready to have people knowing about the baby, and if I move in with you, there'll be questions I don't want to answer."

It seemed so obvious to him, and Sam saw her words as an opening rather than a firm refusal.

"We're going to have to answer those questions eventually, especially after the baby is born. It'll be easier for us to explain if it's clear we're involved from now on, rather than it looking as though we were just sneaking around."

"I'm not moving in with you, Sam." She eased out of his embrace, leaving him with an empty sensation. Leaning against her doorjamb, she gave him a level look.

"This situation is complicated enough without compounding it."

"Think about it," he said, making it a demand when he was inclined to plead. "Please. I want to introduce you to my family, let them get to know you while you're here. It would go a long way to making things easier in the long run."

"We can do that without us living together," she pointed out, those frown lines coming and going. "I just don't want…"

When her voice faded, he asked, "What? What don't you want?"

She took a deep breath and then sighed before facing him again, her eyes wide and luminous. "I don't want either of us to get in too deep. I just got out of a marriage that left me questioning everything about myself—my life, expectations, reactions. I don't think I trust myself to remain objective, especially with the added fact of being pregnant."

He heard the honesty in her tone and wondered if he should match it. Yet did she really need to know about Vicky? And even if she did, it wasn't a conversation for one o'clock in the morning while standing outside her door.

"I hear what you're saying, but I think it would work out to our advantage, so promise me you'll think about it anyway?"

"Yeah. I will," she said with what sounded like a healthy dose of irony in her voice. "'Night, Sam."

After she'd gone inside and closed the door behind her, Sam stood there for a moment lost in thought, before heading back to the elevator.

He wished he could say he knew neither of them were

in any danger of catching feelings, but he was honest enough with himself to admit Chloe had a valid point. The last thing he wanted was to get too emotionally involved, despite the fact she was carrying his child. Chloe seemed to feel the same way, too, worrying that she might find herself in the kind of rebound situation that's hard to make proper sense of or get out of.

No, he definitely wasn't interested in forever, but if he could get her to agree to spending the rest of her time in Jamaica with him, he couldn't see how it could be a bad thing. Everyone would know they'd had a relationship, so the baby wouldn't come as a huge shock.

Plus, he thought as he got back into his car, he'd have the wonderful pleasure of having her in his bed every night, without having to drive her home in the wee hours of the morning.

And that would more than make up for any other risks!

CHAPTER TEN

HOW SHE WAS able to refuse Sam's suggestion that she move in with him was a mystery to Chloe, and she was still shaking her head over that the next morning. And while prepping for morning rounds, only half of her brain was on the workday ahead. The other was still wrestling with the question of *why* she'd said no.

It wasn't as though she hadn't wanted to say an enthusiastic yes. That had been her first impulse. Why shouldn't they enjoy themselves together for the next six or so weeks? They were both single adults, and it would, as he'd pointed out, make explaining her pregnancy to friends and family easier.

Plus after the night before, she was ravenous to get back into his bed.

No matter what, she couldn't bring herself to regret one moment of Sam's lovemaking. There was something about the way he touched her that made her feel like a princess.

No, a queen. Imperious and powerful, demanding her due and getting it.

That was heady stuff.

However, she had another problem.

Sam scared her. A lot.

There was something so compelling and forceful about her reactions to him, she knew it really wouldn't be hard to become attached. A one-night stand was all well and good, but living in his house, sleeping in his bed every night knowing full well the relationship wasn't going anywhere? She wasn't at all sure she was capable of pulling that off and keeping her heart intact, especially since she was carrying his child.

Surely it was better to play it safe? Keeping her own space, seeing him only on her own terms might help her maintain an emotional distance. There was no reason why they couldn't enjoy sex without her actually living with him.

"Dr. Bailey?" Nurse Oliver put her head around Chloe's office door. "Dr. Pullar from psychiatrics sent up for a consult. Dr. Owens is asking you to go."

Thankful for the distraction, Chloe got directions to the psychiatric unit and went on her way. Yet as she made her way across the hospital grounds to the other wing, her thoughts circled right back to the pickle she was in.

Nothing seemed clear-cut to her anymore, leaving her wondering how to figure out if whatever decisions she made were right.

The reality was her experiences with men were limited. Her only real relationship had been with Finn, and she'd fallen for him so hard and so fast that by the time she'd regained her senses, she was walking down the aisle.

Only in hindsight did she realize that in many ways she'd been subsumed by him and their relationship. Although she knew herself to be a competent, modern woman, they'd never really had a partnership. Finn made demands and decisions, and she'd marched in lockstep along with him, sometimes against her better judgement. It was no excuse to say she'd done that to keep the peace or because he'd go and do whatever he wanted to anyway.

It just made her a twit.

She'd always been the peacemaker of the family, smoothing ruffled feathers and keeping things on track, and Finn—knowing that—had taken advantage. Worst of all, she'd let him.

Who's to say Sam wasn't cut from the same cloth?

He'd said himself that he was used to getting his own way and doing whatever he wanted without thought for anyone else. While he'd shown her consideration in many ways, he'd also been overbearing in others.

She wasn't up for that type of ride again, even temporarily—thank you very much—so getting emotionally tangled up with Sam wasn't on.

"Nice to meet you," Dr. Pullar said, after Chloe had found the correct area and introduced herself. While escorting her toward the examination room, he continued, "Is it unusual for you to get a call from a psychiatrist wanting a consult?"

"Not at all," she replied, sending him a smile. "We're very big on cooperative medicine at Royal Kensington, so whatever specialty is needed becomes a part of the patient's team. I'm guessing it's the same here."

"It is," he replied, opening a door and waving her through. "Especially when we get referrals and the patient hasn't been under consistent medical care, as is the case with Ms. Barnes."

Twenty-five-year-old Kadisha Barnes had been taken to a rural hospital by a family member. According to the history they'd gathered there, she'd started to display personality changes a few months before, including extreme mood swings, which had gradually increased. She'd resisted going to the doctor, for reasons best described as paranoid. They'd taken her to the nearest hospital the day before, after she'd suffered extreme confusion and then had a seizure.

"As is sometimes the case because it's difficult to get all the tests done outside the larger centers, she was referred to us for psychiatric evaluation, but I'd like your opinion."

As Chloe took the file from him, she asked, "You suspect physiological disease rather than psychiatric?"

"Yes, from the progression."

Looking at the notes, Chloe could understand why the psychiatrist might think so. Off the top of her head, Chloe could name a number of diseases that mimicked the effects of psychiatric disorders and had to be ruled out before a diagnosis could be made.

"Did the family member list any other changes they may have noticed recently, or has Ms. Barnes been able to answer any questions?"

Calvin Pullar shook his head. "Unfortunately, the history I've given you in the notes is all we have, and Ms. Barnes is frightened and won't speak."

"Have you examined her yet?"

He shook his head. "She's truly terrified, and I decided it would be better to get you down here first rather than putting her through repeated examinations."

"Sensible. Let's take a look."

Kadisha was indeed scared, but there was less of an adverse reaction when Chloe and the female nurse spoke to her, while she shrank back when Dr. Pullar approached, so Chloe took the lead. Although she wouldn't answer questions, Kadisha did follow directions, allowing Chloe to come to a tentative diagnosis.

"I'd suggest both TSH and T3 blood tests," she told Dr. Pullar. "Although there's no sign of a goiter, I highly suspect hyperthyroidism."

He nodded, and thanked her for her time. "I'll call up later and let you know the results."

As she made her way back toward her office, of course Sam Powell wormed his way back into her thoughts, and her blood heated anew as she thought about the night before.

The memories made it hard to think straight and be realistic. How easy it would be to just give in to the desire, without worrying about the consequences. While acknowledging it was best to keep on a friendly footing with him so they could be cordial and pleasant going forward, there could be such a thing as *too* friendly.

Or, more like too *invested*.

She sighed, trying to be logical. Only after the pregnancy revelation had Sam come near her. Didn't that indicate his main interest was the baby, no matter what else happened between them?

With a sigh, Chloe acknowledged to herself that she was in danger of getting in way over her head. What she needed was to cultivate detachment, so it would be easier to walk away when the time came.

Just as she was about to exit the building, as though her thoughts had conjured him, she heard Sam call her name, and her heart leaped. With her hand still on the door, she watched him stride toward her and only just stopped herself from grinning like a fool in response to his obvious pleasure at seeing her.

"What are you doing on this side of the hospital?" he

asked, as he came alongside her and reached out to open the door for her.

"Just examining a patient. Psych asked for a consult," she replied, stepping out into the courtyard and welcoming the wave of heat since she was sure her face was glowing. She knew she should tell him there was no need to accompany her back, but somehow the words wouldn't come out.

"So, how're you this morning?" he asked, as they set off toward the other side of the compound.

"I'm well, thank you," she replied demurely, even though gooseflesh broke out across her shoulders, and her nipples peaked at his intimate tone. So much for detachment! "And you?"

The sound he made was somewhere between a snort and a chuckle. "As well as can be expected, when I spent most of the rest of the night thinking about you."

There went her heart again, jumping and racing like a crazy thing.

"Sam—"

She tried for a quelling tone and apparently succeeded, because Sam laughed.

"Hey, don't go all schoolmarm on me. I'm just speaking the truth. I was wondering… Do you have any plans about seeing other parts of the island while you're here?"

The change in subject surprised her and she paused, looking up at him as she replied, "Yes, but I'm not sure where to go, or how to get there yet. I haven't given it as much thought as I should."

"Okay, let's work something out, and I'll take you."

"You don't have to—"

"I know, but I want to. It would be a shame for you

to come this far and not see some of the island. Where were your grandparents from?"

"Well, Granddad was born in Portland, and Granny is from Hanover."

He chuckled. "Of course. Opposite ends of the island. Well, let me see what I can come up with, okay? What about this evening? Are you doing anything?"

She started walking again, trying to quell the rush of excitement she felt just from talking to him. The man was a menace to her equilibrium, and she forced an airy tone into her voice, trying not to let him see just how off-kilter she was in his presence.

"Oh, I don't know. Rashida usually calls in the afternoon to make plans. She also said she wants to take me shopping on Saturday, and then I'm supposed to spend the night with them and go to Maiden Cay on Sunday."

There was no way to accurately interpret the sound he made, and Chloe wasn't going to ask what it meant.

"Well, if she doesn't call for you to go out with her, want to have dinner with me this evening?"

They were approaching the entrance, and she slowed just a bit while trying to figure out how to respond. Of course she wanted to see him, but hadn't she just been telling herself it was imperative to maintain some sort of distance? That couldn't happen if she were constantly in his company.

Finally, she shook her head. "No, thank you. I have a full clinic load today and I think I'll just go home and relax."

"Well, you'll have to eat anyway. I could bring something over and—"

"Listen," she said firmly, giving him a stern look and stopping far enough away from the doors so they wouldn't be overheard. "You don't need to feel as though you have to take care of me or entertain me, Sam. I'm more than capable of doing that myself, okay? I'll see you on Sunday, for the boat ride."

And then, because she stupidly felt like crying, she turned on her heel and marched to the door, determined to put her mind back on work and forget all about Sam Powell.

At least for a while.

Sam wasn't sure what to make of Chloe's cool, cutting response to a simple invitation to dinner, and his first impulse was to follow her back into the hospital and get her to explain. After the night they'd spent together, he really hadn't expected her to brush him off like that.

Not that he'd thought she'd be suddenly head over heels for him, either, nor did he want her to be. He remembered all too well the way she'd slipped out of his life in San Francisco. Clearly, Chloe Bailey was a master at compartmentalizing and keeping her emotions firmly in check, no matter what she might say to the contrary.

It made him wonder exactly what it was her ex-husband had done, and if whatever it was were to blame for the way she was handling Sam now. That was something else he'd like to corner her and ask her about.

But instead of going after her, he turned and headed back over to the other building. Although it irked him to not demand an explanation, having grown up with sisters and seen how his parents dealt with arguments, he decided to leave her alone for at least the rest of the day.

Not that she'd sounded angry, Sam thought as he headed back to his office. Maybe she was just a bit overwhelmed by everything and needed some space. Everyone handled situations differently, and just because he was itching to have it out with her didn't mean he had the right to demand that conversation.

Perhaps she was even doubtful of his motivations, both for sleeping with her and for asking her to come and stay with him, and that made her overcautious.

In truth, Sam was a little muddled about his motivations himself, so while he chafed at the decision not to contact Chloe Friday afternoon, it seemed for the best. It might give him a chance to figure out what, exactly, he was doing.

The evening found him uncharacteristically alone at home, leaning on the veranda railing, looking out at the city lights. Usually he'd be out somewhere, playing darts or having a couple of drinks since he wasn't on call, but tonight he wasn't up for it.

It wasn't in his nature to unburden himself to others or look for someone else to solve his problems. He'd always handled his business himself. Even after Vicky died, the only person he'd spoken to about her pregnancy was Kendrick, who was his oldest friend. More like a brother, really. In Sam's eyes, there'd been no need to make his parents sadder than they had already been or open himself up to a new, more dreadful level of pity.

Chloe, at least, had told him about the baby immediately, and he had to give her credit for that. She'd also advised him that, realistically, they didn't need him, which was something he both knew was true and resented.

The thought came to him then that not only did he want this baby but he *wanted* to be needed—to be an indispensable part of, if not Chloe's life, then his child's.

Did he have a right to be? Did he deserve that kind of grace?

He'd questioned his fitness to be a father many times since Vicky's death. If she hadn't doubted his abilities to parent, why hadn't she told him about their baby? It was, to him, the only thing that made any sense, no matter how many other reasons Kendrick espoused.

Are you sure the baby was yours?

Maybe she didn't plan on keeping it?

Strange how now those questions brought only a dull ache and a lingering wish to know rather than the grinding anguish they always had before. He'd acknowledged he'd never know the answers—that whatever he thought or suspected would remain conjecture—but this sensation, so much like acceptance, was new.

As new and as unexpected as his overwhelming pleasure at knowing he was going to be a father.

Why he felt so strongly about Chloe's pregnancy, he didn't know and didn't feel the need to dwell on too deeply. He preferred to act rather than navel-gaze.

Taking a sip of his drink, he tried to be logical about what absolutely needed to be done.

With the way things stood, Chloe would be on the island only until the end of the year. After that, she'd return to the UK.

Everything inside was telling him this thing between them needed to be settled, and soon.

Long before she was scheduled to return to London.

She'd turned him down flat when he'd asked her to move in with him, even temporarily, but maybe there was some way to change her mind—other than making love to her until she was too tired to go home?

If he could prove he was someone she could count on to think about what she wanted, who would provide whatever she and their child needed, would that be enough?

For some reason he couldn't shake the idea that if he could just get her to move in with him, it wouldn't be too hard to get her to agree to stay on the island past January first.

Maybe...

His brain faltered, not wanting to think too deeply about marriage. He'd planned on marrying Vicky—had trusted her in a way he'd never been able to trust another woman after discovering her duplicity. When she died, he'd pledged not to get entangled—not to risk himself in that way—again.

Yet fate had presented him with an opportunity he hadn't wanted but couldn't turn away from, and he needed to make sure he didn't blow it.

And if taking care of his child properly meant marrying a woman he desired but didn't love, was he willing to go that far?

Perhaps if he only desired her, it wouldn't be enough, but Sam had to admit he genuinely liked Chloe. He'd go so far as to say she was intriguing, infuriating and enticing. He admired her intelligence and drive along with her dedication to her profession.

And he wanted her physically, with an intensity that often approached the point of pain. If last night was any indication, the passion between them hadn't subsided one iota. If anything, it had heightened to explosive proportions.

Many a marriage had been successfully based on far less. There was no reason to believe they couldn't make a good lasting go of it, especially to protect and properly raise their child together.

But, even *if* he got comfortable with the idea, Sam realized it would make no sense to think about broaching it with Chloe. She'd had no problem shooting him down over something as inconsequential as dinner. No doubt she'd blow him out of the water if he just came right out and said they should get married.

No. He needed a plan. One that would show her the type of man he truly was and convince her they were meant to be together, for the sake of their child.

And he didn't have a heck of a lot of time to think one up and put it into play.

The days were ticking away a lot faster than he'd like. Soon it would be December, and there would be only a month before she was set to leave.

Whatever he needed to do had to be done soon, before he lost the chance completely.

CHAPTER ELEVEN

CHLOE SPENT FRIDAY evening alone and out of sorts as Rashida had taken her children to a birthday party. Grumpy and annoyed with herself for it, she'd sat down to watch a documentary in the evening and fallen asleep, awakening at minutes to midnight.

The nap hadn't refreshed her, though, so she went straight to bed, only to awaken in the morning before the sun was even up, although she usually slept in a little on the weekends. At least she had texts from Cora, complaining about a man she was working with in Sweden, to occupy her, and chatting back and forth helped her spirits. Something about the way Cora mentioned Jonas had Chloe wondering what she wasn't saying…but who was she to pry? Here she was, pregnant by a man she hadn't even told her best friend about and saying nary a word.

The invitation to go shopping with Rashida that morning didn't materialize, either, as her son had a stomachache and needed attention.

That, of course, was perfectly understandable, but Chloe then spent a few hours sulking while taking care of chores. Finally, tired of her own nonsense, she sat down to read up on new research results, sent to her by the team at Royal Kensington, and promptly fell asleep—

again. Awakening sometime later, she sat for a moment, disoriented, wondering what exactly had roused her, and it was only when the doorbell sounded again that she came to completely.

Was this the infamous pregnancy-induced tiredness she'd always heard about? If so, she thought as she stumbled to the door, it rather sucked.

When she looked through the peephole to find Sam on her doorstep, she was instantly fully awake and ready for battle.

In fact, if she were being strictly honest, she'd been ready for battle since their last conversation, expecting Sam either to call her back or try to see her to have it out. He'd taken the wind out of her sails by the simple method of ignoring her, while she'd stewed on both the fact they'd slept together again and that he'd asked her to go stay with him.

Which, in turn, just made her even madder.

So she yanked open the door with a certain level of ferocity, but whatever she'd planned to say died in her throat when she saw the jumble of bags and boxes in the corridor.

Finally, she gestured to them and said, "What on earth is all this?"

"Christmas decorations," he said, picking up a long box in one hand and a couple of bags in the other. "You said you liked putting them up, and I thought you were probably missing doing that this year, so I brought you some."

She was too shocked to do anything but move out of his way as he headed into the apartment.

"That wasn't necessary…"

He put down his burdens and gave her a grin before heading back out the door for the rest.

"No, but some of the best things in life aren't strictly necessary, are they? I just figured that since you'd be here for Christmas, it would be nice for your place to be festive."

"But why?" She was still standing beside the open door like a ninny, watching him stride back and forth with boxes and bags. Had he bought out an entire Christmas store? Did they even have stores like that in Jamaica? "I'll just have to take it all down before I leave on the first of January."

"I'll help you," he replied, shoving the last couple of boxes into the apartment with his foot, then closing the door behind him. "Besides, it's the Christmas season. You might want to invite people over or take pictures to send to your family back in the UK. Would you want the place to be bare?"

"I wouldn't care," she said, unaccountably both annoyed and close to crying, unable to figure out if he were being nice or somehow manipulative. "It's too much bother."

He'd stooped to start opening the box clearly marked Christmas Tree, but paused to rock back on his heels and look up at her.

"I've upset you." Rising to his feet, he shook his head. "I'm sorry. That certainly wasn't my intent. I can take all of this stuff away if you really don't want it."

Now he was making her feel like an ungrateful cow, and Chloe blinked, trying to hold back her stupid tears.

"It's not that I don't want it, it just seems like a lot of trouble to go to when it'll all just have to come back down in a few weeks."

"Bah," he said. "It's not a big deal at all. Please don't cry."

"I'm not crying," she huffed, even though he'd dissolved into a watery silhouette because of the moisture in her eyes. "I don't cry."

She saw him move but wasn't fully prepared when he gathered her close. The immediate jolt of electricity through her system miraculously had her tears drying up, and for a moment, she fought the urge to relax and take the comfort his embrace offered. But her body hadn't got the memo and went almost boneless, even as it heated and tingled, remembering all the amazingly naughty things they'd done two nights before.

"Of course you don't cry," he agreed. "Although I have heard that pregnant women sometimes do things they've never done before—like burst into tears or, in Rashida's case, be nice to their husbands."

Chloe's huff of laughter at his remark about the oft-acerbic Rashida turned into a hiccup.

"You're terrible," she said, sniffling, trying not to pay attention to how wonderful it felt to have his arms around her and determined not to let him know how close she was to dragging him off to her bed. "And I'm sorry. Although it doesn't excuse my grouchiness, I've been up since five this morning."

Sam leaned back so he could see her face, his palms making soothing circles on her back. At least, she assumed they were supposed to be soothing instead of making her blood start rushing through her veins. "Have you eaten?"

"What is it with you and food?" she asked, forcing a little chuckle and trying to ease away from his far-too-tempting body. "You're constantly trying to feed me."

Tightening his grip so she couldn't get away without

a struggle, he tilted his head to one side as though think-ing about it. Finally, he replied, "I love to eat, to be hon-est, so since it's important to me, I guess I figure it is to everyone else, too, and I try to feed the people I care about. I guess food is my love language."

Oh, she wasn't putting even a toe into *that* water, so Chloe fell back on answering his initial question.

"I had something when I got up."

"That was a long time ago, so let's go get something to eat, and then you can let me know whether I should get all this stuff out of your place or whether we're going to decorate."

In the final analysis, it was easier to agree than to argue, but it was also a little scary to realize just how seeing Sam improved her mood.

As she went to change her clothes, Chloe firmly re-minded herself how far she'd come since her divorce and how strong she had to be to protect herself and her baby from future disappointments.

Despite the sparks of desire still firing across her skin from being in Sam's embrace, it wouldn't do to keep fall-ing into his arms—and his bed.

She needed to keep their relationship as simple as possible, no matter how difficult that might be with his sexy smiles and mind-destroying lovemaking. If all he wanted was to keep her sweet, so as to make things run smoother in the future, there were other ways to make it happen which didn't include losing herself in the process.

All she had to do was keep reminding herself of that fact.

Sam took Chloe to the Liguanea Club, which served de-licious food. And since she'd been upset before, which had made his heart ache, he also made sure to keep the conversation light.

Well, as light as possible when you have two doctors chatting together, trying not to bring up the very subjects foremost on their minds.

Like babies. And wanting to sleep together again. And what their relationship should look like going forward—a subject that insisted on taking up far more space in his head than Sam liked, but that wouldn't be dismissed.

"It's stupid, I know," Chloe said, as she spread her napkin on her lap, preparing to tuck in to a plate of *escovitch* fish, mackerel rundown and ackee cooked with salt pork, accompanied by *bammy* and a boiled dumpling. "But I've been extremely surprised at the variety of diseases I've treated since I've been here. I expected the usual ones, like epilepsy and dementia, but I've already seen a number of cases of myasthenia gravis and even one poor young man with a rare one—Alice in Wonderland syndrome."

"What?" Sam was intrigued. "I've never even heard of that."

"I've only ever seen one other patient with it," Chloe admitted, as she cut a bite of fish. "And that was unfortunately caused by a brain tumor. But none of the tests we did on the youngster I saw last week have come back positive, so it seems to be a chronic case with no treatment available. I just hope his mother believed me when I told her it should eventually subside. He's only eleven, and usually these cases resolve themselves within a few years."

"Wait, start at the beginning. What is Alice in Wonderland syndrome anyway?"

She chewed and swallowed before answering.

"It usually manifests as an alteration of visual perception—you know, like Alice saw, where she or things around her got big or small—although there can also be hallucinations and time distortions. With the altered visual perception, objects and even body parts can appear smaller or larger than they actually are. But it isn't permanent. It comes and goes. So for instance, in the young man's case, he suddenly thought his hands had swollen to three times their normal size. When it first happened, he called out for his mother, thinking something was wrong with him, but when she came into the room, he thought her head was swollen too."

"That's frankly terrifying," Sam admitted. "He must have been frightened out of his wits."

"He was," Chloe said, shaking her head. "As was his mother. She told her neighbor, and eventually it got back to the pastor of her church, and he said the child was possessed by demons. They spent who-knows-how-long trying to pray him well before the mother realized he wasn't getting better and took him to the children's hospital. They referred him to Kingston General."

Sam nodded. "I've had a few patients that have come to me only after the prayers didn't work, too, but I'll admit never for something like that. I almost don't blame them for thinking there was something supernatural about it."

She smiled, and Sam realized it was the first time she'd done so freely that day. Seeing it made him feel lighter somehow, as though a weight he hadn't even noticed he was carrying had eased off his shoulders.

"It's one of the stranger neurological disorders, and it's often experienced by people with very specific diseases, like brain tumors, Epstein-Barr, temporal-lobe epilepsy and migraines. When I was reading up on it again, I also found a recorded case of a man with the degenerative brain disease, Creutzfeldt-Jakob, who'd experienced the visual symptoms."

"You said there's no treatment?"

"In his case, I advised against any. There were no signs of underlying conditions that would bring it on, and so, in reality, I had nothing to treat. It took a good deal of time getting his mother to understand that there was no magic pill and even longer to convince the little fellow that no, he wasn't insane nor demon-possessed and eventually it would stop."

Sam shook his head. "Save me from the patient that thinks I'm a magician and one wave of my magic scalpel or pill dispenser will change everything. I have a lady I've operated on twice already for pica. The first time, we saw from her scans that she had a mass in her stomach and feared cancer. It was hair. I removed it and told her she needs to go to the psychiatrist. She asked if there wasn't 'something I could give her' to help her stop. I told her the psychiatrist might be able to, but I couldn't. A year later, she was back."

"Did she ever go to get therapy?"

"I hope so, since I haven't seen her after her final post-op examination, but it wouldn't surprise me if I see her turn up again."

To his surprise, Chloe's eyes started to twinkle, and she laughed. "You realize that if the people at the next table were to hear us talking, it might completely put them off their food, right?"

Sam couldn't help laughing with her.

"You're right. I remember the looks we used to get in fast-food joints when all of us med students would hang out, especially after anatomy class. We even had people get up and leave."

"I'm not surprised. I remember those days well."

Then he turned the conversation to her family, learning that she was the eldest of four, that her maternal grandfather, who suffered from early-onset dementia was still alive but now in a nursing home, and that she was closest to her paternal grandmother.

"She was always strict about how we behaved and carried ourselves but never tried to tell us how to live our lives, if that makes sense?"

"It does. My mother's a lot like that. Which reminds me—every year she has a charity gala and I'd really like it if you'd come with me."

His heart sank as those two little lines between her brows made an appearance.

"I don't think that's appropriate, Sam. All your family will be there, won't they? They'll have questions if they see us together."

The urge to tell her she was now a part of his family was so strong, it took all his control not to say anything.

Where was that even coming from?

Instead, he shrugged as though he didn't care one way or the other and said, "I told you I wanted to introduce you to them, and it would be easier having them all in one place. Besides, it'll be a crowd of people, so it's not like a private family-only affair. Kendrick and Rashida will be there too."

Chloe didn't look convinced. "I'll think about it. When is it?"

"December fourth. She always says it's the kickoff to the Christmas season, and none of us have the heart to tell her anything different. This year's been hard on her, though. She needs hip-replacement surgery, but they're trying to get her to lose some weight first. Sometimes I think she's not following the dietician's plan as a way to put off the operation."

Man, he was trying to keep it all light, but the sight of those lines between her brows was stressing him out.

He hadn't realized how important it was for him to introduce her to his family until she didn't seem to want it, and now he was forced to act as though it was no problem.

She would, he thought as he jabbed his fork into his fish, make him crazy if he wasn't careful.

But maybe she already had, and he just hadn't cottoned on to that fact yet?

That thought made him smile, and he looked up to find her staring at him.

The lines had smoothed out from between her brows, and her lips were curved slightly upward, as though she'd seen something amusing.

"What?" he asked, letting his smile widen, ridiculously happy to see her look so lighthearted. "Do I have toast crumbs on my nose? Rundown sauce on my chin?"

She chuckled, shaking her head, and didn't answer his question, only saying, "I'd like to put up the decorations after we leave here. I think they'll make me get into the Christmas spirit a little more. I've missed feeling—what was the word you used—*festive*?"

And, suddenly, the day got brighter.

"Great," he said, grinning. "You'll love some of the ornaments I found. They're perfect."

CHAPTER TWELVE

CHLOE HADN'T BEEN sure what to expect about Jamaica at Christmas but never in her wildest dreams had it included people in Santa hats and reindeer headbands dancing in the sea. Yet, she thought with a grin, forever after, if the words *Christmas* and *Jamaica* should ever be thrown together in her hearing, this was the scene she'd immediately recall.

Maiden Cay turned out to be nothing more than a sandbar out in the Caribbean Sea, about a twenty-minute boat ride from Morgan's Harbor Marina in Port Royal. It was, though, a popular spot for Kingstonians to party. With a bar and a sound system pumping out reggae, calypso, dancehall and, somewhat incongruously, Christmas music set up on the cay, it was well equipped for fun.

Vessels of various sizes were anchored in two crescent shapes on either side of the cay, many lashed together so people could pass from boat to boat when not in the water or onshore. Marlon Mattison's boat, being bigger than many of the others, had been anchored farther offshore in deeper water by itself.

It was quite a sight, and as Chloe stood waist deep in the water, she couldn't help thinking how lovely it all was. The sea was crystal clear, the sky bright blue with just a few fluffy clouds for emphasis. All around her, people laughed and shouted and sang, seemingly having the time of their lives.

"Hey, grab that for me, nuh?" someone shouted nearby, and Chloe turned in time to see a Santa hat floating near Marlon's boat. As she watched, too far away to help, Sam handed his dark glasses to someone, stepped up onto the gunwale and then executed a flawless shallow dive into the sea. With his broad shoulders and tapered torso, as well as truly masculine, muscular legs, he really did swimwear justice!

With a few easy strokes, he got to the hat. Plucking it from the water, he stuck the sopping thing on his head at a rakish angle and started swimming to hand it back to its owner.

Chloe turned away, not wanting to be caught staring, but there was no way to ignore her visceral reaction. Her skin prickled as though the temperature had suddenly risen, and a low throb started up in her belly, reminding her about the night before and the intensity of pleasure they'd shared.

She hadn't meant to sleep with him again, but somehow it had seemed completely natural after the laughter and teasing they'd shared decorating her flat.

She'd been enchanted as she opened boxes and bags and seen the ornaments he'd brought. While there were the requisite balls, stars and bells, he'd also brought a series of glass ornaments painted with island scenes.

"I thought you could keep those as mementoes," he'd said, as she exclaimed at their beauty. "One of my cousins paints them and I was fortunate enough to get a set before she sold out."

There were six balls in the series featuring Dunn's

River Falls, a market scene, a beach view, Jonkanoo dancers, a raft being propelled down a bamboo-lined river, and finally, Devon House.

As she'd cupped that last one in her hands, she'd been overcome by a rush of tenderness for the man who'd gifted it to her. She'd turned away as she thanked him so he wouldn't be able to read any of what she was feeling in her eyes.

When it came to Sam, her emotions were all over the place, and she didn't know what to do about it.

Propelled by a need she couldn't seem to overcome, she glanced back toward the boat again, forcing herself to take in the entire scene, although her gaze wanted to seek out Sam, and only Sam.

Kendrick and his brother were standing near the cabin door, chatting with one of the other passengers, and as she watched, all three burst into laughter, making her smile.

Rashida was dancing, in no way hindered by her belly, which was at the stage where it seemed to get bigger each day. She seemed to have figured out how to use her stomach as a counterbalance for her shaking booty, and Chloe could only hope she'd be that chipper when she was seven months along.

For a moment the sun seemed to dim, as Dr. Hall's warnings regarding her chances of carrying the baby to term crossed Chloe's mind and had to be pushed away.

No. She was determined to keep a positive attitude. As Granny always said, "Never trouble trouble, till trouble trouble yuh!"

Finally, she let her eyes track toward where Sam was, still in the water at the side of the vessel, looking up and speaking to one of the women on board.

Jealousy fired through her, and Chloe made herself turn back toward the sandbar, although now she wasn't seeing anything but her own silliness.

What right did she have to care about whether Sam was talking to some tiny, cute, perfectly petite and gorgeous woman?

None.

His baby growing in her womb—and her sleeping with him the night before—gave her no hold over him whatsoever.

Now, if her hormones would just settle down and stop making her emotions swing wildly all over the place, she'd be fine.

The music had changed from soca to what seemed to be a very popular reggae tune, and a cheer went up on the cay. Because of the increase in the noise level, Chloe didn't realize Sam was approaching until suddenly he was beside her.

"Here," he said, holding out the wide-brimmed straw hat he'd insisted she buy the day before. "This will shield you a bit from the sun."

Dammit, now she was getting all gooey because he cared enough to be concerned about her getting burnt.

"Thank you," she said, taking the hat with a little smile but not looking at him. Sam, wet and slick from swimming was a far too potent turn-on. Best not to commit that image to memory. "I have on sunscreen, though."

"Yeah, but a hat is even better, although you still get the reflected glare off the water."

She murmured something incomprehensible in reply and set the hat on her head, glad that she'd pulled her hair back into a low, messy bun so it would fit.

"You having a good time?" Sam dipped down into the

water so his head was lower than hers, as though wanting to be able to see her face. "I was worried that the weather wouldn't cooperate, but it's perfect for a beach session."

Chloe nodded. "I'm having a ball. The music is great, and the setting couldn't be more beautiful, although I'll admit it seems strange to see Santa hats and Christmas lights on boats in the middle of the ocean."

Sam laughingly agreed. "Everyone's excited for Christmas this year. Normally people wait until December to put up their decorations, but last year no one felt much of the spirit because of the pandemic, so I think they're trying to make up for it."

"I like it," Chloe replied. "The spirit of the season coming alive around me in a gloriously warm tropical setting."

"I'm glad," he replied, lifting a hand to wipe his face. "You don't mind me hanging out with you here, do you?"

She shook her head, knowing what he meant. Although she didn't know if he'd mentioned their relationship to Kendrick or anyone else, she still hadn't told Rashida or even Cora anything, even though she was tempted.

Was embarrassment holding her back?

She didn't think so. After all, they were all adults—both Sam and herself single—and she didn't think her friends would turn up their noses at her because of her actions.

No. If she were scrupulously honest with herself, there was a part of her that wanted to hug all of it—Sam, the baby, even just the fun afternoon of decorating—to herself for a while longer. Eventually there would have to be explanations and discussions, but for the moment, Chloe liked the sense of being isolated from all of that.

It also gave her more time to figure out what she was doing and to try to decipher Sam's actions in a rational manner.

Part of her wanted to believe Sam was going to be the present, nurturing father he seemed to be trying to convince her he could and would be. The other part, the cynical one that still stung from life with Finn, told her not to get her hopes up.

And then there was the part that melted a little more with each smile he sent her way. Each glance from those twinkling, mischievous eyes. Each touch, accidental or on purpose, they exchanged. Every caress they shared.

That part—which seemed to grow increasingly strong—weakened her resolve to distance herself from him. Instead, it rejoiced each time he invited her somewhere or just called to find out how she was. Not to mention how it exulted at being in his arms and the sense of freedom she found in his lovemaking.

All those bits of her were frankly at war, and she admitted the inconsistency of her thought patterns was annoying. Was that contrariness leading her to make unfortunate choices? She really didn't know what she wanted, so even following her heart wasn't left as a viable option.

"Hey, Sam. Chloe. You want something to eat?"

They both looked back toward the boat, and then Sam lifted an eyebrow at her, making her heart do a silly little stutter.

"Are you hungry?"

Needing to make things light, to break out from the weight of all she was experiencing, she cocked one eyebrow right back at him.

"You want to feed me again, don't you?"

He laughed, but there was a gleam in his eyes that said there were other things he'd rather do just then.

"Always. I can't have you withering away on my watch."

It was her turn to laugh then. "I don't think I'm in any danger of that. I've already put on a couple of pounds since I've been here."

His eyelids drooped, and the look he gave her was incendiary. "You're perfect."

For a long moment, she couldn't breathe, her breath hitching somewhere beneath her diaphragm, her pulse going haywire.

How could he do that to her with just a look and two simple words?

"Come on," she said, the words a little choked. "I should have a little something."

And she struck out for the boat, not waiting to see if he was following.

Once on board, she toweled off and got her food. Purposefully making her way to where Rashida was sitting, she took the last spot on the bench and tucked in, not joining the conversation. Instead, she swung her foot in time to the song now playing, as though caught up in the music. Pretending to listen to what happened when Santa got stuck in a mango tree was better than trying to figure out her complicated life.

Sam really, really wanted to punch Marlon in the mouth, even though they'd known each other since they were in nappies, and he was, through Kendrick, an honorary part of the family.

"Ooh, bwoy. Mi can't tek it. That woman is making me sweat." He turned to his brother, a scowl on his face.

"Explain again why it is she's been here almost a month, an' mi jus' a-meet her?"

His rhapsodies over Chloe had been almost nonstop since the start of the trip. If Kendrick didn't put a stop to it soon, Sam might find himself facing charges of mutiny.

It was very bad form to toss a captain off his own vessel.

He'd finally been unable to keep it to himself anymore and told Kendrick he was seeing Chloe, although out of respect for her, he'd made it sound casual and hadn't mentioned the baby. It had been hard not to say something to his best friend about that, because Sam teetered constantly between insane joy and gut-wrenching fear every time he thought about the pregnancy. Being able to share those emotions with his level-headed friend would surely have gone a long way toward calming him down. But Chloe was adamant about not telling anyone, and Sam knew he couldn't abuse her trust that way.

Now Marlon's drooling was just aggravating him beyond bearing. Rather than let his temper get the better of him, Sam stuffed the last forkful of food into his mouth and tried to tune the other two men out, but it wasn't easy.

The truth was, although he'd tried to hide it from Chloe, he was still annoyed from the night before, and Marlon with his nonsense wasn't improving his mood.

He'd thought he and Chloe had had a good time. No, a great time. She'd seemed so happy and relaxed as they put up the tree and decorated it. And afterward, when he couldn't keep his hands off her a moment more, she hadn't resisted even for a second. In fact, she'd taken their first kiss from sweet to carnal in the blink of an eye.

Then, just when he'd thought everything was perfect, she'd kicked him out and refused to come home with him, to boot.

"You could bring your clothes for tomorrow," he said, while she sat up in bed watching him. He was trying to dress as slowly as possible, hoping she'd change her mind and tell him to come back. "Then we can drive out to the marina together."

"Kendrick and Rashida have already said they'll come and collect me," she'd replied, as unmovable as Blue Mountain Peak itself. "So it's all arranged."

He couldn't help realizing she didn't want him hanging about—and didn't want Rashida or Kendrick knowing they were seeing each other.

Ridiculous to feel used and, frankly, outmaneuvered.

Here he was, trying his best to get their relationship normalized—if that were even possible—and she was ducking it at every turn.

"Woo-ee, look at dat. Look at dat."

Sam had been trying his best not to look at Chloe, but at Marlon's words, his gaze swung right to her, only to see Rashida teaching her one of the new dance steps. Chloe was laughing, her face alight with mirth, while her body...

Oh, Lawd. The swivel of her hips, the way her breasts moved beneath the thin material of her swimsuit made his brain short-circuit and his body grow hard between one breath and the next.

Was he even actually breathing?

From the tightness of his chest, he thought perhaps not but couldn't somehow seem to care.

She moved that way when they were in bed together, with unfettered joy and the kind of innate sensuality that no red-blooded man could ignore.

Sam wanted to go over there, swing her into his arms and dance with her. Or cover her up with a towel and hide her from all the other appreciative gazes now affixed to her luscious body.

Marlon headed that way and Sam watched with building anger as the other man tried to pry Chloe away from Rashida so as to dance with her himself.

"You know, if you murder Marlon, you'll not only go to jail but Mummy will never talk to you again. And she's your biggest fan."

"I won't murder him," Sam replied to Kendrick, while keeping his eyes on the ongoing drama at the stern of the boat. "But I might do him a damage."

Kendrick snorted. "Yeah, but it's your own fault, man. You've hardly said a word to Chloe all day, besides that one little dip together. No wonder Marlon thinks she's a free agent."

Sam tried to shrug but ended up with his shoulders stuck up by his ears for a moment as Marlon put his arm around Chloe's waist and they started moving from side to side in sync.

"That's the way she seems to want it. I asked her to move in with me—just for the rest of the time she's here—and she turned me down."

"Hmm." Kendrick took a swig of Red Stripe from his bottle, as though giving himself time to figure out what to say next. "Rashida told me Chloe's been through a tough couple of years. Maybe she doesn't want any more complications in her life right now. And knowing our families, her living with you, even for a little while, would definitely bring complications. I'd go so far as to say high drama."

He'd pointed out to Chloe that, whether she liked it

or not, the baby would definitely cause both complications and drama, so they might as well get out ahead of it. She'd remained unmoved.

Kendrick gave him a long, solemn look before saying, "I've never seen you like this before. You sure this is just one of your usual flings?"

It was on the tip of his tongue to blurt it all out, but he pulled back at the last moment.

"Yeah, what else could it be when we live an ocean apart?"

"Huh." Kendrick took another swig from his bottle and shook his head. "You tell me."

"Nothing more," he said, shortly. But he'd had enough of watching Marlon pawing Chloe and whispering in her ear. "Excuse me."

Stopping at the cooler, Sam grabbed a bottle of water and went over to where Chloe was now sitting on one of the benches, Marlon looming over her like a John Crow.

Plopping down beside her, he forced a smile and held out the water. "Best to keep hydrated in this heat."

"Go weh, Sam." Marlon sounded genuinely put out, as though he had a chance with Chloe, and Sam was blocking it. "Yuh nuh see me talking to the beautiful lady?"

It would be so easy, so shockingly easy, to just say *Back off, Marlon, she's mine. And she's going to be my baby mother, so you can't have her.*

Sam bit back the words, but they were on the tip of his tongue.

Instead, he just smiled, baring his teeth quite a bit more than was absolutely necessary, and said, "Isn't that Toni over there, looking for you? She was asking about you earlier."

"Lawd," said Marlon, looking around like the guilty man he was, trying to spot his ex-lover. "Hide mi!"

As he hurried off toward the boat's cabin, Chloe turned a laughing face Sam's way and said, "That was pretty mean."

Now he could shrug, unfettered and unrepentant.

"All's fair in love and war. And that was war."

Chloe's laughter shouldn't make him so happy, but it did.

And it was at that exact moment, Sam knew he was in deep, deep trouble.

CHAPTER THIRTEEN

THE DAY AFTER the Maiden Cay excursion, Chloe woke up reaching for Sam in the bed beside her, although she didn't know why. Since the first time they'd been together at his place and fallen asleep, she'd been careful not to spend the night with him. There was something so incredibly intimate about spending the night in the same bed and waking up with him, that she'd been determined not to do it.

It felt like a step too far.

But nevertheless, here she was, her arm outflung, palm down on the cool sheet beside her, feeling lonely.

"Contrarian," she chided herself, rubbing her hand back and forth. "This is what you wanted, isn't it?"

Yet although she'd enjoyed the trip the day before, it had shown that perhaps this *wasn't* really what she wanted.

Sam had made it obvious on Saturday that he wanted her to come home with him and then travel together to the marina the next morning. When she'd refused and gone with Kendrick and Rashida, he'd obviously taken it as meaning she didn't want anyone to know they knew each other and had acted accordingly. Besides the brief moments in the sea, bringing her water a couple of times and rescuing her from Kendrick's brother, he'd paid her little mind. And even after Marlon had scurried away, Sam had quickly excused himself, and that had been the last time they spoke.

She'd half hoped, half expected that he'd offer to drive her home, but once they got back to the dock, she'd seen him have a quick word with Kendrick, and then he'd left. And he hadn't called to make sure she'd got home okay either.

Now, as she got up, she wondered if he'd call as he usually did, to ask how she was doing.

If the boat trip, and that desolate feeling she'd woken up with this morning told her anything, it was that she didn't want to go on the way they were. Sneaking about, pretending there was nothing going on between them.

Spending nights in separate beds.

Moving to this next step was frankly terrifying, but at this point, she had to admit certain truths, if only to herself.

Sam was right when he'd said that if people knew they'd been seeing each other in Jamaica, it would make the eventual baby revelation easier.

Also, although she was leery of getting in too deep with him, there was something between them that couldn't be denied. A scorching passion unlike anything she'd known before that made her feel better about herself, just in its expression. After her divorce she'd wanted to grow, to become stronger, less namby-pamby, and although she certainly didn't know why, being with Sam seemed a step in the right direction.

Lastly—and it had taken her a while to even realize it—once she was back in England and the baby was born, an opportunity like this would never come again. She was determined to devote herself to raising her child and being the best mother she could be. There would be no time for love affairs and grand passions. If she didn't take advantage of this chance to enjoy Sam, and the woman she was with him, it would be lost forever.

She was taking Dr. Owens's clinic that evening, so wasn't scheduled to start work until later in the morning, and was inclined to curse about the extra time it gave her to think. On a morning like this, there would be nothing better than activity to keep her mind occupied, but instead, she was stuck in the flat, one ear cocked, in the hopes Sam would call.

Although what, exactly, she planned to say to him, she didn't know.

And when the phone finally did ring, it wasn't him at all, but Rashida.

"Chloe!" Rashida's voice was at full volume, and Chloe pulled the phone away from her ear while stifling a laugh. "Girl, can you believe it's Monday already? Where did the damn weekend go?"

"There was a weekend?" she teased. "No one told me that."

Her friend laughed. "Remember those two days when you didn't go to the hospital? That's what that was."

"Ah, thank you for the update."

"You're too funny. But listen, I want to make up for missing our shopping trip. Let's get together this evening, and we can go to a few stores. They're starting to stay open a bit later and I still need to do my Christmas shopping."

"Actually, I can't make it this evening since I have clinic from six to nine. But I do need your help, and I'm hoping we can do that shopping trip later in the week? I need a dress."

"Ooh, what for?"

Here was a prime opportunity to get her relationship with Sam out in the open, although she'd enjoyed the intrigue and secrecy of it for a while. If Rashida found out through gossip or from Kendrick, she'd probably be upset and it could cost Chloe a friendship she'd come to value.

"For Sam's mother's gala, next Saturday."

There was a long, pregnant pause, and then Rashida asked, "Sam Powell's mother?"

She said it as though she'd never heard his name before and Chloe sat down, settling in for the interrogation. "Yes."

"I didn't know you knew Sam well enough to be invited to the fundraiser. And if yesterday was anything to go by, I'd still say it wasn't possible you did. How on earth did that come about?"

"Well, Sam and I had met before, at a medical conference, and he's been checking on me since I got here. Well, more than checking on me, really. We've been sort of seeing each other."

"Hold on," Rashida said, her voice rising a little. "You knew each other from before? And you've been *seeing* each other, recently? How come Kendrick never gave me that piece of suss?"

"Maybe he didn't know?"

With a kiss of her teeth, Rashida let her opinion of that statement be understood.

"Those two are thick as thieves. Have been since they were little boys. He knows, and didn't tell me. Hold on. You never told me either!"

Chloe chuckled, even though it really was no laughing matter. "It never came up. Besides, Sam and I are just casual friends."

"Huh…" Chloe could almost hear the gears grinding in Rashida's head. "Well, my advice, my friend, is that you keep it casual. Sam's a great guy but not the settling-down type."

Chloe forced a laugh. "Who said anything about settling down? That's a huge leap, from casual friends to happy-ever-after, isn't it?"

"Just saying," came the swift reply. "He's not a dog—doesn't lead women on—but there's more than one woman who found out the hard way that he meant it when he said he wasn't interested in anything more than a good time. There were a couple who felt that because they'd slept with him and hung out together for a few months, it was going to last forever."

"I harbor no such delusions," Chloe assured her friend, keeping her tone light even though she felt as if a rock had settled in her chest. "Sam's just being kind, and we're just having a bit of fun together. After all, I'm only here for another four weeks or so."

"Long enough to fall in love," Rashida said, her voice positively dripping with warning. "Please, just remember what I've said."

"Don't worry." Making the words casual and breezy was difficult, but Chloe thought she managed it. "I just finished with a horrid divorce, remember? Getting serious about any man is the last thing in my plan, believe me."

And she realized she actually meant it. She'd given her all to Finn, only to have it thrown back in her face. There was no way she'd be willing to risk that again. From now on, if she was giving her all, it would be to her child.

Her little miracle.

And though she was willing to share the baby with Sam, her own heart and life would be off-limits once she left Jamaica.

"All right, my friend." Rashida still didn't sound totally convinced but seemed disinclined to belabor her point. "Just don't get hurt—or hurt Sam." She tacked the last on as though it was an afterthought. "Mind you, it would be great if you both *did* fall in love, and I get to keep you here in Jamaica."

"How do you know I wouldn't convince him to move to England instead?" Chloe teased, and she laughed when Rashida replied with a long, juicy kissing of her teeth.

"Then I'd have to hunt you down and do you damage," she said. "Kendrick would be like a headless chicken without Sam around, and our phone bills would be through the roof. Are you free tomorrow? I know just the place to take you to get an outfit."

After making plans for the following evening, they said their goodbyes and rang off.

It was strange, she thought to herself as she made another cup of tea, but the conversation with Rashida had somehow steadied her mind. Now, even more so than before, she knew for a fact that the only person whose emotions she needed to protect were her own.

According to Rashida, Sam Powell wasn't the type to get attached, and Chloe valued her friend's insight. Rashida had known Sam a great deal longer than Chloe had and could be relied on to provide an honest opinion.

So, Chloe should be able to enjoy their renewed physical relationship and let it be known they were seeing each other without fear—fear for him, at any rate.

But, of course, her foremost thoughts must be for the

future of their child, and no amount of pleasure could be allowed to jeopardize it—or the relationship with its father.

Even if Sam wasn't willing to consider that, Chloe had to.

Sam yawned, more annoyed than usual at the slow pace of the traffic on his way to work. Despite the sun and sea air, which usually had a soporific effect on him, he hadn't slept well.

This whole situation with Chloe had him messed up— bad-bad.

Tossing and turning, alternately angry at the way she'd acted as though she hardly knew him and frustrated because he wanted her in his bed, he'd spent a restless night.

He'd turned Kendrick's words over in his head, wondering if Chloe really was avoiding whatever drama publicly being with him would cause.

Millie Hall had said she should avoid unnecessary stress, too, although she'd conceded that modern life was often inherently stressful, especially when one was a physician.

Perhaps for Chloe's sake, he should back off. Give her enough room to breathe, without him trying to press her into a situation she didn't want?

Everything inside him rebelled at the thought. He wasn't trying to push her to do anything untoward, was he? All he wanted was to make sure she understood he was committed—to supporting her and the baby, at any rate.

But he hadn't ruled out marrying her to keep her and his child in Jamaica or at least have a solid footing on which to move to the UK.

Migration was an idea he never thought he'd ever consider, and realizing it had been percolating in the back of his mind was something of a revelation.

He honestly loved his life. He loved his country, his friends and his family, no matter how annoying they could be at times. Yet here he was, considering giving it all up to be with a woman who clearly wasn't even willing to let people know they were a couple.

That made him snort.

They weren't a couple. At least, not in Chloe's eyes. His reaction to seeing Marlon and a couple of the other men out at Maiden Cay try to chat her up told him he saw the situation much differently, but his opinion didn't seem to matter right now.

It should make him angry, but instead he just felt baffled and a little sad.

So he'd decided to give Chloe some more space. If she wanted to talk, she knew where to find him, but right now, he didn't feel he was in the best frame of mind to seek her out, even with a call.

As the traffic started moving, finally, and he had to navigate around a truck that had broken down, his phone rang, and he answered without checking the caller ID.

"Dr. Sam Powell."

"Sam, you dutty dwag. How you nevah tell mi seh you and Chloe was an item?"

At Rashida's words his heart stopped for a second and then settled back down. Scowling, he replied, "Kendrick told you?"

"No! And you wait till I see him later. I goin' give him a tongue-lashing like you wouldn't believe. I was just talking to Chloe, and she spilled the beans. She said you invited her to Miss Norma's gala, and that the two of you are carrying straw."

Now his heart was galloping, but he'd known Rashida too long to be taken in by her overexuberant style of speaking. Sometimes she played fool to catch wise, saying something she knew wasn't strictly true as a way to get a person to say more than they should.

"Carrying straw?"

Using that particular expression usually carried a connotation of a serious relationship rather than casual.

"Well, okay, she didn't make it sound as though it was that serious. But she said you were seeing each other, and I man vex that I'm apparently the last to know."

Sam couldn't help chuckling. "Rashida, you're only the second person to know, not counting Chloe and me, so you're way ahead of everyone else."

"Huh." She didn't sound appeased. "So, you're introducing her to your fam on Saturday, eh? What are you going to tell them?"

"Nothing, other than her name."

"Sam!"

"What? Is there something else I should tell them?"

Had Chloe told Rashida about the baby too? If so, he was sure it would be all over Kingston—and probably much farther afield—before the day was out.

"I don't know. Is there?"

"No," he said firmly, realizing she was fishing again. "Don't make it out to be more than it is."

Rashida kissed her teeth.

"You know what, Sam Powell? I'm glad Chloe has such a good head on her shoulders and doesn't seem to be taking you too seriously. She's been through a lot, and I just wanted to tell you that if you hurt her—"

"Okay. I get the drift," he said, breaking into her tirade. The last thing he needed was to be reminded of just how tenuous his situation was and how easy it would be to mess up. "Have a good day, and go easy on Kendrick. He didn't say anything because I asked him not to."

"*Harrumph.* Now you're really on sinking sands, my friend, making a man keep secrets from his wife."

Sam only laughed and said goodbye.

As soon as Rashida hung up, Sam texted Kendrick on his work phone, making sure his friend knew that his wife was on the warpath.

And as he finally made it almost to the hospital and the traffic started to flow freely, he realized he was whistling.

Chloe had broken the seal of secrecy she'd put on their relationship, and now Sam felt free to act.

Act how, exactly, he wasn't sure, but he'd figure it out.

CHAPTER FOURTEEN

CHLOE PUT HER mind firmly on work, although her brain wanted, very badly, to wander its way to thinking about Sam. He hadn't called that morning, and she wasn't sure whether to be annoyed, sad or happy.

More of her previously unknown contrariness coming to the fore, causing her all kinds of mental issues.

The first part of the day dragged, with only the news that Kadisha Barnes was responding well to treatment for hyperthyroidism to brighten Chloe's spirits. Then, just before the start of the evening clinic, she found herself tempted to call or text Sam but talked herself out of it.

Realistically, although she felt more sanguine about their relationship and the ramifications of being seen to be involved with him, knowledge of the inherent risk refused to be banished.

There was no escaping habit, and that darned conservative streak so carefully implanted in her by her previous experiences refused to lie down and shut up.

Of course, if things went poorly between them, she could simply walk away. Return home, and leave him to sort out how he was going to react to fatherhood and whether he'd be available for their child or not.

Yet that didn't sit quite right with her. Indeed, she

didn't see in Sam the type of man who would distance himself from his child just to spite or avoid its mother. If anything, he'd be even more intent on making sure he did all he could for his offspring, in as honorable a way as was possible.

He had definite strength of character, and his reactions to news of her pregnancy had given her the idea that he was all in when it came to being a dad.

Talking to Rashida had taken away some of her worries, but Chloe was, by nature, the kind of person who picked and picked at problems until she understood them. Acting without complete understanding—or at least understanding all she could—didn't come easy to her at all.

"But sometimes you have to take a leap of faith," she muttered to herself, while shrugging into her lab coat. "Be brave. At least I'm pretty sure *he* won't be hurt by whatever happens."

And, she also knew her own strength. The breakdown of her marriage, and the realization of how little she'd gained for all the time spent trying to nurture and uphold it, were painful but valuable lessons.

As long as she had her baby, she would survive, and they both would thrive, with or without Sam.

That gave her some peace, and she was smiling as she went in to greet her first patient.

By nine thirty, she had seen the last person on the list and was finishing up her charts when the nurse popped her head around the door to say good-night.

"Thank you so much for keeping everything flowing tonight, Doreen. I appreciate all your help."

Nurse Doreen grinned. "You're welcome, Dr. Bailey. And I have to say, your understanding of patois is coming along nicely."

Chloe laughed with her and thanked her again with a wave. Doreen had been nurse on duty during the Alice in Wonderland diagnosis, and had had to act as interpreter between the boy's mother and Chloe. Although she'd grown up hearing her grandparents speaking patois at home, there were some times when comprehension failed her, badly. And that could be fatal when one was a doctor.

Locking up behind her, she made her way out to the parking lot and looked around for her driver Delroy's car, but it was nowhere to be seen. Instead, there was Sam, leaning on the front of his 4X4, arms crossed, sexier than should be allowed.

He walked to meet her halfway across the parking lot, and Chloe tried to will her heart to slow down but to no avail.

"I told Delroy I was here to take you home," he said. "I hope you don't mind?"

"Not at all."

And suddenly, seeing him again like this, something inside her settled and grew quiet.

They were in his vehicle, heading for her flat when he said, "You told Rashida about us."

"Yes, but not about the baby. I didn't think that was necessary."

He was silent for a moment and then asked, "Does this mean your objections to having people know we're seeing each other no longer apply?"

"I still have some reservations," she replied, trying to be as honest as she could. "But I realize you were right when you said it would make things easier in the long run."

Sam exhaled, and the corner of his lips twitched upward momentarily before settling back into a line.

"I'm glad."

He said it simply. A statement of fact. Yet her pulse started racing, like a crazy thing.

"Why?"

"Because I'm tired of pretending we're just friends."

How to interpret that? Chloe decided not to read too much into it. Rashida had cautioned her, and she was taking her warning about Sam's aversion to serious relationships to heart. She didn't doubt it had taken some determination on his part to not already be married. Any woman with a grain of sense would have snapped him up in a heartbeat.

"Well, you don't need to anymore."

They drove the rest of the way in silence, but it wasn't uncomfortable. It felt…peaceful. As though both of them had reached a place of, if not clarity, then something close to that.

He came upstairs with her, and she wasn't sure whether he would come in or not. But there was something she realized she wanted and was willing to take the chance of having.

So when she opened the door, she turned to him and said, "If you give me a few minutes, I'll pack a bag."

He froze, his gaze searching hers, but she held it as understanding dawned in his eyes.

"We'll have to move the decorations to my house," he said, his eyes gleaming, and a little smile playing across his lips.

"Sure," she said, giving a little shrug. "We can do that when I come to get the rest of my stuff during the week."

His answering grin told her that even if she wasn't doing the right thing, it was what they both wanted.

And that was enough for her, in the moment.

They were back in his car and heading for his home when it struck Sam that there was something very different about Chloe this evening, but it took a while for Sam to put his finger on what it was.

She was more relaxed than he'd seen her since her arrival on the island—chatting casually with him about the clinic that evening and her upcoming newspaper interview that Thursday. The entire time, her voice was serene, occasionally amused but without the edge it so often had.

This was a Chloe he didn't know. The first night they'd met, the conversation was casual—determinedly so—and flirtatious. They'd both kept it light, even when the sexual tension between them became obvious. Since she'd turned up in Jamaica, their interactions had been stressful, unpredictable, and there was no wonder. Just seeing each other again had been a shock. The baby revelation had stunned them. Almost every encounter had been fraught with questions and decisions needing to be made.

Suddenly it felt as though she'd put all of it aside, and he wasn't sure what to make of or how to handle it.

With an internal shrug, Sam decided to just go with the flow. After all, what other choice did he have just now?

He also knew he had a tendency to bulldoze his way through situations, but as he'd told her honestly, he had also been used to only really having to think about himself. Only with his family and closest friends was he willing to compromise and make allowances.

She was part of his family, whether she liked it or not, so he was willing to put his own wishes aside to make her happy.

Not that he had anything to complain about right now. She was in his SUV, and they were on their way to his house, where she would spend the night in his bed. By inference, she'd decided to give in to his request to stay with him for the rest of her trip, which was what he'd wanted.

Was it really giving in, though? Or did Chloe have reasons of her own for the decision?

Did it matter?

Sam considered and decided it did.

Until they started communicating properly, there was way too much margin for error. As a surgeon, he was used to calculating risk over benefit and knew it could mean the difference between life and death. A satisfactory outcome or one that did nobody any good.

"Why did you decide to come and stay with me?"

From the corner of his eye, he saw her head turn as though she was surprised by the question, and she seemed to consider the question for an awfully long time before she answered.

"When I spoke to Rashida, she warned me not to take you too seriously—that you're not the kind to want a long-term relationship. In a funny way, that was reassuring. It let me know that you weren't in danger of getting in over your head."

He didn't know whether to be hurt by his friend's assessment of his character, even if it was true, but pushed the thought aside for the moment.

"What about you, Chloe? You're not worried about yourself?"

"Getting attached?" Her little huff of laughter was,

for some unknown reason, painful. "Sam, I'm a realist. I have to be, with a baby to think about. I'll only be here for another month, and once I go back, it'll be to put plans in motion for myself and my child. I'm not stupid enough to jeopardize it all by falling for you. And even if I did, I'd deal with it."

"That sounds almost cynical."

He wanted to keep her talking, learn how her mind worked, gain some insight into her heart and her soul. It shouldn't be important for him to do, but somehow it was.

"I've already been through the fire. I'm tempered. Hardened, to a degree." She laid her head back against the seat, and when he glanced her way, she was smiling, just slightly. "I'm also aware that this is probably the last time I'll get to do something even slightly crazy, like moving into the house of a man I really hardly know. So, with that being the case, I'm parking my risk aversion and I'm simply going to enjoy myself. If that's okay with you?"

"It is," he said, matching her matter-of-fact calm, even when inside, he wasn't quite as sure as he sounded.

And as he led her up to his bed a little while later, he knew it was more than okay with him.

In fact, having her there was almost perfect.

Frighteningly so, when he took her attitude toward him into consideration.

CHAPTER FIFTEEN

HAVING MADE THE decision to stay with Sam, Chloe refused to second-guess it and, by the end of that first week, realized she was happier than she could remember being for a long time.

Living with Sam was surprisingly easy. Used to Finn's constant demands and complaints, she'd been braced for something similar, but her fears in that regard never materialized. Instead, Sam was considerate and almost ridiculously courteous. Once she stopped waiting for the other shoe to drop and reminded herself she was there for only a short time, Chloe began to really relax.

Kendrick had been surprisingly urbane about the change in her address and assured her he'd reassign Delroy, who was on staff at the hospital, so he wouldn't be losing his job because she didn't need him anymore. Besides that, he made no comment to her, either positive or negative.

Rashida, on the other hand, seemed to be beside herself.

"I've never known Sam to have a woman live with him," she said, on the evening she took Chloe to buy a frock for the charity do. "You sure you two aren't planning something permanent?"

"I'm only here until January first, then I'm gone. This is as permanent as it is going to get."

Rashida had slid her such a look of disbelief Chloe couldn't help laughing.

"Honestly, we're just having a bit of fun. Don't read anything more into it or you'll hurt your brain."

That had made Rashida chuckle, although she still didn't look totally convinced.

Everywhere, there were the signs of Christmas now. Lights twinkled, decorations gleamed and white euphorbias set off the bright reds and gentle pinks of poinsettias. There was a sense of excitement in the air, and the oft-time languid movements of the city folk seemed to speed up until there was an extra bounce in their steps.

For the first time in years, Chloe felt a part of it all rather than the season being a chore of shopping and taking care of everyone else's needs and wishes. When Sam helped her pack up the decorations they'd put up in her flat not too long before, she had a little pang of melancholy, as though it was a harbinger of endings. That faded quickly, though, when he insisted on their doing the entire process all over again, only at his home instead. By the time they had finished, the living room had a jolly, festive air, and Chloe's cheeks ached from laughing at Sam's antics. He, by the simple method of being himself and showing honest enjoyment of their time together, had once more totally transformed her mood.

That Thursday, she had the dreaded newspaper interview, which turned out to be far less stressful than she'd envisioned. The reporter had been overjoyed to find out that Chloe's grandparents had been born on the island since, as she said with a laugh, "We Jamaicans are quite sure the island is the source of all things great."

Then she had her next appointment with Dr. Hall, who started with a physical examination along with lots of questions about how Chloe had been feeling.

"It's been surprisingly smooth," Chloe told her, as the doctor measured her abdomen. "I have crackers beside my bed, just in case, but I haven't had any morning sickness, and my breasts are a little tender but nothing unbearable."

"Still tired?" Dr. Hall put away her measuring tape and began to prepare the machine for the ultrasound. Chloe's heart rate picked up, and Sam shifted position so he could see the monitor better.

"A bit. Those unscheduled naps—the ones that sneak up on me—have abated, though."

"It should get better from now on." She had the ultrasound wand in her hand and sent Chloe a slight smile. "Ready to see the baby?"

"Yes, please," she said, hardly able to breathe.

"I'm guessing it's no use asking you two whether you want to know the sex or not," she said, as she squirted gel onto Chloe's stomach. "You'll figure it out for yourselves, if not this time, then the next."

Neither she nor Sam answered, and when Chloe sent him a fleeting glance, she found his eyes were trained on the monitor, his face intent and somehow stern.

Then the wand was sliding across her skin, and Chloe's gaze flew to the screen.

It took what felt like forever for Dr. Hall to get her bearings, although it wasn't more than a few seconds. And then...

"There."

It took a moment for the swishing sound to register as the heartbeat, because Chloe was mesmerized by the image. Her medical side traced the form, searched, saw nothing but pure perfection in the tiny being nestled inside her belly.

"Oh," she gasped, and felt Sam's fingers squeeze hers. She hadn't even realized he'd taken her hand, until that moment.

"Looks like a girl," Dr. Hall said. "Although it's too early to be absolutely sure."

"A girl," Sam echoed, and there was no mistaking the wonder in his voice.

When she looked at him, he was still staring at the ultrasound monitor, and Chloe could see his eyes were misty.

"Don't you start, Sam," she said, trying for a light tone, even though her throat was tight. "You know it doesn't take much to get me going nowadays."

Millie Hall glanced first at Sam and then Chloe and smiled.

"Yes, Sam, stop your nonsense before you make Mum cry too."

He laughed, but it sounded rusty. "You two leave me alone." And Chloe's heart gave a flip when he lifted her hand to his lips and kissed the back before saying, "If I want to get sappy over the first look at my baby, it's none of your business."

They all chuckled, but the tenderness of the moment stuck with Chloe, through Millicent Hall's recap of the appointment and the declaration that she was satisfied with the progress of the pregnancy. Even her admonishment to make sure they called her at the slightest discomfort didn't dim the glow surrounding Chloe's life as they left with a sonogram picture of their child.

That night when they made love, it was with a slow,

gentle rhythm, as though the evening's events had lulled them into a new phase of their relationship. One that Chloe didn't allow herself to dwell on too much.

None of it changed the inevitable outcome, and she refused to allow future sorrows, fears or uncertainty to cloud the beauty of the present.

Of course, there was still Sam's family to meet, but she just kept reminding herself that she wouldn't be around long enough for their opinion of her to really matter. And whatever trepidation she still felt on the Saturday evening of the gala event melted away under Sam's appreciative gaze when she came down the stairs.

"You look amazing," he said, taking her hand and twirling her slowly around.

Laughing, she replied, "Thank Rashida. She took me to the place she says she shops at almost exclusively when she isn't—in her words—'grossly preggers.'"

And, even without his approval, she knew she was looking her best. The bright yellow silk of the dress made her skin glow, while the fitted bodice and flowing skirt set off her figure to perfection. She'd hesitated over her heels, knowing they weren't the best thing to be wearing, but she compromised by buying a slightly lower pair, telling Rashida she didn't have any with her that would match her gown.

Sam looked magnificent in his tuxedo, and she told him so, having the pleasure of seeing him look almost abashed at her words.

That was something else she'd discovered about him. For all his good looks, intelligence and strong will, he seemed almost unaware of his appeal. It was both surprising and endearing.

When they pulled up to the hotel where the ball was being held, Chloe took a deep breath.

"It'll be fine," Sam assured her, as the valet opened her door. "Just enjoy yourself, and don't worry about anyone."

The ballroom was stunning. Instead of what Chloe thought of as traditional Christmas decor, it was festooned with long streams of white orchids, tied with red velvet ribbons and set among evergreen boughs. That was something of a theme of the Jamaican Christmas, she realized. Because the white euphorbia and red poinsettias bloomed at that time of the year, red and white had become synonymous with the season.

It was crowded as people mingled during the cocktail hour, chatting and laughing. Chloe was a little staggered at the attendees' elegance, although she'd already noticed how beautifully Jamaican women dressed, no matter their occupation or social bracket.

"Come and meet the parents, and get it over with," Sam said, in an obviously teasing tone, putting his hand on her lower back to guide her toward the other side of the room. Partway across, he dipped his head to whisper into her ear, "Do you know how difficult it was for me to leave the house this evening? I just want to take you back home and slowly work that dress off you, running the silk over your skin to figure out which is softer."

Heat rushed down her spine, making her shiver, and she paused long enough to reply, just as softly, "I think, for comparison's sake, it would be better if I rub the silk *and* my skin over you, so you can properly decide."

The look he gave her was incendiary and full of promise.

"Deal," he replied, just as someone called his name, and he turned toward the sound.

"Sam, you finally made it." A woman, almost as tall as Sam, was on them and reached up to kiss his cheeks. She turned an interrogative expression Chloe's way and then, after a brief moment, smiled widely, "Oh, it's Dr. Bailey. How nice to see you again. I'm so glad you came."

"You've already met my sister, Mel?" Sam asked, his eyebrows high with surprise.

"Yes," Chloe replied, wondering how it was she hadn't noticed the family resemblance before.

"Dr. Bailey was at the clinic when I took Ali in for her last checkup, and I think what she said really got through to her. Her behavior has calmed down so much since then. Sam, I'll tell you all about it after this craziness is over. I don't know how Mummy keeps talking us into doing this year after year."

And then she was gone in a swirl of perfume and velvet, making a beeline for a person at the side of the room who was beckoning to her.

"I feel a little silly, having not realized Mrs. Gabaldon was your sister," Chloe said, still stunned. "The two of you look very much alike."

Sam wrinkled his nose. "She isn't as handsome. Or so I've heard. Come on. Mummy and Daddy are holding court just over there."

His parents turned out to be nothing like what she'd expected. Mr. Powell was a head shorter than Sam, although very like him in physique, while Mrs. Powell had "stamped" the children with her unmistakably beautiful features. The couple was comfortably ensconced at the far end of the room, husband on his feet chatting with a group of people, wife seated in a comfortable chair, her walker close to hand.

And although Chloe found herself very much the object of close scrutiny by both, they were nothing but charming and friendly, leaving her to wonder if they knew about their son's current living arrangement.

When she asked Sam, while they were heading to the bar, he shrugged.

"Kingston may be a city, but in many ways, it's just a small town. If Rashida mentioned it to her mother, then mine no doubt will know."

Dinnertime found her and Sam at a table with Rashida, Kendrick and another couple, who were introduced to Chloe as longtime friends.

"Milton went to high school with us," Kendrick said. "And has never wavered in his devotion to the purple-and-white."

She took that as a reference to the school colors and was proved right when the men launched into a spirited debate about various sporting events that went right over her head.

"These damn men, with their Manning Cup and Champs," Milton's wife, Jacinth, grumbled, sending them a hard look. "In their thirties and still arguing about schoolboy sports. You'd think they'd have outgrown the fascination by now."

"What are men but overgrown boys anyway?" quipped Rashida, before taking a sip of her water. "Might as well let them go at it. It's harmless, one way or another."

And their talk turned to another topic of seemingly endless appeal to the Jamaicans Chloe had so far met—food. Specifically, Christmas fare.

"You should see my gungo peas tree." Jacinth all but crowed. "Laden. Positively laden with pods. And the sorrel is already picked and drying,"

"Our sorrel is steeping," Rashida interjected. "It bore

early this year, and I didn't want to wait. Oh, and I got some Jerusalem peas from the country."

They kindly explained, for Chloe's sake, that gungo peas, otherwise known as pigeon peas, used to be available exclusively at Christmas time, so were synonymous with the season. Jerusalem peas, she gathered, were like tiny red kidney beans and were hard to find because they weren't considered a cash crop.

"And you know all about sorrel, don't you?" Jacinth asked.

"Yes," Chloe laughed, familiar with the ruby-red drink, steeped with ginger and allspice and often "sweetened" with overproof rum, ubiquitous during the holiday season among Jamaicans. "Through my grandparents. You can buy the dried petals in the Jamaican stores back home, but British people always get confused by the name. To them, that's not something you use to make a drink but a whole other plant."

The conversation ebbed and flowed through dinner, and afterward, Sam's two sisters, Mel and Daphne, along with Mel's husband, Peter, came to join them.

"You were supposed to sit up at the head table, Lemuel," Daphne said to Sam, giving him a scowl. "We had to put Mr. Harriman and his wife up there to fill the spots."

Lemuel? Chloe mouthed to him, getting a wrinkle of his nose in reply before he answered his sister in the kind of lazy tone brothers know will make their sisters see red.

"It's way more comfortable down here with the plebs," he said, which raised a howl of outrage from almost the entire table.

"Well, you're in for it now anyway," Daphne told him with a smirk. "I heard Mummy telling Aunt Lillian that she's planning to 'have a word' with you…"

Mel giggled. "And we know that one word always leads to many when it comes to our mother."

That led to stories of times gone by, when one or the other of the children—which included Kendrick, Marlon and, later on, Milton—had been caught in one misdemeanor or the other and the consequences thereof. The stories had the entire table, Chloe included, breathless with laughter.

It felt good, she realized, to be in that group. Homey but without the expectations she was so used to having placed on her shoulders. No one looking to her to smooth things over or to take on responsibility for others' lives outside work. She could just be—her.

Even with Sam.

But it was all temporary, and she had to keep reminding herself of that fact. It was no good getting too comfortable, because it was all going to end in a few short weeks.

So when she found Sam's questioning gaze on her face, she just smiled and shook her head, refusing to let any sad thoughts disrupt the lovely evening.

And she kept the tone light on the drive back home, saying, "I'd forgotten your given name was Lemuel. How on earth did that become Sam?"

He slid her a glance, his lips twitching. "Can you imagine what I went through at school with that name? Luckily for me, most people have never heard it before, and it sounds enough like Samuel for the kids to get confused, so they started calling me Sam, and it stuck."

She giggled. "I think I rather like the name Lemuel. I should start calling you that."

"Don't. You. Dare," he replied, which just made her laugh even harder.

Yet later, when they got back to Sam's place and he set about the comparison between flesh and silk, taking her to new planes of ecstasy in the process, there was, for Chloe, an almost frantic edge to the experience. The need to cram as much passion and intensity into that glorious night so the memory would be indelibly carved into her brain.

Never to fade or be forgotten.

CHAPTER SIXTEEN

CHLOE FELT ALMOST as though she were drifting in a time that bore no resemblance to reality except for when she was in the hospital and actively working. Yet that little corner of her brain, which always insisted good things were never easy, and if they were, never lasted, kept niggling at her.

There was something on Sam's mind, and he wasn't sharing it with her, so she worried at that like a dog with a bone.

More than once she'd found him looking at her with a wrinkled brow or staring off into space in the middle of a conversation. But when she asked him if he wanted to talk, he always smiled and shook his head.

"My mind was wandering," he'd say, going back to whatever he was doing or changing the subject.

She knew there was more to it than he was saying, but didn't try to force the issue.

With no way to know whether what was bothering him had anything to do with her, she found herself falling back into the pattern of taking the blame. It was hard not to, since in the last years of her marriage, she'd taken to walking on eggshells and trying to actively head off problems that could cause confrontations.

Finn had never been violent, but his rages had been disturbing nonetheless.

Then a phone call from her sister, asking if she was coming home for Christmas, put her in a bad mood.

"Really, Colette? Mum put you up to this, didn't she? I told you all that I'd be home on January first. Why would I fly all the way to London for one day, just to have to fly back and do it all again in a week's time?"

"Stop acting like it's a big deal, Chloe. You can afford it, and it will get Mum off all our backs. She's been ranting about it since you left, until none of us can stand it. You don't work on Christmas Day anyway, so it's completely doable."

For a moment, just one sickening moment, she almost agreed. It was a knee-jerk reaction, brought on by the old ways and the old expectations.

Her entire family assumed she'd bow to their whims and make their lives easier, no matter what it cost her in time, energy or money.

But now she had her baby to think about, and it was time to put a stop to all the nonsense.

"I most certainly will not fly back for Christmas. It's out of the question." When Colette started arguing, Chloe cut her off. "Listen, I'm not having a tiff with you about it. You all need to deal with Mum however you can, but leave me out of it."

"But it's your fault she's acting up!"

"Well, she needs to get over it. And so do you."

Then, before the call could degenerate into something worse than it already was, she rang off.

But the call, coming on the Tuesday morning as she was getting ready to present a talk to a gathered group of neurologists invited to Kingston General for that purpose, left her rattled.

Was that what she was facing when she went home? All the old stressors and demands? Out of her entire family, the only one she could depend on for advice was Gran, but to get the advice she really needed, she'd have to tell the older woman the entire story.

Was she ready to reveal her pregnancy? Especially to any of her family? Of course, if she asked Gran not to say anything, she wouldn't, but it would have to be faced at some point anyway, so why put it off?

The following morning, she awoke before the alarm as usual and, instead of getting out of bed, turned her head to look at Sam, still asleep beside her.

In repose, his face took on an almost stern cast yet was no less handsome for the lack of mobility, which was what gave him his charm. She could, if she let herself, fall in love with him—more so now than when they'd first met or when they had just started to get to know each other.

Everything he did, even when he was being rather overbearing, seemed aimed at making her comfortable or keeping her and the baby in good health. There were times when she wondered if he was just acting that way because he was on his best behavior, but if it was a charade, it was an exceedingly good one that never faltered.

But he was a force to be reckoned with, both in and out of bed, and no matter how he was presenting himself, she'd seen and been the recipient of the full strength of his character. No amount of mind-blowing lovemaking could make up for being sucked into a relationship and being once more subsumed to her own detriment. It was the last thing on her wish list. Although most everyone else seemed to believe Chloe existed to make them happy or make their lives easier, she was no longer buying what they were selling. For herself, and her child, she could no longer afford it.

Slipping out of bed, she padded downstairs and, after making a cup of tea, fetched her tablet and put in a video call to her gran.

"Hullo darling." Gran's smile was wide, and behind her, the lights of her Christmas tree twinkled. "How are you?"

"I'm good, Gran. And you?"

But Gran didn't answer the question, just narrowed her eyes and said, "You're not all right. I can see it. What's going on?"

Chloe huffed a little laugh. She never could hide from her grandmother.

"Oh, Colette called me yesterday, asking me to fly back for Christmas."

"She lose har mind?" When Gran lost her English accent and fell back into patois, you knew she was upset. "Aren't you coming home in January?"

"Yes. On the first."

Gran kissed her teeth, another sign of great annoyance. "Ridiculous. I hope you told her to go weh."

Chloe chuckled. "Not in so many words, but yes, I told her to go away."

"Good." Gran leaned closer to the camera, as though searching Chloe's face. "And what else?"

It was the moment of truth, and Chloe's heart started thumping so hard, she felt slightly ill.

"Gran, I have something to tell you, and it might be a bit of a shock."

"Go on. Spit it out."

"I'm pregnant."

There was a long pause, during which her grandmother just blinked, her mouth moving but no sound coming out.

Then she said, "Chloe Janice Bailey, tell me yuh neba tek back dat worthless man yuh did married to!"

Shock had apparently completely shattered Gran's carefully cultivated Britishness, and the evidence of that break made Chloe want to laugh, but she squelched the impulse.

"No, Gran. The baby isn't Finn's. I haven't had anything to do with him since I walked out."

"Thank God. He would have had you in his clutches forever if it was, and I couldn't stand to see that."

Chloe had known her grandmother wasn't overly fond of Finn, but that sounded more emphatic than expected.

"I didn't know you disliked him that much, Gran."

Gran sat back, took off her glasses and rubbed one eye, as though trying to decide what to say. Then her lips firmed, and she said, "Chloe, I watched as Finn stood by and let the family bully you, without doing a thing about it. In fact, he encouraged it, because it gave him an excuse to take advantage of you too. And if you think I didn't notice the way he always made jokes at your expense, acting as though you were the village idiot instead of the capable, competent woman you are, you're mistaken.

"He was bad for you, and your parents and siblings liked him because he allowed them to ride roughshod over you with impunity. I was so glad when you left him, I can't even tell you."

Then, as though the initial statement suddenly struck

her again, Gran leaned forward until her nose almost touched the camera.

"But baby girl, the doctors said you couldn't have any children. And if it's not Finn's, whose is it?"

Now for the embarrassing bit, but Chloe wasn't about to back down. Not now. This was a far more pleasant foretaste of what was to come, so she might as well get used to it.

"I met a man at that conference in San Francisco. That's when it happened."

Surprisingly, Gran seemed to take that in her stride. "Does he know about the baby?"

"Yes..." Chloe hesitated for a moment and then decided on full disclosure. "It was the weirdest thing. I came here to Jamaica, and there he was again. So it was easy to tell him, because I didn't have to look far to find him."

Gran's mouth moved, like she was chewing on the words before speaking them, then she gave a decisive nod. "God has a plan for you, that man and the baby you made together. That's why it worked out that way." Then her face fell. "Does that mean you're staying there or planning to move to Jamaica?"

"No, Gran." Why did it hurt so much to say it? It wasn't as though that had ever been a consideration. "I'm coming home as planned. I'm just sort of dreading what the rest of the family will say and how they'll act when they find out."

Gran kissed her teeth again and shook a finger, which would have been in Chloe's face if she'd been there in person. "If I weren't a Christian lady, I'd tell you *exactly* what to tell them if they kick up any fuss."

And Chloe had to laugh, feeling somewhat lighter

than she had before and yet somehow sadder at the same time.

Contrarian!

As Chloe said goodbye to her grandmother and switched to checking her email, Sam considered quietly stepping back into the kitchen and pretending he hadn't overheard her conversation. Yet the anger pulsing under his skin wouldn't let him leave well enough alone.

"Chloe..."

She spun around, eyes wide. "Sam. I thought you were still asleep."

He shook his head, fighting for equilibrium. "I woke up when you got out of bed and came down for coffee."

Her eyes narrowed, those storm-cloud lines forming between her brows, and her chin tilted up as it did when she was about to do battle.

"You overheard my conversation."

"Parts of it."

Lips firm, that chin lifting a notch more, she said, "You're angry because I told my grandmother about the baby—"

His hand slashed through the air, cutting her off.

"No, I'm not. The part that made me angry was hearing how your family—and your ex—treated you."

It had been like listening to a story about someone he'd never met, and yet the traces of that old, familiar life had been there.

Having been self-aware enough to recognize the problem, she'd been fighting to throw off those lingering cobwebs. There'd been some times after she first arrived that he'd been caught in the crossfire when she pushed back at his high-handedness, and he hadn't known why.

Instead of mollifying her, he saw her chin go up even higher.

"I'm not that person anymore, so don't get any ideas about bossing me about, now that you know."

Suddenly, his anger waned, and he couldn't help chuckling, as he shook his head.

"You're kidding right?" The lines between her brows deepened, and he hurriedly continued, "It makes me admire you even more. I know how hard it can be to break away from family expectations, and from what I heard, you're doing that in spades."

The lines smoothed out and Chloe nodded.

"It hasn't been easy. When I finally recognized how everyone was manipulating me for their own benefit, I felt like a fool. I'm finished with all that now. I have to do what's right for the baby."

She probably didn't realize it was her loving heart that had made her such a target of her family's selfishness, but Sam did. Walking toward her, he held her gaze, something warm and sweet filling him, so that by the time he was next to her, he couldn't help putting down his cup and tugging her up into his arms.

"You have to do what's right for *you*," he said, reveling in the way she melted against him, resting her cheek against his shoulder and sighing. "Everything else will fall into place."

"I hope so," she replied, her arms around his waist. "But sometimes everything seems so complicated."

That he could understand and agree with, but he didn't want to get into it right then. All he wanted was to hold her and to make her happy. Maybe getting away from everything, including work, would give her a little time to de-stress and gain some clarity?

"I want to take you away next weekend. To Portland, or even Negril, if you're up for it. It'll be nice and quiet, and you'll get to see some of the island. If things were different, I'd say we could go between Christmas and New Year's, but the hospital is always busy and I'll be on call."

"Dr. Owens has set up a two-day conference on December twenty-eight and twenty-nine, as well, so I couldn't go then anyway. He says he wants to get the most out of my time here. But I'd like to do something with you this weekend," she replied, tightening her hold on him for an instant and then easing out of his arms. "Rashida wanted me to go round to their place and help her make Christmas puddings, but I know she can manage without me."

"You don't want to be involved in anything that pint-size sergeant major is doing," Sam replied, the last of his anger draining away when Chloe giggled. "She somehow talked Kendrick, Marlon and me into building her an outdoor brick oven once and wouldn't leave us alone to get on with it. It felt as though she was everywhere at once, issuing orders and making demands."

She was outright laughing now, and Sam realized he'd be quite happy to hear that joyful sound for the rest of his life—a revelation that struck him dumb for an instant.

Then, words rose to his lips, held back only by the knowledge that she wouldn't want to hear them.

Stay. Stay with me.

Worse than knowing she would reject the suggestion out of hand was the knowledge that, somehow, he wasn't even entitled to ask.

CHAPTER SEVENTEEN

RASHIDA REFUSED TO be gainsaid and changed her baking plan from the next weekend to the one after.

"I should have done it from last month," she told Chloe. "I'm already behind times, and if they're not as rum-soaked as some people like it, too bad. I'd rather spend the time with you, enjoying it, than doing it by myself. We'll do steaks on the grill outside—or the men will—and make a party of it."

"I can't remember a busier Christmas than this one," she told Sam, after informing him that the sergeant major had spoken and moved their baking date. "But I haven't done my shopping. In fact, I'd go so far as to say I haven't even thought about it. Have you done yours?"

She was thinking that maybe they could go together, and if she saw anything for him, get Rashida to take her back, but Sam had the nerve to smile a little smugly and say, "Actually, I have. I bought most of my gifts in San Francisco, so I could get it over with. Besides, then I know no one would get the same thing from someone else."

"Well, you're one up on me. Mind you, I didn't think I'd need to buy gifts this year at all, besides a few souvenirs to take home. Who would have thought I'd have made so many friends while I was here?"

"I don't think anyone would expect you to buy gifts, Chloe."

She shook her head, giving him a smile. "I want to, though. Everyone's been so nice to me, and so welcoming."

It was on the tip of her tongue to say she'd miss them all, but something held her back. Probably the knowledge that she'd miss Sam most of all.

Work was busy that week, and Dr. Owens explained why. "The neurological department is mostly closed between Christmas and New Year's, with each of us taking turns to be on call. There are no clinics or scheduled appointments, which is why I put together that two-day symposium."

"I've contacted my head of department at Royal Kensington and he's sending me some additional information from other research teams, so I hope to make it as interesting as possible. There'll be ample time for Q and A sessions too."

Luckily, her boss had warned her that she'd be expected to do a number of seminars, so she'd come partially prepared. With a bit of work over the next week, she'd get the rest of the information pulled together and be ready to go.

But she was looking forward to her weekend away with Sam. He'd decided to take her to Portland, her grandfather's home parish, and she was excited to go. They planned to leave on Friday afternoon and come back on Sunday, going over Junction Road through the mountains on the way there, and back on the longer route, which went around the coast.

"What time do you think you can be ready to leave this evening?" he asked on Friday morning. "Barring emergency, I'll be done by about four."

"I'm doing a clinic with Dr. Owens this morning and then a presentation to a group of neurological nurse practitioners after lunch. It's slated to finish at three, and then I should be done."

Sam chuckled. "That means you won't be done until four, or haven't you caught the Jamaican vibe yet, where everything goes longer than it should?"

Chloe couldn't help laughing with him. "Very true. I had noticed."

"I'll drive over to the east wing and wait for you outside."

And, as annoying as it was to admit it, Sam was right about the presentation, as she didn't leave the building until four fifteen.

At least Sam had the grace not to say "I told you so."

They'd packed their bags in the car that morning and set out straight from the hospital.

"We have to drive past the house, so we can stop there if you want to change," Sam said, but Chloe just settled back in the seat, prepared to enjoy the drive.

"This is pretty comfortable," she replied. She'd specifically chosen a loose, flowy skirt and cotton shirt and paired them with flats, just for that reason.

Once they left Kingston, the road twisted and turned and climbed up and up into the Blue Mountains. The scenery took Chloe's breath away. Hillsides densely treed would suddenly part, revealing swaths of grassy slopes with stands of bamboo waving feathery arms to the sky. Sam pointed out Castleton Botanical Gardens as they passed, and the name rang a bell.

"I think my granddad mentioned it as somewhere they'd go when he was young, on a Sunday or holiday."

"It was a popular place for day-trippers back in the day. I even remember going there on a school trip once, many, many years ago. What did he say about it?"

"I don't remember," she said with a pang of sadness. "I used to spend quite a lot of time with him when I was young and my grandparents looked after us when we got off from school. Granddad had an old road map that he got in the eighties, which was the last time he was here, and a topographical map, too, and he'd point out some of the places he'd been. He always said that when I got older, we'd come to Jamaica together and see them all."

"Is he still alive?"

"No, unfortunately. He died almost two years ago. He'd had a stroke a few years before and never fully recovered and then had congestive heart failure."

"I'm sorry." He probably recognized the lingering pain in her voice. Sam, she'd noticed, had got surprisingly good at ferreting out her moods, even when she tried to hide them. "And I'm sorry you didn't get a chance to discover the island with him."

"Me, too," she replied. "It would have been a lot of fun. But this trip has been, and continues to be, one of the best I've ever taken, and I'll be remembering him when I see some of the places he talked about."

He murmured agreement, then said, "I finally spoke to Mel, and she told me about your appointment with Ali."

To her ears, he sounded particularly bland, as though the conversation hadn't been a good one.

"Oh?"

"Yes. She was so happy that you seemed to get it through to Ali that while it's okay to hope that she outgrows her epilepsy, she should still be making plans to mitigate seizures, in case she doesn't."

Relieved that the feedback had been positive, Chloe replied, "I just wanted to be honest with her. Puberty is difficult enough for people without chronic diseases, but in her case, she needs to learn how to calm herself down rather than give in to the temptation to let fly over every little thing. I think she understood what I was trying to say."

"It sounds like she did. She got her mother to enroll her in a yoga class, and Mel says she's taken to it like a duck to water. It's smoothed her out, somewhat."

"Amazing. I'm glad. You know, it'll stand her in good stead, epilepsy or no."

"And give her parents a break too. She was turning into a bit of a brat."

Chloe laughed. "That might have more to do with puberty than anything else. She's pretty much there."

"Don't remind me," Sam groaned. "I can't believe she's twelve already. I swear she was just born. After growing up with two sisters and seeing what's happening with my nieces, I dread the thought of having a daughter."

"Do you?" This was a subject they'd never discussed. "You'd prefer a boy?"

He was silent for an instant and then said, "I just want the baby to be healthy. I don't really care about anything else."

She believed him. There was a strange tone in his voice. One she'd never heard before and couldn't interpret. It made her want to ask him what he was thinking at that moment, but she didn't feel as though she had the right.

This situation was too strange to be demanding confidences or confessions. The only thing she could do was agree but without further comment.

In all, the drive to Port Antonio in Portland Parish took a little over two hours, and it was completely dark when they got to the villa Sam had rented for the trip. Clean and spacious, it was decorated in the colonial style, and Chloe actually gasped when she saw the massive four-poster bed draped with mosquito netting and complete with steps to climb up into it.

"The mattress is higher than my waist," she said, standing beside it for comparison. "I've never seen a bed like this before."

"We'll have to try it out later and see if it's as sturdy as it looks."

That was the start of a glorious couple of days spent swimming, exploring and making love. Sam, as it turned out, had a special affection for Portland, and took Chloe to a number of places, each one more dazzling than the last. Reach Falls and rafting on the Rio Grande were her favorites, although Blue Hole was spectacular and the entire parish, including the sleepy town of Port Antonio, entranced her.

Also during those two nights, Sam seemed more determined than ever to make her crazy with desire. Not that he'd ever failed to satisfy and to leave her love-drunk when it was over, but there was in his touch a different timbre—one that took her to the edge and kept her hovering on the precipice without immediately letting her fly.

It was purposefully done, of course, meant to sharpen need to a razor's edge and intensify the final slash of ecstasy.

But she had her revenge as they made love one last

time on Sunday afternoon before embarking on the trip back to Kingston. Taking control, she led him in a slow, erotic dance that promised the pinnacle of release if he could just hold on to his control a little longer. And then a little longer yet.

Once, twice, she almost precipitated the crisis herself, her orgasm springing to the fore almost in full flower, and she had to stop moving so as to regain her equilibrium.

The sound Sam made—pleasure-laden and pleading, both—was almost her undoing, but she wasn't ready to end their journey just yet.

There was a sublime power in looking down at his damp chest and tight face, in feeling the hard grip of his hands on her thighs and the strength of his body beneath hers. It made her light-headed and elated, able to take on anything and everything the world flung her way.

Rocking against him, she gave a soft cry as the perfect angle was achieved, and the hard upthrust of his hips made it sublime. Slowly, with short circles, she started them climbing again, but this time, the ascent was swift, a rocket of sensation and want that was too intense to be denied or forestalled.

She flew straight past the point where she'd meant to halt and shattered around him, shuddering and almost sobbing. Then, before she could get her head back out of the clouds, she was on her back and Sam was above her, his expression ferocious and heartbreakingly beautiful.

She felt his release, the hard pulse of it, but then he was moving with long, hard strokes, somehow causing another rush of sensation that led, amazingly, to another mind-bending orgasm.

And, just then, Chloe knew she'd never have another

memory as sweet, both full of promise and yet with that shadow of heartache yet to come.

Three weeks were all that were left, and she was determined to ring every last scintilla of joy and pleasure and *life* out of them.

Lying next to him, satiated and content, she let her mind wander, flitting from subject to subject until it alighted on one she'd been meaning to bring up with him but had let slide before.

"Have you given any thought to baby names?"

She felt him turn his head, as though looking down at where she nestled against his side, but was too languorous to move to meet his gaze.

"Not really," he said softly, with a hesitant note in his voice.

She snuggled closer, putting her leg over his. "You sound surprised I should ask."

"I am, a little," he confessed, his arm tightening around her.

"Well, you shouldn't be. This is your child too."

He didn't reply to that but bent to kiss the top of her head before asking, "Do you have any names picked out?"

"I have a few I like, subject to your approval. I really feel as though this is something we should agree on, you know?"

He stroked her arm and made a little hum of agreement.

"Well, let's hear them."

"For a girl, Adrianna, or Antoinette. I also fancy Olivia and Zara. But I'm really leaning toward my gran's middle name—Victoria."

She felt the change in his body, the way it jerked and then grew stiff, as though zapped with electricity.

"Not Victoria." He didn't sugarcoat it, just flat out refused, and that had Chloe rolling over so as to be able to see his face.

It was ashen, his eyes fierce, and a shiver ran down her spine.

Leave it alone, or ask for an explanation?

The old her would have backed off so as not to upset him more, but the new her, the one who was determined to be strong and forthright, couldn't let it go.

"That's the only name that has any sentimental meaning for me, so I'll need more information before I cross it off the list."

They'd left the mosquito netting open, so there was nothing stopping Sam from rolling over to sit on the edge of the bed, his back to her, stiff and almost preternaturally still.

The silence, broken by only the slow, melodic swish of the overhead fan, seemed to thicken until Chloe felt as though she couldn't breathe.

"It wouldn't be appropriate," he finally said, in a wooden, almost mechanical tone. "That was the name of the woman I planned to marry."

Something inside her shriveled and retreated from his words, but Chloe didn't allow herself to give up.

A voice within was telling her not to react the way she really wanted to, which was to batter him with questions until he was as bruised as she felt. Instead, she kept her voice even, although the effort to do so made her slightly nauseous.

"I guess that's a good reason, especially if she's still in your life."

And might realize through our child's name that you're still in love with her...

Sam got up and walked to the window to stare out for a moment before turning and facing her across the room.

"She died, almost nine years ago." His voice was still flat, but his eyes sparked with so much pain Chloe could hardly bear to keep holding his gaze. "Along with our unborn baby."

CHAPTER EIGHTEEN

SAM WATCHED CHLOE'S FACE, wanting to see her reaction, needing something from her, although he wasn't sure what.

He'd almost convinced himself that he'd never have to tell her about Vicky and the baby. It was, he reasoned, old news. A history that had no bearing on the present. He'd been content—determinedly so—to remain unattached and aloof from romantic ties of any kind. Wallowing, if truth be told, in the old pain. Reluctant to revisit it, in even the remotest sense.

Chloe had mellowed the ache, simply by being herself, and offering him a redemptive chance.

Her eyes were wide, and Sam tried to interpret the emotions he saw flickering in their dark depths, but they were too fleeting.

"I'm sorry, Sam."

She meant it. The sympathy in her voice was unmistakable, yet he also felt as though a new distance yawned between them, and he didn't know why. He'd opened up to her in a way he'd never done before, but instead of it bringing them closer, he thought she was pulling away.

"It was a long time ago, but I'm not going to say the pain went away. In fact, I held on to it and used it as a crutch and a life lesson. I didn't plan to ever marry or have kids. I think what I really wanted was to avoid even the chance of being hurt like that again."

"And my pregnancy being high-risk brought it all back." She nodded, as though she'd reached a decision. "I'm sorry for that."

"Don't be." Sam felt suddenly on shaky ground. The weekend had been so wonderful, but now he felt everything slipping away. "You weren't to know. And it's not like any of this was planned."

"No." Chloe slipped from the bed and headed for the bathroom. "You're right about that, but I would have been more sensitive about the name issue if I'd known about your ex beforehand." Sam took a step toward her, although he didn't have a clue what he was going to say, but she paused in the doorway and looked back. When he saw the lines between her brows, his heart sank even further. "Not that it's any of my business, mind you," she continued, giving him a smile that didn't quite reach her eyes, before stepping into the bathroom and closing the door.

Shutting him out.

Suddenly angry, he let her go and set about getting dressed.

He'd bared his pain to her , and she'd walked away. If she wanted to be unreasonable instead of talking things out, then there was nothing he could do about it except wait and let her cool down.

It wasn't as if she'd been terribly forthcoming with him about her past either. Oh, she'd told him she was divorced and that it was because her ex had cheated on her repeatedly, but only when he'd heard her conversation with her grandmother had he learned the whole truth.

He heard her come out of the bathroom as he was pulling on his shirt and couldn't resist glancing her way as she rummaged in her bag for some clothes.

Even in profile he could see her lips were tight, and he was sure those lines would be back between her eyes. His anger bled away, leaving him mentally scrabbling for a way to make things right.

"Listen, I'm sorry I never mentioned it before, but I honestly didn't think it had anything to do with our situation. With us."

Her head tilted slightly, as though she was considering his words, and then she nodded.

"Sure, I can see why you'd think that."

"What does that mean, exactly?"

He had to pin her down, make sure they weren't talking at cross-purposes.

She turned then to face him, and her expression made his heart stutter. It wasn't angry, or upset, but blank. Closed to him in a way he'd never seen before.

And she shrugged, the movement casually dismissive.

"The reality is, that besides our baby, we have nothing. We agreed to have a bit of fun while we were figuring the rest of it out, so no—your prior relationships really are none of my business."

For a moment he couldn't speak, the sting of her words raising a rush of prickling heat over his skin.

"Do you really classify what's happened between us as *nothing*?"

The corners of her lips tipped up in an ironic, hurtful little smile.

"Well, the sex has been terrific," she said, and there was amusement in her voice. "But, seriously, we knew going in that it was just a crazy coincidence that brought us together and we'd be going our separate ways in short order."

"But…"

Sam faltered, the words he'd been about to say sticking in his throat.

He'd been about to tell her that he wanted her to stay in Jamaica. Maybe even confess that he'd thought about marriage and them making a home together, here or in England, but she'd just said there was nothing of substance between them. So why even bother?

"Exactly," Chloe said, that slightly mocking smile still on her face, her eyes dark and unfathomable. "Come on, let's get on the road. You said you wanted to get back to Kingston before nightfall."

And with that, the conversation was apparently over.

It was only when they got close to the city, after an almost silent drive, that he realized the worst of the fallout was yet to come.

"I'm going to stay at the apartment," Chloe said, her tone conversational, as though it didn't much matter what he thought. "I just need to get some clothes for work and I'll grab a taxi."

He wanted to tell her no. To say that wasn't what he wanted—wasn't what was right for them. Maybe even play on that sweet, conciliatory side of hers to get what he desired. Anger rose, luckily choking him before any of the words were said, and he inhaled a long, deep breath, fighting for control.

"Sure," was what he finally got out, past what felt like barbed wire in his throat. "But I'll drop you off when you're ready."

And it was only after he'd done just that, and watched

her walk into the apartment building, that he realized the choking sensation wasn't born of anger.

But of fear.

She'd known what she was getting into with Sam Powell. She'd been warned and had even said it herself. He was her last chance at a no-strings-attached fling. One without everlasting commitment or complication.

But, standing in her Christmas-denuded flat, Chloe realized she hadn't listened.

Not to Rashida nor to herself.

Instead of keeping her baby's father at an emotional arm's length, she'd dropped her guard and fallen for him—hard.

It was, she knew, all on her. Yes, she was hurt and upset with Sam for not telling her about losing his ex-girlfriend and their baby, but if she'd stuck to the original plan, it wouldn't have been so painful.

Now she could understand all too well his reluctance to become involved with another woman. And it was just as well he'd made that choice, because no one could compete with a ghost.

Chloe wouldn't even try.

She'd been a willing—if somewhat unwitting—doormat in her previous relationship. There was no way she'd be a poor replacement for a deceased woman in her next.

And now she also understood Sam's obvious worry about her pregnancy and both his willingness to accept that he was about to become a father as well as his concern for her well-being. It had all been out of fear of losing another child.

What Chloe had seen as evidence of his growing care

for her, personally, and a developing relationship had been born out of that fear.

His feelings for her—beyond the sexual attraction— were strictly because she was the receptacle for the life she carried in her womb.

Going out onto the balcony, Chloe came to the realization that for the baby's sake, not to mention her own, some hard decisions had to be made.

What she wanted was to walk away completely, leaving Sam—and hopefully this heartache—behind, but that wasn't possible. He was still the father of her child, and some contact with him was inevitable. She just couldn't handle it right now when she was raw and heartsore, with every nerve exposed.

Tears made her neighbors' twinkling lights shimmer, as though mocking her misery, reminding her what she'd just lost.

Even if it had just been an illusion, she'd been so happy living it. More content than she could ever remember being in her life. Now she had to face the fact that it was over.

Forever.

Using the tips of her fingers to wipe away the moisture from her eyes, she straightened her back and tried to find the elusive silver lining she knew had to be there somewhere.

Falling back on the benefits she'd thought of after her divorce—her job and freedom to do whatever she wanted—didn't bring the joy they had before. But that was what she had. At least until the baby was born.

Cupping her palms over the slight bump of her stomach, she whispered, "We'll be okay."

Saying it more to herself than to the baby.

She didn't expect Sam to call her over the next couple of days, but he did, and she didn't answer. After the second time, he sent her a text, telling her to phone him when she was ready to talk.

That made her snort. If he left it at that, he might never hear from her again. While she was able to hold it all together at work, despite constantly looking over her shoulder in case Sam was around, just the thought of talking to him made tears flood her eyes.

She really had to get herself together before that particular conversation.

Not feeling up to socializing or explaining to Rashida what was happening, Chloe sent her friend a text on Monday morning, saying she was working on her presentation for the next few days. The person she really wanted to talk to was Cora, but from the sounds of it, her friend was having her own problems, and Chloe didn't want to burden her with anything else.

On top of it all, there was the growing sense that she needed to handle this all herself, as a testament to her inner strength. She didn't *need* Sam or anyone else to make it through life, she reminded herself stoutly, even though the thought brought with it a hard pang of sadness.

Getting ready for bed after three days of hard thinking, she came to a decision.

The following day she'd call Sam and arrange a meeting with him. She needed to get the rest of her clothes from his house anyway, and it was a good excuse to sit down and talk this all out.

At some point, before she left, they'd have to get everything settled, and the anticipation of that conversation was causing even more stress than just having it and being done would.

Settling under the sheet, Chloe pulled up the information her colleague in London had sent regarding neuro-fibromatosis research and started reading through. Although she'd used getting prepped for the seminar as an excuse to avoid company, she was well pleased with the amount of work she'd actually been able to do.

And before long, she felt sleep creeping up on her and turned out the light, somehow more serene than she'd been for days. Making up her mind about how to deal with Sam had lifted a weight off her spirit.

When she awoke, it was to darkness and a sensation both familiar and unwelcome.

Back pain, excruciating and unrelenting, bad enough that she held her breath, too afraid to even exhale, in case it got worse.

Still trapped in a somnolent state, she recognized it as the start of her period and tried to remember where she'd left her pills.

Then the rush of awareness, the fear—more potent and grinding than the pain itself—had her reaching for her phone on the bedside table.

Mindless with terror, she didn't even think, just pushed the button.

When Sam answered, all she could do was gasp, "Call Dr. Hall. I have to go to the hospital."

CHAPTER NINETEEN

SAM PUT HIS hand on Chloe's shoulder, needing to feel her warmth under his palm, but there was little sensation in his fingers.

Millicent Hall was speaking, and he forced himself to listen.

"It really is an old wives' tale that pregnancy is a good way to get rid of endometriosis. While some women get some relief from the symptoms during pregnancy, others don't."

She looked down at the chart in her hand, flipping a page back and then forth again.

Sam wanted to shout at her to hurry up, to tell them whatever the hell she had to say.

Chloe shifted, and the brief touch of her cheek against his fingers steadied him slightly and made him realize his grip on her was probably too tight.

He loosened his fingers.

"All the tests have come back negative. There is no bleeding and the ultrasound showed no abnormalities or masses. Chloe's temperature is within normal range, so I'm tentatively confident there's no infection."

He must look even worse than he felt, Sam thought,

because Millie was speaking to them as though they were ordinary people instead of doctors.

No bleeding, instead of "spontaneous abortion."

No abnormalities or masses rather than "hemoperitoneum" or "endometriomas."

Not "sepsis caused by intestinal perforations or changes in endometriotic lesions due to decidualization," but just plain old *infection*.

She didn't say the words, but she didn't have to, because Sam's brain supplied them itself, running through all the possible permutations until he thought he'd go bonkers.

Damn him for researching the condition and its possible effects on the pregnancy, once he knew Chloe had it. A little ignorance would be bliss just now.

"I think what we're seeing is simply a manifestation of Chloe's underlying condition. A continuation of her symptoms rather than a clear-and-present danger to her pregnancy. Endometriosis during pregnancy can almost be distilled into a battle of hormones. If the progesterone wins, there's a relief from symptoms. If the estrogen wins, there isn't. Tonight, the estrogen was stronger."

"Can I go home?" Chloe's voice was faint, faraway, but knowing she didn't mean his house made him, ridiculously, want to weep.

"I'm going to keep you in," Millie said. "To monitor your condition overnight. But if all goes well, you'll be discharged in the morning."

Then with a nod, she left.

Sam was rooted where he stood. The adrenaline surge he'd felt when Chloe woke him up had waned, leaving him cold and shaken. He couldn't even remember the drive from his house to the hospital. Knowing he wasn't in the best of conditions to drive, he'd arranged for an ambulance to pick Chloe up, but he'd arrived at the same time and hadn't left her side since.

Chloe put her hand up and her fingers were as icy as Sam's.

"Why don't you go home?" she said. "And get some rest. I'll be okay."

Did she really want—*expect*—him to leave?

Should he ask or just take it as a given that she wanted to be alone?

A nurse bustled in at that moment and gave them a smile, as though the bottom hadn't dropped out of his *rass* life and been carried away by gut-tearing fear.

"Doctor said I'm to give you something to help you sleep."

"See," Chloe said, her voice strangely calm, yet she sounded almost as numb as Sam felt inside. "There's nothing more you can do here, Sam. Go home."

He bent, meaning to kiss her cheek, but found himself resting his forehead on her hair, his fingers still gripping her shoulder, reluctant to let go.

"Sleep well," he finally said, aware of the nurse watching them and the sympathy in her eyes.

With a soft kiss on her cheek, he left the room and stood outside the door, unable to get his feet to go a step farther.

Millie had met them at Andrews Memorial, a hospital Sam knew well, but which now seemed as unfamiliar as the shadow world of a dream. Objectively, he knew he was suffering from shock or, at the very least, the tail end of the adrenaline dump, but he couldn't seem to figure out how to treat it.

Physician, heal thyself.

The old saying rose in his brain and drifted away again.

"Dr. Powell?" He turned at the sound of his name to see another nurse coming toward him. "Dr. Hall said to tell you that there's an empty private room just down the hall, if you want to stay and need to lie down."

"Thank you," he said automatically, but instead of following her pointed finger, he wandered down the corridor and, taking a back route, went outside, behind the main building.

The night was cool, but Sam was already shivering before he got out the door, so a little night breeze meant nothing. Walking along the edge of the carpark, he found a spot behind a tree where the streetlights couldn't reach and sank down onto the ground.

The look on Chloe's face when he'd rushed to the stretcher, the stark terror in her eyes would stay with him forever.

He'd known then that she thought she was losing the baby, and her fear had infected him like a superbug, bringing with it all the grief and agony he'd endured before.

Even now, his hands shook and his entire body felt like jelly,

And yet he had to remind himself, the worst had not happened. The pain and terror would pass, and they still had a chance to...

To what? What do you want, Sam?

The moment of truth was upon him, and he knew it but couldn't corral his faculties enough to think it through.

Every nerve and sinew in his body strained to go back

inside and be with Chloe. To protect her with life and limb and whatever else he had to bring to bear.

He hadn't wanted a child. Had even less wanted to feel the way he did about Chloe, but this wasn't a choice anymore.

It was all there, lying in that hospital bed, and although he knew full well none of it was his for the taking, he wanted it—them—nonetheless.

Chloe had filled a hole in his heart, and in his life, that he'd hardly dared to admit even existed. Looking back, he'd kept busy with work and all the extracurricular activities a man could ever want, but when he went home at night, there'd been no joy, no meaning to any of it.

The weeks with Chloe—weeks of fear and fun and infuriation—had meant more to him than the last ten years of his life.

When Vicky died, he'd felt cheated—not only out of being a parent but out of all the little steps leading up to it too.

The excitement of hearing they were going to have a child.

The first trip to the doctor and the plans for the future—everything from choosing names and nursery colors to where would be the best place to raise the baby.

The first sonogram, where they could see the new life in its very beginning stage.

Vicky had, for whatever reason, deprived him of all of it, and he'd resented her for doing that.

Chloe had had every opportunity to do the same but hadn't.

She'd told him about the baby as soon as she'd known herself and allowed him into Millie's office, when she could very well have asked him to stay in the waiting room. Allowed him that first glimpse of the life they'd created together.

She'd even wanted to consult with him on the name.

Everything he'd been deprived of before she'd lovingly given of her own accord.

And given of herself too.

Not just her body, but her sweet, practical, loving spirit too.

She was one in a billion.

A hundred billion.

His first impulse was to go in there and snatch at it, make demands and issue ultimatums. But he knew that wouldn't work, and even if it did, it wouldn't last.

The one thing he wanted most of all was the one thing he didn't think she'd be willing to give.

Her heart.

Hospitals are no place to get well.

As she drifted up from her blessedly drugged sleep, Chloe found herself wondering who'd first said that, even as she acknowledged the truth of it. How difficult it was to consider getting better when there was always some type of racket going on.

For the patient who simply craved peace and a quiet place to think, the wards—even a private room—in a hospital were the worst possible place to be.

Lying on her side, she could see the window where a thin stream of murky light came through the blinds to one side. Weak sunlight, she thought, rather than streetlamps with their harsh glare.

She knew where she was. The sounds of a hospital in the morning were nothing new. What *was* new was this feeling of utter impotence, of rage, that her body—even having been given this precious gift—continued on its path of betrayal and fearmongering.

Sam's face.

She could hardly bear to think about his expression, the absolute agony she'd seen in those moments when he'd run to her side. Thinking, no doubt, about those he'd lost before, terrified their child would be added to the tally.

He'd rallied, of course. He was used to emergencies and knew how to put his own fear aside so as to give the support she'd needed.

That was the kind of man any woman would be proud to have beside her—one who would always have her back, no matter what.

The man she would love for the rest of her days.

"You're awake."

His voice had her closing her eyes, not to pretend sleep but to battle back the tears she'd been about to shed.

When she rolled over, he was there to reposition her pillows and pull up the sheet, his hands tender and careful.

She lifted her chin, facing him, looking straight into his face for the first time since he'd spoken.

He looked pale. His eyes were red, as though he hadn't slept.

"Did you get any sleep last night?"

He gestured to the chair beside her bed.

"It wasn't terribly comfortable, so no."

Her silly heart leaped with the knowledge that he'd stayed, but she forced it to calm.

"You should have gone home. There was nothing you could do here."

The look he gave her was long and searching, then he shrugged.

"On the contrary, there was a lot I could do. I watched you sleep and made sure that if the pain woke you up, I'd be here to get you the help you'd need."

"That's what the nurses are for." It was hard to dismiss his words, but Chloe knew she had to. This thing between them couldn't go on. Not like this.

Not when it hurt both of them so much. The last thing she wanted was to add to his pain.

He shook his head and looked as though he would perch on the side of her bed, then thought better of it. Instead, he brought the chair closer and sat down.

"No, that's what I was for last night." Before she could speak in response, he continued. "I know all too well what it really means not to be able to do anything at all for someone you care about, and that wasn't the case last night."

He cared about her.

Again her silly heart leaped, and again she subdued it. Of course he cared. For the baby, perhaps even for her, as a friend, a lover. Nothing more.

"I didn't tell you the entire story about Vicky, and I need to, so you'll understand."

He paused, but didn't look away, keeping his dark, pain-filled gaze on her until Chloe was sure her heart would break. Something told her she didn't want to hear any more, and she should stop him from telling it, but no words could pass the tightness of her throat. Instead, she nodded, knotting her fingers into the sheets so as not to reach out and try to smooth away the lines around his eyes.

"She died in a car crash and..." Now he hesitated,

and she saw him swallow. "It was only when she was gone that I found out she was pregnant. Four months pregnant."

"Sam—"

Words failed her, even as questions rushed through her brain and a cold, sinking feeling settled in her stomach. He'd not only lost the woman he'd loved but she'd betrayed his trust too.

How could he ever get over that?

She saw it now, the final blow poised above her head, but Chloe refused to bow before it. Hadn't she, oh-so-stupidly, told herself she could handle whatever came her way? Well, this was the chance to put her money where her mouth was and keep her dignity.

"You don't have to say any more, Sam. I understand."

He cocked his head, and his eyes narrowed. "Do you?"

"Yes." How ridiculous to be proud of the firmness of her voice, when inside she was already wailing. "I don't want you to be hurt again either. Before you know it, I'll be flying back to England and out of your hair."

He got up so abruptly the chair scraped across the floor, and he scrubbed his hand across his jaw, as though trying to take off the skin.

"If that's what you think—" He broke off, and cursed under his breath. Then he inhaled, and said, "If that's what you want."

"I do." There, it was done. Over with. If the blasted man would just leave so she could cry in peace, she'd be okay.

"Chloe…"

"Just go, Sam. Don't make it harder than it needs to be."

"Harder? For whom?"

The spurt of anger was welcome and Chloe embraced it.

"For you. For me. For all of us. If you need to leave, then go. Don't let some ridiculous sense of responsibility keep you here."

He was beside the bed, but she couldn't see him because she was crying. Angry with herself, and with him, for reducing her to this state of weakness.

"I don't feel responsible for you, Chloe." His tone was hard, and it hurt enough that she dashed away her tears so as to glare at him as he continued, "You're a grown woman, competent and smart. You can, and have, taken responsibility for yourself. Why should I try to take that away from you? But what I do feel is love, and I don't want to go."

He hadn't said *love*, had he? Not with that stern, forbidding expression on his face?

"Wh-what?"

"I love you, Chloe. And I love the baby you're carrying, and I don't want to go, and I don't want you to go back to England either. What I want is to be with you, through the good or bad. Life isn't easy, but you make everything in my life better, and I want that to continue, forever."

She knew she was gaping at him like a fool while the blood rushed and bubbled in her veins, like champagne.

"I'll only go if you tell me there's no chance in hell that you would ever love me back, because if there's even the slightest hint—"

"I love you too."

The words slipped out and couldn't be recalled even if she wanted to do such a thing. Sam pulled her into his arms and kissed her until her head swam, and she knew she'd never be whole without him again.

"Oy!" The nurse sounded as though she couldn't decide whether to be angry or amused. "None of that, you two. This is a respectable place, not a motel."

And Chloe could only bury her heated face in Sam's chest and laugh her joy aloud.

EPILOGUE

Zara Lucinda Powell made her way into the world, via scheduled cesarean section on a hot, humid night in June and came out wailing as though completely over the entire experience already.

"Beautiful," Millie Hall said, as she laid Zara on Chloe's chest and Sam cut the cord. "Nothing wrong with her Apgar score, I'm sure."

Still dazed, Chloe looked down at the perfect little being, murmuring encouragement, relieved beyond words that, even with everything that had happened, this moment had finally arrived.

Not endometriosis nor placenta previa, which had caused the C-section, could dim the joy.

Zara stilled, looking up into her mother's face, and Chloe got a thrill of pleasure when she realized their baby had Sam's eyes.

"She's perfect," Sam said, and the wonder in his voice matched her own. When he reached out a finger and smoothed it across the baby's head, Chloe fought back tears. "Perfect, just like her mother."

"Mama, can I take her for a minute? I'll bring her right back," the nurse said, smiling and holding out her hands—asking but really telling, in that way good nurses know how to do.

When the nurse whisked their once-more screaming offspring away to weigh her and give her a quick cleaning, Sam reached down and rested his cheek on Chloe's head.

"Good job, Mrs. Powell," he whispered into her ear. "You came through like a champ."

She snorted. "All I had to do was lie here. Millie did all the work."

Dr. Hall looked over the drape and laughed behind her mask. "Tell me that two days from now when the incision site makes it hard to even cough."

But even that couldn't stop Chloe from grinning behind her surgical mask.

How could she not be happy?

She and Sam had been married on Boxing Day in Kendrick and Rashida's garden, and their life together so far had been magical. Chloe, after long discussions with Sam, had decided that living in Jamaica would be best for them all and had taken a post at University Hospital, where she was also lecturing.

And now, their sweet little girl had finally arrived.

"It's worth it," she said, smiling up at Sam, who was watching what the nurse was doing with Zara and didn't notice. "It's definitely all been worth it."

He looked down at her then, and they shared one of those looks that always made her melt.

"Yes," he agreed softly. "Every minute worth it, for all this."

* * * * *

DECEMBER
REUNION
IN CENTRAL PARK

DEANNE ANDERS

MILLS & BOON

This book is dedicated to
boss extraordinaire, Debbie Charlton,
and the best of co-workers, Stefanie Porche.
I will always be appreciative of your support.

CHAPTER ONE

ENDLESS CLOUDS FLOATED by as Dr. Scott Thomas looked outside the plane that was taking him home. Home? Was it still home? Despite how hard the last year and a half had been, he'd come to think of London as home. But still something was missing. No, make that someone. His home hadn't felt the same since he and Felicity had dashed off to New York to be with her parents. He'd not known at the time that she wouldn't be coming back with him.

He punched the pillow he'd been given earlier and tried to reposition himself. The transatlantic flight was going to be rough on him the next day if he didn't get some rest, and he wanted to be at his best when he arrived to work the next day. The chance to help another hospital set up a specialty cardiac unit like the one at his own hospital, the Royal Kensington Hospital, was something that excited him, and it had been a while since he'd been really excited about anything.

Nothing could have surprised him more than to be offered this chance to be part of The Kensington Project, and while a part of him had been only too happy to return to New York, another part of him worried about what he might find when he finally made it to his hometown.

His parents, of course, were thrilled with the opportunity to see him, especially since he'd be remaining in New York till after the holidays. And then there was Felicity. Would she be happy to see him? Or would she wish him on his way, as she had the last time he'd seen her? Where exactly had they gone wrong?

"Is there anything I can get you?" A soft voice came from beside him.

Looking up, he saw that one of the flight attendants was standing over him. She'd spoken to him earlier in the flight, offering him a blanket and pillow.

"No, I'm fine, but thank you," he said. It had been pretty apparent that she wanted to start a conversation with him, though he had been careful not to encourage her.

"You sure?" she asked. "You seem a bit…distracted."

Her badge said her name was Kristen, and she made an attractive picture in her trim navy suit with her honey-blond hair and golden sun-touched skin that hinted of time spent in much warmer climates than those with which he was familiar. And just like every woman he had met in the last eighteen months, he wasn't even tempted to ask her for her full name.

"May I?" she asked as her hand indicated the empty seat next to his.

"Sure," he said as he repositioned himself more upright in his own seat.

"I take it from your accent that you're from the States. So am I. Are you headed home?" she asked.

There was that word again. *Home.* It had never seemed as complicated as it had in the last few months.

"I grew up in New York, but I work in London now," he said. "Is New York your home?"

"It is right now," she said. "I move around a lot. So, married? Single?" she asked with a smile that could be dangerously sexy, he was sure, but still he felt nothing.

What would it take to make him feel that heart-pounding adrenaline-buzz attraction again? He feared there was only one smile that would ever get that kind of response from him.

He realized she was staring at him and still waiting for his answer. "I'm single. I mean… I'm not married."

"A girlfriend, then?" she asked him.

The conversation was making him a bit uncomfortable, but he knew it wasn't her fault.

"It's complicated," he said, hoping that this would end her interrogation.

"Isn't love always complicated?" She gave him another smile and moved to get up. Apparently she had heard all she needed to hear. "Maybe we'll meet again sometime and things won't be complicated."

He watched as she walked back and joined the other attendants at the front of the plane, then adjusted his pillow once more. Love, complicated? It had never seemed to be that way for his parents, but the last few months had proved to him that emotions made people, even people you thought you really knew, unpredictable.

He stretched his seat back and closed his eyes. Immediately his mind got caught up in thoughts of complicated love and memories that seemed to be burned into his brain on a movie reel that he had replayed over and over for the last eighteen months.

It always opened up the same way…

A perfect moonlit night at that little sidewalk café that was her favorite; laughter while they sipped wine and talked about their day. Then they'd walk through the English garden in the park just blocks from his London home.

He could almost smell the sweet scent of the hydrangea blooms as they walked hand in hand and talked of everything and nothing, never tiring of hearing what the other had to say. It was always as if they were two strangers meeting for the first time and wanting to know everything about the other, instead of two people who had grown up together from childhood.

And even when silence fell between the two of them, there was no sign of awkwardness. They'd continued their walk until they stopped to share a kiss that seemed to change everything—a change they embraced as one kiss led to another until they were both racing to his place, together.

If only he could stop the memories there...

Scenes of kisses and touches played over in his mind: a vision of her stripped bare for him; the sight of her stretched out in his bed; the feel of her in his arms as they lay sated from their lovemaking.

He twisted in his seat and tried to will his mind to stop there. To leave him with that last happy memory of brushing long blond hair from sleepy blue eyes and wishing her a good night as they fell into slumber together, wrapped around each other for the first time.

But, no, there was no happy ending for the movie his mind insisted on playing for him each night as he tried to sleep.

There was always the insistent ringing of a phone, and the words his father had choked out as he gave Scott the news that had brought his life to a screeching halt—Scott's best friend, and Fliss's brother, was *dying*. Suicide, his father had said, though Scott refused to believe that this was possible, arguing with his father that he had to be mistaken as his father pleaded for him to find Fliss and break the news to her in person so she *wouldn't* be alone.

He'd looked down at the woman lying in his bed, the one he was falling in love with, and had known instinctively that nothing would ever be the same.

Finally the last scene replayed itself.

In his arms, he held his lover and friend, whose tears and sobs broke what was left of his heart after the loss of his friend.

Scott's eyes flew open. Looking around the plane, he was glad to see he hadn't drawn anyone's attention. He looked at his watch. He had three more hours before they landed at JFK and there was no way he was going to sleep now. Dragging out his laptop, he dug into the reports he'd been given on Brooklyn Heights Hospital's new cardiac unit. He might be tired when he showed up the next day, but at least he'd be up to date and ready to get to work.

It had finally happened. She'd lost her mind. That was the only excuse she had for why she was standing in the middle of the emergency-room hallway, staring at the back of some man's head. It had been bound to happen at some point. She couldn't continue to work seven days a week, twelve to sixteen hours a day, without this happening. Of course, she could see why this man had gotten her attention. That thick head of dark chocolate-brown hair in that specific close-cropped cut was like a magnet for her eyes—eyes that were apparently tired from lack of sleep, because no matter what they were telling her, that man couldn't be Scott.

She looked around the hallway. It was the same New York City crowded hallway where she had spent most of her hours in the last year. It was definitely not the Royal Kensington Hospital elite cardiac unit in London, where Scott could be found.

Clenching her hands, she felt the vial of medication in her hand. She had to get back to her patient. She didn't have time for this nonsense. There had to be plenty of men that could resemble Scott from the back.

She two-stepped it down the hallway, dodging stretchers and wheelchairs, but a sense of unease still followed her back to her patient's room. It had been a strange experience to react to a man that way, especially when she could barely see his profile.

Entering the room, she noted that the young woman's heart rate was still tachycardia and had gone from running in the one-eighties to the two-hundreds now.

"It's going to be okay, Jenny," Felicity said to the young woman who was even more pale and diaphoretic than she had been when she first arrived.

"The vagal maneuver hasn't helped?" she asked the emergency-room doctor.

"No. Go ahead and draw up the adenosine," he said.

Drawing up the medication, she wiped down the IV port and then attached the syringe. "Has Dr. Campbell explained how adenosine works?"

"He said it should make my heart slow down, but also that I might feel some chest pain and dizziness." Jenny's bright green eyes shone with a look of panic that Felicity was used to seeing in the emergency room.

"I'll be right here with you," Felicity said as she took Jenny's hand into her free one, preparing to inject the medication into the IV line.

"Are you ready?" she asked her patient, then looked over at the doctor who nodded his head for her to push the medication that would basically stop Jenny's heart before it returned into a normal rhythm.

She squeezed the young woman's hand and pushed the medication. Everyone's attention went to the monitor above the bed as the cardiac rhythm began to slow until there was a pause.

"Oh," the young woman said as she clutched both of their hands to her chest, bringing Felicity's attention back to her. Pain and panic filled the woman's eyes.

"It's okay. The worst is over, I promise. Just hang on a few more seconds." Felicity looked back up at the monitor to see that the heart rate was gradually slowing to a normal sinus rhythm. "Is it better now?"

Jenny nodded her head, but Felicity could tell that she hadn't totally recovered. At least some of the young woman's color was returning now. "Can I get you something?"

"No, I'm better now." The young woman's voice trembled, but she let go of Felicity's hand and closed her eyes. "I'm just going to rest a minute."

"I'll be right here if you need anything," Felicity said as the rest of the staff began to leave the room. She would remain in the room with her patient until she was assured the young woman was stable and then have her transferred to the cardiac floor for observation and more testing to find the cause behind her tachycardia.

She was turning to get her patient a blanket when her eyes came to a stop as she saw the man from earlier standing outside the glass doors of the trauma room. Who was he, and why did he have to be here in her ER, upsetting her now when she needed to be concentrating on her patient?

Yes, the man was at least as tall as Scott and they did share the same basic build that included a pair of very wide shoulders. And, yes, this man did have the exact same haircut that Scott had always favored, but it was more than that. Something deep down inside her told her she knew him.

Turn around. Let me see your face.

Her heart was beating as fast as her patient's had earlier.

For a moment she let herself imagine that it was Scott. That he had come back to see her. But how would he have known where to find her? Unlike the years when they had been separated by colleges in different states, there had been no late-night calls that went on for hours, nor had there been the funny texts that they had shared for years as they checked up on each other. Felicity had known they needed a clean break. Ignoring his calls and texts had added more heartache to her life, but she would never have survived hearing about Scott's life without her.

"Are you okay?" Dr. Campbell asked as he came to a stop at the door, blocking her view. For a moment she thought the doctor was talking to her patient before she realized he was speaking to her.

"Yes, we're good. I'll let you know if there are any changes in her rhythm." She had to get herself together. She had a job to do and it did not include daydreaming.

She took a blanket off the shelf beside the stretcher and covered the young woman before allowing herself to walk over to the doorway. If Scott's doppelgänger had ever actually existed, he was gone now. It was official. She was losing her mind.

Checking her patient's vital signs again, she made herself concentrate on getting her charting done. There were only a couple of hours left in her shift and then she had to go to the new unit and check on progress there.

"Hey, Felicity, Jodi said I should relieve you so you can go to a meeting Dr. Mason just called," said Matt, startling her, a few minutes later. One of the new nurses who had been hired to take the place of the nurses who were going to the new cardiac center, he moved extremely quietly for being a giant teddy bear of a man at six feet six inches, with the large build to match.

In the last two weeks, Dr. Mason had begun making a habit of calling these last-minute meetings that were making it difficult for her to help fill in while the rest of these new nurses were being trained.

"I'm sorry. I have to leave you." She checked the monitor and saw that Jenny's heart rate had settled into a normal sinus rhythm in the nineties. "But Matt's going to take great care of you. He'll get you admitted and transfer you to the cardiac unit."

"Thank you for taking care of me," Jenny said before shutting her eyes again. The poor woman had been through a lot today. She deserved her rest.

"Believe me, I'd rather be here taking care of you than going to another meeting," Felicity said as she gathered her stethoscope. When she'd accepted the brand-new position of nursing manager at the new clinic, she'd had no idea the number of meetings and the piles of paperwork that were necessary to start the new department.

"Thanks for helping me out. Dr. Mason can be difficult if anyone misses one of his meetings." Felicity couldn't help but feel guilty about leaving her patient with another nurse at this point, but there was nothing that could be done about it. She'd taken the extra shifts in the ER to help out, but everyone knew her first priority had to be her new department.

"No problem," Matt said. "I saw him in the unit introducing some new hire to the ER docs. Rumor says he's some hotshot from London."

A wave of tiny pinpricks rushed over her, making her skin sting and tingle. It was just a coincidence. That was all. New doctors were arriving at Brooklyn Heights every day. Besides, why would Dr. Mason pull everybody in for a meeting concerning some new doctor?

Unless this doctor was a cardiac doctor who had been involved with a specialty ER department. Unless he had been one of the leading members for such a program in his own hospital. The Royal Kensington Hospital in London had such a program. Scott had been there for the planning and opening of that program. Was there a possibility that Scott was actually here?

With the sound of her heart drumming a staccato rhythm in her ear, she tried not to rush through her report to Matt before she hurried off to the meeting room. Her steps became faster as she approached the door. And there, standing once again with his back to her, was the man she had seen earlier in the emergency room. This was getting ridiculous. Was it Scott or not?

Stopping outside the door, she took in everything she could see of him—the perfect cut of a well-tailored suit, one of Scott's indulged weaknesses since graduating from medical school; the broad shoulders, which he'd developed while playing high school football with her brother; and the confident stance, shoulders back and feet solidly planted, which invoked leadership. All these things she could see in this man.

And then he turned, and suddenly her eyes were locked with a pair of hazel ones that mirrored the shock she knew had to be in her own. He was here. Dr. Scott Thomas had returned to New York.

CHAPTER TWO

SCOTT WAS AT a loss for words. Yes, he'd planned on getting up to Hudson to see his parents as soon as possible. And he'd planned, or hoped, to run into Felicity while there, but this? Never had he imagined that he'd find her here in a hospital where he had agreed to work for the next eight weeks.

"Well, this is a surprise," Felicity said as she took a step toward him.

"Scott, this is Felicity Dale, the nurse manager that we've hired to run our new cardiac unit," Dr. Mason said as he walked over to them.

"Scott, why are you here?" Felicity asked him, both of them ignoring the other doctor.

"He's here to help with the opening of the new unit. I told you I was trying to find someone after Dr. Kane had to go on family leave to take care of her mother. There's no telling how long it will take for the poor woman to walk again after her hip fracture. Dr. Kane could be out for months," Dr. Mason continued as the tension between the two of them hummed through the air. Couldn't the man hear it? Feel it?

"I didn't know you were working back in the city," Scott said as he started to recover.

"You know each other?" Dr. Mason asked.

"We worked together in London," Felicity said quickly before Scott had a chance to answer.

He waited for her to add more, but she didn't, which shocked him almost as much as seeing her here. That was it? No mention that the two of them had grown up together? No mention of all the years they had spent as the best of friends?

"Now that I think about it, I do remember something from your résumé about you having experience in London. What a coincidence! This is great! With Dr. Kane having to go on leave, I was so worried about us being ready by the grand opening. But with the two of you working together, I know we'll make it," the older man said as he wrapped one arm around each of their shoulders. "Now, let's get this meeting started."

Dr. Mason moved away from the two of them and headed for the front of the room, giving Scott no choice but to follow him. Hesitating for a moment, he moved closer to Felicity, whispering in her ear, "We'll talk later."

"Sure," she mumbled, before moving away from him and heading for a chair at the large executive table—as far away from him as she could manage.

What was wrong with her? Rather than catching up with an old friend, her tone made it seem like he had suggested that she face a firing squad.

He'd respected her choice to end something that had barely started between the two of them, though he had never understood it, but he'd also given up on understanding why she'd decided to end their friendship too. And now she wanted to pretend that they were barely acquaintances? Was she just still reeling from the shock of this new position they found themselves in?

"I know we're all a little out of sorts with Dr. Kane having to go on leave, but she wanted to tell everyone..."

Scott tried to concentrate on what Dr. Mason was saying. His role in The Kensington Project was to help with the final steps of opening the new cardiac unit in New York City that was being modeled after the London hospital's own center. Part emergency room and part procedural area, it had been highly successful in London and promised to be just as successful here. He'd thought he was ready for the job. Excited, even.

But this? There was no way he could have prepared himself for finding Felicity here in the same hospital as him, let alone having to work on the same project together.

But here he was, sitting at the table with the woman who had once been his best friend, with neither of them even acknowledging that relationship. Were they supposed to go on like this the whole time he was here? She had to know that wouldn't work for either of them.

"And with the experience he has assisting with the setup of the Royal Kensington Hospital's hybrid cardiac center, I know he is the perfect person to help us with the opening of ours. And I've just learned that he and our own Felicity Dale, the nurse manager for our new unit, have actually worked together before in London. With the two of them leading the way, I'm sure we are in for a very successful grand opening and, just as important, a new opportunity to serve our community." Dr. Mason seemed to beam with pleasure every time he mentioned the new center. It was no secret that this was one of the last things the older physician wanted to see completed before he retired. It was one of the first things he'd told

Scott that morning when they met. "So now I'm going to turn the meeting over to Dr. Thomas."

Scott stood and looked around the room, his eyes stopping on Felicity. "It's nice to see all of you here and I look forward to us working together."

He made his eyes move on to the next person beside her and then around to the rest of the staff, but they kept coming back to Felicity. "As Dr. Mason has said, the grand opening of the cardiac center here in New York will be an advancement for patient care that will serve a great need in this community. It promises to streamline the care of cardiac patients, as it will drastically lower the time from ER arrival to intervention, increasing the patient's chances of survival while at the same time helping to decompress the general emergency room, allowing other patients to be seen more quickly. We've seen this happen in London and I'm sure you will see the same results here. Does anyone have any questions?"

He answered a few questions, mostly about the cardiac program in London, then turned the meeting back over to Dr. Mason. After a few reminders concerning the next week's agenda, the meeting was closed and Scott worked his way around the room, stopping as he went to acknowledge introductions from staff members with whom he would be working. Finally he made it to the one person he needed to speak to.

"Fliss, do you have a moment?" There'd be no way for her to deny how well the two of them knew each other with him using the nickname he'd known her by most of his life.

"I can't believe you're here. Why didn't you let me know you were coming?" The blush that followed her statement was an acknowledgment that she was the one who had insisted it would be best if they didn't stay in contact. Of course, he'd refused to accept this until it had become apparent that she wasn't going to take his calls.

Where had things gone so wrong between the two of them? Yes, she had lost her brother, but so had he. Somehow, something that should have brought them closer together had sent the two of them off in different directions. And it seemed by her reaction to his return to New York that she wished for it to stay that way.

"I thought you were still working in Hudson." Hadn't that been the reason she'd refused to go back to London with him? She wanted to be closer to her parents, which was understandable under the circumstances. It had hurt, though, to learn that while he'd been thinking they were starting a new phase in their life together, moving from friends to lovers, she had been planning a life in the States without him.

Before she could answer him, a phone began to buzz, and she pulled the hospital-designated phone out of her lab jacket and read the message out loud. "'Cardiac arrest. Male, fifty-five. ETA fifteen minutes.' I've got to get back to the ER."

"We need to get together." He wasn't going to let her run off without agreeing to talk to him later. There was a lot for the two of them to get caught up on and not just with their personal lives. He had to get up to speed with this new program as well and he needed someone to help him. "Dr. Mason said that the group was getting together at a place across the street after work."

"I can't. I'm still working some shifts in the ER, and when I finish my shift tonight, there are some emails regarding the new unit that I need to address." She glanced back down at the phone in her hand, no doubt figuring out how much time she had till the patient would be arriving.

"I'm sure Dr. Mason is expecting you to attend." While he knew this was true, he did feel a bit guilty about pressuring her to come. He couldn't help but see the dark circles under blue eyes that used to sparkle. There was no sparkle there today.

"Bernard's?" she asked, glancing back at her watch.

Did she really find it that uncomfortable to look him in the eye?

"Yeah, that's the place. We'll talk there." And before she could refuse, he turned and walked away. She wasn't the only one having problems dealing with this situation. Having Felicity here was going to be a complication for which he was in no way prepared, but if they were going to work together, they needed to start off on the right footing. They didn't have any time to waste to get things back on track for this grand opening. It was important for their careers that everything went smoothly. They were both professionals. They wouldn't let any personal issues get in the way of their jobs.

Now, if only he could convince the knot in his stomach to believe that. And if only he could convince himself that he was going to come out of the next eight weeks without his heart more bruised than the last time he had left New York.

Felicity tried not to get caught staring at the man sitting in the seat beside her. The noise from the crowd at the pub made talking almost impossible—something she was glad of right now. She needed to get her mind wrapped around the fact that Scott was here.

Four hours ago she'd been getting on with her life,

working her job in the emergency room and preparing for her new position as manager of the cardiac center. It had been her dream job. Her everything. She'd been so proud of where her career was going. She had a future to look forward to. She'd applied for the job, hoping it would give her life more purpose.

Yet here Scott was, making her question all the decisions she'd made in the last year and a half, because no matter how much she'd like to deny it, she still felt the same heart-pumping attraction she'd felt for most of her life whenever she was around Scott. It had been hard to fight during her teenage years and had only gotten harder to ignore during her college years. As an adult with no love life for the last eighteen months, she was finding it even harder to ignore now.

But it was only physical. That was all. And Scott would only be here for eight weeks. It wasn't like she was suddenly going to throw herself into his arms. She'd spent most of her adult life ignoring that particular desire. Except for that one crazy night when they'd broken all the rules of friendship and finally slept together.

No. That wasn't true. They'd taken their relationship into dangerous territory weeks before when what had started as some innocent flirting turned into an attraction that neither of them could ignore. Nights out as friends had suddenly turned into dates in romantic restaurants where they'd become even closer.

It was the change teenage Felicity had always dreamed of for their relationship, while it made the adult woman she had become worry about what this new connection between them would mean for their friendship if things went wrong.

And then there had been that night when she'd thrown

all her fears away and embraced everything her body had told her they could have together. And it had been even more than she had ever dreamed of.

Memories flashed through her mind of tangled legs and passionate whispers, her body arching against his as they both cried out their release.

A shiver ran over her skin as it responded.

"Cold?" Scott reached over and handed her his jacket. "It is a little chilly in here."

Unable to tell him where her thoughts had taken her, she didn't argue. Taking his jacket, she draped it over her shoulders. The warmth from the wool and Scott's own body heat made her stomach tighten even more.

"How long have you been here?" His warm breath tickled her cheek as he leaned into her side. His hazel eyes seemed to be searching her face for something. But what? Not that it mattered. She'd developed a good poker face in the last few months; a necessity as she'd started to see the concern in her parents' faces each time she went to visit.

"A year in January." She raised her voice over the noise of the crowd instead of leaning closer as Scott seemed to prefer.

"I thought you were going to stay in town?" He had moved even closer. She blamed the heat from his body and his jacket for her damp palms.

She didn't want to tell him that she'd found the slow pace of their hometown upstate New York community hospital unbearable after the excitement of working at a London hospital—something that he'd told her would happen.

"They made me an offer I couldn't refuse," she said, quoting from what she knew was one of Scott's favorite movies. She watched his lips lift into the half smile that had never failed to charm her. Her own smile couldn't be hidden.

"Okay, so you were right. The pace of a small hospital was too slow for me. Not that the people weren't nice—they were. I just didn't fit in there." She didn't have to tell him that her work life was all she'd had then. All she still had.

But it's important work. My patients need me and that's what matters. It's enough.

Then why did it seem she was having to remind herself of that now? The last eighteen months had been hard. The loss of her brother had been hard on all of them, but she'd made it through by concentrating on her parents and her work. And now she had her dream job and it was all the future she needed right now, no matter how much that stupid voice in her head kept telling her she needed more.

Their waitress began passing out their group's orders and Scott leaned back into his seat. She took a deep breath and would have relaxed except she caught the scent of spicy deep woods and salty sea breezes.

He still wore the cologne she had given him all those Christmases ago.

He'd been a senior in high school that year, and the crush she'd had on him had been growing for those last two years. She'd saved her babysitting money all that fall and gone alone to the department store where she spent over an hour looking for the perfect gift for Scott.

The memory of how her brother, Leo, had made fun of the gift was bittersweet now. But wasn't everything bittersweet when it came to her and Scott? There was so much of the two of them entangled with her memories of Leo that she found it impossible to think about one without thinking about the other. They'd both been the most important people in her life except for her parents. And now she had neither one of them.

"You're not eating," Scott said as once more he leaned closer to her.

She cut a piece of the medium-rare steak she had ordered and studied it. Her stomach churned at the thought of eating it. She couldn't do it.

Suddenly it was too much. All of it. The surprise of seeing Scott. Knowing they would be working together again. The memories of Leo with the two of them. It was just too much.

"I need to go. I'm sorry. I forgot about an email that must be sent out tonight," she said to the group along with Scott as she handed him back his jacket. If she sat there one more minute, she would lose it, and she wasn't going to embarrass herself in front of her colleagues like that. Opening her purse, she put several bills on the table, then stood up. Without another word she headed for the door that would lead her out to the street where she could lose herself in the crowd. Not that she thought Scott would follow her. He wouldn't. He was too much of a professional to rush off and leave the rest of the group, even if he wanted to.

Besides, why would he after the way everything between the two of them had ended? Scott had undoubtedly moved on with his life by now. If only she had the strength to do the same thing. Because eventually she would have to face Scott, and it would be a lot easier for both of them if she could put all the old feelings she'd always had for him behind her so that maybe at the very least the two of them would be able to work together again without letting their past get in the way.

CHAPTER THREE

SCOTT WATCHED AS Felicity rushed out the door. Had he said something to upset her? He'd tried to keep things light and friendly without bringing up any subjects that could cause issues between them, yet still things had gone wrong. Could it have gone any worse?

Of course it could. All it would take was one conversation with Dr. Mason and she could have him sent back to London. Not that he thought she would do that. While he couldn't seem to recognize this woman Felicity had become now, he knew inside that she was still the same fair person she had always been. They just needed to find some safe ground where they could communicate.

He'd spent hours imagining what it would be like to see Felicity again, but nothing had prepared him for this.

He'd imagined seeing her on the street of their hometown. She'd turn and see him, her eyes lighting up with joy, and then she'd walk into his arms.

He'd imagined casually dropping by her parents' home and finding her there. Once again she'd be happy to see him and once again she'd walk into his arms as if the last few months had never taken place.

Ever since he'd been told he would be returning to the States, he'd thought of scenario after scenario and, yes, unrealistically each scenario had ended with her in his arms. Not once had he imagined that she would instead be running out of a restaurant to get away from him.

He wanted to blame it on the fact that neither of them had been prepared for seeing each other this way. Just like they hadn't been prepared the morning they got the phone call telling them that Leo was dead. If they'd had a few more days, a week or a month before that call, maybe things would have turned out differently.

But they hadn't been given that time. And now they were both back in New York and once more they didn't have a lot of time. But he couldn't make this about him and Felicity. This was about the job and getting it done right and on time.

There wasn't time for him to spend wondering about what might have been. From the way Felicity had acted when she had seen him, that would be a waste of both their time. She would come around to the idea of working with him again. She was too much of a professional not to. And they'd always made a good team, so there was nothing to worry about there. All they needed to do was concentrate on the task ahead of them and leave their personal problems out of it. But first maybe they needed to clear the air.

He stood and excused himself.

"Fliss, wait!" he called as he caught up with her a moment before she made it out the door. For a minute he thought she hadn't heard him. Or was it that she was pretending not to hear him? "Hold up."

She stopped and turned toward him. His gaze was again drawn to the dark circles around those blue eyes that had once stared up at him with pleasure. Where was the sparkle? The laughter? The welcoming smile that was as much a part of her as her own name? There was no welcoming smile for him now.

He couldn't help but feel anger toward his lost friend. Had Leo even thought about what he was doing to the lives of the people who loved him when he'd taken his own? Scott knew that wasn't fair to his friend; Leo had been in a dark place inside his own mind, but at times Scott couldn't help but feel anger toward Leo for leaving them this way.

"We need to talk," he said, moving out of the way so another diner could exit the restaurant. When she didn't argue, he looked around the lobby for a more appropriate setting for this conversation. Finding a small corner away from the door, he walked toward it. For a moment she gazed out the door, and he thought she wouldn't follow him. She seemed to gather herself, her back becoming straighter and her chin coming up. This was more the woman he knew.

"I'm sorry if I was a bit abrupt. It's been a long day and I really think it would be better if we talked later. This has all been a bit of a shock," she said.

He recognized that stubborn look in her eyes. He'd seen it many times over the years. There would be no getting her to change her mind right now.

"I'm in meetings all day tomorrow. What about dinner after work?" He wasn't going to let her go without pinning her down on a time. He'd known things wouldn't be straightforward between the two of them when they did meet again, but he hadn't expected this. Of course, he hadn't expected the changes he saw in Fliss either.

She gave a short laugh and shook her head. "I barely have time to sleep right now. I still have shifts to work in the emergency room until I go full-time on the new unit. Plus, I'm working almost full-time hours trying to keep everything going so that we can make our grand opening on time."

"All work and no play…" He left it open to finish. It was a stupid game of quotes and proverbs they'd played when they were in school and continued through the years.

"…makes Felicity a successful leader in her new manager role," she said as she rolled her eyes at him, a sign that the old cocky Fliss was inside this woman somewhere. He just needed to be patient, though that was the last thing he was feeling right now. There was so much he wanted to say, but she was right. Meeting like this had been a shock to both of them. They'd both be more prepared to deal with this after a good night's sleep.

"Okay, I'll see how my schedule goes tomorrow. Maybe we can get together before you leave for the day." He'd make it happen one way or the other. Whether she thought so or not, there were things that needed to be dealt with between the two of them if they were going to be able to work together again.

"Sure, tomorrow sounds great, but I think you need to get back to your dinner now. Dr. Mason isn't the most patient of men. Good night," she said as she hitched her purse up on her shoulder and headed away.

He waited until he saw her disappear into the sidewalk crowd before he made his way back to his table.

"Is everything okay?" Dr. Mason asked from across the table. The older man was not a fool. He had to have noticed Felicity's reaction to Scott.

"Everything's going to be fine," he answered with confidence, trying to convince himself as much as his new colleague. Something told him this would be the most difficult assignment he had ever been given.

Because this job and the chance he had of any type of future relationship with Felicity depended on it.

"There you are," Scott said from beside her. "I thought I'd missed you."

Felicity looked up from the computer where she'd been finishing the charting on her last patient for the day. It had been so long since she'd seen him dressed in his white lab jacket. He was every bit as handsome as she remembered. She tried to ignore the shiver of recognition that ran through her. This was something she was going to have to get used to now and she didn't dare let Scott see how his presence affected her.

"I was just about to leave. It's been a long day," she said as she started shutting down the computer. The holiday season was close, and with tourist numbers in the city growing, the number of people seen in the ER would increase till after the first of the year.

"Maybe I can walk you out?" Scott asked as she stood.

"That's fine." She had planned to catch a taxi outside the emergency-room entrance, so at least it would be a short talk.

A cold wind blew through the ambulance bay as the doors shut behind her. She wrapped her arms around herself as they stopped for a crew of EMTs to roll a stretcher loaded with a man who looked as miserable as she felt right then. Tired and cold were not a good combination.

"I'm going this way," she said, pointing toward the line of taxis as he started in the direction of the car park.

"I can give you a ride. It will give us more time to talk," Scott said as his hand came up behind her to rest on her back. She started to move away from him when suddenly she was pulled into his arms.

The weight of his arms around her as he clasped her tight to his body brought back memories that made her head swim, but the screech of tires and a woman's screams for help brought her right back to reality.

"I need help!" the woman cried as she threw open her driver's door, then moved to the back door of the car. "My son, he's not breathing."

As Felicity grabbed a stretcher that had been left by the door, Scott rushed to the woman's side.

"What happened?" Scott asked as he pulled the young boy out of the car and laid him down on the stretcher.

The boy's color was a dusky blue and Fliss checked for a pulse before starting compressions. There was no sign of trauma that she could see and teenage boys did not just go into cardiac arrest.

"It's my fault," the woman cried as Scott pushed the stretcher into the entrance and began calling for help. "It's my medicine. He took all my medicine."

"I've got this," one of the EMTs Felicity had seen earlier said as he took over the compressions. Other staff members joined them as they rushed the boy into the first empty room.

"Felicity, find out what it was he took," Scott called out to her as he told another nurse to draw up some Narcan.

"Got it," she called back as she put her arm around the shaking woman and led her aside. "We need your help. Can you tell me what happened? What did your son take?"

"It was my pain meds my doctor prescribed me when I hurt my back. I think it's called Norco. I've only taken it once and I keep it put away. I guess he found it in my dresser when I was at work. Is he okay? Is he going to be okay?" the woman pleaded. "He's been so depressed since that girl broke up with him, but I didn't think he'd do this. Not my Butchy. He's too smart for this."

A cold chill ran up Felicity's spine as she realized this hadn't been just another kid suffering from an accidental overdose while experimenting with their parents' medication.

"Is he going to be okay?" the boy's mother asked again. "Please tell me he's going to be okay."

"We've got his heartbeat back," Scott said as he joined them. "The emergency-room doctor is in with him now, but he'll give you an update as soon as he can. Come this way and I'll show you where you can wait."

The trip to Felicity's apartment was quiet with neither of them talking after she gave Scott her address.

"I checked with Dr. Adams before he left. The boy's going to be okay," Scott said as he parked the car in front of her apartment.

"I know. I checked with his nurse. He's already fighting against the ventilator." She'd made sure the boy's mother would be let in as soon as possible too. She knew what it was like to sit in that room and wait for news of whether your loved one was going to survive or not. "His mom said this was over a girl. A girl. He wanted to give up living because of some teenage girl. What sense does that make?"

"It's not ever going to make sense to us," Scott said. She knew they were no longer talking about the boy they'd left in the ER.

"If we understood, would it make it better?" she asked.

"It's all those questions of why and what you could have done to stop it that eat at you. They never stop."

"But there comes a time you have to let it go," Scott said. "You know that."

She did know that. She just didn't know how it was possible. Letting go of the guilt and pain would be like letting go of her brother. Let go of the big brother who had always been there for her? It would be like giving up a piece of her heart. She wouldn't be able to live without it.

"If life were just that easy," she said before unbuckling her seat belt and opening the car door.

"Look," she said as she turned back to him, "you don't have to worry about the job. I've got my part in opening the new unit under control. And as far as working together, maybe putting our past behind us is what we need to do."

"Can you do that?" Scott asked. His eyes held hers and she fought against looking away. Somehow she had to convince him that she could work with him without it affecting the job they'd been given.

"Sometimes, you just have to let it go." Turning, she rushed out of the car and ran into her building, shutting the door behind her before the first tear fell.

"We're going to take care of you. You did the right thing calling 911 when the pain started," Felicity assured the man clutching his left arm as she applied the pads of the cardiac monitor. She'd bet her bachelor's degree that the man was having an ST-elevation myocardial infarction, which meant time was not on their side. The sooner the interventional cardiologist could confirm her suspicions, the sooner they could get this patient to the heart cath lab.

She looked at her watch and wrote the time the patient had arrived down on her paperwork. One of the first things Scott had taught her in the cardiac department in London was how important door-to-balloon time was in achieving the best outcome for the patient. It had been just a little over thirty minutes since the man's chest pain had started.

This was why it was so vital to get the new cardiac center open. With its emergency triage abilities and its new procedural area, they could streamline the process, which meant cutting the time a cardiac patient spent in the regular emergency room. From the web meetings she had attended in the last week, she knew Scott was spearheading the procedures to identify these patients when they arrived in the emergency room.

"It's a STEMI," she said to the ER doctor who had come to stand by her as they both studied the monitors.

"Okay, let's start the chest pain protocol and get an EKG to confirm. I'll go call the doctor who's on," he said as he walked away.

"Where's the doctor going?" the man asked, his voice cracking with pain and fear. "Can I see my wife?"

She started applying the EKG pads so that the strip would be available when the doctor returned.

"You need a specialist, so he's going to go call the cardiologist who'll be here in just a few minutes to check everything out. As soon as I can, I'll get your wife in to see you. Try to be still for just a few seconds."

She waited for a second, then hit the button, and the strip started printing. Studying the rhythm displayed on the paper, she knew she had been right. It was a classic MI. She sent the electronic record to the patient's chart so that the two doctors could review it, then looked at the clock over the stretcher. It had only been fifteen minutes since the patient had rolled into the room, but it seemed so much longer.

"I'll be back with something to help with the pain, and the cardiologist will be right in." The fact that she had to leave the room to get the medication while what he really needed was her at his bedside was another reason that the new cardiac center was so important. She'd met some resistance from the pharmacy about having a medicine dispenser in each of the new state-of-the-art exam rooms, and the department's budget had taken a big hit, but she'd won that fight.

Returning to the room, she found the heart cath team already preparing to transport her patient.

"That was fast," she said to Sandy, one of the nurses who soon would be part of her own staff.

"Dr. Thomas reviewed the chart and agreed that it was a STEMI. He's waiting to talk to the patient. Can you bring his wife over for us?" the other nurse said as she switched the patient to a portable monitor.

"I'm going to get her right now," Felicity told her patient as she arranged the blankets more securely around him. "Dr. Thomas is one of the top cardiologists I know. He'll explain everything to you. You're in the best of hands."

She watched for a second as the patient was rolled out of the room. Then she headed to the waiting room to find her patient's wife. The fact that Scott was picking up some of the shifts in the intervention cath lab, which had been left empty when Dr. Kane had taken leave, was not a surprise. While he seemed to be comfortable with the administrative details he would have to handle with this project, she knew his heart would always be in patient care, and she had no doubt that Dr. Mason had considered his procedural experience and reputation when hiring him.

Somehow she had been able to avoid Scott for the last four days, but now with the new center on track to open soon, it was the last day she would be working in the emergency room. Instead of attending meetings remotely and working on the new unit following her shifts in the ER, from now on all her time would be spent getting ready for their grand opening. Of course, part of her was just like Scott; she preferred the hands-on patient care, which wouldn't start till after the opening.

Preparing herself for both an upset wife and a doctor whose mere presence set loose a bucket of butterflies in her stomach, she headed out into the waiting room. She wouldn't be able to avoid seeing Scott any longer.

Scott left the cath lab feeling good about his patient's outcome. It helped that Felicity and the ER doctor had diagnosed the patient quickly and that the rest of the heart team had responded, making the patient's door-to-balloon time below the ninety-minute threshold that was the standard. The group he had been sent to work with here in New York were all professionals, which was making his job a lot easier. But he couldn't help but notice the way Felicity had fled the room as soon as he finished talking to her patient's wife. He knew she was busy in the always-crowded emergency room, and bless her for helping out with their staffing crunch, but that wasn't the problem. She was still avoiding him, and it had to be dealt with if the two of them were going to work together.

He'd tried to clear the air between them, but she remained distant. He'd given her space to accept the fact that he was here in her hospital, and now it was time for them to move on. There were a lot of details they needed to go over on the nursing side of the new center. As the nursing manager, it was her job to work with him, and that was impossible for them to do if she kept avoiding being in the same room with him. Enough was enough.

Placing a call to the emergency room, he requested that Fliss come to the office—*her* office—that Dr. Mason had him using in the new department. He had no doubt that seeing him sitting behind what was supposed to be her desk was something that would set her off. She'd always been the first one to call him out on acting privileged just because he had a medical degree hanging on his wall. He couldn't wait to see her reaction to the fact that he had moved in and made himself at home, since the only time she seemed to use the office was after he had left for the day. The office was big enough for the two of them to share, though that didn't seem to be something that she would do. Thirty minutes later—and, yes, he was sure that Fliss had kept him waiting on purpose—there was a knock at his door.

"You wanted to see me?" she asked as she stepped through the doorway.

Seeing her standing in front of him wearing those bright blue scrubs that had always been her favorite, he was struck by the truth of those words. Yes, he'd wanted to see her. He'd wanted to see her every day since he'd left New York. He'd spent every day of the last eighteen months missing seeing those blue eyes that seemed to sparkle with humor and those just-a-little-bit-too-wide lips that had seemed to smile with joy whenever the two of them had been together.

But those eyes showed none of that humor today. Instead they had a wariness that he had never seen before. And there certainly was no joy in her smile. He watched, fascinated, as her teeth came out and bit down on her bottom lip. Was she nervous about seeing him? Then her face lost all signs of emotion, as if she had suddenly taken control and she had to hide whatever it was she was feeling from him.

But he knew that it had to be killing her to hold that blank mask in place. Fliss had never been one for holding back her feelings or opinions. It was one of the things he had always admired about her. If she was pissed off at you, you knew it. There was no game you had to play to find out what had upset her. The fact that she was holding everything in now was not a good sign. He wanted his old Fliss back, the one who would be chewing him out right now for his high-handed demand that she come see him.

But she wasn't his anymore and he needed to remember that. He needed to treat her just like another member of the team.

"Please, take a seat." This time he saw a spark of anger as she narrowed her eyes at him. Then it was gone and the new all-business version of Felicity returned. "I thought this might be a good time for the two of us to talk. I've been able to speak with everyone involved with the grand opening of the new unit, except for you. For some reason you've turned down every invitation I've emailed you, and every time I try to talk to you, you deny there's a problem or you run away. We used to talk about everything." She'd given him no option but to bring up their past. Hopefully it wouldn't make things between them worse. "I understand that my presence here was a surprise, but it's time for us to move past that. I need to know if you're going to be able to work with me on this."

She blinked rapidly with a deer-in-the-headlights look that told him nothing of what was going on behind her bright blue eyes. What was it going to take to get past this wall she had built around her emotions? And more important, why did she feel she needed that wall between the two of them? Finally she took the chair in front of the desk.

"I apologize," she said, her eyes now meeting his and holding. "I have been busy trying to help with the emergency-room staffing, but today was my last shift. I'll be able to put all my time into preparing for the center's opening now. And, yes, I understand that we will need to work closer together from this point on."

She hadn't given him much, but it was a start. Still, it would be better if they came to a clear understanding.

"I'm not saying that you haven't been doing your job, Fliss." He saw the small jerk of her body when he used her nickname. It seemed she didn't want any reminder of the relationship that the two of them had shared in the past. If she didn't like him calling her by the name her family and friends used, he would have to respect that. If it helped for the two of them to work together, he'd avoid it from now on. "I've seen the emails. You've done a remarkable job organizing the department. But I'm sure you're aware that with just five weeks left till we open the new unit, there will be more hands-on work needed from both of us. I need to know that it isn't going to be a problem. I need to know that the two of us can work together."

"There won't be a problem," Felicity said, her chin coming up with a look of determination that he had seen many times. "I plan to do everything possible to make this grand opening perfect. This is *my* hospital. I'm invested in its success."

Staring into those deep blue eyes, he knew that she was telling him the truth. She'd do whatever she had to in order to make her department the best. Even if it meant working with him.

But he wanted more than that. He wanted the way it used to be when they worked together. He wanted the two of them to be a real team. Together they could make this project the best one he had ever been involved with. He could go back to London knowing he had made a difference when his time here was over, and that was important to him.

No, he had accepted that they could never go back to the way things were before Leo's death, but was it too much to ask for the two of them to at least get along while he was here?

"Okay, then. How about we do a walk-through of the unit together? I'd like to see the nurses' side of the patient-flow process," Scott said before standing. It was time to see if this unspoken truce between the two of them would hold up.

Felicity wasn't sure how she found herself with Scott in the deserted new unit when she'd spent the last four days doing everything she could to avoid him. But she had known that eventually she would have to face the fact that they would be working together.

While most of the remodeling work had been completed earlier in the month, late equipment arrivals and some changes that had been required after the approval of the medicine-dispensing machines meant there was still some construction work being done. Unfortunately the crews that had been working had already gone for the day.

"I like the fact that you've provided for supplies to be kept in each individual room, but what about the restocking?" Scott asked as he opened one of the built-in glass-doored cabinets.

"Each nurse will be assigned a set of room numbers each shift. It will be their responsibility to restock their rooms when they turn it over before the next patient arrives," Felicity said as she moved around the room, trying to concentrate on the work that had been finished as well as what still needed to be done before the rest of the equipment was installed.

But like the night at the restaurant, the sight of Scott brought back too many memories. No wonder Scott was afraid she wouldn't be able to work with him. Every time they were together, she became overwhelmed with emotions that she hadn't felt for months.

After Leo's death, she had felt nothing. She'd been numbed by the shock of his suicide and the loss of the big brother to whom she'd always been so close. It was all she could do to put up a good front for her parents so that she could support them. Then the numbness had been gone and all the pain had rushed inside of her. Not only the pain of losing Leo, but the pain of having to send Scott back to London without her. She'd had to accept that there could never be a future for the two of them with his life in London and her place in New York with her parents. She'd made the right decision sending him back to a job to which he had dedicated his career, but she'd had to work hard to find a way to deal with the pain and still function. After six months of barely surviving while also helping her parents cope with their own pain, she'd been able to make a life here at work, which gave her a sense of belonging and purpose and took her focus off the pain of her brother's loss that would always be there.

Now Scott was here disturbing the peace she had found. Because every time she saw him, all she could think about was their time together in London when they had finally both been in the right place at the right time. They'd taken the chance on having more than just the friendship they'd shared since childhood.

She'd spent her whole adult life waiting to have Scott see her as a woman instead of as his best friend's little sister or as a best friend in her own right. And even though she'd first been concerned about what it could mean for their friendship, it had been worth it. It had been intense and magical and everything she had known in her heart it would be. And then it had to come to an end with one phone call.

Now she didn't even know how to carry on a conversation with the man whom she had once dreamed of spending her whole life with. But for the next two months she needed to find a way to make this work, because she'd made the hardest sacrifice she could imagine by sending Scott away, and she didn't know if she would be strong enough to watch him leave again.

No, she could and would do this. She set her mind back to the job at hand. She would make this work. This unit was the most important thing she had in her life right now. She just had to find a way of dealing with Scott as she would any other coworker. She'd managed to hide her feelings for him all through high school when he'd spent most of his time at her house, hanging out with her brother. She'd spent hour upon hour trying to listen through the thin wall between her and her brother's rooms, waiting to hear Scott say something, anything, about what he thought of her. Until finally she'd realized that he had no deep thoughts about or longing for her as she had for him. Still, she'd been happy with the friendship that had grown between them as she had gotten older.

All she needed now was to do the same thing for the few hours that she was at work. She was older and wiser. His place was in London and her place was here, where she could watch over her parents. Nothing had changed in the last eighteen months. It was time to grow up. She was an adult and she needed to act like it. She had responsibilities to her parents now that Leo was gone.

She embraced her pep talk and turned her attention back to her job and the exam rooms they were discussing.

"I like the color," Scott mentioned as he motioned toward a wall where monitors were being installed.

The painters had begun covering the walls with the pale gray paint that would match the furniture, which had been ordered months earlier but still hadn't arrived. She made a note on her computer pad to give the warehouse a call the next day. "We didn't want to go with the same white of the emergency room. We felt this would be more calming."

"And the new monitors are going to be amazing. I've sent the manufacturer information back to our purchasing agent in London so that when it's time to upgrade our unit, we can get a price on them," Scott said as he moved out the glass door and into the hallway that would take them back to the office. "And having the medication dispensers in each room will be amazing. I still don't know how that was managed. That many machines, even though they're smaller, must have been expensive."

"It was the first thing I lobbied for when I got the position. I felt like it was something that had to be there so that the nurse could not only give the medications quickly, but also remain in the room with the patient as much as possible." She couldn't help but feel a bit of pride that she had impressed him.

"I'd love to review the list of medications that will be stocked," he said as they made their way back to the office.

"I had all the medications that would be kept on the unit approved by Dr. Kane before she left," Felicity said.

"And she consulted with all the cardiologists that will be working on the unit, I'm sure, but we both know things get forgotten or overlooked. It wouldn't hurt to give the doctors another look so that when we do open, there won't be any complaints."

He had a valid point and Dr. Kane hadn't informed her which doctors had been allowed to see the medication list that had been put together from their own past experiences. There could have been someone left out, and doctors did not like being left out of decisions that impacted their patients' care.

"I can email you the list before I leave today," she said.

"It's looking good, but I think we can agree that there is still a lot to do before opening next month," Scott said as they stopped outside the office door.

She looked down at the list she had compiled in the last hour. There was a lot to do, but it was very doable. "True, but we're still on schedule."

"But it's a tight schedule. One thing goes wrong and we'll be playing catch-up for the rest of the month," Scott said as he opened the door. "Now, how do you want to share the office now that the two of us will be working the same hours?"

Share the office? That would never work. "I really don't need the office right now. It's mostly here for me to have any private conversations I might need with the staff or the physicians. Most of the time I'll be working with them in the unit."

She'd be happy to work in the nurses' lounge as long as it put some distance between the two of them.

Sitting down behind the desk, he leaned back in the office chair and studied her. It seemed they had come full circle and ended right back where this conversation had started.

"We're going to be working together closely, and I'll be honest—I don't understand why it should be that difficult. To be exact, it should be simpler. We've worked together before without any problems. But this time things are different. *We're* different. You've agreed that we have to put the past behind us, but I don't understand it, or what happened, and I'm worried that it's going to affect this project," Scott said, his eyes never leaving her.

She remembered the pep talk she had given herself earlier. She couldn't keep letting old emotions and memories cloud the here and now.

"If we concentrate on the job, I know we can make this work," she assured him.

"So, we go at this with a fresh start. A new beginning?" he asked.

"Yes," she agreed, "a new beginning."

He continued to study her for a minute before he nodded his head. "Okay, let's get together tomorrow after lunch and go over the rest of the construction details.

The last thing we want is for something to come up that will cause a postponement of the opening."

Felicity nodded her head in agreement and then headed back into the ER to finish her shift. It was going to take more than a pep talk to prepare her for the next few weeks, but the thought of a new beginning with Scott did show some promise, even if working close to him would not be easy. Because no matter how much she talked bravely of putting their past behind them, she knew there would always be a part of her buried in that past.

CHAPTER FOUR

FELICITY COULDN'T BELIEVE how much work was involved in starting up the new unit. She'd spent every day for the last two weeks juggling staffing schedules, attending meetings and having very heated discussions with the purchasing department that was still negotiating with the delivery of the unit's furniture. And that didn't take into consideration all the last-minute details and decisions the construction crew had started coming to her to solve.

And then there was Scott. He was everywhere she turned. She wasn't sure when the man had become so needy. He was always needing questions answered, always needing progress reports. And now there was the multitude of doctors that he had brought to her because he needed her to orient them on the new process of triaging chest pain patients in their new location. It seemed that it would never end.

But along with his apparent neediness had come her ability to deal with him better on a professional basis. She was so used to seeing him now that his presence was no longer causing the heart-thumping reaction that it had two weeks ago.

Okay, maybe there were still a few palpitations when he sat a little too close to her like he was right now in the crowded meeting room, but all in all she thought she was handling things a lot better than she had hoped. All she had to do was make it through this last meeting of the day and she'd be off for the long Thanksgiving holiday.

"My mother called this morning," Scott said as he moved closer and whispered.

"That's nice," she said through gritted teeth as those irritating palpitations returned. Why did the man feel so welcome to invade her personal space? Oh, yeah, because he had all but lived there before.

"She spoke with your mother last night." He seemed to be waiting for her to respond, though she wasn't sure why. She was very aware that their mothers spoke daily. The two of them had been close since their own childhood.

"My mom was keen to assure your mother that I would be very happy to give you a ride home tomorrow," he said.

She choked on nothing but air as she took in his words. Covering her mouth, she cleared her throat and took a sip of water as the staff members in front of her turned around, embarrassing her even more.

She cleared her throat again until she could find her voice. "You don't need to take me. I've already bought a Metro ticket."

"What and have our mothers mad at me the whole time I'm home?" he whispered back to her, giving her no doubt that it hadn't been his idea. He probably had no more of a desire to spend his morning stuck in a car with her than she did with him. But that didn't change the fact that their mothers would not understand why they couldn't share the ride.

Finally the meeting came to an end, giving her a chance to escape.

"Whoa," Scott called out as he grabbed her hand. "We need to talk about this. You can't leave me taking the heat when I show up without you."

"There isn't anything to talk about. I've made arrangements. I don't need a ride to my parents' house." Her voice sounded whiny and childish even to her own ears as she pulled her hand from his while trying to ignore the buzz of attraction that had always run through her when Scott touched her.

"That's fine. I just need you to call my mother and explain that to her," he said as he moved back to his seat and retrieved his computer.

All signs of attraction disappeared. "I can't do that. You know how she and my mother are. They never take no for an answer."

One dark brown eyebrow lifted as he stared at her.

"Can't you just tell her that you didn't see me?" Not that his mother would take that as an excuse.

"You want me to lie to my mother?" he asked.

"What? Like you've never lied to your mother before? What about the time you and Leo sneaked out to meet Allison and Sarah out by the lake?" She realized her mistake as soon as the words were out.

"How do you know about that?" Scott asked as they joined the group exiting the room.

"I guess Leo told me." There was no way she was admitting that she had been listening through the door that night. Maybe there had been a time she would have been okay confessing her less-than-honest deeds, but not now. Besides, they weren't supposed to be bringing up their past. Of course, it had been her who brought it up first.

That darned eyebrow rose again.

"Okay, just tell her that I had already made plans," she said. And what explanation would she come up with for her own mother, who would see this as an act of extreme rudeness? Being stubborn wasn't a good reason for upsetting her mother. Her mother had hounded her for months for details of what had happened between her and Scott after he'd returned to London and they lost contact. Both their mothers were undoubtedly thrilled they were working together again.

There was no way she was going to win this one. The trip would be uncomfortable, that was for sure, but it would make her mother happy to see the two of them together, and that was what really mattered.

"There's no getting out of this, is there?" she asked as they moved down the hall together.

"I'll pick you up at eight," he said as he looked down at his watch. "See you then."

She watched him as he hurried out of the building toward the doctors' parking lot, unable to keep from wondering where he was off to in such a hurry. Did the popular Dr. Thomas have a date? And where had that thought even come from?

She was supposed to be concentrating on their work, not their past, and it was proving to be much harder than she had thought. She felt like she was back in middle school, where the green monster of jealousy had consumed her every time she'd seen Scott out with one of his high school dates. But that was the past. She was a grown woman now and he was a grown man. That thought didn't make her feel any better. They had definitely been two grown-ups sharing very grown-up actions when they had spent the night together.

And that was definitely not something she wanted to think about right now. Groaning, she pulled her coat on, then shoved her knitted cap on her head. The weather station had called for the temperatures to dip into the twenties. She'd have to pack some extra layers, as it would be even colder in their small hometown of Hudson.

Suddenly she stopped in the middle of the sidewalk. People passed on each side of her while she thought of what had just happened.

No matter how uncomfortable her thoughts were now, she and Scott had actually had a conversation. Not the conversations they had been having for the last couple of weeks that had been centered round their work. They'd had a personal discussion that had included their lives outside of work—at least, as it pertained to their parents—and it hadn't been awful. Was it possible that by starting anew, they could someday return to being friends? Could she accept friendship after losing the chance of having so much more? She'd accepted that friendship was all they could have years ago and had found a way to make it work. Was it possible for her to do it again?

Starting back down the sidewalk, she suddenly felt lighter than she had in weeks. Maybe there was some hope for the two of them to find a way to have some type of relationship once his time here was over. But at what cost? Could she let herself get close to him again without wanting more? Could she lower those fragile walls she had put up to protect herself from being hurt again and take a chance on a friendship that had meant so much to her? It wasn't like she was looking for more than friendship. Nothing had changed since he had gone back to London. Whether her parents wanted to admit it or not, they needed her close by.

It was going to be a long drive back to their hometown. All she could do was wait and see what spending more time alone together would bring. Hopefully, at least for their parents' sake, they would be able to make this work.

The strain of trying to keep up a conversation with Scott without touching on any subjects that would bring up a past that they had agreed not to discuss had Felicity closing her eyes and pretending to sleep while they traveled north in the high-end sedan that Scott had rented for the time he was in New York.

The first hour had gone by quickly as they'd discussed some of the projects to which they'd agreed to give priority status once they were back at work on Monday. Then Scott informed her that their parents had planned a dinner together tonight at his parents' house and it had been decided that Christmas dinner would be at her parents' house this year. After that, the conversation had sagged and she hadn't wanted to risk the comfortable mood between the two of them by bringing up the fact that it would be the first year they'd have Christmas at their house without Leo.

So now she sat, eyes closed, her head resting against the back of the seat while her mind brought up memory after memory of Christmas in her childhood home with her parents and Leo. Christmas without Leo was impossible to imagine. Last year they'd all still been suffering from an all-consuming grief and the holidays had been easy to ignore. But this year they would have to face it.

Her parents would take it hard, but she would be there for them. They wouldn't go through it alone.

"I know you're not sleeping," Scott said from beside her.

He was wearing the cologne she loved, and she breathed it in as she tried to make her body relax into the seat.

"My parents know this year will be hard for you and your parents. They'll be there to help. We all will."

She heard the concern in his voice and wanted to crawl deeper into the seat. She wasn't stupid. She knew her parents were as concerned about her as she was about them, and she had no doubt that her mother had expressed those concerns to Scott's mother. She was once again glad that their parents had never known the change that had taken place in her and Scott's relationship before they'd learned of Leo's death. Having both of their mothers involved in their love life would have made it even harder to send Scott away. Neither one of them would have understood how helpless she had felt thousands of miles away from her parents when they needed her the most. Nor would they have understood the guilt she felt about being so far away from her brother when he too had needed her. She'd let her brother down. She would not make that mistake again. The only other option would have been for Scott to move back to the States and she wasn't going to let that happen. They'd all been so proud of him when he'd been offered the job at the Royal Kensington Hospital. Giving that up for her would have been wrong.

She'd been so confused about what had happened to her brother that she'd been in no condition to make any type of commitment to a relationship, even if it was to Scott. It had seemed that everything she believed in was shattered. How could the brother who had always been so happy on the outside been so depressed on the inside that he took his own life? And why hadn't she noticed it during their weekly phone calls? She hadn't noticed it because she had been too tied up in her own life instead of looking out for her family.

And if she had been so wrong about her brother, what was to say she wasn't wrong about how she felt about Scott? What if she was just one more relationship to Scott? There had been no mention of a commitment. She'd watched him with girls, then later women, and had always wanted to know what it would feel like to be the one who won Scott's heart. But she had no reason to think he wouldn't have moved on from her just like he had dozens of times before with others. No, it was best that things had ended the way they had without their parents being involved.

"Your parents have been great. A lot of people I thought were my parents' friends came around at first, but then they kind of disappeared. I think the grief they were going through was just too much for others to deal with," she said, trying to return the focus to her parents.

"And you? Did you have someone to support you?" he asked.

Just what was he asking? Did he want to know if there was someone else in her life? He had to know that hadn't been true—at least, not when Leo died. She'd been in London and spent all her time with him. There was no way he could think that she had broken things off because of another man.

"I would have been there if you'd let me," he murmured softly.

"I thought we agreed not to talk about the past." He had no right to bring this all up again.

She'd known he loved his job in London, and even

though he might not have understood it then, time had to have shown him that they'd made the right decision to break things off between them. Besides, it was water under the bridge now. There was nothing good for either of them that could come out of reliving that decision.

"I know you're aware that caregivers are the last ones to ask for help when they need it," he said.

She felt a tiny stab in her heart. He hadn't been asking about her as his once-upon-a-time lover. He was just showing concern for a coworker and old friend.

"I have my parents," she said as she turned her head to stare out the window, looking for something to change the subject. "Look, there's a Christmas tree farm."

She squealed as he hit the brakes, then quickly turned the car into the small parking lot that was already crowded with families looking for that one perfect tree. "What are you doing?"

"Isn't that pretty obvious?" Scott asked as he opened his car door, letting a gust of wind into the car. "Better grab your hat and gloves—the temperature's turning icy. Dad called this morning to say they had a lot of snow overnight."

Grabbing her coat from the back seat, she pulled out gloves and her hat, then opened her door. Her eyes immediately went to the small stand that was selling hot chocolate. She turned around and pulled her purse from the car, then shut the door.

She got a glimpse of Scott over at a stand selling Christmas wreaths as she stood in line for the warm chocolate magic that she hoped would heat both her hands and her stomach. After paying for the drinks, she began her search for Scott again.

Avoiding the children who ran in and out of the trees

that had already been chopped down, she started down the middle aisle, finally spotting Scott in the last row, where a group of smaller blue-green trees stood together.

"Your mother will never settle for a tree that small. Besides, you know she likes the Douglas fir better than the Fraser." Scott had told her once that the biggest argument his parents ever had had taken place after a trip with him and his brother to get a Christmas tree.

"I picked up a couple wreaths." He motioned to where two large wreaths decorated with red bows and pine cones sat propped against another tree. "I was thinking this would be a good size for your apartment."

"For me? What would I do with a tree? The last thing I need is a real tree in my apartment. I'm never there. It'd be dead in a week," she said as she handed him his drink. She waited for him to take a swallow.

"It's chocolate," he said as he smacked his mouth.

"Of course it's hot chocolate. We're at a Christmas tree farm." She bent down and picked up one of the wreaths, then waited for him to grab the other.

"Is there some rule that they can't sell coffee at these places?" He gave the drink a suspicious sniff. "I bet if they added some coffee to this, it would be good."

She'd never understood what the man had against chocolate. Of course, it had paid off at Easter when he'd traded his chocolate for her jelly beans, since Leo had always refused to trade with her. "It's delicious and it's warm. Come on. My mom will already have something to say about me not being there to help with the cooking. I don't want to listen to my dad complain about them having to hold dinner for us."

"What about the tree?" he asked, turning back toward the little tree as he picked up the wreaths he had bought earlier.

"If you want to get it for your hotel, buy it. I'm fine without a tree," she said, turning away and heading back to the car. There was no way she was going to let him talk her into taking it home with her. Her apartment was fine just the way it was.

By the time they were back on the road, their earlier conversation had been forgotten and they had returned to comfortable topics. As they pulled into his parents' driveway, she looked down the road where she could just see her own parents' home. When she'd first moved back to the city, she'd made the trip home every weekend she wasn't working. But lately, with the cardiac center nearing its opening, she'd only been able to make it once a month. Her parents had surprised her by encouraging her to stay in the city and assuring her that they were fine without her hovering over them. She'd wanted to point out that she'd learned that talent from the two of them, but hadn't. If the two of them wanted to ignore the fact that they were getting older, that was understandable, but she saw people their age come into the emergency room every day. She couldn't ignore it.

As he parked the car, she started to get out, then realized that Scott hadn't moved. They both sat and looked at the pink-bricked two-story that had always seemed like a second home to her.

"It's your first time home since...since Leo's death." She didn't know why she felt the need to say it out loud, but she did. Reaching out, she covered his hand with hers, something she wouldn't have dreamed of doing just days ago. They'd agreed to put the past away, but this was different. This loss that the two of them shared went deeper than anything else that had happened in their lives. They couldn't ignore the fact that when they walked into the house, something would be missing.

"Come on," she said as she released his hand. "Your parents are going to be so excited to see you."

CHAPTER FIVE

"FLISS, WOULD YOU mind going with Scott to take a plate of food down to Ms. Connors for me?" Scott's mother asked as she packed up a plastic container.

Felicity finished drying the last of the large platters that had been used to hold the massive amount of ham that had been served for their Thanksgiving meal as she eyed the container being held out for her to take. It wasn't that she minded running the errand—she had always been fond of her old science teacher—but the fact that throughout the day both her mother and Scott's mother had made a habit of pairing her and Scott together.

But was that really unusual? When Leo had been alive, the three of them had always done things together.

Or was it because things had been strained between her and Scott since Leo's death that their mothers had decided to get involved? It couldn't be that they knew about what had happened between the two of them in London. No one knew that. No one except the two of them. There was no way Scott had told his mother that they'd ended up in bed together, because if Scott's mother had known, her own mother would have known as soon as the woman could have reached a phone. And then there would have been questions to answer. Lots of questions that she wouldn't have been able to cope with, questions for which she still had no answers.

Realizing she hadn't answered the request, she put down the dish towel and took the container. "Sure. I'll grab my coat and get him."

Walking out of the kitchen, she found Scott in a tall armchair, his eyes shut, though he still held his phone in his hand.

"What?" Scott said, not opening his eyes as she shook his shoulder.

"It's finally happened. You've turned into one of *them*." She motioned to their fathers, both sleeping in a pair of recliners across the room.

Scott opened his eyes and looked over at the two men, then turned his warm hazel eyes back to her as they roamed over her with an intensity that filled her stomach with a warmth that had nothing to do with the hot cider she'd been sipping in the kitchen.

"Nice fashion choice, Mom," he said as he stared at the old floral apron she had forgotten she'd put on.

Yanking it over her head, Felicity pushed both the apron and container of food into his arms before heading to the front door to get bundled up to go out into the cold.

"Your mother needs us to take this over to Ms. Connors's place," she said as she started layering on her sweater and coat.

"Are you sure I should go? Ms. Connors always liked you more than she liked me and Leo," he said as he followed her in getting his own coat on.

"If I'm going, you're going." She opened the door and a cold gust of wind blew into the foyer. "Besides, you need to work off that second piece of pumpkin pie I saw you eat."

"It's snowing again," Scott said as he closed the door behind them.

Big white flakes fell all around them, making her glad she'd worn her sturdy boots as they made their way down the block. The snow was soft and calming as it fell, and the neighborhood was quiet as other families shared their own Thanksgiving meals.

"And why didn't we take the car?" she asked as she wrapped her scarf tighter around her neck and tucked it into her coat as the wind pulled at the strands of hair she had tucked inside her hat.

"You're the one that said I needed to work off the pie. Besides, look around you. It's beautiful. And smell that air." He stopped and took a deep breath as Felicity let herself fill up that need she'd always had to look at him. Being home together was bringing back emotions and memories that made her miss those years when everything had seemed so simple.

But things aren't simple anymore. Everything has changed. We aren't the same people we were before Leo's death. This is how life is now.

She started back up the road. There was nothing good that could come from reliving what had been between the two of them. They both had their own separate lives now, which were thousands of miles apart. They didn't even live on the same continent any longer.

Ms. Connors had always lived in one of the older homes in the neighborhood, but she'd always kept it well maintained and all the children in the neighborhood knew to stay out of her garden. The sound of her voice was enough to put fear into any child or adult. They waited on the small covered front porch for the elderly lady to turn the lock on the door.

"Come in, come in," Ms. Connors said as she led them into a front room where she moved a stack of books to the side, leaving only a small space for the two of them to sit.

"Mom sent you this," Scott said, handing the food container to their former teacher, then taking a seat next to her.

Felicity tried to shift the stack of books farther to the side, only to find them leaning against her until no more than her shoulder kept them in place. Glancing down at the floor, she looked for a place to move them but found yet more stacks leaning precariously against the sofa. She held the opinion that her former teacher had a hoarding problem, which she had once mentioned to Leo, only to be told that having a room overflowing with books was not hoarding. It was called collecting.

She wished her brother were here now to see how the stacks of books had grown. But then maybe he was right. It did seem that the rest of the room was clean and orderly.

She pushed against the stack once more as Scott squeezed farther back into the sofa, leaving her nowhere to escape from the touch of his body against hers.

"We missed you today," she said as she tried to take her mind off the feel of Scott's warm shoulder against hers.

"I was sorry to miss it, but the weather's just too cold for me to tolerate right now. My arthritis, you know, it acts up every year at this time." Ms. Connors held up a notebook with fingers that looked painfully twisted. "And of course I'm busy working on cataloging all the books I collected while I was teaching."

Looking back around the room, Felicity hoped the woman planned on living a very long life.

"And it's so good to see the two of you together again. Now tell me, what's new with the two of you? I've missed your visits so much. And of course I've missed your brother, Felicity. He was always so good to come by and fill me in on all the gossip from the school."

Felicity felt a deep ache in her heart as she remembered Leo telling her about his visits to the elderly teacher after he had taken a position at their old school.

"He enjoyed those visits as much as you did. He told me once that your guidance helped him learn his way around all the politics in the school system." Her throat tightened with the words, but she managed to get them out. Felicity always found it hard to talk about her brother, but she knew Leo would want the woman to know how much he had appreciated her.

"Mom said you were thinking about moving," Scott said as he quickly drew the woman into a discussion of the advantages of living closer to her sister.

Thirty minutes later, after listening to Scott describe his job and home in London and respond to the older woman's own memories of once visiting the United Kingdom, Felicity was glad to walk back into the cold. The snow had stopped and left everything blanketed in a thick layer of pristine white.

"Come on," Scott said as he caught her hand and pulled her away from the path that led back to his parents' house.

"What are you doing?" It was only the warmth of his hand that had her holding on to him.

"Hear that? Everyone's headed to The Hill," Scott said, the laughter in his voice warming her even more. His ability to enjoy the moment was one of the many things she appreciated about him. He always had a knack for having fun wherever he went.

As they turned down a path that led away from the road, the screams of the neighborhood kids got louder. Teenagers shot past them as they raced each other to be the first one down the snowy slope. Scott helped her as they climbed up the back of the hill that was the highest point in the small community, moving to the side as more children ran past them, toting old wooden sleds and brightly colored tire tubes as they all headed to the community park.

At the top of the hill, they stopped and took a breath. The hill was covered in a deep layer of snow and it looked like every kid within ten miles had come to try out the new snowfall. Scott let go of her hand and headed toward two teenage boys.

"How about renting me your sleds? Twenty dollars apiece?" he asked the boys, each holding red wooden sleds that looked as if they had been handed down for generations.

"What are you doing?" He couldn't really think she was going to go down the hill on one of those.

"Just handling a little business deal with these two young men," Scott said before turning back to the boys and pulling out his wallet. "What do you say?"

"You're crazy." And he was very much mistaken if he thought she was going to go along with his plan.

A sharp scream cut through the air from the bottom of the hill and she ran back to the edge, only to find a group of kids engaged in a snowball fight. Both children and adults cried out as they shoved off, sending their sleds and tubes speeding down the hill. Others built snowmen farther down into the park. It was a snowy heaven.

She looked back to where Scott still bargained with

the two boys. He turned and motioned her over. Or was it instead a snowy hell?

"I'm not getting on that thing," she said as he handed her one of the sleds. "It's old and rickety. What if it falls apart halfway down the hill?"

"I dare you," Scott said with a wink.

She looked down at the sled in her hand as more screams and laughter floated up from the bottom of the hill. This was stupid, but she had never been one to turn down a dare. "One time down the hill and then I'm done."

Fifteen minutes later she was launching herself down the incline on the flatbed sled and holding on for dear life. She heard Scott's whoop of joy from behind her, and crisp, cold air filled her lungs as her own laughter bubbled out of her. She dived down the hill, feeling as if she were six years old again and this was her first ride.

She saw the bump in the snow right before her sled hit it, sending her airborne for a split second. Then she crashed down into the snow, hurtling even faster toward the bottom of the hill.

She pushed back, extending her feet into the snow as she tried to slow her speed, only to have her sled slide to the right and dump her out beside Scott. Brushing away the icy slush from her face, she took the hand Scott offered and pulled herself up.

"You want to go again?" he asked with a smile that said he already knew her answer.

Grabbing her sled, she took a deep breath of clean, brisk air as Scott had done earlier that day. Happiness flooded through her, and for the first time in forever, she felt the heavy blanket of grief and responsibility lift from her shoulders.

With a squeal she hadn't known she was capable of,

she turned and started running back up the hill. "Last one up has to pay for the next ride."

She heard his shout of laughter from behind her as she began the climb back up the hill. It was as if the clock had rewound and things were back to when she and Scott had been the best of friends. It couldn't last, of course. They'd have to go back to the real world soon. But for now, for today, she was going to enjoy this time they had.

Felicity placed the last of her clothes into her weekender bag, then set it off to the side of the bed. It had been a good weekend, spending time with her parents and helping her mother plan the main menu for their Christmas dinner. She hadn't seen Scott since Thursday and she assumed he was spending time with his parents as she was with hers.

Flopping onto her back, she stared up at the ceiling. She had a love-hate relationship with the room. While the bright pink floral curtains and spread from her pre-college days were comforting in their familiarity, her grown-up self resented the throwback to a time when she had believed anything was possible. What had happened to that girl? She'd had so many dreams back then. Going to college. Becoming a nurse. Going off to London to work with Scott. And Scott. There had been so many dreams about Scott. And for a moment it had looked like all those dreams would come true.

And then Leo had taken his life and the world she thought she knew had suddenly made no sense. The fact that her parents needed her had kept her strong throughout the first few weeks after losing him, though most of the time she felt as if she was just stumbling from one day to the next. Only later had she been able to ask herself what had happened.

She remembered the last time she'd seen her brother as she'd been about to board the plane to London. He'd told her to be happy as he'd hugged her. She'd seen the sad smile on his face as he waved goodbye from the window after she'd gone through security and she thought it had been because he was going to miss her. But now she knew that there had been more. Had he had the same smile ever since the injury that caused the end of his football career? Had she been so wrapped up in her own life that she hadn't noticed? They'd all known he'd been depressed after his injury, but they'd thought he'd moved past it when he started his teaching job. Why hadn't she been able to see how bad his depression had become? What if leaving had made things worse? What if she had stayed home instead of running away to London to be with Scott? What if she'd stayed home and been there for her brother?

What had she missed? Was there anything she could have done to save him? She would always think that things would have been different if she'd remained near home. She was a nurse. Surely she would have seen some sign that she needed to get help for her brother.

Though she was learning to live her life again, the questions never stopped. And neither did the guilt of knowing the one night her brother had needed her to be there for him, she'd been in the arms of his best friend.

If only she could understand what had happened to her brother. Maybe if she understood why he had taken his life, she would be able to go on living her own. Even with her new job, she felt as if her life was stalled. Her life was suspended in a time known to her as *After Leo's death* versus the vision she'd had for her life in the time *Before Leo's death*.

And now, with her brother's room just feet from her, the memories of all the time they had spent together seemed to be centered here. All around her. Constant and bittersweet in a house that used to bring her comfort and peace.

Her parents had asked if she wanted to help them go through Leo's things, but she hadn't been able to bring herself to do it yet. While she knew it needed to be done, she was too afraid to let go of the past. Too afraid that she'd lose her brother's memory if she let the past go. And the guilt? How could she let that go when she knew things would have been different for all of them if she'd been there for him?

Something hit the bedroom window and she jerked to attention. It wouldn't be a bird this late at night. Before she could get to the window, something knocked against it. It couldn't be, could it?

She raised the shade. Scott's face was only visible with the light of the full moon. The window creaked as she slid it up and she stopped, afraid she'd wake her parents.

Shaking her head with disgust, she finished opening the window. She was acting like a teenage girl, afraid her parents would ground her for sneaking a boy into her room. She stood back so that the *boy* sneaking into her room could climb through the window.

"What are you doing here?" Her mind went to several reasons he could be climbing into her window, most having to do with the bed that occupied the room.

"I wanted to talk," Scott said as he looked around the room.

"You lost your phone? You forgot where our front

door was located? You just felt adventurous and wanted to take a chance getting shot by my dad?" she asked. "What possible reason could you have for climbing that ladder in the dark? You could have fallen to your death."

"I didn't want to wake your parents," Scott said. "Come on. I want to show you something."

"Not even I am naive enough to fall for that line." Her heart hammered against her chest as his lips turned up in a smile of which any wolf would be proud. What had she been thinking letting him into her room? "Okay, Doc. What's up?"

"Just trust me," he said as he began climbing back out the window.

"You know you're crazy, right?" she asked as she climbed out behind him, not daring to look down. Not that she hadn't used this same ladder herself to get in and out of the house when she was younger, much younger than she was now. The frosty cold air filled her lungs and bit into her skin the moment she stepped onto the ladder.

"Wait. I need my coat." She reached back inside the window and pulled it off the chair where she had laid it.

Backing down the ladder slowly, she stumbled on a step and Scott's hand shot out to steady her, then remained on her back, leaving her feeling anything but steady.

She climbed into his car, then laughed when he turned on the engine but didn't turn the lights on until they had pulled out of her parents' driveway. "What are we? Sixteen?"

"I have a reputation to uphold, you know," he said as he turned back toward the highway that would take them out of town.

As he took the next right, she realized where he was

taking her. She was suddenly aware that she wore only a pair of button-up pajamas under her coat. "Getting caught at Make-Out Lake is not going to help that reputation you're so worried about."

"The kids probably don't even call it that anymore. And I'm pretty sure taking a drive out to *Stone Lake* is probably not going to get me in trouble," he said. His eyes never left the road, but she could see the smirk on his face. He was probably remembering all those nights he'd sneaked out to the lake with his high school dates. That thought made her stomach tighten with her old friend the green-eyed monster again.

But she knew she didn't have any right to feel that way. She'd put her romantic feelings for Scott aside. There was no future there and she wasn't going to waste her energy on something that could not be.

They turned off the road that led to the lake and took a path that was just wide enough for a car. In the headlights she could see the outline of trees, but it wasn't until they came out of the dark woods that she could see the lake itself.

The full moon reflected off the still body of water, giving the whole lakefront a magical glow as snow piles carpeted the trees, twinkling like fairy lights as the branches swayed in with the winter breeze.

"It's beautiful," she whispered, not wanting to spoil the moment. Everything seemed so peaceful here. It was as if the whole world was frozen in place.

Just as your life has been frozen in place.

She shivered as that truth settled around her.

"It is very beautiful." Scott had known when he'd driven down here earlier that evening that he needed to share this with Fliss. But did she see what he saw? "It's so peaceful, yet at the same time I'm afraid to breathe because it looks so fragile."

He didn't say that it was the same way he felt about their friendship. That he was afraid to say too much, to feel too much, because of the fragile new beginning that had finally emerged over the weekend.

But some things did need to come out in the open if they were going to have any chance of a future relationship, though he regretted the pain he knew that it could cause the two of them.

"Your parents are worried about you." He waited for the explosion that he had expected from her for inserting himself in her affairs, but it didn't come. Instead she just stared out into the dark as if he hadn't spoken.

"I called him about us," Scott said, surprising even himself with his words. It wasn't as if he had ever intended to keep it to himself. He just hadn't had a chance to discuss things privately with her before the funeral. And afterward, when she had told him she wasn't returning to London with him, there hadn't seemed to be any reason to bring it up to her.

"What do you mean?" Her voice was quiet, but there was a tension in her body that hadn't been there earlier.

"The night before our first real date, I called him. I had to, Fliss. It wouldn't have been right to have him find out any other way. I owed it to him."

"You make it sound like the two of you were going to face off at dawn over pistols. Leo loved you, Scott. He would never have been mad at you."

Scott was glad to see that some of the tension between them was gone, but there was still so much for them to discuss.

"What did he say?" she asked, her voice once again quiet, as if she wasn't sure she wanted to hear the answer.

"You mean after he cussed me like a dog and pretended to warn me off?" He smiled at the memory of the colorful words his friend had used.

"He didn't seem surprised, really. He told me to take good care of you and he threatened my life if I broke your heart." And hadn't that been a bit hypocritical of his friend when only days later he had broken both Scott's and Fliss's hearts?

"He seemed...okay, then?" she asked, then shivered.

He turned the heat up in the car. The snow had begun to fall again and the temperatures outside were dropping.

He'd gone over his conversation with Leo word by word and there hadn't been any sign that his friend was depressed. He'd seemed happy and upbeat just like he had always been when Scott talked to him. Only now Scott knew that it had all been an act. His friend had to have been suffering to do something as drastic as taking his own life.

"Yes. He seemed happy with the news. There was nothing he said that even hinted he was depressed."

"You know, he didn't seem surprised when we became closer friends after he went off to college. I've always wondered if he had anything to do with that." She had turned toward him now and the light from the moon that lit the sky shone across the light blond hair that cascaded down her back. Her eyes, turned up toward his, shone with a sapphire light all their own. She was as beautiful as the landscape outside.

"He might have suggested that I keep an eye on you, but that was all," he said. Then, without thinking, he pulled her close so that her head rested on his shoulder.

"It's still hard to believe he's gone. I think of picking up the phone and calling him whenever the Yankees bite the dust, and then I remember he's not here anymore."

"It's not fair," she said, her voice steady, though he could feel the dampness of her tears through his shirt.

"It never is." The truth of the words hit him hard. It wasn't fair that he'd lost both Leo and Fliss at the same time either.

What if they'd had this conversation before? What if he had demanded she let him help her through this grief before she locked him out of her thoughts and emotions? What if they'd worked through Leo's death together?

The what-ifs were piling up like the snow outside the car. There was no going back to the way things had been before Leo's death, but they both could move forward as friends again. His body's own reaction to her nearness protested against that thought. He couldn't lie to himself. He wanted more than friendship, but he would be glad to take what he could get right now because the time they'd spent together this weekend had given him hope that there could be more between them someday.

"My parents have no reason to worry about me. I'm doing great. The new job in New York is more than I could have hoped for." She moved away as she spoke, then turned back toward him. "I'm excited to see everything we've worked for put into action. Not only is it going to make a difference to the way the whole cardiac department is run, it's going to free up space in the ER for other patients."

There was no denying the excitement in her eyes. The only time she really seemed like her old self, the happy Fliss he'd grown up with, was when she talked about her work. The only other time he had seen that look in her eyes had been when she'd been flying down the hill on the sled he'd rented.

"Can you just do me one favor before we leave? I never... I mean, when we were growing up, I didn't get to..." she said as he started to put the car into Reverse. "Can you just kiss me before we leave?"

Putting the car back in Park, he tensed as she undid her seat belt and moved closer.

"I know it sounds stupid, but..."

His lips sealed over hers before she could say anything more. It had been so long, too long, since he'd tasted her. What had brought on her request, he didn't care.

Her lips opened to his and his hands tangled in her hair as he swept inside her mouth, his tongue beginning an intimate dance with hers, touching, retreating, then tangling together.

She pulled away from him, her lips as bright red from his kisses as the color that filled her cheeks. Only the binding of the seat belt kept him from following her to her side of the car. Her chest rose and fell with the same desperate need for air that he was experiencing. He wasn't the only one shaken by what they had just shared.

"What I was going to say was that I never had the chance to be kissed at Make-Out Lake and I always felt like I had missed out on one of those teenage milestones." She straightened her clothes, then buckled her seat belt.

He knew this was true because all the boys in her classes had been warned off by both him and her brother.

He decided it was time to leave before he got it into his mind to educate her on all the other things that had gone on at their high school make-out spot. Just thinking about doing them with Fliss made the drive back to her parents' home very uncomfortable.

He waited while she lifted a small pot in her mother's garden for a hidden key, then went inside the house.

Driving away, he couldn't help but hope that there was some way the passionate woman who had been in his arms for just those few moments, the one he had fallen for in London, would somehow find her way back to him before it was too late and they were separated again.

CHAPTER SIX

SCOTT GLANCED OVER to where Felicity slept in her seat next to him. From the few grunts she'd made since he had picked her up and started driving back to the city, it was obvious that she hadn't slept much better than he had.

Unable to forget the feel of her lips against his, he'd spent the night wondering how they had managed to mess things up between them so quickly. Yes, Leo's death changed both of their lives forever. But shouldn't that have been even more of a reason to turn to each other?

Even when she sent him away, he'd not believed that she meant for it to be permanent. She just needed some time to deal with the loss of her brother before she could return to London.

But when six months had passed and she still wouldn't talk to him, he had let his pride get the best of him. Instead of flying to New York and demanding that Felicity talk to him, he'd accepted that not only had he lost Leo, but he'd lost her too. He could see that had been a mistake.

Now those old what-ifs had wound their way back into his subconscious, as they had after Leo's death, until they had worn a path so deep that he couldn't seem to get away from them. Like Felicity, it had only been his work that had pulled him from the abyss. But he'd realized over the last few months that it wasn't enough anymore.

And just one taste of Felicity had shown him that he wanted more. He wanted the future that he had glimpsed for just a few wonderful moments. He wanted the woman he had fallen in love with in London.

He saw the sign for the Christmas tree farm that they'd stopped at earlier in the week and an idea formed in his head. He missed the happy, spontaneous woman who had lit up his world. And that woman had always loved Christmas. His mother had told him there was magic in Christmas if you only believed in it. He was pretty sure that Fliss had lost the ability to believe in anything. But maybe he could believe enough for the two of them.

He turned the car into the parking lot. Somehow he knew that helping Fliss find the magic of Christmas again was the key to her also finding herself and moving on with her life. Maybe then she would find her way back to him.

Felicity woke at the slamming of the car door. Scrambling up in the seat, she looked around her and was surprised to see that they were once again at a Christmas tree farm. No, not *a* Christmas farm—it was the same one they had stopped at before. Dragging her coat and scarf on, she went to look for Scott, only to find him waiting in line while a young boy tied twine around a small tree much like the one he'd admired before.

"I hope you're not buying that for me," she said as she followed the two of them to the car, where they worked on tying it to the luggage rack on the roof.

"I know it's a little small, but it should fit perfectly by

the fireplace," Scott said as he checked the knots holding the tree in place.

"I told you before, I don't need a tree. I'm hardly ever home. It's just a waste." And when had he picked out a place for it in her apartment? He'd only been inside once, the day they'd left for the weekend. "Look, it's sweet of you to think of it, but seriously, I don't need it."

"Of course you do. And don't worry about decorations. I'll pick some up for it."

Had he always been this high-handed? Or had that kiss, the one she was trying hard to forget, given him the wrong idea? Why had she done it? Was it because she had spent so many nights lying in her bed, knowing that Scott and Leo were out at the lake with their girlfriends while she was home alone, secretly wishing she'd been the one Scott had chosen? She had to admit that his kiss had been even better than the ones her imagination had dreamed of. All of their kisses had been better than her imagined ones. Her mind flashed back to the night they'd spent together. Her lips. His lips. Everywhere.

She loosened the knot of her scarf, hoping to let the icy air in to cool her skin. She was not going to think about it. It was in the past, where it needed to stay.

Refusing to argue the point with him any longer, she climbed back into the car. He might have insisted on buying it, but that didn't mean she had to accept it.

Thirty minutes later she couldn't bite her tongue any longer. "Why is it so important to you that I have a tree?"

"It's Christmastime, Fliss. You've always had a tree. It's not the first tree we've picked out together. Don't you remember the lot we went to in London?" he asked. "The poor thing couldn't have been three feet tall."

"And it still barely fit in the living room." It had been

more of a bush than a tree, but it had held a small string of lights and enough balls to qualify as a Christmas tree. After they'd finished decorating, they'd gorged themselves on popcorn and watched a lineup of British Christmas movies. She'd been homesick for her family during the holiday season, but that night Scott had made her feel like she was at home. He'd taken care of her then just like he was trying to take care of her now.

How could she explain to him that, to her, Christmas was just one more day to get through now? "I do appreciate the thought. I just don't think I'm ready for it this year."

"Whether you're ready or not, Christmas is coming," Scott said as he moved his hand over hers where it rested on the console.

"You've moved on with your life." She didn't mean the words as an accusation. She was just stating a painful fact that she found hard to understand.

"Would you rather I hadn't?" he asked.

Would she rather he still be mourning her brother? It embarrassed her that her first thought was that she wished he hadn't moved on. Because she wanted him to be just as miserable as she was? No, not really. It was the fear that Leo would be forgotten if they all went on with their lives.

"It doesn't mean I've forgotten him, Fliss. I never will." That his words were so tuned to her thoughts didn't surprise her. It had always been that way between the two of them.

"Spend Christmas with me," he said.

"I have to be at my parents' for Christmas. They'll need me. You know that. Besides, your parents will be there too." She wasn't sure what Scott was planning, but she knew it frightened her.

"Not the day. The season. Let me show you that you can still enjoy Christmas." His words held so much hope.

"Scott, if I gave you the wrong idea by asking you to kiss me, I'm sorry." It was important that they didn't have any misunderstandings between them. They still had a professional relationship that they had to return to the next day.

"No expectations. Just two old friends enjoying the Christmas season together," Scott said as he pulled his hand away from hers, and the cozy comfort of the car that she had been enjoying seemed to disappear. "For old times' sake?"

How could she turn down his offer when she knew all he wanted to do was help?

"Okay, Doc. I'll go along with this plan of yours." She'd take the tree and agree to some shopping if it would get him to change the subject. "Now turn those hazel eyes of yours back to the road and concentrate on getting us back to the city. Vacation time is over. Tomorrow it's back to work for the both of us."

It was the smell of paint that drove her into Scott's office the next day. Well, technically it was her office. At least, it would be when Scott returned to London. Moving a small table that she had originally planned to use for organizing file folders, she set up an area for her laptop and the stack of envelopes and invitations that she had started addressing after her lunch meeting.

"There you are," Scott said as he came into the office. "I'm glad you finally joined me."

"What do you mean?" He made it sound like she had been avoiding him. Of course, that was what she had been doing when he'd first arrived. She'd surrendered her office to him without a single complaint. It had seemed like the best thing for both of them while things had been so tumultuous between them.

"I didn't mean to throw you out of the office. Like I told you before, it's big enough for the two of us to share, I would think." He began to move his folders and papers as he cleaned off a spot on the desk.

"Until the painters finish in the lounge, we will definitely be sharing, but I'm quite happy over here. There's plenty of room for what I need." She studied the list she had made of hospital board members and medical officers who would be invited to the grand opening that would take place in just two weeks' time.

"Did you have a chance to review the list of invited guests?" Though she knew he wasn't familiar with most of the people in the hospital, she didn't want to leave off anyone Dr. Mason might have mentioned wanting to invite.

"I did and I ran it by Dr. Mason at our meeting this morning. He was happy to see that you had included some of the vendors. It's always good to keep a good relationship in the community, especially when they go into other hospitals," Scott said.

"Dr. Mason just wants to spread the word about the program, I'm sure." And make sure that all his colleagues in the city ended up green with envy at what he had been able to accomplish with the new center.

A knock came on the door, and Theresa, one of the new charge nurses who had volunteered to help unpack supplies, stuck her head into the room.

"I've finished stocking the nurses' station, but I wanted to see if you wanted to join some of us from the ER. It's tree-lighting day at the Rockefeller Center, you know."

The words bubbled out of the woman and Felicity couldn't ignore the way she was staring hopefully at Scott. "I know you're from upstate New York, Dr. Thomas, but I wasn't sure if you knew about the lighting."

"Felicity and I have attended the lighting several times," Scott said. "If we missed the lighting, Fliss would insist that we stop by the tree at least once while we were in the city during the holidays."

She wasn't certain whether he had purposely brought her into the conversation to cool down the woman's interest in him or whether he was just being friendly.

"Really?" the woman asked, glancing over at Felicity with a look of disbelief.

Was it possible that there was one person left in the hospital who wasn't aware that she and Scott were old friends?

"I'm sorry, Theresa, but I really need to finish these invitations, or we'll have a very lonely grand opening." She went back to work on the invitations. If Scott wanted to go with the other woman, she wasn't going to stand in his way. It wasn't like she needed his help to finish with this project.

"I'd love to, but I've got a few charts to sign off after my shift in the cath lab before I leave tonight. But thanks for the invite. Maybe next time," Scott said.

The possibility of him attending the ceremony with her another year seemed to satisfy the woman as she hurried out the door with a smile on her face. Felicity didn't mention that next time the famous Christmas tree was lit he'd be halfway around the world.

And where would she be next Christmas? Working these same late shifts just to have something to help pass the long, lonely hours? Okay, now she was just being maudlin.

Minutes ticked by as they both worked quietly. While addressing envelopes wasn't what she'd dreamed of when she'd taken the new position, it was a bit exciting to see the stack of invitations pile up. There was a lot of pressure coming down from administration for this grand opening to go well, especially with the board members planning to attend.

But the real excitement would be when the unit was finally open to the community. Getting the word out that there was a fast track through the emergency room that would increase the survival chances of a patient with a cardiac emergency was just as important as showing the unit off to the bigwigs of the hospital.

"Let's do it!" Scott said, startling her.

"Do what?" she asked as she straightened a stack of envelopes she had knocked over.

"Let's go to the tree lighting. You always loved it when the three of us got to be there," Scott said. "I can come in early and finish the few charts I have left."

She didn't bother to tell him that it wasn't the three of them anymore. He had to realize it wouldn't be the same without Leo. He knew she avoided everything that reminded her of her brother. She looked at her phone where it lay beside her. "It's too late. We'd never make it through traffic now."

"We can take a car service and…" His phone rang, interrupting him. It was clear there was some type of emergency.

"There's a patient coming by air. The crew called in a STEMI, but then the patient lost his pulse. If they can get him back, they want to go straight to the cath lab, but Dr.

Turner is tied up with another emergency." Scott grabbed his go bag that she knew contained a fresh pair of scrubs.

"I'm going to meet them on the roof with the ER staff."

"I'll make sure the lab is ready. I can assist if needed. Just call and let me know if you're coming straight over." She grabbed the shoes she had kicked off under the table earlier.

"Will do," Scott said, running out the door.

Heading out of the office, she stopped for a second and admired the shiny new nurses' station. This was why this unit was important. If they'd been open, the patient would have been able to come straight here, where they would work to stabilize him before taking him to the cath lab next door.

Fifteen minutes later she stood at the control booth and watched as Scott inserted an intra-aortic balloon pump. She'd watched on the monitors as he opened up the blocked artery that had likely been the cause of the man's MI, but she knew the damage to the man's heart was extensive if Scott was having to put him on the device that would help his heart continue to work.

"The man's a miracle," said the technologist in charge of the monitors and documentation.

"Not many survive the widow-maker," she said, referring to the man's blockage in his main coronary artery.

"I'm not sure this guy is going to survive, but at least we've given him a chance now. I mean, Dr. Thomas. There's something about his technique that makes it all look so simple," the man said before turning back to his monitors.

The pride she felt at the compliment on Scott's behalf was the same she'd felt when they'd been working together in London and she would overhear comments on the special ability he had to make his procedures go off so easily for the staff and the patient.

That time in London seemed so long ago now, though she did think about it often. There'd been a certain magic to the city with the charm of its history and people. But that was a lifetime ago, and there was no reason for her to relive those memories now. She was glad she had them—most of the time—but she knew she'd made the right decision to stay with her parents.

She turned away from the monitors and headed back to the office. There was a lot of work left to do before she could finish for the night.

CHAPTER SEVEN

Scott was happy to find Felicity back in what hopefully would now become *their* office. He knew they were both tired, but the last case had drained him more emotionally than physically. He didn't feel like going back to the hotel by himself. Not yet, at least. "You ready to go?" Scott asked as he gathered his own laptop into his briefcase.

"I was just heading out," she said. "How did it go with the wife?"

"It's always hard to tell someone's loved ones that the patient might not make it. They have a set of twins away in college. She was calling them when I left her with the chaplain." He knew he'd done everything he could for the man, but it didn't make it any easier to watch the wife break down when he told her she needed to call their daughters so they could be here if their father didn't survive the night.

"Let's go. We have an appointment," he said as he shut the office door behind them.

The look she gave him was not a surprise. Of course, Fliss had never liked surprises. It was the reason her family had refused to put out her Christmas presents even after she was too old to believe in Santa Claus. She'd been caught red-handed more than once with a half-unwrapped present.

"Have you forgotten the breakfast meeting with Dr. Mason in the morning?" she asked.

"It's not that late," he said as they stepped out of the side entrance that led to the parking lots. He spotted the car with his hotel's insignia across its door. He just hoped the concierge had been able to arrange the rest of his last-minute request. Taking her arm, Scott guided her through the other cars that waited for their fares.

"You know we've already missed the tree lighting, right? And I really do need to get home. Maybe you don't need your beauty sleep, but some of us do," Felicity said as she scooted over in the back seat for him to climb in next to her and began to give her address to the driver.

"I just had to tell a woman that her husband might not make it through the night. Life's short, Fliss. You have to make time for more than work," Scott said as he laid a hand on her arm. "Just go with me on this one. Please?"

He waited as she considered his request, finally relaxing when she settled back into the car seat as she made sure there was plenty of space between the two of them so they weren't touching. He hoped the space would be gone by the time the evening was over.

They rode in silence, Fliss undoubtedly trying to figure out what he could have planned for the night. Sitting back, he let himself enjoy the view of the city that seemed even more alive now that darkness had fallen. Lights of every color shone from the small businesses that lined the street as they prepared for the coming holidays. Looking up into the sky, he could see the larger buildings whose lights always made up the backdrop of the city. It was truly The City That Never Sleeps. And he loved everything about it.

When the car stopped, he made arrangements with the driver to return, then took Felicity's hand. "This way."

He waited for her reaction when she reluctantly exited the car. The smile she gave him more than compensated for the lack of sleep from which the two of them would be suffering the next morning.

"You've always said that one day you wanted to take a carriage ride through the city." He didn't have to say how corny the whole carriage in Central Park had seemed when he was a young teenager. He'd been afraid that she was going to force him and Leo to take a ride with her. Now he couldn't wait to take this ride with her. Looking at the wonder and happiness he could see in her eyes, he knew he'd take a carriage ride up the entire East Coast if it made her this happy.

"Which one do we take?" she asked. "Can we take the one with that big black horse? The one with the white carriage?"

"Let's find out." Still holding her hand, he pulled her along with him till they came to the beautiful black mare that stood with its driver at the front of the line. Minutes later they were loaded inside and headed down the path out of Central Park.

As he tucked the blankets in around her, Felicity moved closer till their shoulders touched, the movement more instinct and habit than intentional, he was sure. He had missed the warmth of her on those cold nights in London.

There had been so many changes to their relationship after she had come to London. The longtime companionship he had enjoyed with her had quickly turned into something more. He had enjoyed each new experience as their relationship had changed, becoming more intimate and deeper than anything he had felt before. It was as if they had discovered something new about each other every day as they explored their new romantic interest in each other.

And explore they had. They'd spent many nights talking for hours in their favorite English pub. And then there had been the even longer good-nights at her door until finally he'd gotten the nerve to make the move for that first good-night kiss. Just one kiss and he'd known things would never be the same between them. When she'd sighed into his mouth and opened her lips for him, he'd known there was no going back. Never again could he look at his best friend without thinking of the sweet taste of her lips.

It was the kiss that had had him waking Leo up with the call he'd known he had to make immediately. While the two of them had taken different paths after high school, they had still remained close and he didn't want anything to endanger their friendship. The fact that Leo hadn't been surprised that there had been changes in his sister's relationship with his old friend just showed how well he knew the two of them. And with Leo's blessing, he'd had the courage to explore this new connection with Fliss.

If he had only known what the future held for the three of them then.

"Look, you can see the lights from the Saks window display." Felicity moved closer as she pointed down the street to their destination. Sally, the black draft horse pulling their carriage, clopped slowly down the street as

Felicity bounced up and down beside him as if she could help the horse go faster.

Putting his arm around her, he pulled her close. The smell of honeysuckle hit him, reminding him of the bottle of shampoo that still sat in his shower where she'd left it the morning they'd flown out of London.

"Relax. The store's not going to go anywhere. You don't want to spook the horse." He pulled her closer against him. It was probably wrong of him to use the poor horse as an excuse to hold her.

While there were still plenty of people on the streets, they had a good view of the store as thousands of color-coordinated lights ran up and down the building. The driver slowed the carriage and Scott pulled his phone out to take a picture of Felicity's face as she took in all the lights. He'd send it to her mother the next day.

When the tree at Rockefeller Center came into view, they both moved up in the seat. The lighting of a tree was a long-held tradition for the city and it seemed that each year the tree got more spectacular.

"Do you remember the first time we came to see the tree?" Felicity asked.

"I remember it was cold. Too cold for anyone with any sense to be outside." Both he and her brother had complained about the trip, only going with her because she had insisted she would go alone if they didn't come.

"And you and Leo whined about it the whole time we were here. It was New York in the winter. It was supposed to be cold. What I remember is how excited the crowd was when we were counting down. Then when the tree lit up and the choir started singing, it was magical." She sat back in the seat, her face lit with a smile.

"It is still magical," he said as he looked down into

her eyes. If only she could see the magic that still surrounded the two of them. He bent his head to hers before he could think too hard about what he was doing and brushed his lips across hers, letting them linger there for just a moment. It wasn't much more than a peck on the lips, but he knew he was playing with fire when for a mere second her lips opened and he enjoyed the taste of her before she pulled away. He saw the uncertainty in her eyes before she turned her face away from him. His heart stuttered for a beat as if it knew it was in danger. Fliss had broken it when she'd sent him back to London alone, and there was no reason to doubt that she would do it again. But was it possible for them to at least have these next few weeks together? If this were all he could ever have of her, would he take it?

She turned back to the lights of the street as if nothing had happened between them. Had he just ruined what he had been so carefully building between the two of them? Would one kiss, one night, one Christmas together be enough for him?

They turned the corner and St. Patrick's Cathedral came into view, its Gothic architecture always awe-inspiring. As they left the crowded streets and headed back to Central Park, the rest of the trip was spent in silence as they both seemed occupied with their own thoughts.

By the time they returned to the cab, they both were dragging from the length of the day. As the car drove the two of them back toward the hospital, he was relieved when Fliss leaned against him once more.

"I'm glad we're friends again," she said as she closed her eyes.

It wasn't much—and definitely not the declaration he

had hoped for—but for now it would have to do. They'd come a long way, but they still had far to go.

Felicity glanced around her small apartment to make sure once more that everything was in place. Agreeing to Scott's request that he bring over decorations for the tree he had insisted on buying her, she'd had to rush home to straighten up before he arrived. Now, dressed in a soft pair of jeans and a warm sweater, she stood in the middle of her small apartment and found herself thinking about the times Scott had hung out in her even smaller flat in London. With a kitchen too small to do any real cooking, she'd lived on takeout, until one night when she'd decided to cook a meal for Scott. It had been a disaster from the moment she'd put the small chicken in the tiny oven to the moment the fire alarm in the building had gone off. As usual, Scott had pitched in and helped with the cleanup without commenting on the fact that she was a disaster in the kitchen. Instead he'd picked up the phone and ordered takeout, acting as if that had been the plan all along. Of course, since he'd experienced her cooking before, it might have been.

She hadn't thought much of her apartment in London recently. Or at least she had tried not to think of it. She'd left it so suddenly. Her thoughts at the time had only been for her parents. It wasn't until after the funeral that she'd known she couldn't return to London. Her parents had been too fragile at the time. She'd made the hardest decision of her life in a matter of hours, knowing that if she took too long to think about it, she might not be able to do what she knew was best for all of them. She'd had to stay with her parents. And she'd had to let Scott go to live out his dream of working in London. After seeing where her brother's failure to achieve his dream had taken him, she couldn't be responsible for Scott's dream ending because of her.

Her apartment doorbell buzzed, and checking the camera, she opened the door for Scott, who carried two large boxes.

"That seems a bit much for such a little tree, don't you think?" She took the top box from him, then placed it on the small kitchen table. When a whiff of ginger and garlic met her nose, she opened the box, revealing multiple small cartons. "You remembered?"

"That we always vetoed your request of Chinese and substituted pizza and beer when we decorated the tree?" He laid the other box next to the tree, then took off his coat. "It wasn't really fair using our two-guy votes against you all the time."

It had been enough to make her scream at times when her brother and Scott sided against her, but she'd eat all the pizza in the world if things could go back to the way they were then.

"Besides, it's time for some new traditions. And I'm starving," he said as he moved the pizza takeout menus on the table out of the way.

They ate in silence, as they both had missed lunch due to a last-minute meeting called by the hospital plant operations department, who had felt the need to discuss the new fire security doors that had been added during construction.

"I know this sounds crazy, but I can't wait till I'm back to taking care of simple things like a patient having an MI," she said, then laughed. "I guess that sounds heartless. I don't mean I want someone to die. I'm just tired of all these people in suits thinking that the color of the tile in the staff bathroom needs five meetings and six pages of reports filled out."

"I know exactly what you mean. All the bureaucracy can be hard to deal with," said Scott, "but in the end you'll see that it's been worth it. Brooklyn Heights is going to be the talk of the cardiac community once the new unit opens up."

"Don't you miss working with your patients in London?" She waited for his answer, knowing he would never lie to her. Why did she feel the need to know that sending him away before had been the right thing to do? It didn't matter now.

"London is spectacular. You know that," he said.

The fact that he didn't say more confused her. He'd always been so excited about his job with the cardiac team at the prestigious hospital in London.

"And your job?" she asked, pushing for more.

"I love the job. The hospital is state of the art in its cardiac department and the staff is phenomenal, as you know," Scott said, then turned toward the box he had brought with him. "I know you prefer white lights, but these just seemed right for this space."

He pulled out a small string of blue mini lights. "I have another string of white ones in here in case you don't like these. And I also picked these up."

He pulled out another box, then took out a small ornament and handed it to her. Holding the crystal snowflake up to the light, she watched as prisms of all the colors of the rainbow danced across the bare walls of her apartment.

"They're beautiful." She carefully placed it down, then reached for the string of blue lights. "Let's put them on."

In minutes the tree was quickly transformed into a

spectacular winter arrangement. The pale blue of the lights reflected off the ornaments and walls, turning the small room into a winter wonderland that brought back the memory of their trip to their parents' homes.

"It's perfect," she said as she sat back and admired the small tree. Scott's choices had transformed it from a small forgotten bush in the corner of the room to the room's centerpiece. "How do you always seem to know what something needs?"

Or what I need?

It had always been that way with him. He consistently seemed to know what she needed and exactly when she needed it. In high school, he'd known when she needed that bit of encouragement to step out of her comfort zone. In college, she could always count on him for a phone call right when she was feeling overwhelmed with exams and clinicals. Sometimes it had seemed that he knew her better than even her brother or her parents. It was like he knew what she needed before even she did.

And then there was this little tree that seemed to drive out some of the gloom that had settled over her lonely apartment. It was perfect.

"Wait," she said as she jumped up from where they sat around the tree and ran toward the front door. She flipped the switch to both the living room and kitchen. The room went dark except for the pretty pale lights of the tree.

"Now it's perfect," she said as she took her place in front of the tree. Minutes passed as they both just watched the lights and their reflection in the crystal snowflakes, but there was no awkwardness in this silence. Instead the moment was one of shared peacefulness. The crowded streets of the city and Scott's hospital back in London were both thousands of miles away right then. For now there was just the two of them with this brightly lit Christmas tree and it was enough. And if a little bit of Christmas spirit eased its way into her heart, she wasn't about to admit it to him.

CHAPTER EIGHT

"WE COULD HAVE just driven over to the mall," Felicity grumbled. They had agreed to make an early morning start, which would have been fine except for the fact that she hadn't slept more than a couple of hours the night before. She wanted to blame the Chinese food, but knew it was more than that. She'd spent a long time in front of her newly decorated tree after Scott had left, going over all her memories of past Christmases that she'd spent with both Scott and Leo. She'd been able to block out all those memories the year before, but this Christmas season was different.

Because of Scott. He was forcing her into the present, but all she wanted was to keep looking back at the past. It seemed better to look back to the past than to think about the future.

"But you've always loved shopping the market fair. You think Dad would like this?" Scott asked as he picked up a small carving of a sailboat.

"It's nice, but I like that one better." She pointed to the slightly larger one that reminded her more of Scott's father's boat.

"Nice." Scott picked it up and examined it. "I like the sail work on it."

"I'll take it," he said as he handed it to the salesperson.

"See, this is why I need you," he said as he turned toward her. "You have this great knack for picking out the perfect gift."

"Are you talking about that awful sweater you were going to buy your mother? Anyone could have told you that was all wrong. What woman is going to wear a sweater with a huge sequined fish?" It had truly been the worst sweater she had ever seen.

"I thought it was cute," Scott said as he paid and they moved on. He stopped at a small jewelry shop that had been set up temporarily in Grand Central.

How a man who had picked out and decorated her Christmas tree so perfectly could think that sweater was cute was impossible for her to understand. Of course, his gifts had always been more quirky than traditional.

She spotted a nice light green crocheted afghan that she knew her mother would love. She held it up to the light. Each stitch was precise and the yarn was a soft wool. She was handing it to the salesperson when Scott walked up with a jewelry bag in his hand. She wanted to ask him what he'd bought but stopped herself. What if it was for someone back in London? A woman? Was it possible he had someone waiting for him in London? He'd certainly had his share in both high school and med school. It shouldn't have been a surprise to her if there was someone in his life now.

And the kiss they'd shared the night of the carriage ride? She'd assured him that it had only been a kiss between friends, but it had felt like more. So had the kiss at the lake.

"I'm starved. Do you want to get something to eat?"

he asked. "How about lunch at Macy's? I know you wanted to shop for some new ties for your dad."

She forced herself to smile and nodded her head, unable to think of anything but what the small jewelry bag in his hand could contain while he sent out a request for the car service.

She was being ridiculous. It only made sense that Scott would have a woman in his life. It had been over eighteen months since their breakup—if you could call ending a relationship that had lasted one night a breakup.

But wouldn't he tell her if there was someone else? Over the last couple of weeks, they had been finding that close friendship that they had enjoyed for most of their lives. Wouldn't he at least have shared something about a new woman in his life? And there was still that kiss. It was hard to believe he would have kissed her, even as a friend, if he'd been involved with someone else.

By the time she was taking a seat at the small restaurant inside Macy's, she knew she had to know if there was a woman. Not that it would really make a difference in their relationship. As a friend, she had no right to anything he didn't want to share with her.

She managed to wait until after the waitress had taken their orders before trying to bring up the subject. She didn't want to appear too interested or to cross some line that would make it uncomfortable for the two of them to continue with the new friendship they had managed to find.

"You haven't said much about London. Tell me all the gossip," she said, trying to play it off as a natural interest in her former coworkers. She immediately thought of a brown-eyed beauty that had made it clear to Felicity from day one that she had an interest in Scott.

No. There was no way he could have fallen for Katie. He was too intelligent to get involved with a woman who made it clear that she was husband-shopping for the man with the biggest wallet.

And that didn't sound jealous at all. Nope. Not one bit.

"There's not a lot of gossip to tell you about. Dr. Matthews is getting a divorce. You were the one who pointed out all the signs to me, if I remember correctly. The poor guy is dating Katie Callahan now." Scott took a drink of his water while she silently celebrated this news.

"I'm not surprised by the divorce, but I am about Katie." Dr. Matthews was a nice guy, but if Katie was the type of woman he wanted, then she would wish the two of them the best of luck.

"There's no explanation for some people's taste." Their drinks came, along with an appetizer of crispy oven-roasted vegetables. Her mouth could all but taste the cauliflower and pine nuts, but her stomach was still filled with nerves.

She served herself and then pushed the vegetables around on her plate. This wasn't the way she did things— at least, not with Scott. They'd always been able to talk about everything. She'd even been known to give him advice on women, even though the cost had been high to her own morale. There was no reason, if they were going to be friends, that they couldn't talk about their involvement with other people. She was just going to have to face this square on. She could do it. She'd listened to him talk about other women in his life before, so what was the difference now?

Maybe the fact that for a very short time she'd been the woman in his life? Her heart squeezed as tight as a fist at the memory.

This wasn't working. She needed to just come out and ask him.

"Scott, are you dating anyone?" The question sounded ridiculous now that she'd voiced it. Did she sound like a jealous ex-lover? If Scott had wanted to tell her about someone in his life, he would have done so.

He slowly lowered his glass without taking his eyes from hers. "Why would you ask that?"

"It just seems… I mean… I'm sorry. I know it's none of my business." She took a swallow from her own glass.

"Do you think I'm the kind of guy that would kiss another woman when I was in a relationship with someone else? After all these years, after everything we've been through, do you not know who I am?"

"I didn't… I mean… It was just a kiss. A kiss between friends." Unable to bear his look of disappointment and anger, she looked away. She *had* known better. She *did* know better.

As the waitress delivered their meals, she looked back at him. His hazel eyes no longer danced with the laughter they'd shared earlier in the day. Instead they stared back with a hardness she had never seen before. This was her fault. She had messed up. It had been a good day, a great day, with the both of them easily falling back into the comfort of their longtime friendship. And now she'd let her jealousy ruin it. Jealousy to which she had no right. Jealousy that she could never admit to him without revealing the feelings she still had for him. Feelings that could ruin the friendship they were working so hard to mend.

And she wouldn't do that. Scott's friendship was too important. She couldn't let her old teenage desire for more destroy this one last chance they had to make things right between the two of them. She needed his friendship too much. Over the last few weeks, she had come to realize just how much she needed him.

Scott tried to fight back his anger as he walked Felicity to her door. He had tried to let it go, he really had, but just thinking about her questioning him about another woman made him even angrier. How could someone who had known him so well think that he would kiss her if he had someone he was involved with back at home? It didn't make sense.

Had their time apart changed him so much that she didn't recognize him for the man he was? He didn't think so. She knew him, *really* knew him. She had no reason for asking him something that questioned the very principles he lived by of being honest and up-front with everyone.

And then there was that comment she had made about it just being a kiss between friends. There had been nothing friendly about the kiss, as far as he was concerned. Maybe it hadn't been as passionate as some of the kisses they'd shared before, but it had meant more to him than what she seemed willing to accept.

And that just made his blood boil. She seemed so sure that all there was left between them was friendship, when he knew there could be more.

"Do you want to come in?" she asked as she unlocked her door.

Walking inside with her right now would be a mistake. He was too wound up in emotions that could explode at any minute. So what, he was going to just keep all this inside? No. He'd show her just how honest and up-front he could be.

He took a step inside and could immediately tell that she'd hoped he wouldn't. As usual, this new Fliss wanted to avoid anything that could complicate her world. Well, tonight he was going to be her complication.

"I'll make some coffee," she said as she moved past him toward the kitchen.

Her body brushed against his, and that was all it took for his body to burst into flames. He caught her wrist with his hand and very gently pulled her close to him. He didn't want to scare her. He would never do that.

"I think we need to set a few things straight." Her body relaxed against his. There was no way she could ignore the proof of his desire as he held her against his hard body. Had she really thought that all the desire he'd felt for her before they'd parted had just died away? Had she thought that because she had decided that she needed to end things between them, all the emotion and desire that he'd felt for her would cease to exist? That he could have just replaced her with someone else that easily?

It was as if, unknowingly, he'd spent half his life waiting for Felicity Dale. For her to grow up. For her to come to London. For her to realize she'd made a mistake when she'd sent him away. He was tired of waiting.

"What are we doing, Scott?" Her voice was husky with a sound he'd only heard once before. The memories of the night they'd shared in his bed made him rock-hard.

"I think it's time we quit avoiding the elephant in the room. We slept together, Fliss. And we both enjoyed it. A lot. That attraction, that desire, it's still there whether you want to accept it or not. That's a fact. Now it's up to you to decide what you want to do about it. I know what I want. You know what I want. It's up to you if we take this any further, but while you're thinking about it, you need to think about this too." He lowered his head to hers and waited for her to pull back. Instead she moved toward him, her lips already parting for his when they met. The taste of her filled his mouth, and he immediately remembered all the other parts of her he'd tasted that one night they'd pleasured each other.

His body went hot with a need he hadn't known since the last time he'd held her. He ran one hand through her silky hair and pulled her closer with the other that remained around her waist. He wouldn't do more. Not tonight. He wouldn't take what he needed from her just because of the heat of the moment. She needed to accept that there was still something between them before they could move any further.

Her moan was the sweetest sound he'd ever heard. Yeah, she still wanted him. He softened his hold on her and stepped back as he raised his head. Her lips were wet from his kisses, her blond silky strands tangled in his fingers. Her eyelids slowly opened, revealing soft blue eyes heavy with what he knew was desire for him.

It hurt from his groin to his heart to step away from her, but he knew it was the right thing to do. Fliss had never been one to make spontaneous decisions.

And after the way she'd sent him away before, he needed to know that she wanted, *needed*, him as much as he needed her. It was Fliss's decision if they went any further. He'd left New York feeling unwanted and unneeded. It had been a blow not only to his pride but also to his heart. He didn't want to leave here feeling that way a second time.

He took another step away, then walked back out the door. He'd wait for her. He just hoped she didn't make him wait too long. Their time was quickly running out.

CHAPTER NINE

"IT'S MISSING SOMETHING," Dr. Mason said as he looked around the new cardiac center.

Felicity scanned the area. There was nothing missing. The new center was beautiful with everything so shiny and new. The light gray walls perfectly complemented the faux-wood floors with their gray tint. The chrome-and-glass light fixtures worked well with all the state-of-the-art monitors displayed at the modern glass nurses' station. Even the signage on the walls had been designed to be practical but also decorative. There was absolutely nothing missing.

"The contractors have assured us that all the paint touch-ups will be done by the end of the day and the bio-med team will have the display monitors up and running by this afternoon," Scott said, then turned back to her. "Is there anything you're aware of that hasn't been completed?"

"No. The stocking of supplies is complete and you can see that all the furniture has been placed properly," she said. It had been a fight to get the furniture here on time, but it was done.

"No, that's not what I meant. The unit is beautiful.

It's everything I and the board hoped for. It's just…" Dr. Mason looked back around the unit.

Scott looked over at her and shrugged his shoulders. She had checked everything off her lists. It was all complete.

"It just needs a bit of Christmas, I think," Dr. Mason said. "That's it. That's what it's missing."

"But, Dr. Mason, it's a beautiful unit. It's perfect just the way it is now." She'd fight the man before someone hung a fake garland or a bunch of giant red balls on her brand-new unit.

"The rest of the hospital's been decorated for weeks now. We can't open up here without a little bit of Christmas cheer." Dr. Mason turned in place as he took in the whole panorama of the unit before stopping in front of Scott and Felicity. "You've both done a great job here. And I know the important thing is going to be the great difference we're going to make to the community once we open. But impressions are important, and I know we're going to make a great one on Monday when we do our first tour. It just needs a touch of the season to warm it up. Nothing flashy, just a touch. I trust you two to know what it needs."

They waited until Dr. Mason had left the unit before looking at each other.

"Okay, Father Christmas. What's your plan? Because I can tell you right now, we are not going to clutter this place up with some gaudy decorations, no matter what he wants." They'd worked too hard to let their grand opening be ruined by Dr. Mason's need for some Christmas cheer.

"I agree, but we can't just ignore his request," Scott said as he walked over to the nurses' station.

"And it's a little late to try to find decorations from

the warehouse. Everything's already been taken by the other departments." She watched as Scott walked back to the automatic doors that opened into the unit, then turned and studied the nurses' station again. She was glad he was at least busy concentrating on something besides her. She'd caught him watching her several times over the last week and it had been unnerving. She had started to remind him that they needed to concentrate on the job, but that would have meant having a personal conversation, and she wasn't ready for that. Right now she preferred for all their concentration to be on the new unit. It was safer that way.

Not that all her own concentration had been on the job. She'd spent several nights that week wide-awake, unable to keep her mind from playing over the kiss that had almost had her begging Scott to take her to bed. She was working sixteen-hour days, but the moment her head hit her pillow, all she thought about was the way Scott had felt pressed against her. So hard. So ready to take their friendship to another level, somewhere they had been only once before. But was that what she wanted?

Yes, she wanted it. Physically, she knew they were good together. But where did they go from there?

And that was the problem. She never could just accept the here and now. She always worried about the future. She always had to know what the plan was going forward. Maybe that was part of the reason she'd sent Scott away. There'd been no plan. They'd taken their friendship to a place where it could be changed forever. And it had done just that. But that had been her choice. Just like Scott had left it up to her whether they took things any further now.

"I think we can do it," Scott said, startling her.

"Do what?" Her head whipped around to where he was standing. Had he read her mind? That was one of the scary parts of their relationship: he knew her too well.

"All we really need is a little something as you first enter the unit. Just a touch of decoration that warms the place up—just a little bit of sparkle," he said, studying the area he had chosen in which to make a statement.

"A touch of sparkle? Like the crystal snowflake ornaments you got for my tree?" she asked. She could see it now. "Blue lights—pale blue like the ones on my tree. We could string some around the outside of the nurses' station here, then a small tree over here."

She walked behind the front desk and cleared a spot where a small basket had been stored for keeping discharged patient files. She still felt the unit was fine as it was, but if they had to decorate, at least this way it wouldn't detract from its clean, modern look. "If we can't find a tree or the ornaments, I can donate my tree."

"It will have to be an artificial one to pass the fire code. There were still some small artificial ones at the hobby shop where I picked up your ornaments. I'll run over there now. Do you want to go?" Scott asked.

"I can't. I still have an appointment," she said. He sent her a look that said he didn't believe her. "I have a late interview for that last open RN position."

"Good. You can help me when I get back, then." He smiled at her for the first time in days. "Dr. Mason was right. With just a few decorations, it will be perfect."

"It's perfect now," she grumbled as he left the unit. But she had to admit, she was looking forward to seeing how it would look once they added just a little bit of Christmas.

The interview went well, and by the time Scott returned she had made the job offer and emailed all the paperwork to the human resources department.

"Did you buy out the store?" she asked as she took one of the bags from him.

"Just the lights—the blue ones, that is. We need a lot more to go around the nurses' station than we did for your tree." He set the rest of the bags and boxes down on the counter. "If you want to start on the lights, I've got some of those hooks with the suction cups that won't leave a mark."

By the time he returned with a small tree, she had all of the lights pulled out of their boxes and strung together. They worked as a team and quickly had the lights hung and the tree decorated. When they both stepped back, she was happy to see that Scott had been right. The decorations were perfect.

"It's perfect. Look at it. The whole place looks perfect," Felicity said as Scott plugged in the lights. "Though I still think it looked fine before."

"It did look fine, just a bit empty," Scott said as he came around to stand by her.

"What it needs is patients and staff. I can't wait till this opening is over so we can finally make use of the space. One of the emergency-room nurses I talked to yesterday said the wait time to be seen yesterday was up to four hours. Can you imagine sitting in the waiting room that long?" She started to walk through the unit, turning off lights as she went.

"Just be prepared for there to be some problems. When we first opened our unit in London there was a real learning curve concerning which patients to send to the ER and which need to come straight to the cardiac center," Scott said as he followed her.

"I know, but my staff is up for the challenge." She noticed just how quiet the unit was as they walked back to their office to lock up. This evening had been the first time they'd been alone since he'd left her apartment the day they'd been shopping together. She'd expected it to be awkward for the two of them to work together, like it had been when he'd first arrived. Instead Scott had treated her as if nothing had happened between the two of them. As if he'd never kissed her, then walked out, leaving her to decide where their relationship went from there. And where could it really go? He would be leaving in less than three weeks. Of course, they could become lovers until then.

"About the other night…" she started, then stopped. Was this really the time and place to start this conversation?

"Yes?" Scott said. Of course, he wasn't going to make this easy for her.

"I just wanted you to know…" Know what? That she had visions of jumping his body every time she shut her eyes to go to sleep? Why was everything so difficult between them now? Why couldn't she just tell him how much his kisses had affected her? How much she wanted him to kiss her again?

"Look, Fliss, I wasn't trying to pressure you into something you don't want. I just felt like you needed to know where I was coming from. I want you, and I think you want me. But I've been wrong about us before."

His reminder that she had ended things between them stung, though she couldn't fault him for it. He had never understood why she'd wanted to end things between them, even though he had understood that she couldn't leave her parents. He'd never understand how hard that had been for her or why she had thought it would be best for him if the two of them had a clean break.

"It's late and we've got a big day tomorrow. We can talk about this later," he said. He turned the last of the lights out behind them as they walked out.

As they left the hospital and went their separate ways, her excitement for the grand opening the next day was forgotten. All she could concentrate on was where things stood between her and Scott. She was torn in two different directions. One part of her wanted to do what she knew the old Felicity would do: decide what she wanted and go for it. But the other part of her, the one she had become over the last year and a half, that Felicity wanted to do the responsible and safe thing.

No matter what decision she made, there was one thing neither one of them could forget. Scott would be leaving the day after New Year's Day. Their time together was running out. He had left it up to her what happened between them. Was she brave enough to make a decision that could cause them to lose everything they had rebuilt in the last few weeks?

And if she let this chance with Scott go?

You will regret it for the rest of your life.

It was strange sitting at the new nurses' station with the rest of the staff, waiting for a sick patient to arrive. Usually they'd all be enjoying a break in the action, but not today. Scott stretched his legs out in front of him and adjusted his seat. He'd never been one for waiting for something to happen.

The grand opening that day had gone by fast, with

the morning dedicated to giving tours of the unit, first to the hospital board members and then to other staff members, until after noon, when the department officially opened for business.

The phone rang and Felicity quickly answered it. "Brooklyn Heights Cardiac Center."

Scott waited as she took down some notes. "Bring him over. We're ready."

"Fifty-five-year-old male. Shortness of breath. Chest pain radiating down his left arm for thirty minutes. ETA by ground ambulance, ten minutes," she said as she stood and, with the charge nurse, headed to the triage room they had decided would be used for their first patient.

Minutes later two paramedics came in with the expected patient. After helping them move the patient over to the exam table, everyone began to work on the man at once.

"Hi, I'm Dr. Thomas. How are you feeling right now?"

"Not good. This pain is bad. Real bad." The man's voice quivered as he spoke.

"We're going to give you something to help with that right now." Scott nodded to one of the nurses as she drew up the morphine.

"Do you see a cardiologist—" Scott looked down at the paperwork the EMS crew had left "—Mr. Lawrence?"

"Yeah, I had a couple stents put in about a year ago," the man said.

Scott leaned over the patient and began to do his assessment. His skin was damp and his color had become cyanotic. It was clear he was in distress.

One of the nurses who had been left to man the desk stuck her head into the room. "The ER just called. There's a woman in triage with atypical chest pain with EKG changes. They're on their way now. I'm putting them in room three."

"I'll be right there," Felicity said as she started to pull off her gloves.

"You stay here. I'll take this one," said Anna, the charge nurse, as she left the room.

"Is someone getting a twelve-lead?" Scott called out as he studied the rhythm on the monitor on the wall. It clearly showed he was having an MI.

"I've got it," one of the nurses said as she ripped it off the machine and handed it to him.

"Fliss, call the cath lab. I need him there now," Scott said. The EKG clearly showed ST elevations. "We'll use the new room. I just need a team," Scott said as Felicity picked up the phone and punched in numbers. With the cath lab and new center working side by side, this man had a better chance of survival.

"He's gone unresponsive," one of the nurses called. "Blood pressure falling along with heart rate."

Scott quickly checked for a femoral pulse. It was weak but it was there. He noted how cool the patient's skin was against his hand.

"He's going into cardiogenic shock," Scott said as he began pulling the monitors off the man. "We need to go now."

"Have the cath team set up for a balloon pump," he said to Felicity.

"Already done," she said. She joined him and the rest of the staff as they rushed the man's stretcher toward the back entrance to the interventional lab.

"Good luck," Felicity said as she left him.

He looked down at his watch. It had been less than ten

minutes since the patient had arrived in the new unit. It looked like luck was already on his side.

An hour later, when Scott had returned to the unit, almost every room had been filled. Joining Felicity at the front desk, he looked over the central monitors, where he could observe the vital signs and cardiac rhythms from all the patient rooms.

"Welcome to our grand opening," Felicity said with a smile.

"Looks a bit different from this morning, doesn't it?" Scott said as he took a seat.

"Apparently rumors are already circling. Dr. Mason has been back down here and he was very happy when I told him about our success with our first patient," she said.

"The patient has a long way to go, but at least we gave him a good chance. The fact that he made it to the cath lab so fast is definitely a point in his favor." There was no doubt in Scott's mind that if the patient had been kept waiting in the emergency room, he wouldn't have made it.

"Anyone I need to see first?" he asked.

"We called the on-call cardiologist for orders on the woman in room three that came in after Mr. Lawrence and started serial cardiac enzymes on her. She's stable." She pulled up the strip so he could review it. "There's an older man in room five that you should probably see next. He stopped his diuretic and is in new onset atrial fibrillation."

"Okay, that's my next stop, then. If there are any issues, just text me," he said as he headed back down the hallway.

He'd always enjoyed this part of the job. Working

shoulder to shoulder with the nurses and giving direct care to his patients was more satisfying than any other part of his job. The fact that he was getting to share this with Felicity made the experience even more enjoyable, as they'd always been so compatible at work. It was like she knew what he was thinking before he did, which was a bit disturbing considering some of the things he had been thinking lately when he had been around her.

But there was nothing he could do about that. There was more than just mere attraction between the two of them. There always had been. But how long was it going to take for her to accept that? He just hoped she didn't wait too long. The opening of the unit and his work here was almost complete. In less than three weeks, he would be on his way back to London, and this chance to find out what was left between them would be gone.

Felicity had worked many long shifts on cardiac units and later in the emergency room, and none of them had been more demanding than the last twelve hours. Now she sat back at her desk and stared at the computer screen that showed her the day's payroll information, which she needed to approve by the next morning. Finally, when it began to look like the little squiggly lines were chasing each other across the screen, she knew she had to take a break. Closing her eyes, she rested her head on her desk for just a moment.

Too many restless nights caused by memories of that night they'd shared in London were catching up with her and it was all Scott's fault. If he hadn't kissed her that last time in her apartment, those memories would have been left buried. Instead, each night she closed her eyes, she was reminded of every touch, every kiss, that they had shared.

She had planned the rest of their lives around that one night. Their engagement would take place on a romantic trip someplace in the English countryside and their wedding would be an event that their hometown would talk about for days. She'd even planned the children she knew they would have in the years to come: a boy and a girl with their father's dark hair and her blue eyes. It had just been silly musings as Scott had lain next to her. But there had been such a happiness in her heart that night, which had given her hope that finally the two of them would have a future together.

Who could have known that in a few hours both of their lives would change in such a horrible way?

But she wasn't going to let herself think about that right now. She just needed to rest her eyes. Just for a minute.

"Fliss, wake up," Scott said from somewhere beside her.

"No, go away." She turned her head away from the voice that was disturbing her dreams. She wanted to go back to that deep, soft bed where a warm and naked Scott lay next to her. "So nice."

"Fliss, honey, you can't sleep here tonight."

She felt a warm hand run up and down her arm. Opening her eyes, she met soft hazel ones only inches from hers. She recognized those eyes. She leaned over and kissed their owner. "Hey."

She lifted her head up so she could see him better, then noticed his green scrub top. "You've got clothes on."

His strangled cough and laugh stirred something awake in her mind. She made herself lift her head and look around the room. This wasn't Scott's apartment in London.

She groaned and tucked her head between her arms. She'd fallen asleep and had been dreaming. Maybe if she stayed this way, he'd leave her to die of embarrassment alone.

"Do you want to talk about it?" Scott asked. He'd moved away from her, but she could still hear the amusement in his voice.

"No. I want to go back to sleep." She refused to look up. Eventually he would have to leave. She'd just have to outwait him.

"So you can go back to sleep and dream of me without my clothes on?" he asked, his mouth now close to her ear.

She jumped up, connecting with his face.

"Ouch," he said as he put his hand to his jaw, then gave her a wicked smile. "You awake now?"

"Yes, I'm awake, thank you." She moved away from him as she talked. This sexy, flirty Scott was dangerous. "And now I'm going to go home."

She grabbed her computer and started stuffing it into her bag. She'd finish whatever it was that she'd been working on when she got home. Right now her priority was to get away from Scott.

She'd kissed the man and revealed that she'd been dreaming of him without his clothes on, all while being alone in her office. Her work office. And now he was grinning at her like the big bad wolf who wanted to take a bite out of Red Riding Hood.

She just didn't have words. There were none that could undo this embarrassment. She started toward the door.

"You might want to take your coat. It can be cold out there if you don't have enough clothes on."

She went back to the hook beside the door and grabbed her coat before slamming the door behind her. She heard the laughter coming from behind the door and groaned.

She had made it out of the hospital and halfway down

the block to the subway before she slowed her steps. The man was never going to let her live this one down and she couldn't blame him. It wasn't something she would likely forget herself. She'd embarrassed herself many times before in her life, but this would be one for the records.

There was no way she could hide the fact that she wanted to be in Scott's bed now. It was so tempting to just come out and tell him that she wanted to sleep with him. She'd all but told him so tonight. He'd made it clear it was up to her to decide where they took their relationship next. And just because she wanted to become sexually involved with him again didn't mean that there would be any talk of a future. Scott knew her reasons for staying in the States just like she understood that his place was in London at the job he had worked so hard for.

They were two adults who were attracted to each other physically. There was no reason that they couldn't enjoy each other's company physically. Wasn't that just what they had been doing while she was in London? She might have had big dreams about a future after they'd slept together, but neither of them had made any mention of such a future. There had been no talk of love.

Maybe all Scott wanted was a physical relationship. That was okay. She could agree to that. Couldn't she?

All she had to do was go into things with an acceptance that this was just a temporary relationship between the two of them. Maybe this was what she needed in order to move on with her life. To move past her crush on Scott.

Now all she had to do was find some way to tell Scott that she wanted him without making an even bigger fool of herself than she had already.

CHAPTER TEN

SATURDAY MORNING, FELICITY was shocked to find herself out shopping with the rest of the holiday-weary crowd on the last weekend before Christmas. She had always prided herself on getting her shopping done long before the desperate shoppers hit the stores. But here she was, seven days before Christmas, with eyes glazed over from too much window-shopping and feet that would be sporting blisters the next day.

The opening week in the new cardiac department had been a huge success. There had been some issues, mainly on the physicians' side, with policies that needed to be addressed—such as which patients would be escalated to the cardiac center after originally being seen in the emergency room—but Scott had been there to handle those while she had concentrated more on her staff and their patients. And to ensure she didn't find herself being caught asleep at her desk again, she'd started bringing all her administrative work home with her. Not that it mattered—they'd both been too tied up to do more than greet each other in the morning and say good-night as the next shift came in to relieve them.

She'd therefore not had a chance to approach Scott

with her decision to take their relationship further—at least, that was what she was telling herself.

She'd stopped to admire the display of assorted Christmas trees made up from colorful men's ties in bold solids and multicolored stripes. Looking at the store's name on the sign above the door, she realized that this was the small department store she had visited all those years ago as a teenager, shopping for a special present for Scott. The one where she had discovered the scent that she now associated with him.

Had she stopped and admired the store's window display that year? She couldn't remember. Staring at the window, she caught her own reflection. She'd changed so much since then. There were physical changes, of course. Those irritating braces that had plagued her teenage years had been replaced by the straight white teeth the orthodontist had promised and she'd finally moved out of the training-bra section when she'd made it to her sophomore year in high school.

But there was more than that. She'd been a shy teenager, which was one of the reasons she'd followed her brother and his friends around so much, always hanging in the background, never wanting to bring too much attention to herself. Now she stood a little straighter and she was a lot bolder than she'd been before. She had become more confident, something she owed to Scott's encouragement, when she had become a nurse. And she'd been willing to work hard for what she wanted, which had paid off when she had applied for her new position. So why couldn't she make herself move on with her personal life?

Because she was afraid. She'd built up her idea of what her perfect life was going to be, and when she'd lost Leo, she'd lost that perfect dream. She was a nurse. She knew life was messy and difficult and sometimes ended in heartbreaking ways, but for some reason she hadn't ever thought that would be her life. But now she knew that, like every other human, she had no guarantee. And without that guarantee she was too afraid to take the next step.

She turned to face one of the mirrors on the shop wall and looked herself in the eye. It was time for her to move on, and the first thing she needed to do was grab this opportunity to be with Scott for the short time they had together. She looked over to where the ties dangled from a tall, thin tree. To start, she would find the perfect present to show him that she did still care for him.

As the store doors opened and she entered, she felt a little bit more Christmas spirit awaken inside her. This might be the only Christmas they would ever get to spend together. It wouldn't be perfect, not without her brother here, but she was going to make great memories that she could relive for the years that were to come. And for now that would just have to be enough.

Felicity waited till the end of the day to approach Scott with her invitation. He'd spent most of the day on the unit, only having to take one patient over to the cath lab for an intervention, but she'd never found quite the right opportunity, and with the next day being Christmas Eve, time was running out.

"About Christmas," she started, as he stepped into their office.

"We're not back to that again, are we? There's no reason for you to take a train when I'm already making the trip in the car." Scott's voice held a note of agitation she wasn't used to hearing, but they were both tired, so she let it go.

"No. It's not that. I was thinking…" she caught herself looking down at her shoes and made herself look up "…maybe you'd like to come over the night before and we could just leave from my place the next morning."

She knew the moment he realized she was inviting him to spend the night with her when his eyes shot to hers and didn't leave.

"Are you sure?" he asked as he walked toward her.

He stopped in front of her with only inches between them. Desire sparked between them with an energy that shocked her heart into a dangerous rhythm.

"Oh, yeah. I'm very sure." Her voice was thick with a passion she'd denied for too long. She wanted this man, no matter what the outcome might be. If only she had admitted this to herself earlier. She'd wasted so much time fighting it.

He pushed a small strand of hair that had come loose from its tie behind her ear and let his finger linger as it traced a path from her ear down her neck. Was he remembering how sensitive her neck was to the touch of his lips? How she'd cried out for him when he'd bitten that perfect spot between her neck and collarbone as she came? Did he remember every touch, every kiss, the way she did?

Her breath caught in her throat and she stepped closer.

"Not here. Not like this," he said as he brushed another unseen hair back from her face, then stepped away. "Tomorrow. We'll have the whole night."

She took a deep breath and calmed her breathing. He was right. This wasn't the place.

"I'm only scheduled for half the day tomorrow, so I

can take care of supper." She moved as far away from him as possible while she gathered her bag and coat.

"I'll make a bargain with you. If you can help me wrap a few presents, I'll bring dinner," Scott said.

"You haven't wrapped a thing, have you?" Felicity couldn't help but laugh at his guilty look. His mother had always spoiled him by wrapping his presents for him.

"I had most of them wrapped at the store. It's just the ones when we went shopping together at the market that need to be wrapped."

"Okay, dinner is on you," she said as she opened the door to leave.

"And after dinner?" he asked.

"That's all on you too," she said before shutting the door. She'd done it. She'd made a decision that would move things forward with Scott. And if the last few minutes were any sign, there would be no waiting till after dinner.

Scott knocked on Felicity's door and waited. It felt like he had done a lot of waiting for Felicity. And after her reaction to him the night before in the office, waiting for tonight had been especially difficult. Everywhere he had turned that day, he'd seen her, and his mind happily sent him memories of the two of them together that one night in his apartment in London.

He repositioned the box he held in his arm, then switched the takeout bag and his duffel bag into his other hand so he could check his jacket pocket. He felt the length of the small jewelry box and relaxed. Of all the Christmas gifts he had bought, this one was the most important to him.

The door opened and he fumbled the box in his arm.

Dressed in a red formfitting dress that skimmed the tops of her knees and matching high heels that had his mouth watering, Felicity was a sight even his imagination had been unable to dream up. Gone were the boxy hospital scrubs and the comfy jeans that he associated with his friend Fliss. Instead some beautiful blonde heartbreaker stood in her place. He could do nothing but stand there and stare.

"Here, let me take some of those," she said as she moved toward him.

He cleared his throat, then entered the apartment while making sure that he kept some space between the two of them. "No, I've got them."

Scott looked around the room. There had been some changes here too. A poinsettia sat on the table along with two red candles and a small nativity scene on the fireplace mantel. Pillows in soft blues lay on the couch with a throw blanket that matched. The apartment had seemed so sterile and unwelcoming the first time he'd seen it, and he'd been shocked at how different it had looked compared to the homey little place she had rented in London. But now, with the small changes she had made, he could see her living here.

"The place looks nice," he said as he crossed the room and placed the rest of the items by the couch.

"Thanks. Someone told me Christmas was coming, so I decided I'd better get ready." She smiled at him as her eyes danced with merriment and his heart turned over. This was the woman he'd been waiting for, the Felicity Dale who was a little bit cheeky and a whole lot of excitement. Somehow she'd found her way back to him and he wasn't willing to wait another minute.

"How hungry are you?" he asked as he slowly made his way over to her.

He came to a stop with barely an inch between them and she didn't move away. Instead she stepped closer, laying her hand on his chest. Did she feel his heart as it hammered in his chest? Did she realize that it beat just for her?

He wrapped his hand around her neck and pulled her closer as he angled his mouth over hers. She opened at the first touch of his lips and he filled his mouth with the sweet taste of her. He wrapped his other arm around her waist and pulled her against him so she could feel the hard length of him. It might be too soon to let her know how much he cared for her, but he wanted her to feel just how much he wanted her. She rubbed her body against his and her moan was more than he could take.

Remembering all those sappy romantic movies she used to make him watch with her, he lifted her up in his arms.

"Wrap your legs around me," he said as he adjusted her body against his, then headed for the only door that led from the room. He placed her on the bed, then unwound her legs from around him one by one. He unstrapped one high heel, then ran his hands up her leg, massaging her calf and trailing his fingertips higher up her thigh until he could go no farther before placing that leg down and then repeating his movements on her next leg. When he got to the top of her thigh this time, he glided his hand over the red panties she wore. The soft silk was damp from her desire for him and he lingered there for a moment, stroking her gently when she opened her legs for him. Her moans became louder when he pressed the palm of his hand against her and he followed the path of his hands with his lips, stopping when he reached the inside of her thigh.

"Scott." She moaned his name and something broke inside him. He remembered the way she had called out his name when he'd entered her for the first time. He'd taste every inch of her before the night was over, but right now he just needed to be inside of her.

Pushing her dress up, he trailed his lips up her chest to her mouth. Their kisses became desperate and demanding. She helped him pull her dress over her head and her lacy red bra followed. Moving back to the end of the bed, he made quick work of his own clothes and then stood for a moment, taking in the sight of the passionate woman who lay on the bed before him. She was clad only in red silk panties, her sapphire eyes flashing with desire. Her lips, bruised from their kisses, stood out against her pale porcelain skin. He'd never seen a woman more beautiful than Felicity Dale.

He covered her with his body and they both moaned as he entered her. He took a moment to take in the vision she made as her eyes burned into him. He bent his mouth to her ear and whispered, "Never forget this. Never forget the way I feel inside you, the way we fit so perfectly. Promise me that."

"Yes," she moaned as she arched against him. "I'll always remember."

She arched against him again and he sank into her. He wouldn't let her forget him again.

He began to move inside her as she rocked against him. He fought for control. He wanted this night to last. She cried out his name and he lost the battle. She shattered around him, and time stood still as all breath left his body and he broke into a million pieces inside her.

When he was able to pull himself back together, he rolled over, taking her with him until she rested on top of him. Brushing his hand against her soft hair, he closed his eyes and let himself drift off.

Felicity had watched Scott from afar for so many years, but she'd never seen him like this. His body relaxed and his respirations were deep and even. At that moment he appeared so vulnerable. She rested her head on his chest and listened to the steady drum of his heartbeat, trying to relax her own body. He'd made her promise that she wouldn't forget the way they fit together and how could she? Never had a man made her feel so desired. Never had she ever felt so much desire for another man. There had never been another man for her.

That thought cleared away the rest of the sexual haze that had engulfed her. That was a dangerous path that her mind wanted to take, and she wasn't ready to find out where it would lead. Too many obstacles lay in the way of this being anything but a fling for the two of them. Nothing had changed since she had sent Scott back to London without her. She still wasn't willing to leave her parents alone. London was so far away. That was what she needed to remember.

But she wasn't going to let that ruin the time they had right now. They had only a few days left together and she wasn't going to waste them. Tomorrow they would spend the day with their families, but the next day they would return to the city, where most of their time would be spent at work. There were only a few hours that they could spend alone together, and they needed to make the most of those. After he was gone, she could sit alone and feel sorry for herself. But not now. Right now she needed to live in the present and enjoy every moment they had left together.

She closed her eyes and rested her head against him. For now she was just going to enjoy the warmth of him against her.

When she opened her eyes later, she was greeted with the spicy smell of tomato sauce. Stretching, she climbed out of bed and grabbed the first thing she saw—Scott's long-sleeved shirt—before she headed into the bathroom. After putting herself back together, she rescued her red panties from the bedsheets, then headed for the kitchen, where she found Scott fighting a piece of Christmas wrapping paper as he tried to cover the small sailboat he had bought his father.

"Hey," he said as he started to get up from the table. "Did you come to rescue me?"

"I think it's your father's present that needs rescuing. Let me see if I can find a box for it," she said as she returned to her bedroom.

When she came back with a small box, the sailboat and wrapping had been removed and plates piled high with red sauce and pasta had taken their place. He had lit the candles and turned the lights down. With the Christmas tree lights and the glow from the fireplace, the room had an intimate feel that was just the mood she had wanted to set earlier in the evening.

"Ready to eat?" he asked as he poured them each a glass of a Moscato wine—her favorite. Still shirtless because she had refused to give him back the shirt that she had on, he'd pulled on only his pants and left the top button undone. He looked good enough to eat himself. Her stomach growled, but she wasn't sure it was from her need for food. They'd both starve to death if she didn't get her mind on something else.

"Sure. Then you can do the dishes while I take care of the presents," she said as she looked over at a mess of Christmas wrapping paper that had been pulled out and piled up on her couch.

They talked about everything—their work, of course, and then their parents' plans for the next day, and Scott even talked about his work in London. They talked about everything, except what she was sure was on both of their minds. But what was there really to say? They'd both enjoy this time together and then things would go back to the way they were before Scott had come back to New York.

No, that wasn't true. She'd changed in the last few weeks. She'd taken a step toward returning to a life that held more for her than just work, and she didn't think she could go back there again.

As she finished wrapping Scott's presents, she glanced over at the opening to her kitchen, where she could see him washing her dishes. He was the proof that there was nothing as sexy as a man doing dishes. Was it wrong to wish for more dirty dishes just so she could continue to watch him? No, not at all.

Making a decision, she pushed the wrapping paper aside and stood. There was only one present left to wrap and it could wait until the morning. The clock on her mantel showed it was fast approaching midnight and she couldn't think of anything she wanted more than Scott for her Christmas present.

Wrapping her arms around him from behind, she ran her hands up his bare chest. He stopped with his hands still holding a serving dish, his body tensed under her hands. The feel of his muscled back against her breast had her rubbing against him just like one of her mother's old cats. Thinking of those cats, she put her mouth to his earlobe and bit down lightly before licking away the sting and whispering into his ear, "It's almost Christmas and I've finally decided what I want."

"And what would that be?" Scott's voice was as tense as his body.

"All I want from Santa this Christmas, right here, right now, is you," she said, moving back as he turned in her arms and placed his soapy hands under her bottom, pulling her against him.

"I think that's something I can take care of without Santa's help," he said as he bent his head to hers, making all her Christmas wishes come true.

CHAPTER ELEVEN

THEY'D HAD TO rush the next morning to get ready to leave for the Christmas dinner at her parents' house. As she packed her bag for the trip, she tried to keep her mind off the fact that she would have to spend tonight alone. There were so few nights left for them that the thought of spending one apart seemed unbearable.

"It will be fine," Scott said as he took her hand and squeezed it as they sat outside her parents' house. "Your parents know what they're doing. If they thought they couldn't handle Christmas at their house, they would have told my parents."

They had held hands on the journey, but when they had stopped in her parents' drive, she had pulled away.

"And I'll be here too," Scott said as he opened the door to his car and climbed out.

"I know," she said when she joined him on the sidewalk.

After making their way inside the house, she found her dad in the living room, watching a football game. She left Scott with all the men as she went into the crowded kitchen and pushed her way past aunts and cousins.

"There you are," her mother said as she pulled Felicity to her for a hug. She let herself relax against her mom's shoulders. Her mom was a strong woman, but Leo's death had shaken her. There was no way for them to get through this holiday get-together without being reminded of her brother.

Felicity pulled away and looked her mom in the eyes. "Are you okay?"

Her mom gave her a watery smile. "It helps that everyone is here."

"You sure?" she asked.

Her mother nodded, then hugged her again. "You smell nice. Kind of woodsy. New perfume?"

"I wondered when you were going to show up," Scott's mother said as she came up behind her.

She'd known that kiss she'd shared with Scott right before they'd arrived had been a mistake.

"Yeah, it's different, right?" Felicity said to her mother before she turned to Scott's.

"Scott's in the den with the rest of the freeloaders waiting for food to magically appear," Felicity said as she tried to move away from the two of them. She had no doubt Scott's mother would recognize her son's scent. Of course, she could use the excuse that she had been closed up in his car on their drive there.

Her mom nodded before she was pulled away to handle someone's question concerning something that had just come out of the oven. Unfortunately Scott's mother remained.

"Your mom is doing fine," she said as they both stared after Felicity's mother. "She's strong. So is your dad. You don't have to worry about them."

"I don't… Okay, I do," Felicity admitted. "It's just so hard, especially around the holidays. I can't help but worry."

"I know, but you need to understand that they worry about you too. You're their little girl, no matter how old you are," Scott's mother said. "And I'll always be there for your mom. Just like Scott will always be there for you."

Did his mother suspect what was going on between Felicity and Scott? The woman was as intuitive as her son. Did things like that run in families?

"We're actually looking into taking a couples' cruise together for Valentine's," she said, shocking Felicity even more.

Her parents on a cruise? Wouldn't they have a ball, especially with their best friends along with them.

But what if they got sick? They could end up in some primitive hospital that wouldn't be able to take proper care of them. There was that special travel insurance that they could get that would fly them back to the US with a medical flight team.

She realized Scott's mother was waiting on her to say something. Did Scott's mother think she was going to try to talk her parents out of a trip that they deserved? Okay, maybe it had crossed her mind.

"They'll love that," Felicity said as she laid her hand on the other woman's arm and squeezed. "Thank you for being there for Mom and Dad. It means a lot to me to know that you're here for them. I'm still a couple hours away. We're all so lucky to have you close by."

Afraid that her mother would catch sight of her senti-mental tears, Felicity excused herself and took the back stairs out of the kitchen and up to the second floor. She stopped at her brother's door. Her parents were going to be okay. They'd survived the last year and they were starting to put their lives back together. Was she holding them back?

"Hi. Mom said I'd find you up here," Scott said as he came up behind her and put an arm across her back. To someone else, they would just look like two friends comforting one another, but she knew the difference now. She leaned into him and rested her head on his shoulder.

"Do the two of you have some type of special power?" she asked, then realized how crazy that sounded. "Don't answer that. It was a stupid question."

"My mom, no. But if you let me in your window tonight, I can show you all my special powers." He wiggled his eyebrows at her and she laughed.

"There's no way you're spending the night with me in my room with my parents downstairs, no matter what your special powers might be," Felicity said as she moved away from him.

He pulled her back into his arms and kissed her with just enough heat to make her consider pulling him into her room right then. "What if I use my special power of being super quiet?"

"Not even an invisibility power is going to get you in there tonight," Felicity said as she took a deep breath and tried to calm her heart.

"We could go down to the lake," Scott said as she started to move away from him.

"And get caught like a bunch of teenagers? In our hometown, where everyone knows us? It would not only embarrass our parents, but it would shock the granny panties off Ms. Connors." She moved farther out of the reach of his arms.

"Why did you have to say that?" he said as he headed

for the stairs. "The woman's downstairs and you have to bring up her underwear?"

She followed him down the stairs as he grumbled some more about her ruining Christmas with images of his old schoolteacher that he didn't want to see. Laughing, they joined everyone else who was already gathered around the table, waiting for her father to lead the blessing of the meal. Then chaos broke out in the room as everyone began to pass the food. Scott slipped his hand into hers under the table, and if anyone noticed that Scott seemed to suddenly be eating with his left hand, no one commented.

The merry crowd moved into the living room, where her parents' tree was surrounded by presents, which were quickly given out, and the crowd was dispersed to different areas to start cleaning.

"I love this cookbook," Scott's mother said as she leafed through the yellowed pages. It had been a lucky find in one of the vintage bookstores in the city. "My mother had one just like it, but my sister laid claim to it when we were taking care of my mother's estate. And, Scott, the sweater you bought me is so soft. I've never had real cashmere. And I love this pastel blue color. It's so unlike your usual presents."

"I told you," she said after Scott's mother moved off to thank someone else for their gift.

"And I didn't argue. I'm really not good at buying gifts. Except for yours. I think I did very well with yours," Scott said as he moved in closer and bent down to whisper in her ear. "And I can't wait till I can give it to you."

She and Scott had decided to wait till that evening

when they could find somewhere to be alone to exchange their gifts for each other.

Leaving him talking with one of her cousins about the stock market, she went looking for her father, who had bought her a soft brandy-colored leather tote that she could use for work. When she couldn't find him in the living room, she returned to the dining room and found him sitting in a dining-room chair, rubbing his chest.

"Daddy, are you okay?" She rushed to him as she called out for Scott.

"I'm fine, baby girl. It's just a bit of indigestion," he said, though he continued to rub at his chest.

"What is it?" Scott asked, bending down beside Felicity as she took her father's pulse. She counted out the beats as she looked at her watch. His pulse was at a regular rate and rhythm; his skin was dry and his color was good.

"He's having chest pain," she said as she counted her father's respirations. "I need my stethoscope. I think we should call 911," she said as she turned toward Scott.

"Hold on a moment, Fliss. It's not my heart," her father said as he began to stand, only to find her pushing him back down into the chair. "Look, calm down. I just ate too much today. Go get your mother and tell her I need my medicine."

"You're taking medicine? What kind of medicine?" As far as she knew, her father didn't have any health issues.

"I'll go find your mother. I'll be right back," Scott said as he started out of the room, pushing past a crowd that had gathered at the door to the dining room. Felicity hadn't noticed. "Everything's fine now. He just needs to sit for a few minutes."

Her father was a quiet and proud man, and she knew

he wouldn't want this kind of attention. This was her fault. She had panicked and now she had made things worse for him.

"I'm sorry, Daddy. I didn't mean to cause a scene." She leaned her head against her father's shoulder.

"It's okay. I should have told you I've been having some stomach issues." Her father looked uncomfortable, but more from embarrassment than pain. "I've got this hiatal hernia and the doctor thinks I need to have a surgical procedure. He's going to do one of those laparoscopic procedures next month."

"Why didn't you tell me?" she asked, though she already knew the answer.

"You worry too much, baby girl. And you've got that new job you're so excited about. We were going to tell you when the time came." Her father looked up as her mother came into the room, carrying a bottle and a glass of water.

"I told you not to overdo it today," her mother said as she handed him the pills and water. "He's supposed to eat smaller meals, you know. But it's Christmas and I didn't want to scold him."

Her father rolled his eyes behind her mother, making Felicity smile.

"It wasn't him. I'm the one that panicked, though I'm glad he told me about the surgical procedure." She turned her eyes back to her mother. "Is there anything else you haven't told me?"

"Of course not, honey. The doctor assured us he would be fine. It's a common enough procedure," her mother said as she patted her husband's hand. "To be honest, it's worrying about upsetting you that's given us the most trouble."

Felicity stared at her mother and father. Had she been hovering so much that now they felt the need to tiptoe around their problems so she didn't become upset? "I'm sorry. I don't mean to worry. And I certainly don't mean to worry the two of you."

"We know that," her father said. "We just want you to live your life and be happy."

She moved away from him. Why did everyone think she wasn't happy?

"While your father's medication starts working, why don't you go with me to run Ms. Connors home?" Scott asked from beside her. "If that's okay with your parents?"

"Of course it's okay. We appreciate you running Irma home," Felicity's mother said. "I'll sit here with your daddy, Fliss. You go with Scott."

Scott took her hand and pulled her up. "She's waiting at the door for us."

Felicity grabbed her coat and helped the older woman down the steps to the sidewalk. She let Scott take charge of the conversation as he drove. She didn't want to talk. She wanted to think.

"I never intended to make things worse for my parents," she said when Scott returned from helping Ms. Connors into her house.

"You didn't make things worse, Fliss. They just worry about you, like all parents worry. My mother worries that I'm going to grow old all alone. My father worries that I'm not preparing for my retirement. Different worries, I know, but they can really get wound up about it." Scott put the car into Reverse, but instead of turning back toward her house, he turned out of the neighborhood and took a road that led into the park. He parked where they could watch some of the kids try out the new sleds they'd just received that morning from Santa, while those more experienced shot past them as they slid down the hill.

"I wanted to give you this here," he said as he handed her a small jeweler's box. He hadn't attempted to wrap it. Instead it had red ribbon that he had tied into a neat bow around it. She recognized the insignia. It was the same one that had been on the jewelry bag that had caused her so much jealousy over another woman who didn't exist.

"I don't have yours with me. It's back at the house in my suitcase," she said as she turned the box over in her hand. "It doesn't seem right opening this without you having yours."

"You can give it to me when we get back to your parents' house. Just open it already. You know you want to," Scott said. He was watching her with so much pleasure. Whatever was in the box had to mean something special to him.

Sliding the ribbon off, she opened the box and stared at the beautiful white-gold snowflake that was covered in small diamonds, with one larger one in its center, hanging from a delicate white-gold chain.

"It's beautiful."

Suddenly it made sense why he had brought her here to give it to her. He wanted it to be a remembrance of their time together in the snow.

"I love it," she said as she bent over the console of the seat and kissed him. Their lips touched and lingered together for a moment, and then he reached for her. As one hand tangled in her hair, the other cupped her face. Letting go of the small box, she opened her mouth and her hands slipped around his neck, curling into his hair.

A child shouted close beside the car and they broke

apart. Looking around, they both laughed when they saw it was only a child calling out for his mother.

"I really like my gift," she said as she settled back against the car seat.

"I'm glad," he said as he relaxed into his own seat.

They watched the kids in the park until the sun started to go down and everyone began to head home. By the time they made it back to Felicity's parents' house, the crowd had gone, along with Scott's parents. After checking on her dad, Scott excused himself so he could spend some time with his own parents before he had to return to the city. It would be the last time he would see them before he returned to London.

It wasn't until she was getting ready for bed that she remembered the present she hadn't given him.

There was a tapping sound coming from his window. Scott turned over and groaned. He'd been tossing for two hours and now this. Had some bird gotten caught up in the screen? Climbing out of bed, he opened the curtains, but couldn't see a thing in the darkness. Suddenly a bright light blinded him and he stumbled back against a chair. He was about to shout out to his father that there was an intruder when he saw Fliss's face pressed against the window.

"Everything okay, son?" his father called from the room next door.

"Sorry, just got up for…something…and slipped," he said as he put his finger to his lips to warn her not to make a sound. When his father didn't answer him back, he figured it was safe to assume he'd fallen back to sleep.

Scott slid the window up carefully and was greeted by a small wrapped package in a gloved hand that was shivering.

"What are you doing here?" he asked, as he leaned out the window into the cold air. The weather channel had called for temperatures in the twenties, but the windchill meant it felt much colder.

"I wanted you to have your Christmas present before Christmas was over," she said as her teeth chattered.

"Get in here," he said as he reached out for her, but she pulled away.

"I've got to get back before my parents miss me." She leaned in and kissed him with lips as cold as ice. "I hope you like it."

Before he could say another word, she turned and headed off into the dark. He waited for a minute, hoping she'd come back, before finally shutting the window. Picking up the package, he removed the carefully wrapped paper, then opened the small jewelry box. Lying on a white cushion was a tiepin in the shape of a Christmas tree with a small diamond sitting on its top. Too awake to sleep now, he sat on the bed and stared at the small Christmas tree. It wasn't something he would have chosen for himself, but he knew he would wear it every Christmas for the rest of his life in remembrance of his and Felicity's time together.

Finally he put the box down and climbed back into bed. He knew he'd dream of Fliss tonight. He just didn't know if it would be memories of their time together or fantasies of a future he wasn't sure they would ever have.

CHAPTER TWELVE

SCOTT FOUND FELICITY in the storage closet with a clip-board and a pen. He pulled the door shut behind him.

"Hey," she said as she turned when he came into the small room. "Are you already finished for the day?"

"I am, but I can wait for you," Scott said. He moved behind her, placed his arms around her and nuzzled her neck. "Because you're definitely worth waiting for."

"Scott," she said as she pulled away from him. "My nurses are right down the hall."

"I shut the door," he said, laughing at the shocked look on her face.

"It doesn't have a lock. Anyone could come in." She moved over to another shelf of medical supplies and pre-tended to ignore him.

The hospital had been busy after Christmas and it was no surprise to either of them that their time together had been limited to quick conversations in passing at work.

But the nights… They'd made the most of every mo-ment of those. He'd checked out of his hotel the day after Christmas and moved in with Felicity that night so that there would be no wasted time going back and forth. Instead, each night they would rush home and cook together—okay, he did most of the actual cooking—and then they'd fall into bed together, both of them anxious and desperate for that first moment when they would come together, skin to skin. They'd free their passion for each other from the chains they kept in place while pretending to be only coworkers to everyone else around them. Only, it still wasn't enough. There was still something missing when they came together, something that Fliss was holding back from him.

"All right, I'm done," she said as she closed her clipboard and moved toward him. "The rest can wait till tomorrow. Let's go home."

Home. Didn't that sound nice? But where was his home? His parents had set down roots in the same town and in the same house where they had first married. In some ways that house still felt like home. Not the small bedroom where he'd spent his childhood, but the comfortable atmosphere that told him this was where he belonged. This was where he could be himself. He'd almost achieved that in his own apartment in London. But there always seemed to be something missing.

Except for that one night with Felicity.

That night had made everything in his life feel right. Just like tonight when they'd enter her small apartment and everything would feel right. Like he had come home.

"I received an interesting invitation from Dr. Mason today," Scott said as he started the car. "One of the board members is having this high-class New Year's Eve party tomorrow night and invited us to attend."

"Us?" Felicity said as she turned toward him. "Or you?"

"Where I go, you go," he said, then winced at the words. Not that he didn't wish the words were true, but that would have to be Fliss's choice. He wouldn't demand that she come anywhere with him, no matter what it might cost him.

And he knew that if he pushed her, she'd run—or more likely push him totally out of her life. He'd let her do that before. It wasn't going to happen again. He'd fight for their friendship if that was all they could have together.

And he'd fight for the future he could see for the two of them, but he wouldn't let himself be hurt again. The loss of Leo and then of Felicity had been too much. His first months back in London had been miserable for both him and the people around him. It was only his work that had saved him then. He wasn't prepared to revisit that pain. He had picked himself up and started over once. He wasn't sure he could repeat it.

"The invitation was for two, but I could tell that Dr. Mason was expecting you would be the plus-one." The older man was very astute, something that had surely helped him climb the ladder to the cardiac medical chief position.

"Where's the venue?" she asked, then whistled when he told her the name of the hotel. "That place is amazing. I don't have anything to wear to a place like that."

"You have that red dress. You look amazing in that dress." Just thinking about that outfit was enough to set his body blazing with his need for her. They would definitely be having another late-night dinner. Some things a body needed more than food and sleep.

"Too simple. It needs to be dressier. I'm thinking something classic for a party at a place like that," she said, as she looked out the car window, then turned back to him. "Don't worry. I know the owner of a little vintage store that's bound to have something."

But her smile seemed sadder than he had expected, not excited like he had thought she would be at the opportunity of a night out on the town.

"It's okay if you don't want to go," he said. He parked the car, then turned to her. "It will be fine. I know you're too busy at work to have to worry about getting prepared for a last-minute invitation to a party."

"It's not that. Any other time I'd love to go to a swanky New Year's Eve party." She bit down on her lip before she continued. "But we only have three more nights before you leave. I don't want to share you with all of those other people."

He grabbed her hand and pulled her into the apartment building and up the stairs. "And I don't want to share you with anyone else either. I'll just tell them we have other plans."

"You can't do that. Dr. Mason is expecting you. Maybe we can just stay a little while. If we slip out early, no one will notice," she said as he took her keys and opened her door.

"That will work," he said as he pulled her inside the apartment. "I've just got one question."

As soon as the door shut, she was in his arms. "What's that?"

She had wound her arms around his neck, and his body was instantly aroused. "What would it take to get you back into that little red dress?"

"Wow," Scott said as she turned in a circle, letting the hem of the long blue sequined dress brush against the floor.

Finding the perfect dress for such an occasion on New Year's Eve day had been a miracle and a hit to her monthly budget, but seeing that look in his eyes made it worth curbing her daily trips to the specialty coffee shop across from the hospital. With the dress's open back and low neckline, along with its fitted waist, it looked as if it had been made for a night on the red carpet. Of course, the fact that she'd found it in a secondhand store meant that it could actually have walked one of those red carpets.

"But it has sequins," Scott said as he joined her in front of the mirror, wearing a classic black suit and snowy white shirt. She knew they would make a stunning entrance tonight.

"You don't like sequins?" she asked as she made one more attempt to get a good look at the back of the dress. The salesclerk had assured her that the dress covered all the necessary parts, but there seemed to be a whole lot of dress missing in the back. She could only hope that the heating would be turned up in the ballroom.

"I like sequins," she said. "They're very glamorous. That doesn't mean they should be arranged into the shape of a fish and worn on some poor woman's chest."

"I'll never understand," Scott said as he moved to the dresser, then returned and handed her the little Christmas tree tiepin she'd given him.

It might have been after Christmas, but with her wearing her snowflake necklace, it seemed right that he wore her gift too. She attached the pin, then turned and picked up her wrap and clutch purse.

"Is it too late to cancel?" Scott said as he pulled her into his arms. He ran his hands down her bare back until they came to rest where the dress draped across the top of her bottom. When his hand slid inside, a shiver ran up her spine, followed by a flush of heat.

"Rain check?" she asked as she raised her lips to his for a short kiss that quickly became hot and demanding.

"I can think of so many ways to get you out of that dress," he said as he walked her back toward the bed.

Turning quickly, she ducked under his arm and headed for the front door. She'd almost made it when his arms caught her and pulled her back against him. "I'll give you until midnight. Then that dress is coming off. For both our sakes, let's hope we escape this party before the ball drops. Otherwise we're going to shock more than the granny panties off poor Ms. Connors."

When they stepped into the ballroom, Felicity was surprised at the number of people she recognized. There were senators and business moguls that she had seen on news reports on television, along with actors and actresses she had never dreamed of meeting.

"Are you sure this is the right place?" she asked as she took a glass of champagne from a waiter.

"Our names were on the guest list, so I'm thinking it has to be," Scott said as he took his own glass from the waiter. "There's no way they would have missed us if we hadn't shown up."

"Don't be so sure. I see Dr. Mason heading our way," she said.

"There you are, Scott. And, Felicity, you look lovely this evening. I'm so glad you could make it. And I know you'll have a lovely evening. Mr. Bernhardt always throws the best parties. He's been throwing a New Year's Eve party for as long as I've been at Brooklyn Heights. Most of the board members are here with their spouses, and of course there are a lot of people who have made donations to the hospital this year," Dr. Mason said as he looked around the room. "There he is. Do you mind if I borrow Scott for just a minute?"

She watched as Scott was dragged away to meet a nice-looking older man who seemed to be holding court in the middle of the ballroom. She had met most of the board members, but she didn't recognize this particular one.

While she waited for Scott, she wandered over to where a buffet had been set up. She had to admit that Dr. Mason was right. Mr. Bernhardt did throw a nice party. Pulling her phone out, she searched for their distinguished host and was surprised to find he was a self-made billionaire who had earned his fortune in construction.

"I feel like a trick pony," Scott said when he joined her.

"Really, what tricks do you do?" she asked.

"Ha ha," Scott said as he picked up a small cracker and popped it into his mouth. "At least I'm getting some treats."

"I don't know if he's showing you off or if he's courting you," she said as they began to move around the room, making a game out of seeing how many celebrities they each could find.

"Maybe," Scott said.

"I can't wait till I can call my mom tomorrow and tell her about all the people we've seen tonight."

"Can we leave yet? I'm pretty sure Dr. Mason has forgotten all about us," Scott said as he looked down at his watch.

"And take me home without even one dance on New Year's Eve?" she asked as she took his arm. "What kind of date are you?"

"A date that wants to be alone with you." He tapped the face of his watch before he pulled her into his arms. "We have less than two hours till midnight."

For the next hour, as the room buzzed with conversations that would be spread across the tabloids the next day and million-dollar deals were formed, the two of them danced as if they were the only two people in the room. And as far as Scott and Felicity were concerned, they were.

They made it back inside her apartment with fifteen minutes to spare. Her dress now lay puddled on the floor at the front door, along with his jacket and tie. She'd stripped him of his white shirt in the dining room. His pants lay in the doorway.

"If I'd known you had nothing on under that dress, we never would have made it out of the bedroom," he said as he kissed his way down her chest.

"I had on a thong," she said, then moaned when he took one of her nipples into his mouth and sucked it.

She gripped his back and knew tomorrow he would find where she had marked him with her little love scratches. His hand moved between her legs and she arched her body against his talented fingers.

"Yes, there," she moaned as she covered his neck with her kisses. He knew her body so well, touching her in just the right spot at the exact, perfect time. But then he had always known what she needed and when. It was his superpower.

His fingers became more insistent and his thrusts more demanding. He filled her up until she overflowed with a pleasure that consumed her, body and soul. She had been so empty before, but as pleasure overwhelmed her, it was too much to contain. She anchored herself to him with her arms and her legs. She wouldn't let go. She needed him too much. She screamed his name as wave after wave of pleasure rolled through her.

As the sound of "Auld Lang Syne" filled the room, Scott followed her into the New Year.

He woke her up later with soft kisses trailing down her spine, before he flipped her over onto her back. Their lovemaking was slow and easy this time, with intimate touches and kisses that soothed rather than excited. When he entered her, she wrapped her arms around him and pulled him down on top of her. She needed to feel every part of him against her. As they slowly moved together, she knew she would never be loved by another man like this one. It was as if they had been made to fit perfectly together. They matched each stroke, until their bodies gave way to a warm pleasure that was just as satisfying as the demanding lovemaking they had shared earlier that night.

As she dozed off to sleep, she rested her head against Scott's chest and listened to the strong, steady beat of his heart while tears ran down her cheeks. Only here in the dark, while he slept beneath her, could she admit how much she was going to miss this...miss him. In a day he would be gone and she would be left with the memories of their time together here in her apartment. Would they haunt her the same way her memories of Leo did?

How was she to go on alone after all they had shared? How was she supposed to learn to settle for the life she'd had before Scott had returned to New York? She knew things wouldn't go back to the way they'd been before. Even though things had changed after they'd become sexually involved, they still had a friendship that neither one could deny.

When sleep finally pulled her under, she dreamed of ballrooms and dances with princes, but then the clock would sound that it was midnight and suddenly she found herself back in her apartment and her Prince Charming was nowhere in sight.

CHAPTER THIRTEEN

"FLISS, WAKE UP," Scott said as he gently shook her. There was no reason to make this any harder than it was going to be by startling her out of sleep. "Honey, you have to wake up now."

Sleepy blue eyes blinked open, and his heart dropped into his stomach. He didn't want to be the person who had to do this. Not again. Hadn't she lost enough already? Hadn't they both? Would it be too much to ask to have everything go right for one more day?

He thought of the small jewelry box he had tucked into his suit pocket the night before. He should have shown it to her last night.

And he was a selfish jerk thinking of his own happiness right now.

"Honey, I need you to sit up and listen to me." Scott moved over so she could reposition herself.

"What's wrong?" she asked, her voice still hoarse from sleep, her innocent eyes still foggy.

There was no way to say this without her panicking, he knew that, but he wanted to avoid it as much as possible. "Your mother just called. They've taken your father to the hospital."

"What?" she asked as she moved away from him. "What's wrong with him? Is it his stomach again?"

"No, honey, the doctor in the emergency room at home says it's an MI. They're going to take him to the cath lab." He watched as her face went pale. "I told them we would meet them at the hospital."

"We have to go. I need to be there. I should have been there," Felicity said as she jumped off the bed and headed to the bathroom, shutting the door behind her.

He waited outside the door, ready to step in if she sounded like she needed him. When she opened the door, her face had more color, but her eyes had lost the sparkle from the night before.

It took only minutes for the two of them to dress and pack a bag. Not knowing what they would find when they arrived at the hospital, they wanted to be prepared.

"When exactly did my mom call?" Felicity asked him as they buckled their seat belts.

He pulled out of the parking place and was happy to see that traffic was light. Most people were still in bed, sleeping off all the celebrating they had done the night before. "About two or three minutes before I woke you." He looked down at his watch. "About thirty minutes ago. She said she'd call back as soon as she knew something. I told her to call my cell phone."

"She called my phone," she said. "You answered my phone?"

"You were asleep. I thought it was probably the hospital. When I saw it was your mom…" He didn't have to say any more.

"And now she knows we're sleeping together. What if she tells your mother?" she said.

"If? My parents were at the hospital with her. I'm sure

my mother has already been told," he said. And was that such a bad thing? Their parents were smart people. He'd be surprised if they hadn't already figured out something was going on between them.

"It doesn't matter now. The only thing that matters is my father," she said, though it seemed she was talking more to herself than to him.

Glancing over at her, Scott saw that she was staring at the phone she had clutched in her hand. "Call her. Maybe she has some news."

She hesitated for just a moment, then made the call. From the side of the conversation he could hear, it seemed her father was still in the cath lab.

"It's okay," Scott said when she hung up the phone. "You know sometimes these cases take a while. They would have informed your mother if there had been a change."

He went to take her hand, but she had turned away from him to look out the window. A chill that had nothing to do with the upstate New York winter seeped into his heart. Was he losing her again? He knew this would be a setback to the plans he had begun to make, but he wasn't going to give up on them again. There had to be a way to make things work between them.

He thought about the conversations he'd had with Dr. Mason over the last week and the night before at the party. It was a long shot, but he'd take it.

"I need to call London and let them know I won't be coming back tomorrow," he said.

"Can you do that?" she asked as she turned back to him. "You have a contract with them."

"Someone can cover for me. They'll understand. I

won't leave until we know your father is going to be okay," he said.

"He has to be okay," she said as she turned back toward the window. "I should have been there."

"You can't stand guard over them, Fliss," he told her. "You have to live your own life."

"You don't understand. I wasn't here when Leo needed me. If I'd been here, things would have been different," she said.

"Do you really believe that?" He was tired of hearing her blame herself for something she had no part in. "You think just your presence would have made the difference in his life?"

"It could have. I would have seen that something was wrong if I'd been there."

"Like your parents saw it? Like the teachers he worked with saw it? No, Fliss, if Leo hadn't wanted you to know how bad things were for him, you never would have known either way. He had a mental disorder that he hid from everyone. You can't live the rest of your life carrying the responsibility of his death."

"You can't understand," she said, her voice lifeless now. Where had the woman he had held in his arms this morning gone?

"Why not? Because I've never lost anyone? I lost my best friend. And then I lost you because of this crazy responsibility that you think you have to make sure you take care of everyone else." He tried to keep his voice down, but the emotions he had kept bottled up seemed to have taken over. "You didn't even give me the choice of staying here with you."

"And if I had?" she said as she turned to him, her eyes now sparking with anger. "Were you going to throw away all the work you had done to get the job in London for me? And what for? Because you'd slept with me once?"

"It could have been more than that, Fliss, and you know that." He made himself ignore the pain he felt at her words. She was upset about her father.

"It doesn't matter now. Your life is in London and mine is here in the States. What we've had here has been great, but we both knew it was only temporary."

He felt her withdrawal from him as she turned back to the window, taking away any hope that he'd had for a future together.

By the time they pulled into the hospital parking lot, it had been almost three hours since her mother's first call. She'd called to tell them Fliss's father was out of the cath lab, but he'd been taken to the cardiovascular intensive care unit and they had not been allowed back yet.

"Why haven't they let Mom back to see him? We always get the family back with their patient," Felicity said as they rushed into the hospital.

They found her mom in the waiting room, along with Scott's parents. A tall man in a white lab coat that she didn't recognize sat beside them.

"Fliss, I'm so glad you're here," her mother said after they exchanged a tight hug. "This is Dr. Nelson. He's the doctor that performed the heart cath on your father."

"It's nice to meet you. Your mother says you work at Brooklyn Heights in New York in their cardiac unit," the doctor said.

"Yes, I do. And this is Dr. Thomas. He's a cardiologist temporarily here from London," she said, then got down to business. She didn't have time for these unnecessary pleasantries. "What did you find when you did the heart cath on my father?"

"I was just telling your mother that your father is stable for the moment. We put in a stent, but his left main artery is significantly blocked. The bottom line is that he needs open-heart surgery and the sooner the better," the doctor said. Standing, he turned to Scott. "I can show you the scans if you would like."

"If it's okay with everyone." Scott turned and looked at her and her mother. They both nodded their agreement.

Felicity would have liked to have seen the scans herself, but she knew Scott was the professional who had more experience in the cath lab. Besides, it was likely that her father's doctor would talk more openly with another doctor.

"Good. I'm available right now if that's okay with you," Dr. Nelson said. "And if the rest of you will remain here, I'll let the staff know that they can take you back to see Mr. Dale."

Felicity watched as the doctor and Scott walked off together. She'd felt almost numb for the last three hours, but now all the panic she had been able to hold back wanted to rush through her. Her daddy needed open-heart surgery.

"I should have made him go to the emergency room on Christmas Day," she said aloud, finally voicing the thought that had haunted her since she'd first heard about her father's heart attack. If she'd had him checked out, all of this might have been avoided.

"This wasn't the same, Fliss. He woke me up and told me that this was something different. The pain was different. That other pain, it does make him feel sick and it does give him some bad nights with reflux, but this was different," her mother said as she put her arm around her daughter. "It's going to be okay. The doctor was telling us before you got here that he should recover within weeks of the surgery."

Felicity knew that open-heart surgery was very common. She worked with patients who had the surgery and recovered without any complications all the time. But this was different. This was her father.

A nurse came to get her mother and take her to the intensive care unit to see her husband. Felicity quietly sat in her seat and waited her turn.

Had it only been a year and a half since she had sat in a waiting room much like this one? Her brother had been declared brain dead as soon as he had arrived at the hospital, but he had remained on life support until her parents had accepted that he wouldn't be coming back to them. After agreeing to organ donation, she had waited with her parents for a nurse to come and tell her that her brother was truly gone. His organs had been harvested and she knew his heart had been given to another young man not much older than her brother.

"What did you find out?" she said, jumping out of her seat as Scott came back into the room.

"Dr. Nelson is a sharp man. He's right. Your father's left main has a large block. I'd suggest he goes to open-heart as soon as possible too." Scott reached out and took her hand. Unable to help herself, she let him pull her into his arms. It wasn't like they had anything to hide from their parents now.

"I want him transferred to Brooklyn Heights," she said against his shoulder.

"I told him you would say that. As long as your mother

agrees, he will get it arranged." Scott held on to her as they joined his parents.

When her mother returned, she explained how to find the unit and Felicity made her way to her father's room.

"Daddy?" she said as she walked over to his bed. When his eyes opened, she felt some of the fear leave her. "How are you doing?"

"I'm fine, baby girl. I just need a little rest and I'll be right back to normal." His smile was weak, but she was glad to see that he was in good spirits, though some of that might have been from the meds he'd been given.

Her mother had asked her to be the one to tell him that he was going to need another surgery. She took a deep breath. She'd gotten her stubbornness from her father. If she didn't phrase this exactly right, he would likely give them problems. Not that it was an option. He would have the surgery no matter what. There wasn't a choice at this point.

"I met your doctor, Dr. Nelson. He seems to know what he's talking about and he let Scott take a look at the films they made during your heart catheterization when they put the stent in."

"I only got one stent? My boss at work—you know Mr. Stone—he got three of those stents and he was back at work in no time." Her father reached out his hand to her. "I'm going to be okay. Don't you worry."

"It's not just the stent, Daddy. It's more than that. Scott and Dr. Nelson saw a large blockage to your left main artery and it's preventing the blood from reaching your heart. You need to have open-heart surgery and they want to do it as soon as possible." She waited for her father to say something, to try to blow this off as something that wasn't that serious, but he only looked down where he held her hand.

"You think I need to have this done?" he asked, his voice almost too soft to hear with all the noise from the machines and pumps in the room.

"I do. And I want you to come to Brooklyn Heights to have it done," she said. The fact that he wasn't arguing with her told her that the chest pain he'd had before he came to the emergency room had been bad.

"Can you send Scott in to see me, please?" he said as he let go of her hand. "I'd like to talk to him for a few minutes."

She kissed his cheek, then headed back to the waiting room, where her mother stood talking to some of her father's coworkers who had come in while she had been with her dad.

"He wants to talk to you," she told Scott. "He's taking things better than I thought. He didn't try to play things down or try to argue with me. I think he just needs to hear from you that he needs the surgery."

She walked together with him to the unit, then waited for him outside the doors. The lack of sleep from the night before and the stress of the day were beginning to wear her down. She leaned against the wall and closed her eyes. A few minutes later the doors to the unit opened and Scott walked out, wearing a smile.

"Did things go that well?" she asked when they started back to the waiting room.

"What do you mean?" Scott asked.

"You're smiling. He must have agreed to the surgery and the transfer, right?" she asked.

"Oh, yes, he agreed. I'm going to call Dr. Nelson as soon as we get back to the waiting room." He took her hand as they walked back to join the others. "Why don't you go close your eyes for a few minutes? I'll make the phone call and start making some arrangements in New York."

She was too tired to argue. She took a seat next to Scott's dad, who had found a magazine to read, and she shut her eyes, only to have them open again when Scott took the seat next to her. "Back so soon?" she asked.

"I was gone at least thirty minutes," he said.

She could tell that the lack of sleep was catching up to him too.

"Where's my mom?" she asked as she sat up and looked around the room.

"She's with your father," Scott's father said as he looked up from his magazine.

A few minutes later, when her mom and Dr. Nelson walked into the room together, she stood. There was something about the way the doctor was bending over her mother, comforting her, that told Felicity there had been a change.

"It's okay, Fliss. Your father's just having more chest pain," her mom said as she tried to reassure her. "Dr. Nelson was telling me that if we're going to transfer your father, we need to do it now, before it becomes an emergency situation."

"I just got off the phone with the doctor on call at Brooklyn and he's just waiting for your call, Dr. Nelson. He assures me there will be a bed available within the hour and he can call in the surgical team as soon as Mr. Dale arrives," Scott said. He rested his hands on her shoulders. "Brooklyn has offered their helicopter service for transport if you don't have it available."

"I'll call our transfer center and the doctor now," Dr. Nelson said before leaving the room.

"I can't thank you enough, Scott, for helping us," her mother told him as she leaned over and kissed him on the cheek.

Finally the word came that the helicopter would be there within the hour. It wasn't until she and Scott were in the car and headed back to New York that she realized what was supposed to be Scott's final day in New York was almost over. He'd been so busy. Had he had a chance to call London? But she couldn't think about that now. She was already too close to falling apart, and she needed to be strong for her mother. She had to make sure her father was going to be okay. That was what was important right now. Everything else would have to wait.

The sun had set before they arrived back in New York and the nighttime traffic was heavy as they slowly made their way to the hospital. He'd let Felicity sleep during their ride back to the city.

"Wake up, sleepyhead," he said as he nudged her awake. "We're almost there."

"Has the hospital called?" she asked as she sat up. Her face was marked with wrinkles from where she had leaned against the seat, and her hair had come down from the twisty knot she had wrapped it in that morning.

"I received a text less than an hour ago from Dr. Mason, who said your father had arrived safely and was being prepped for surgery." He wasn't going to tell her about the other part of the doctor's message. Dr. Mason had been very specific that he didn't want anyone to know about the negotiations he was in with the Royal Kensington Hospital to extend Scott's time in Brooklyn Heights. So far there had been no response from the London hospital and it had been arranged for him to leave the next evening.

"Where's Mom and your parents?" she asked as she turned to look at the traffic behind them.

"They're not far behind." He parked his car and they made their way into the hospital and up to the cardiac floor.

"Let me find out where they took him while you wait for your parents. From what Dr. Mason said, they were already getting his lines put in for the surgery, so he's probably already been taken to pre-op," Felicity said and then headed down the hall and through a door that said Staff Only.

Fifteen minutes later she returned looking more pale and tired than she had before. "They've already taken him to surgery. They said he became short of breath and Dr. Hyland felt he needed to go to surgery right away."

"George Hyland is a very good cardiothoracic surgeon. Your father is in good hands. You know that," Scott said as he took her hands in his.

"You know we say those words to people all the time, but on this side of things, it doesn't seem to help. I just wish I'd been able to see him before they took him in for surgery. What if…?"

"There are no what-ifs here. Your father is a healthy man. There's no reason for us to think he's not going to do well in the operating room. We just have to be patient," Scott said. The waiting room was empty, as being a holiday, there were no scheduled surgeries. Taking a seat in a corner of the room, they prepared themselves to wait. He thought about the plans he'd had to talk to Felicity today about their future.

This was not the place to do this. But what choice did

he really have? He'd been given a few extra days, but as soon as Fliss's father got through recovery, they were expecting him to return. Thinking about heading back to London should have excited him. He did love his job there and it was the job he had dreamed of for years. But he'd learned over the last year and a half that without the woman he loved beside him, he would never be happy.

"You know..." he started, then stopped when he saw his parents and Felicity's mom.

"Have you seen him?" Felicity's mom asked them.

"They've already taken him into surgery," Felicity said, then explained that her father's condition had deteriorated and the doctor had felt he needed to start before they arrived.

"I was about to go to the OR and make sure they knew we were here," Felicity said as she started to stand.

"Let me go. The last thing we need is a turf war between you and the OR staff," Scott said as he stood and stretched his legs. "I'll be back in a few minutes."

But he didn't go right back. After checking in with the OR and finding that there was nothing new to report back to Felicity and her mom, he wandered back through the hospital to the office he had been using in the cardiac center and started making some phone calls.

CHAPTER FOURTEEN

FELICITY STOOD IN the doorway of her father's intensive care bed and watched him sleep. Scott had been right. Her father was a healthy man and the surgery had been declared a success. After a few weeks of recovery time, he'd be right back to work.

Scott had arranged for rooms for both his parents and her mother at a hotel only a block from the hospital. At some point Scott had disappeared and she assumed he had found an empty doctor's sleep room.

"Ow," her father moaned as he tried to turn in the bed.

"Daddy, don't," she said as she rushed into the room. "You're attached to a bunch of lines that could get pulled out."

"Fliss?" he asked. He still looked weak, but color had returned to his face, and with the smile he always had for her, he at least resembled her father.

"Yeah, it's me. You had surgery. Do you remember?" she asked as she sat down in the small plastic chair beside his bed.

"Of course I remember. I remember the trip in that helicopter too. I'd rather not repeat that one," he said. "Where's your mother? Is she doing okay?"

"She's at a hotel down the street. Scott pulled some

strings and got her a last-minute room." She adjusted the sheets around her father.

"That Scott is a good man. You won't find better," her father said. "Did he tell you about our conversation?"

"About the surgery?" she asked.

"No. I didn't need him to tell me about the surgery. If you thought I needed the surgery, that was enough for me." Her father tried to turn toward her.

"Let me help," she said as she guarded the lines, then assisted him to roll onto his side. "Better?"

"Much better. This bed is as hard as a concrete bench," he said. "Look, I know me and your mom should stay out of your life...but I think we need to talk."

"Maybe this should wait till later, when you feel better," she said.

"No, this can't be put off," her father said. The monitor above his bed alarmed, showing that his heart rate had increased.

"It's okay, Daddy. I didn't mean to upset you," she said.

"No, I did it myself. I should have said this earlier, and now with things the way they are with you and Scott... We didn't say anything after Leo died and you decided to move back home. And I'm sorry about that. At the time, it seemed that you needed to be here and we sure needed you. But now, looking back, it was a mistake..."

"No, it wasn't, Daddy. I needed to be here with you," she said as she moved closer to her dad. "You need to rest now."

"No, baby girl. There's still things I need to say. It was a mistake for us to let you give up the life you had made in London. And then there's Scott. We knew there was something wrong when you avoided talking about him, but we didn't know… Well, maybe at some point we had hoped… But I can see it now. You gave up Scott to come home for us," her father said, then pinned her with a look that wouldn't let her be anything but honest with him.

"It was nothing, really. We'd just started to see each other, that way," she said. She looked up at the monitors and pretended to study them.

"And now?" her father asked her. "Don't bother denying that you two are involved. I've already talked to Scott."

"Daddy, you know Scott's life is in London and mine is here," she said as she stood up and stepped away from the bed. This was exactly what she had feared would happen when her mother found out she and Scott were involved.

"Why?" her father asked.

"Why? Because Scott loves his job and I love you and Mom. Look at today. What would have happened if I hadn't been here with you?" She made herself calm down. She wouldn't upset her dad no matter how hard this was for her.

"I suspect I would have had the surgery and you would have caught a plane as soon as possible so that you could be here to hover over me like you're doing now," he said as he reached out to her.

"I'm sorry. I don't mean to hover. It's just that I love you and Mom so much. I don't want to lose you. Not like I lost Leo. If I'd been here, then…"

Her father squeezed her hand. "I was here, Fliss, and I couldn't stop what happened to your brother. If you're to blame, your mother and I are even more to blame."

"No, Daddy, it wasn't your fault," she said, moving closer to his bed.

"And it wasn't yours either. You can't stop living because of some misplaced guilt you feel about your brother's death, honey. You have to move on now. Life's hard. Everyone needs someone in their life they can count on, someone who will always be there for them. For me, that's your mom. I think Scott could be that person for you, if you'll let him." Her father closed his eyes. Their conversation had worn him out.

In a few minutes, his breathing became even and she slipped out of the room. After making sure that the nurses had her phone number, she left the unit. She started to go back to the waiting room, but after the last twenty-four hours, she needed a change.

She stepped out of the front entrance of the hospital and onto a sidewalk that was covered in the slush that had been yesterday's snow. As the cold air rushed through her lungs, she pulled her coat around her, then walked across the street to a small all-night diner.

She had ordered a cup of coffee and a cinnamon roll to keep her going when her phone sounded with a text from Scott. After giving him her location, she ordered another cup of coffee. Her father had been right about many things. She had spent the last year and a half trying to be the perfect daughter who was always there for her parents when the truth was that her parents didn't need her. Not that they didn't love her. She had no doubt they loved her.

But after Leo died, she'd let her pain and guilt drive her into thinking that she needed to always be close to her parents so she could keep them safe. She wouldn't let them down like she had let Leo down.

Scott took the seat across from her and picked up the coffee she'd ordered for him.

"Do you know why I moved out of my parents' house and went to the city?" she asked him.

"You said you were bored at the hospital in Hudson." He took a sip of the coffee.

"I was, but I would have stayed there anyway to be close to my parents. No, the reason I moved out was because my mom told me I needed to get a place of my own. She said I was cramping their style."

Scott choked on his laughter as his coffee splashed against the table. "Really?"

"I know. Sad, right? My parents have more of a life than I do." She set her coffee down. No matter what happened next, she needed to say this. "I'm sorry for how I ended things after Leo died. I don't expect you to understand, but I couldn't have gone back to London. Not then. No matter how strong my parents might be now, they needed me then. And I needed them too. But ending our friendship like that was wrong."

"And now? What is it you want now?" he asked, his eyes intense as he studied her.

And that was the million-dollar question, wasn't it? But she knew what she wanted. She wanted it all. She wanted what she had with Scott now, but she also wanted more. She wanted the kind of love her parents had. She wanted to know that the person she loved would always be there for her, just like she would always be there for him.

"I want a friend," she said as she looked up from her coffee.

"I'll be that friend," he said, never taking his eyes off her.

"I want a lover," she said as she moved her hand over to where his rested on the table.

"I'll be that lover," he said as he joined their hands.

"I want a father for our children," she said. She brushed her tears away with her free hand.

"I'll be that father, Fliss," he said as he lifted her hand to his mouth.

"Okay," she said, then giggled. "Did I just ask you to marry me, Scott Thomas?"

"I think you did," he said as he leaned across the table to kiss her. "You wouldn't happen to have a ring with you, would you?"

"No, I'm afraid I didn't see far enough ahead to bring a ring," she said as she wiped more tears away. While she had dreamed of being Mrs. Scott Thomas most of her life, she'd never imagined she would be the one to propose to him.

"Well, I guess it's a good thing that I thought far enough ahead for the two of us," he said as he pulled a jewelry box from his jacket pocket and placed it on the faded laminate tabletop.

Opening the box, he revealed the most beautiful ring she had ever seen. And as he slipped the ring onto her finger, in an all-night diner in the middle of the night, Dr. Scott Thomas made all of Felicity's childhood dreams come true.

EPILOGUE

SHE RECOGNIZED HIM the minute she walked into the room. That head of dark hair that she loved to run her fingers through, those wide shoulders that she knew she could count on to hold her up when things went wrong and that perfectly tailored tux that she had finally gotten him into were enough to assure her that this was the man she was looking for.

The organ began to play and he turned toward her, smiling in the way that had always sent butterflies racing through her stomach, and suddenly they were the only two people in the cathedral.

"Ready?" her father asked her.

She stared back at the man who stood at the altar waiting for her. Ready? For this? For him?

"I've never been more ready," she replied as she took that first step that would begin the rest of her life.

Later, when the vows had been said and the cake had been cut, they left the dancing couples and sneaked away to a small alcove where the two of them could be alone.

"So what is this surprise you have for me?" Felicity asked as she looked around.

"I've spoken to our parents and they've all agreed

to come over to London for Christmas. I gave them the tickets right before the wedding," Scott said.

Throwing her arms around him, she kissed him. "Thank you so much. I can't wait. We'll have to take them shopping in Covent Garden. And we can go to that cute little market and get a tree. I've already shipped the snowflake ornaments, but we'll want a bigger tree for your place, so we'll need to order more. I hope—"

"We have six months till Christmas. Why don't we get through the honeymoon and get moved back before we start decorating?" Scott said as he fingered the small snowflake necklace she had insisted on wearing, even though it was a June wedding.

"I know. And there's going to be so much for you to get caught up on at work. A lot of things have probably changed in the last six months," she said. The fact that he'd arranged to have his contract extended so he could remain with her while her father recovered and while she and their mothers planned the wedding was a true testament to his love for her. "And there'll be even more for me to catch up on in the cath lab there."

"And I still don't know where we're going on our honeymoon," he said.

She'd had to work to get him to agree that since she had done the proposing, she should get to plan the honeymoon. She knew he was going to love the cabin she had rented in the Catskill Mountains where they could hike and fish all day and then spend long nights in an isolated paradise.

"It's tradition that the honeymoon is a surprise. Can't

you wait just a little longer?" she asked as they made their way back to their reception.

"For you, Fliss, I would wait a lifetime."

* * * * *

COMING SOON!

We really hope you enjoyed reading this book. If you're looking for more romance, be sure to head to the shops when new books are available on

Thursday 25th November

To see which titles are coming soon, please visit

millsandboon.co.uk/nextmonth

MILLS & BOON

Coming next month

CHRISTMAS MIRACLE AT THE CASTLE
Alison Roberts

'Here… catch, Abby.'

But the mistletoe didn't quite make it into her waiting hands because it snagged on some lower, outer branches. They were just a few inches too high for Abby to reach, even standing on tiptoes.

'I'll find a stick.'

'I can reach it. I'll just get this smaller one before I come down. Maggie's bound to have plans that need more than one weird bird's nest.'

Abby hadn't moved by the time Euan shimmied down from the tree only a minute later, with a smaller ball of mistletoe in his hands. His nose and cheeks were reddened by both the physical effort and the cold and he was breathing hard.

'You look like a dragon,' Abby told him. 'Puffing steam.'

'Hmph.'

She was getting used to that grunt that was clearly an important part of Euan's vocabulary. He reached over her head to unsnag the first mistletoe he'd harvested and, as it began to fall, Abby also reached up, to catch it. So she was looking up, with her arms above her head, as Euan looked down to see where the ball had gone. He was much closer than Abby had realised. So close that…

... that the moment suddenly froze.

She couldn't move. Euan seemed to be as still as she was. It was a blink of time but more than long enough for something to click into place.

It wasn't conscious. It had to be the result of a lot of things. Things like how excited Abby was to be here, in this spectacular place. The way Euan's story had captured her heart so firmly and her determination to try and do something to help him. The fact that, despite his outward grumpiness and the impression he wasn't that happy to have her here, there was a level of attraction that was the final catalyst for what Abby realised might be the perfect way to make this Christmas more enjoyable for this man.

She hadn't lowered the mistletoe and that was the perfect excuse for what she did next.

Abby stood on her tiptoes and kissed him.

She'd only intended it to be a friendly sort of kiss. A brief, under-the- mistletoe, Christmassy sort of kiss. One that wasn't going to be significant in any way.

But the instant her lips touched his, everything changed...

Continue reading
CHRISTMAS MIRACLE AT THE CASTLE
Alison Roberts

Available next month
www.millsandboon.co.uk